Beneath Juliette

a novel by

John Wilsterman

Wave Writer Publications, LLC
john@johnwilsterman.com

1

Published by Wave Writer Publications, LLC
www.johnwilsterman.com
Townsend, GA
Printed in the United States of America

Dedicated to my loving wife, Jean.
Without her devotion, inspiration and encouragement
this book might have remained forever buried

Beneath Juliette

Chapter 1

Had I not gone fishing with Remy Robillard that night in October, the tale of Frank Robillard and TV Swanson might have remained buried beneath Juliette forever.

At the time Remy was my cameraman, someone I worked with at the television station. He was just a good old Georgia boy and quite a contrast to the rest of us star-power on-camera personalities. I'm really not much of a fisherman, especially at night, being prone to seasickness and easily spooked in the dark. But Remy's a charismatic kind of guy so before caution and good sense squelched the whole thing I said sure, why not?

It was Friday night and neither of us had dates. Around midnight we sat in his boat in the middle of Lake Juliette. A full moon blazed in the sky over our heads. Our conversation was sparse but not our consumption of fishing fare: Budweiser, Vienna sausage, and Spanish peanuts. The moment was peaceful, the calm lake mirroring moon and clouds. The only signs of civilization were blinking red lights on the four turbine towers of a nearby power plant. Somewhere in the boat an old transistor radio murmured country music.

With a sharp lurch of the boat, Lake Juliette began emptying like the flushing of a giant commode.

"What was that?"

"Nothing natural," Remy said.

Maybe I didn't know much about fishing, but our boat shouldn't jerk like that -- like it was rammed by a gator or a swamp thing. But gators don't swim north of Macon, Georgia. And if a swamp thing existed or even the rumor of a swamp thing, I, Brendan Macbean, local television reporter of stories bizarre and folksy, would have put it on the "News at Six" a long time ago.

Tiny, expanding waves rippled the surface of the lake, twirling our boat slowly. A hundred yards away the shoreline seemed to revolve. "What the hell?" I expected Remy to explain it or shrug it off – but instead he grabbed his seat, hunkering down like he was going for a carnival ride.

"Hang on, Bren. This is going to be one *bad* ride!" He spoke with a strong "ZZ Top" inflection. Flashes of moonlight glinted off his teeth, but I couldn't tell if he smiled or grimaced. I opened my mouth to say something, but a sudden, reckless twisting of the boat effectively choked me off. My fishing pole clattered to the bottom of the boat with the mono-filament line still hanging over the side.

Sudden acceleration flattened my lungs. A roar of rushing water grew in volume and blotted out all other sound, while the middle of the lake depressed into a shallow bowl. The onset of a tornado might have produced this much violence, but I saw only the clear night sky and moon overhead. The boat lunged against the anchor rope like a bad dog going for a walk. It parted and snapped toward me like a whip barely missing my face. Now free, the boat spun into the throat of a full-fledged whirlpool. Lake Juliette churned with fury, chugging up tree limbs and other junk, which we crashed into like floating bumper cars. Looking defiant, Remy rode the stern like a bull rider, glaring at the rising rampart of water.

I wedged my body deeper into the bow. The things in the boat -- the cooler, the radio, the minnow bucket -- flew around, pelting me with cruel jabs. I clung with slippery, weakening hands to whatever I could hold on to, but the centrifugal force slowly pulled me away, tearing at my grip, twisting me around. One of my legs slipped over the side, and I felt my shoe flick against a spinning wave.

"Bren, No!" Remy gripped my arm and yanked me back. My shoulder wrenched with pain. He flung my body to the bottom of the boat and flopped on me like a pro wrestler. We both rolled against each other, hugging like two manatees in a weird mating dance.

The force departed as quickly as it had come. Our bodies careened painfully against the sides of the boat. The lake's surface subsided into choppy mounds of water. The sounds of the night returned - crickets and frogs. The moon came out from behind a cloud and cast a vivid light. I lay pinned under Remy's body barely able to draw a breath. My nose caught his body odor and his dumpster fume breath. I felt his warmth, even though we were both soaked. After the threat of imminent death the ordinary nature of these things brought hot tears to my eyes, and with the strongest resolve I stifled the unmanly sobs rattling in my chest.

Remy stood, shifting as the boat rocked. He spat into the lake and returned to his seat at the stern. Except for being wet, he looked invigorated. He let out a huge breath, and his shaking hand conjured a pack of Marlboros, which by some miracle still held a dry one. A flash of his Bic brought it to life. I saw his chest expand followed by an exhale of smoke, a blossom of white in the moonlight. While staring at the distant shoreline he said, "Shit." The smoke made the word sound throaty and harsh.

Trembling like a man in a seizure I lay on my back watching him. The moon behind Remy's head wreathed his face in shadows. With a sudden spasm, I sprang to the side of the boat and vomited the junk food I'd eaten only minutes before.

After a while, I splashed the cool black waters of Lake Juliette on my face.

Through a gravely throat burning with stomach acid I said, "Maybe the fish will like that food better than I did." Uttering weak jokes at inappropriate moments seemed to be a trademark of mine.

"There ain't any fish in Lake Juliette," Remy replied. The boat wobbled in lazy circles. The red lights of the power plant passed behind him. A slight smile elevated the cigarette hanging in the corner of his mouth.

"What? Huh?" I'm sure I said something similar.

"What?" Remy asked.

Adrenaline, asphyxiation and mortal terror make for an unstable mix. A grin struggled to unlock my face frozen for so long in a mask of terror. A laugh followed the grin. Remy nodded and laughed too. In seconds we were both laughing on the waters of Lake Juliette with no one around to call us crazy.

The night became quiet again, all thoughts of fishing forgotten. A lost Budweiser rolled against my foot. I reached for it and with a hiss and spew of foam yanked off the top. I took a long draught, the best I'd ever tasted. I blasted out a substantial belch and felt like a man again.

"Well, I've been fucked," I said, sprawled in the bow of the boat, "about a thousand times."

"Yeah." Remy drew out the word.

At some unseen signal, we both stared at the middle of the lake. Just below the surface glowing green shapes appeared. Like the slow eruptions of a lava lamp, the shapes swirled with the remaining current forming an amorphous column emerging from the lake, a gaseous haze with shadows and features. Moonlight illuminated the shape. The hairs on the back of my head stood and goose bumps covered my arms. I swear it looked like a fuzzy hologram of an old woman in a nightgown.

9

The green light faded into the night air, and after a few seconds, I wondered if it was ever there at all.

I pointed toward the middle of the lake. "What... was that?"

Like nothing could impress him Remy said, "Swamp gas. The whirlpool sets it off. You know what it is. Phosphorescent methane or something."

"It looked like an old lady coming up out of the lake."

Remy puffed his cigarette, looking who-knows-where in the dark. "I heard folks say they sometimes see Miss Nora out here."

"Miss Nora?"

"They say the old biddy haunts the lake. She lived here." He waved at the water. "Her house was right down there. She was my dad's music teacher or something. Helped raised him. I don't know." Remy stopped for a second as if trying to recall more. "It's just swamp gas."

"Your dad?"

"They say she killed him here... oh, about when I was ten."

"Killed him?"

"When the engineers built the lake they had to evict some folks. My dad was the policeman in Juliette, that little town over there. It was his job to make sure those folks all moved out.

"The last one to go was this spooky old woman named Nora Potvin. All these small towns got one like her. Dad let her stay the longest, I guess because they'd had some kind of relationship. But Nora didn't want to go. She put a curse on him when he came to get her, 'and all his scion,' which means me. Then she beaned him with a frying pan and sat in her rocker while the water came up and drowned them both. Anyway, that's the story. According to the legend, she got him then and now she's after me. If you read my fortune cookie, it says, 'Beware of old ladies coming out of the lake.' Ha!" Remy's laugh gently rocked the boat.

A tiny breeze wafted over the lake, and I shivered. "Remy, this whirlpool thing could make a great story. We need to bring the camera out here. If we could get the swamp gas... My god, that's amazing! Monday we can start hyping the spot, maybe show it Thursday just before we go to network."

"I don't want you to do a spot on the whirlpool."

"Are you kidding? This is what we do."

Remy twisted around in his seat. "Right here there used to be a pretty nice valley around a little old stream called Rum Creek." He flicked his cigarette butt into the lake and spat again. "They dammed up the creek to build the lake and to get water for the power plant over there." He nodded to the flashing lights on the four towers.

"There ain't enough water in the creek to fill up the lake in a hundred years, so they pumped it in from the Ocmulgee River. State natural resources people have tried to get fish to take here, but it's too warm for them. I think the plant heats up the water. There's too much temperature change for the fish."

"Thanks for the background," I said. "If there's no fish, then why are we fishing?"

Remy barked a short laugh. "Bren, you ever had a ride like that?"

I stared at him wishing we'd gone hunting instead.

"Maybe I'm stupid, but drowning is not fishing."

"Over by the plant they have a big holding pond for the water they use. Every now and then they let water back into the lake."

"That causes the whirlpool?"

He let the question hang for a moment and nodded. "Maybe if they let out too much, but it's rare. They release some water every day. The whirlpool might not happen again for months. Not too many people know about it, but I'm sure there's engineers over there trying to figure it out. It's dangerous. They can't let boaters out here or there'd be a lot of accidents."

"You're damn right. We *were* an accident!"

"So they don't let people on the lake after dark."

"Except for us?"

Remy grinned. "Well, they don't allow us either."

"Damnit! I'm breaking the law."

"When I was a kid, my dad and I roamed these woods." His arm circled the lake. "We used to look for this cave. Dad's uncle showed it to him when he was a boy. It was hard to find, but one day we sort of stumbled on it, just a long crack in the ground under a rock ledge. I remember trying to look inside. Dark... you couldn't see nothing. Cool air flowed out and it felt good 'cause we were hot and sweaty. You could hear the sound of rushing water like when you hold a seashell to your ear. There must be a huge air chamber inside the cave. When the lake level gets high enough, a lot of water floods in, creating the whirlpool."

"Can't they fix the cave? Close it up or something?"

"Nobody knows where it is. Like I said, it was hard to find, even then. Now it's under fifty feet of water. They've been trying for years.

"When Dad moved old Nora out, the whirlpool drowned both of

them. By the time anybody looked, the water had come up. They brought in scuba divers and all."

"What did they find?"

"There was nothing down there. No house. No old lady." Remy lit another Marlboro. It sputtered apparently not as dry as the first. "They found his pickup all crunched up at the bottom of the lake near the dam. The doors were ripped off. He wasn't in it, but they found pieces of him all over. Brought us his bloody shirt, all tore up with his badge still pinned to it."

"But what happened to the house?" I said. "Shouldn't it still be down there?"

Remy nodded. "I think the force of the water just swept it away and my dad and Miss Nora with it. They both drowned and the whirlpool sucked what was left of them into the cave. They never found a trace of Miss Nora. Neither hide, nor hair, nor a set of dentures. All that talk about hitting him with a frying pan was just talk. Nobody really knows what happened."

My mind swirled like the whirlpool. "Why did you bring me here if not to do this story?" I asked. "You wanted to see if I could swim?"

"Can't be sure about the whirlpool. Doesn't happen regularly. I didn't bring you here for that, anyway. We just got lucky, I guess."

"Lucky!" I snorted. "Like we got lucky and drowned."

"Bren, the way folks in Juliette talked about my dad, you'd think he was a hero. I was ten years old. Mom and Grandpa don't talk about him anymore. Nobody else does either. It's like he never existed. I kept waiting for it to hit me, his dying and all, but I don't think I ever grieved."

I had to interrupt him before I went bonkers. "Remy, stop the soap opera. You want something. What is it?"

He made another short laugh. "Bren, maybe my dad was a hero. Now he's gone. He died under mysterious circumstances in a small town in Georgia. Even without the whirlpool, it has all the earmarks of a Brendan Macbean 'Georgia Legend.'"

Remy wanted me to do a spot on his dad. He didn't just invite me out here to scare the shit out of me. He wanted to get me hooked, if you'll pardon the fishing pun, on a story about his dad.

I took a shaky breath. "Why your dad and not the whirlpool, Remy? I'm sure he was a nice guy and all." That sounded a little cold, but sitting in a boat at night in wet clothes had ruined my social skills.

12

"Bren, everybody in Atlanta likes your spots on the news." He then gave a passable impersonation of my close-out, "This is Brendan Macbean with another 'Georgia Legend.'

"Bren, I want you to do the piece on Dad. The whirlpool is just icing on the cake. I figured you could dig up the rest of the story. If my dad turned out to be a good guy, I'd feel better about it after all these years. A whole lot better."

"I can't do a story just to make you feel better."

I noted the posture of his dark shape in the stern of the boat, leaning slightly toward me. Was there anything about his dad to bring in the whirlpool? I needed something to grab the viewers, to hold them through the commercials. I began to create the spot in my head. Start with a shot of the lake going into flush mode. Fake a granny in a nightgown swimming under water. Background narration: "Is Lake Juliette the lake of death? Did the ghost of this woman murder a Georgia policeman? Exclusively on News at Six. Reporter Brendan Macbean uncovers the gruesome tale of the witch that killed the cop."

I shook my head.

"Remy, do you think Bud's going to buy this?" My producer was a difficult man to please. He didn't really like my feel good, local weirdness stories. But they were popular, and I got more than my share of spots.

Remy chuckled. "Bren, drop it if there's no story. I won't feel bad. But I bet you'll find something interesting."

"What was his name? I have to start somewhere."

"Frank Robillard, football star, war hero, baseball coach, police officer. My dad."

A bolt of lightning hit me. "A policeman in Juliette? Back in college I got a speeding ticket somewhere out here in the sticks. I was coming home from school. Could it have been him?" I strained to remember.

"Hmmm... let's see." He told me the year.

Memory flooded back to me. I had been driving home from Georgia Southern. I-75 was one long traffic jam north of Macon. I was zooming down an alternate country highway. The radio blasting "Statesboro Blues" or something. Wind was whipping through the open window. Blue lights flashed in my mirror, but I hadn't heard the siren for the music. A big guy in a khaki uniform climbed out of a police cruiser. While walking up to my car, he kicked a road-killed animal on the side of the road, a possum or a coon. Not just once but several times, like he

13

was mad or something. That agitated me so much I couldn't talk my way out of the ticket.

The irony seized me. I may have actually met this long-dead guy. Now I'm sitting here talking to his son, the result of a cosmic coincidence.

That's all Remy could give me. I got back to Atlanta an hour before sunrise, itching to get more from the internet. Would an unsolved murder mystery and a haunted lake be enough? How do you connect it all to a Vietnam Vet who gets killed by his music teacher?

But connect it, I did. A simple internet search gave me plenty on Frank Robillard. It took the rest of the weekend to do it, but what I found hooked me worse than smoking crack.

Frank turned out to be an amazing whiz kid, who'd somehow avoided notoriety in the world outside Juliette. He was smart, athletic, and maybe even good looking. But after high school, news about Frank Robillard slowed to a trickle. He played football for UGA, dropped out to go to Vietnam. Then nothing. A decade passes with zilch except his obituary.

Does the trail run out? Not by a damn sight. A search on the town of Juliette revealed the most stunning mystery yet.

Lots of articles about Lake Juliette. Georgia Power engineers declared they were having "lake level problems" in an article about Plant Scherer, the only public mention of the whirlpool phenomenon I could find. They never actually used the word "whirlpool."

But, ho-ho, just before the lake filled up an escaped convict from Ohio was captured between Juliette and Forsyth, one Theodore Vincent Swanson, but no mention of Frank. Had he died before the capture? The name Swanson sounded familiar. I vaguely remembered it from a piece I'd done on cop killers. So I searched the name, and the internet dropped a bomb on me.

Theodore Vincent Swanson currently sat on death-row in the Mansfield Ohio Correctional Institution. Every state including Ohio rewrote their death penalty laws when the Supreme Court reinstated it in 1976. Ohio was the only state that had never actually executed anyone in all those years. But they were about to stick the needle into Swanson.

TV Swanson proved to be a compelling lead. None of this information contained anything about Frank, except for the date of Swanson's capture, May 25, 1980, which curiously coincided with the date the coroner gave for Frank's death. Mere coincidence? I'm sure

Juliette did not have a huge number of policemen, so why no mention of Robillard if Swanson was captured there? TV Swanson had killed two cops in Ohio and fled to Georgia. Maybe Swanson knew something about it. I would need permission to interview him. The process was tricky, but a reporter has ways.

That's pretty much all I had when I got involved with this story, one that never made it to the six o'clock news. It seemed so little considering the obsession was about to consume me, and no hint of the personal agony that was coming. The story of Frank Robillard and the commitment I made to his son, would haunt me more than any old swamp-gas ghost. It would strip me of my job and toss me into the human wasteland of depression. I did not know it then, but I was about to drown in all the secrets buried beneath Juliette more than if the old lady herself had dragged me into the cold, dark lake.

PART ONE – TV's TALE

Chapter 2

TV Swanson derived his nickname from his first and middle names, Theodore Vincent. Someone had connected his surname Swanson, with America's favorite brand of TV-dinner. TV made a career of stealing things and selling drugs, minor stuff compared to his last caper. He did several stints in jail including juvenile detention, the Ohio State Pen, and the Lima Hospital for the Criminally Insane. After his murder conviction, he was sent to death row in Mansfield, Ohio.

He began life in Pineville, West Virginia. His dad had been an automobile mechanic. Before TV reached school age, they moved to Akron, Ohio. His dad ran a filling station until he died of a heart attack in the early sixties. TV dropped out of school in his teens. His adult criminal career began with auto theft, for which he served time in the Ohio State Penitentiary. Several years later he was sent to the Lima Hospital for the Criminally Insane, a plea won for him by a public defender. Considering Lima's reputation for prisoner mistreatment, this couldn't have been much of a deal.

With his murder conviction, the prosecutor stated that TV Swanson committed this last crime with "extreme malice, with a sane and rational mind." Interviewing this guy scared the crap out of me. Even under the prison guard's protection, I expected him to spend the whole time trying to intimidate me, and I was already plenty intimidated.

At the Mansfield Corrections Facility, where Ohio housed their death row inmates, a string of bureaucrats reviewed my credentials before letting me in. The warden delivered a dreary homily about the news media's "liberal slant" before handing me over to Mr. Bedoe, a no nonsense Yankee with an "Ohio" accent. He rattled off our agenda like an experienced tour guide.

"We're gonna go down this hallway and take the elevator to the guard room. There you will go through a metal detector, just like the airport." He smiled showing yellow teeth. The rest of his lecture degenerated into a stream of "blah - blahs" until some vocal subtlety indicated he had finished.

The unavoidable odor of closely packed men assaulted my nose. "Do you ever get used to the smell?" Bedoe ignored my banter and shrugged again.

We arrived at corridor C, death row. Here prisoners awaited the executioner, and the penitentiary went all out to accommodate them. Death Row had its own interview room, infirmary, and kitchen. There was a small exercise plaza where the inmates could stretch their legs and get a little sun. The actual executions would take place at the Southern Ohio Corrections Facility, about fifty miles away.

As we walked down Death Row, a few of the condemned put their faces to the little meshed windows in their doors. Some made comments. "Hey Bedoe! You bring us a new lawyer?" "Who gets the little guy?" I had expected more rowdy behavior, but I didn't get it. Whether they considered themselves guilty or innocent didn't matter. These were society's bottom feeders; the unlucky and the stupid. Even in America death row was a tough place to get into. Eventually the state would get around to killing them, and this fact shadowed every second of their existence.

The visitor's room was well-lit and air-conditioned, with furniture consisting of two metal chairs and a table bolted to the floor. The room contained no other entrance or windows, and nothing obvious to separate me from the murderer. Otherwise the room was empty except for a large guard who seemed to be in a trance, not even nodding at our entrance.

"Ernie's here." Bedoe nodded to the living statue. "I'll come back in an hour."

"You're not going to stay for the interview?" I tried to quash the panic in my voice.

Mr. Bedoe smiled without warmth. "I got work to do. I seen this crap a thousand times."

His departure doubled my discomfort. Bedoe was a jerk, but he was my protector in this world of punishment. Could the stoic guard be counted on for anything? The moment stretched into minutes. Sweat seeped down my neck. My underwear cinched up. My eyes watered and my jaws cramped from unconscious clenching. I heard footsteps outside. Wait! It's too soon.

The door opened.

By the time Theodore Vincent, a.k.a. TV Swanson entered, my resolve had been erased by panic. I couldn't think straight. He walked in

18

as if he had arrived alone, but I knew there must be an escort. I peered around him to assure myself there was another guard, but he stood between me and the door. I forced three deep breaths.

At least he looked relaxed. I couldn't take my eyes off of him. He was the ugliest, scariest looking guy I'd ever seen. His head was shaped like a top, wide near the hairline and narrow at the chin. The front half of his scalp was gleaming bald, the back had graying brown hair that hung down several inches. His chin pointed like a gnome's. His long nose hooked down over thin lips. Now in his mid-fifties, he had a paunch. He was average height, but still taller than me.

TV glanced at the guard and sat down like he knew the drill. He slouched a little in his chair and rested his left hand casually on the table top. His sleeves were rolled up and I expected to see his arms covered in tattoos. I was disappointed. He offered nothing but a predatory stare and a silence that stretched long enough to squeeze out even more sweat. I tried to endure his eye contact challenge, but when he noticed, he shifted abruptly on his chair.

"You a reporter for television?" He spat out the words like bullets.

I reeled as if struck. It took a moment to realize that he hadn't hit me.

"Well, yes, a reporter."

"Are you or not?" His hand came up and I flinched. His efforts to intimidate made me angry and scared that I could even be angry.

"I am a TV reporter, TV. May I call you that? Or do you prefer Ted?" I hoped my voice sounded calm. My heart hammered like a runaway train.

"You can put a story on television?"

I leaned back, awkward with the chair bolted to the floor and folded my arms over my chest. "You have a story?"

He responded with the same predatory stare. "You're goddamn right, I got a story. They got the wrong man in here. They're gonna fry Mr. Bad. Just so's they can protect Mr. Big." He folded his arms matching my posture.

"Mr. Big?"

He looked sideways at the guard, Ernie. "I ain't gonna spill it here, you dumbshit."

"Well, why don't we have lunch?" His lips tightened at my weak humor. "I don't think Ernie's even awake."

TV leaned forward and kept his voice low. With him moving his head in so close, I felt like I was sidling up to kiss a crocodile. "These are power guys," he whispered. His breath was surprisingly fresh, like he'd recently brushed his teeth. "It'll be church, for sure." I took that to mean, like somebody's funeral. "They could come after you too, if you made this stuff public. But it's good shit for television. Blow the lids off some big cans of worms."

His story tumbled out in carefully assembled sentences, the familiar tale of conspiracy, persecution, and the downright meanness of our legal system. I listened to this crock until my head ached. Looking at the killer sitting across from me I knew he didn't believe it, yet he expected me to believe every word.

This man had been in jail for twenty consecutive years. Before that, he spent another eight years behind bars. He was fifty-six years old, and he had been in jail half his life. TV Swanson had constructed an intricate con for somebody like me to come along and believe it. Being a television reporter meant I could exploit him. And no, I didn't feel sorry for the S.O.B. He wanted to get on the tube and, hey, that's what I do.

"Incredible!" I said shaking my head. It was time for some play acting. Would he buy it?

"Everyone thinks that you murdered those cops and all those other crimes. All conspiracy stuff. Man! This'll be a huge scandal. But you know what? You could get some good publicity from this, but I'll have to know everything. Everything."

I said this with my best poker face.

Chapter 3

WEDNESDAY MAY 21, 1980

Lenore Avenue in Akron, Ohio, dead-ended with a chain link fence stretched across the asphalt and a sheer cliff that dropped down to the rail yards of the B & O. The neighborhood consisted of plain frame houses, all built during WWII. At one end of Lenore the homes were well kept and trash free, but litter and derelict cars had collected at this end, and made the neighborhood look unheeded and unloved.

The upper floors of the last house on the right were built above a concrete block basement with a steel door secured by padlocks and dead bolts.

Upstairs, a powerful stereo blasted out Jimi Hendrix's "Fire." Unopened boxes of additional stereo components lined the walls. TV Swanson sat at his coffee table making up twenty dollar bags of marijuana. Other types of drugs surrounded him, including amphetamines, cocaine, and heroin.

A fellow thug named Coon sat on the floor in front of him with his eyes half closed. His head swept in a slow arch, and he drew deeply from a sooty glass bong. Smoky exhale seeped from his nose and mouth, prompting a few muted sneezes.

TV's wife, Corky, lay at the other end of the room, a corpse-like pile of tightly stretched jeans, tee shirt and dirty brown hair. The picture was so familiar to TV, that he paid her no attention. In their nine year association TV remembered few days when she had remained sober. Tonight TV had plenty of drugs, and after she had swallowed a pint of vodka, he had given her enough to put an end to her sniveling and to keep her out of his way.

"This is the finest fucking shit I've ever had," Coon said. He exhaled a lung-full of smoke. "Where'd this shit come from?" His red eyes flushed tears.

"I guess it came from Columbia. But I got it out of a washing machine like one of them we got downstairs."

Coon looked confused. "The shit came out of a washing machine?"

21

TV gave him a wink. "Our Italian brothers bring in this shit inside a new washing machine, which they stash in their warehouse. They got a guy, Guido somebody, who works down there. He unpacks all the appliances. He gets a phone call with a number. That number's on the box that has the shit in it. He's supposed to open that box, take out the shit and give it to Mario What's-his-name. Only now the stuff ain't there. Somebody's snuck into the warehouse and got the shit out of the box. "

"The shit was in the box," Coon repeated. "Cool, man. Who got the shit?"

"I got the shit, you dumbshit. You're smoking the shit. Jesus!"

Coon thought that was terrifically funny and snorted white clouds through his nostrils and mouth. Then his face became deadly serious. "This here's the Dago's shit?" He used the all-inclusive nomenclature for the Akron branch of organized crime.

TV nodded. "Yup. Only I sealed the box back up after I heisted the shit out of it so's they don't think nothing's been stolen."

"But when they can't find the shit, ain't the shit gonna hit the fan?" Coon asked.

"That's Guido's problem. He'll think he got the number wrong or something." TV looked smug. "How they gonna know where it went? Maybe the truck driver took it. By the time they track it down, it'll be all over the street. I'm gonna make sure the blame goes on somebody else."

The plan's subtlety seemed to be lost on Coon. He took another hit off the bong and held his breath until the tears streamed down his cheeks. "Man! I am wasted!"

TV's stomach growled. He'd had nothing but a few donuts that morning. There was too much at stake on the coffee table to go out and get something. If he sent Coon after some food, he might never find his way back. Well, he had suffered through much worse than this. Missing meals was no problem.

He allowed himself another smile. TV, old buddy, you're riding a winning streak, he thought to himself. It felt pretty good, almost comfortable. His business in stolen appliances, stripped motorcycle and car parts did okay, but selling drugs netted lots of cash. He intended to keep it low profile so that the heat would not come down on him.

After being out of jail for nearly five years, TV finally had it together. A pretty damn tough road it was, too, he thought. He'd had more than enough of prison life. The last time he walked away from the Ohio State Penitentiary, he came home to a five year old boy he didn't really know and soon had another kid on the way. Corky remained faithful while he served his time, but he wished she had run off with a truck driver. Coming home to Corky had been a big mistake and making Teeny had been another. The only reason for keeping Corky and the kids with him, was so that Corky's old man couldn't have them. He'd probably try to rehabilitate her and put the kids in a private school. TV snorted and laughed. Across the table, Coon laughed with him.

TV finally felt good about doing his own thing. "But keep low and don't get caught," he muttered to himself, the only person in the room conscious enough to have listened.

Jimi Hendrix finished "Fire" and went right into the heavy intro for "Foxy Lady." That's how TV missed the sound of police cars filling up the street.

****

Detective Sergeant Kevin Neri of the Akron Police Department held his watch to the glow of a street lamp. It was half past midnight. He had driven the length of Lenore Street at a crawl, followed by six more cars and two police vans. Thirty policemen, dressed in SWAT outfits, quickly assembled around the house. Neri whispered orders through an epaulette mounted radio.

It took only a second to smash down the basement door. The policemen flooded in, weapons drawn and ready. The team thundered up the stairs and charged into the room. Two policemen wrestled one of the room's occupants to the floor. The main target of the raid fled up the stairs. Several of the swat team grabbed his ankles and pulled him down. They spread him out face down on the floor, pinning his arms and legs. Batons battered his back and the notorious TV Swanson lay helpless on the floor.

Detective Neri came into the room and turned toward the staccato beat of batons.

"That's enough. Put the cuffs on both of them and read them their rights. What's that?" He pointed to Corky lying on the floor. One of the cops rolled her over with his boot.

"Cuff him, uh, her, too. Get them all in the wagon."

At that moment, one of his crew came down the stairs carrying two children, still asleep, resting their heads against the cop's shoulder and holding on to him as if he were their grandpa.

"Hey, Sarge! These two were upstairs."

Neri looked at the kids and shook his head.

"Put them in the back of my car and stay with them until I get there. The rest of you guys, don't touch anything and get the hell out. Leave everything like it is for the crime scene guys."

The children were an unexpected complication. Neri would have to get them checked out at the hospital. Then he would have to drive them over to the county home. He had expected a sleepless night. But now he could count on a sleepless day.

Chapter 4

Bill "Tuck" Wallace sat at his desk looking at a pile of pink "While you were out" slips from yesterday, a typical stack from customers and sales managers. The morning's coffee on his desk wafted a comfortable aroma. While wondering who to ignore first, his secretary yelled at him from the front office.

"Ted Swanson on line one," Tuck had considered installing an intercom, but he felt the hollering added a personal touch.

"Ted? You mean Corky."

"No, Tuck. It's Ted and he wanted to speak to you."

"To me?" Tuck mumbled, staring at the blinking light on the phone. He had plenty of reason to be confused. He could recall the entire text of every conversation he had had with his son-in-law. The last, nearly nine years ago had been particularly threatening. From the beginning, their feud had grown, and his feelings for the father of his grandkids went far beyond hate. The thought of his daughter and his grandkids in TV's clutches filled him with deep anger. He could never understand why she had chosen to spend even a second with that monstrous miscreant.

Occasionally Tuck did see his grandkids, Harry and Teeny. Corky brought them over and let her father spoil them. Always after their visits, Tuck felt terrible, having to send them back to the degradation they lived in. He felt a profound revulsion toward the lousy, scary son of a bitch who had knocked up his only child and ruined her life. Now after nine years, TV wanted to speak to him!

Tuck took several seconds to calm his pounding heart before he picked up the receiver. He placed it carefully to his ear as if somehow his son-in-law could sucker punch him through the phone. He said nothing, but TV must have sensed that he was there.

"Tuck? Tuck, I'm in jail. I need help. Tuck, are you there?"

Tuck took another deep breath. "Just a second, Ted. I'm having an orgasm."

Ted gave him more than a second. "That's funny, Tuck. But really, they came and arrested me last night. The cops busted into our home and hauled me off to jail. They're letting me have my one phone call now." TV let the silence go on for a few seconds. When it became obvious that his father-in-law would not respond, he resumed. "Aren't you going to say something?"

"Ted. This is so unexpected. So they arrested you. What a surprise! Life is so unfair. Now why in the world would the police arrest you Ted? You haven't done anything, have you?"

"Go ahead, Tuck. Have your fun. I'm really in trouble."

"Good. I know the mayor. I hope they lock you up in the smallest, darkest cell they have. For several decades at least. I'll send you cigarettes. Maybe you'll get lung cancer and die. Hey, this is great! I feel like I just won the Florida Lottery. No, this is much, much better."

"So, you won't help me?" TV asked.

"Help you? Ha! That's really funny." Tuck's hands twitched. "Ted, I knew that you were a fool, but until this moment. I had no idea how..."

"They arrested Corky too."

Tuck stared at the pink slips on his desk. He slammed down the phone, then picked it up and dialed his attorney, barking instructions into the man's answering machine. He slammed the phone down again, grabbed his jacket and ran past his startled secretary.

"Cancel my appointments this afternoon. Call the police and tell them that there is a robbery in progress at 2865 Lenore Street. Do that first."

"What? A robbery? How do you know that?"

"Call them now. I'll give you the story later. That's Corky's house."

The windows of the front door rattled, and he sprinted around the building to his car. At fifty-eight, Tuck was a fit man. He served thirty years as a fighter pilot in the Air Force, retiring as a full colonel. Now he sold insurance. It was an easy life and a simple one. He missed flying, but his ears had aged faster than the rest of him and ruined his equilibrium.

His daughter, Corky, had fulfilled none of his hopes. But even admitting a dose of low self-esteem could not explain the tailspin she had fallen into. He felt responsible for her situation. Maybe the Air Force had taken him away from home too much. If not for his grand kids, she'd have little to reason see him. Her pregnancies had put ugly permanent pounds on her petite frame. Tuck could have accepted that, but her involvement with drugs challenged even his undying love. Her once sunny expression had turned vacant and alien. She became nearly impossible to talk to or reason with. Only the kids held them together. They should have been the gems of Corky's existence, but her criminal husband and her use of drugs refuted that. Tuck blamed no one but TV Swanson. Without that bastard's influence, she might still be helped.

Tuck's knuckles turned white on the steering wheel as he drove through the crowded streets of Akron, running red lights and stop signs, ignoring the horns of other motorists. He careened through the turn off of Market onto Lenore, sped down toward the end and slammed to a stop in front of Corky's house. Tuck had never been invited to this house, and the sight of the dilapidated structure filled him with guilt.

An old delivery truck angled across the driveway. The sides of the van were crudely painted over and it badly needed all kinds of repairs. Tuck Wallace parked his car cross-ways in the street blocking the truck.

Thugs were looting Corky's house. One of them loaded a large box into the back of the truck. Another man emerged from the house with a hand cart carrying a refrigerator. Tuck deliberately blocked his way, earning him an angry stare.

"What the fuck you doin' here? You better get the fuck out here." The man was about a foot taller than Tuck. His head sprouted bushy hair and beard in all directions. He smelled strongly of gasoline and sweat.

"Turn around and put it back. That's not yours," Tuck said trying to sound like the Air Force officer he used to be.

"Get out of my way, you little shit. I'll run this thing over you."

Tuck stood his ground, causing the man to rest the cart, with obvious annoyance. He stepped around the box. "I'm gonna bust your face against this here wall, and then you won't be no more trouble."

He took another step and reached out toward Tuck's throat. Tuck's right hand flew up, jamming his stiffened fingers into the man's eye. The man bent forward and howled in pain. Tuck hooked his right foot around the back of his leg and pushed hard against the round stomach, toppling him backwards. The man's head hit the asphalt. Tuck delivered a solid kick directly into his ear. He kicked again and his victim shrieked, hands alternating between his eye and his ear.

Tuck bent over and grabbed the man's greasy hair with both hands, pulling his head off the pavement "You had enough big guy?" He bashed the man's skull into the pavement. "You want me to keep hurting you?" Tuck's voice shook with adrenalin.

He let go of the man's hair, grabbed the handcart and swung it around, jamming the box back into the door. The box was almost too wide for the door, but the hand truck wedged the whole assembly tightly in the frame. Tuck heard profanity coming from inside the house as the looters came down the stairs and found their exit blocked.

Tuck saw another bearded head appear above the top of the box. The head gave him another dirty look.

"Hey! What the ....? Where's Bone?" the man said through brown and broken teeth.

"He's out here. And he's hurt."

The man on the inside started pushing the refrigerator box, but the handcart wedged it tightly in the door. Jarring thumps against the box failed to clear it. The head appeared again above the box. Making a quick assessment, the man began climbing out through the space above the top of the box.

The handcart had a heavy webbed strap, used to hold bulky freight. Tuck waited until the man was halfway out and looped the strap around the guy's shoulders. He then inserted the other end of the strap into a ratchet device and cranked until the tension trapped him against the top of the box.

"Hey! What the fuck are you doin'?" The man's head came up like a turtle's and his hands sought to reach the strap. "Lemme loose. I'll kick your ass, you son of a bitch!" His head twisted and his hands flailed, but the sides of the door prevented him from getting a hold on the straps. Tuck caught his breath and stepped back.

"You're not going to kick my ass. You can't kick anybody's ass if you can't move," Tuck said. "But, I could kick your ass, or at least the front end of you. And I will if you don't stop struggling."

Tuck heard a sound behind him and turned to find a gun pointed at his face.

Chapter 5

Just for the sheer pleasure of punishing Corky's dad, TV Swanson had wasted his one phone call. He knew once Tuck got his daughter out, she would pester her old man to get him out as well. He might as well sit tight until then. He still faced arraignment and a bail hearing. Although he hoped to get a smartass public attorney who might find some way get him out, having an alternate plan did not hurt. "I'll get out all right, and then there's gonna be plenty of hell to pay." TV muttered.

They had locked him up in a holding cell with the rest of the Thursday night thugs and closed the cell door with a crunch. TV ignored the other rough looking characters and sat cross-legged on the concrete floor.

He was screwed, royal. His whole enterprise had been brought down. The law now had enough evidence to keep him locked up forever. He wanted to pace, but he kept himself calm. He needed his head clear. He needed to think.

The urge to pace made him think of his father. His father used to wear out a circle in the living room carpet with his pacing. He was a man of few moods, most of them bad. His pacing was often a prelude to a beating. TV's father had beaten him so often that he remembered little else about him. His old man used to beat him just to quiet his own rage, his right hand descending like a hammer until little Ted confessed to something, anything, even if he had to make it up.

At age eleven, the police caught Ted stealing from a neighborhood store and he spent two years in the Canton Road Youth Correctional Facility. There he learned what a superb kid beater his dad was. The beatings he received at Canton Road Youth facility could not compare to his dad's. The place had recreational facilities and classrooms but they worked more than they played. What they did learn, they learned from each other. Ted learned to steal without getting caught. He learned to stay out of trouble by getting others into trouble.

After Canton Road, Ted managed to stay out of jail for a couple of years. He turned his momma's hair gray, getting into fights, and getting kicked out of one school after another. When he was fifteen, he started stealing cars. Stealing cars was serious business, and eventually he ended up in the Ohio Penitentiary, a giant step down from Canton Road.

The Ohio State Penitentiary gave you plenty to fear. The warden completely lacked mercy. The guards brutalized the inmates to enforce the rules. The cons themselves lived without pity or rules of decency. Lifers and hard timers left little turf for the newcomer, who could expect nothing except slavery and humiliation. But by the time Ted turned seventeen, he had acquired some size along with the ruthlessness to protect himself.

When they let him out of the State Pen, the only life available was in the criminal world. He could work hard when it involved someone else's loss. He struck like a thief in the night and stayed invisible during the day. But eventually he got caught again. His next send-up was the Lima Hospital for the Criminally Insane, where consistent beatings, terrible food and filthy cells gave him yet another demotion in what the criminal justice system could do to him. For punishment, the Lima guards locked him up in a building resembling an outhouse, where the only floor consisted of a thick wire screen that allowed his wastes to fall through into a trench below. There was not enough room to lay down, no space for a bed, and no plumbing. Nothing but heat in the summer and cold wind in winter. Thinking about Lima triggered memories of the Christian missionary.

Every spring, an association of ministers chose Lima as their pet project. The ministers received some kind of religious credit for their visits. The inmates would be cleaned up, given haircuts and new clothes. For a whole week, the most despicable, degenerate prison was made to look like a sanitarium. The inmates would be treated like human beings, solely for the purpose of impressing the preachers.

Within the prison population they sought a few miserable mongrels of mankind to hear Jesus' call. They came to banish the darkness in these men's lives and tell them about salvation. But a few of the ministers came for something else. Some of them used Lima as a recreational junket. If an inmate participated, he'd be rewarded with a few more days of privileged treatment. But only if that inmate could keep his mouth shut.

One missionary took a bizarre liking to TV. He could still remember the guy's voice, a high pitched Southern accent. The minister never lost his religious facade. He wanted TV to frighten and humiliate him, and TV was only too happy to oblige. After lights out, when all the other prisoners were in their cells, TV would be conducted to this guest's room. After some inane preliminaries, the minister would strip and get on his elbows and knees. During his ordeal, he would scream, weep and pray to God. And afterward he'd deport himself with complete righteousness. He could stand before their motley assembly and preach the gospel without any outward sign of shame. The minister had pledged to help TV when he got out. "I'll help you get a job. I'll help you find the Lord, no matter what you've done. God can forgive. You can be salvaged for this Earth and saved for heaven."

Of course TV knew it was an empty promise. Once the preacher had gone back to his normal life, he'd would think no more about Lima. He never really expected that TV would someday show up for Sunday service.

Back to the problem at hand; TV had run afoul of more than just the police. He had ripped off some big criminals. TV had broken his own rule and did one too many heists, enough to get him noticed. His trouble far exceeded a mere jail sentence. What he had done would get him killed. The big crime bosses would never let him live. They must have connections within the police department. What better moves than to tip off the police, recover their drugs, and have him killed while awaiting a trial? TV would never make it to a witness stand, where he could talk about where the drugs actually came from.

TV looked at the other men in the cell. No one looked particularly dangerous. But the holding cell prisoners came and went continuously. More than likely the place would be empty before his killer showed up. TV's death would be ruled an accident. Who would care? TV could think of nobody who would weep at his passing except the miserable bitch, Corky. Well, she ain't going to be that lucky, he thought. Old TV's going to be around a few more years, and that's everybody's bad luck. Especially all the assholes that deserved payback.

With that conclusion, a great peace came over Theodore Vincent Swanson. As he rested on the cement floor with his back against the graffiti splattered walls, his head drooped against his chest, and he fell asleep with a slight smile on his thin lips. He didn't know what he was going to do. He just knew he would prevail.

Chapter 6

The man holding the 9mm automatic looked about twenty years younger than Tuck, and was dressed in a plain, but wrinkled suit. He had a tired, wary look about him, and Tuck concluded that he was not dangerous.

"Isn't it a rule that you're required to identify yourself? You can't just hold a gun on me. You have to tell me who you are, or I'm free to defend myself. Right?" Tuck said.

The gun lowered an inch. "What are you, the one man wrecking crew?" the stranger asked nodding at the thief strapped to the top of the refrigerator box. The man's voice sounded tired and thick from lack of sleep and too many cigarettes.

"I asked you to identify yourself," Tuck snapped back at him. "I'll give you five seconds before I disarm you."

The other man smiled slightly. Suddenly his face grew stern and he swung his gun to the left. Tuck turned and saw that the big man, the one the other had called "Bone," was trying to get up. As they watched, he managed to get to his knees, then tried to stand. He fell heavily and yelled in pain.

"Don't worry about him. He's down for a while," Tuck said casually. "You may want to cuff him, though. Charge him with burglary."

Tuck saw his chance to take away the man's gun, but he trusted his instincts and did nothing. The man placed his gun in a shoulder holster and held up a shield.

"Sergeant Neri. Akron Police. May I ask you who you are?"

"Bill Wallace. This is my daughter's house."

"Is your daughter Irene Swanson?" Neri asked.

"Yes."

"We arrested her last night. She's in jail," Neri said.

"I know." Tuck turned and waved at the two thieves. "There are a couple more inside. They were emptying the place out when I arrived."

Neri nodded. "My guys are covering the other side of the house. Do you mind telling me what you're doing here?"

Tuck looked him straight in the eyes. "Was she committing any crime when you arrested her? What are the charges?"

"She was stoned out of her mind when we went in. We charged her with possession. But she's probably just high. It's TV we wanted." Neri replied.

Tuck shook his head. "So you just ran her in for nothing. She was in the same house with the criminal and you just ran her in?"

"Look, Mr. Wallace. Your daughter was completely unconscious when we entered the house. There were two kids upstairs. Your grandkids, I presume. We couldn't leave them here. She needed to be in a hospital. She was that close to an OD." Neri held up two fingers together. "We took the kids to the county home. What else could I do? Now," Neri forced a tight smile. "Will you please tell me why you're here?"

"I got a call from Ted at work today. He told me he was in jail. When he told me that Corky, my daughter, was also in jail, well, I started thinking about what was going to happen to this place with the cat being away. I drove over here to make sure that TV's buddies didn't steal what wasn't nailed down and pry up what was."

'TV called you? Not his lawyer?" Sergeant Neri pulled on an earlobe. "Are you two close?"

Tuck snorted. "Not hardly." Tuck looked over Neri's shoulder at the run down house. "Why *did* he call me? I wouldn't help that S.O.B. if God Himself asked me to." Tuck thought for a second. "He called just for the pleasure of telling me Corky was in jail."

"Who's Corky?" Neri asked.

"My daughter, Irene. But, with him in jail, I knew his buddies would loot the place bare."

Neri smiled. "I got a call that there was a robbery in progress. I see you parked your car sideways blocking them in."

"Why didn't you post a guard at the house? That bastard might not have owned all this stuff, but isn't it evidence?"

Neri shrugged. They both turned to look at the plastic yellow tape marked with "Police Line - Do Not Cross!" stretched across the door. It, of course, had been broken when the thieves entered the house.

"Not enough men to guard the place. There's a team from Robbery coming here later to catalog all this stuff. It'll take them a couple of days. These guys got here first."

They both turned to watch Neri's men walking a pair of scruffy suspects toward their squad car. Neri said to them, "Get that one down off the box and cuff the guy on the ground. He might need medical attention."

Tuck turned to Neri. "I have to get my daughter home and go get the kids."

"OK, Mr. Wallace. Thanks for phoning us. Good luck with your daughter."

Tuck ran to his car. He heard Neri muttering. "Thank you, Officer Neri. You're welcome, Mr. Wallace."

Chapter 7

TV Swanson waited in the dim light of the holding cell, detached from his surroundings and unconscious of the actual time. He realized that it was now too late in the day to appear before a judge. No one had come for him. One after another, his cell mates had been removed. The waiting had created a surreal state of expectancy. He relaxed his body with knees drawn up, arms draped over his legs, head lowered as if asleep. His mind raced with thoughts streaming like cars on a freeway. He registered everything around him, the floor he was sitting on, the wall at his back, the air he drew in through his nostrils. He even noted the quality of the silence. Jails were usually noisy places full of undisciplined men. But the holding cell had become like a coffin.

During his last stint in prison, TV had witnessed a killing. The killer did the deed in a dark corner of a crowded hallway. The onlookers pushed away pretending not to look. The victim had violated one of the ever-changing laws of prison life. The poor guy found himself suddenly cornered, his head twisted around by powerful arms, his last breath released. The killer paused only a second to make sure and calmly walked away. TV had unwittingly gazed into the killer's eyes for a brief moment. The silent communication they exchanged had filled his brain with sudden fear and revelation. TV quickly looked away, shaking. What he had seen in his eyes both terrorized and fascinated him. At once TV knew murder took guts and boldness beyond anything he had ever done, but it promised sensations more exquisite than anything he'd ever felt. The years had not erased the knowledge taken from the killer's face. Now a murderer approached, someone who would take his life. A man who had killed before. A man who knew about that feeling.

The killer probably counted on the fact that TV didn't know he was coming. But TV had voluntarily entered a new realm of his life. He decided he would be the one to do the killing. For him it would be a graduation ceremony. When his assassin arrived, TV would summon his own boldness and feel the ecstasy that belongs only to killers.

After hours of dark silence, TV heard padding footsteps far down

35

the empty corridor. He saw the man out of the corner of his eye as he came around the end of the holding cell and paused before the steel bar door. The man was not tall but had a wide barrel chest. His arms hung longer than average, and his fingers curled into hooks. The man was dressed in jeans and a sweatshirt, his face hidden by a dark baseball cap. From his street fighting experience, TV could tell the dangerous ones, but smiled to himself, knowing the error his enemies had made.

The killer scanned the cell and nodded, seeing what appeared to be a man sleeping on the floor. He inserted a key into the door lock. The lubricated mechanism withdrew the bolt with a muted click. The door hung on ball bearing hinges and swung open. The man entered and turned around, making sure the lock didn't re-engage.

TV was off the floor in a blink. He ran his shoulder into the man's back with all his strength, slamming into him, knocking the door open. The would-be killer fell to the floor, his face making direct contact with the concrete, his baseball cap flying out into the hall. For a moment the killer lay sprawled across the frame of the cell door, stunned, but struggling to get up. TV stepped lightly over him and grabbed the door with both hands. Driving it shut, he jammed the killer's head in the door. TV pulled it open and bashed the heavy metal frame against the man's head again.

TV stood over his helpless victim and felt the first hit of the promised sensations tingling his body for the first time. But he knew that he wasn't finished. The man's face, distorted with bloody grooves where the door's steel frame had cut into it, looked up at him, the eyes locked into his, questioning. Blood spread across the floor. Quickly TV slammed the door a third time, a fourth, a fifth. He couldn't tell when the actual killing occurred, but he wanted to thrust the door again, hoping those feelings would keep gushing through him. For one delicious second he viewed his act. Blood splattered the floor and walls and spread at his feet. The killer's body quivered no more.

With his foot TV pushed what was left of the man inside the door and slammed it shut. The automatic lock clicked. He picked up the baseball cap and put it on, leaving bloody fingerprints on the brim. TV glanced at the surveillance camera on the ceiling staring at him with a black glass eye. He gave the camera the finger, but the red light was off. Somehow he knew that no one would be looking. The architects of his murder wanted no witnesses and had suspended such surveillance. He ran, pausing at every intersection, expecting guards to stop him. The word had gotten out. The halls were empty.

Shaking his head with amazement, TV ducked into an isolated men's room and saw his own face in the mirror. He stared into the eyes of a new man. Haunting eyes, emptied of humanity reflected back at him, and only for another sensual second did he revel in his blood streaked hands, face and clothes. Washing quickly and turning his sweatshirt inside out he exited the bathroom dripping tainted water from his fingertips.

He spied a red exit sign and strolled out the door into a parking lot. Evening had arrived. TV eased into a dark shadow behind a dumpster and paused grinning, breathing the clean air of freedom. He knelt against the cooling metal of the dumpster and closed his eyes. Like a lover finishing a good date, he hugged himself and relived his recent experience.

TV knew that this kind of freedom would not last. He strolled out of the parking lot and down the sidewalk without choosing a specific direction. A quick search of his pockets revealed that he had absolutely nothing. All his possessions had been confiscated, his wallet, his money, even his fake Rolex. He looked around, expecting to see a squad of police charging after him. No one paid him any attention. Even police cars passed by, arriving and departing city buildings. Not one of them looked his way. Why should they? He felt invincible, invisible and cunning beyond belief.

A bus pulled up right in front of him, and he hopped on. The bus driver gave him a glance but said nothing.

"Do you have change for a twenty?" TV asked.

"Tokens or exact change only," the bus driver said as he pulled away from the curb.

"I don't have it," TV replied.

"Get out at the next stop. You get the exact change or buy some tokens. Catch the next bus." He pointed to the sign next to the glass box where passengers dropped their fares. The sign read "Fare - $.60 - Exact Change or Token. The Driver Will Not Make Change." TV reached into his pocket. "Wait a minute. I think I do have the change." He fumbled around in his pocket for several seconds. Out of the corner of his eye he noticed that they were passing the next stop. The bus driver ran a yellow light. "Nope," TV said with a grin. "Nothing."

The driver gave him another look. "Okay, Buddy. Have a seat. Catch me next time."

"Thanks. I really appreciate it." He gave the driver his most charming smile.

TV thought as he sat down, Five minutes ago, I turned a guy's head into chopped meat. Now I'm charming the Metro drivers. Is there no end to my talents?

He paid no attention to where the bus was going, not caring as long as it took him away from jail. He needed to make plans. Without a doubt, his run in this town ended last night. The Akron police would soon react to his escape. This time, he needed to disappear for good. He had murdered. His heart fluttered wildly at the recollection. I'm a real bad ass now, he thought. But real bad asses always come down hard when they fall. His first priority was to gather up his family and split. The thought of splitting without them was unthinkable. Taking Harry and Teeny away from his father-in-law would agonize the old goat, and yes, Corky too. The thought of hurting Tuck made him smile. He slouched in his seat, laid his head back and closed his eyes.

"End of the line. Hey, buddy!" the bus driver yelled from the front.

TV woke up with a start. He looked around quickly. The bus had taken him all the way to Summit Mall in West Akron. He stood, stretched and walked on sleep-stiffened legs toward the front of the bus.

"Thanks for the ride," he said to the driver.

"Don't forget to catch me next time," the bus driver quipped at his back. The bus roared on trailing diesel smoke.

On TV's right was Summit Mall. Across West Market Street were a K-Mart and other stores. He darted through traffic toward the K-Mart.

Few shoppers were in the K-Mart's parking lot. The store itself offered nothing he wanted, and TV was not stupid enough to risk shoplifting when he had just won his freedom. He needed cash not junk. He walked around the lot until he found an unlocked car, a 1974 Buick Century, just beginning to rust. It was a perfect car for his purposes. No one would give it a second look. The owner could return any minute, but it was worth the risk. He opened the Buick's door and quickly sat behind the wheel. With the edge of the driver's seat belt clip he pried open a cover plate on the steering column. He plucked a bundle of ignition wires from the interior, pulled one from the cluster and connected it to another. He removed some of the insulation from another wire and flicked it against a contact. The engine turned over but did not catch. He tried it again and repeated until it caught. He sat in the driver's seat with the door open and let the car warm up. "In the driver's seat," he mumbled to himself. Smiling, he drove the Buick away from the K-Mart at a deliberate pace. When he moved onto the highway, he accelerated, knowing that slow driving attracts as much attention from the police as going too fast. He drove back to the center of town keeping the car just over the speed limit.

TV expected at least one member of his association of thugs to be at the Penguin Bar on Arlington Street, but it was still too early for the whole gang. He saw a chopper belonging to one of the gang parked out front. TV put the Buick on a side street and entered through the back door. The place was empty, except for Pigman, his thug buddy and Clem, the bartender.

TV looked at his old hangout with new eyes. A pool table, dirty mirror behind lines of liquor bottles, a row of vinyl covered stools along the bar. The place was nearly as dark and empty as the night outside. Few patrons came in this early. And any that did would clear out as soon as his gang arrived, which they did every evening just before midnight. Pigman wore an extra large denim jacket with the sleeves removed. He perched on a barstool, resting his huge arms on the bar.

"You got your sickle parked in my spot," TV said. He nodded to Clem, who poured him a beer, placing the sloppy wet mug on the bar. Pigman turned around on the stool.

"TV!" he said with a deep voice. Although he was as big and hairy as a gorilla, his face had given him his name, particularly his nose. "I thought they'd busted you."

"Word travels fast. That would have been last night. Busted Coon too. They took Corky and my kids."

"They got your kids in jail?" Pig asked.

"No Dumbshit. They're somewhere's else. Probably some foster home or something. They threw Corky in jail, but her old man probably got her out by now. Can't let the princess get soiled."

"What they got on you?"

TV took a deep breath, glancing at the beer. He suddenly felt tired, hungry and terribly thirsty. He drained the mug in a series of throat bobbing swallows. He slammed the glass down. Clem immediately refilled it.

"What don't they got me on?" he said. "I ain't been arraigned yet."

Pigman looked puzzled. He knew the procedure. Arrest, arraignment, and then you make bail. "How come you out?"

"They left the door open." TV thought this was funny and started laughing. His laughter tumbled down a slope spiraling toward hysteria. Waves of hilarity rolled through him. He inflated his lungs, and deep spasms of his mirth echoed off the bar's ceiling and walls. Pigman and Clem exchange looks. "They got me on everything. Burglary. Dealing. Possession. Grand theft auto. And they leave the door open." He wiped his eyes on his sleeve. "Everything but murder. They don't have me on that. Yet." He barked a few more laughs.

"You lucky you walking," Pig said.

TV's eyes darted toward him as if he had said something significant. Pigman squirmed on his stool.

"Pig, you got any money?"

"I don't know, TV. Maybe a few bucks. My rent's due." His eyes fell to the floor.

"Hand over your fucking wallet. You're going to be late with the rent." Pigman looked deeply into TV's eyes and after a moment, handed over a small leather purse secured to his belt by a chain. "Always glad to do you a favor, TV," he mumbled.

TV opened it. Inside were handfuls of twenties and some ones. He stuffed all the bills in his pants. He dropped the leather case, and it dangled on the chain. He glanced at the bartender. Clem shook his head.

"No way, TV," Clem said in a simple voice. TV stared at him for a few seconds. Clem's denial started a roaring in his ears. He knew he could go through this room like the wrath of a vengeful god. He had known Clem for years, but knew nothing about him. Did Clem have a family? A mother, maybe? Clem had always put up with their shit and never complained. TV's body twitched but his internal storm passed. He would let them both live, and that brought a surge of feeling to his head, to his body, but not nearly as good as that other feeling had been. TV put a steadying hand on the bar and breathed the smoky air of the room.

Pigman and Clem again exchanged looks.

TV turned around and quickly went out the back door. Yes, it was good to be walking.

Chapter 8

At the county home, TV Swanson plucked his two children away from a pair of placid staff workers. They offered only superficial resistance.

"We're closed," one of them said, blinking.

"I'm here to pick up my kids," TV said.

"You have to come back tomorrow."

TV shook his head. "I've got to get them tonight. It's an emergency."

"Daddy!" His five year old daughter, Teeny jumped up from a couch full of kids into his arms. He shrugged and grinned at the staffers.

Harry, his ten year old son, stood on the other side of the room and stared at him. The look on Harry's face froze TV for a minute.

"Come on kids. We're going." He looked at the two staffers. "You got a problem?" They turned back to the television.

TV carried Teeny out to the darkened parking lot and the stolen Buick. Harry followed a few steps behind.

"Where'd you get that car, dad?" Harry asked.

"K-Mart parking lot near Summit Mall. Do you like it?"

Harry climbed in the front seat, his privilege since their mom wasn't with them. Teeny scrambled into the back. TV twisted the wires on the steering column. The engine started, rocking the car. "Fasten your seat belts!" He roared out the Swanson family inside joke. No one in the Swanson family ever fastened their seat belts. They pulled out into sparse evening traffic.

****

Harry's father drove a few miles to their run-down home. He parked about a block away from their house, shut the engine and lights off.

"Are we going home, dad?" Harry asked.

"Not for long. We're moving. I just need to get a few things."

"Moving? What about my stuff?"

Instead of answering, TV barked a command. "Get down. Now!"

41

They all ducked out of sight, ears pressed to the car seats, a move the whole family had practiced many times. TV had spotted a police cruiser in the rear view mirror pulling onto Lenore Street behind them. The police moved slowly past the Buick and kept on going. Harry inched his eyes over the dashboard to get a look. The cruiser stopped at their old house and raked it with floodlight beams for about two minutes. Then they turned around and headed back up the street past the hiding Swansons.

When the police had driven out of sight, TV said, "You kids did good. I owe you a Dairy Queen." Teeny said, "Yippee!" Harry shrugged. His dad owed them a multitude of Dairy Queens.

The kids followed their dad around to the back of the house. Squatting down, TV bumped open a basement window frame with the heel of his hand. It was a tight fit, but he squeezed himself inside, helped the kids and closed the window. He whispered, "Stay away from the windows. Okay?" Harry and his sister both nodded. "Go get two sets of school clothes, shirts and pants. Get one set of play clothes. Harry, you got that? You need to help Teeny get the right stuff." Harry nodded. "I'll be up in a little while with something to put it in." The two kids scrambled up the steps, hunched over like proper skulkers. "Hey! Make sure that you close the closets and drawers. We don't want the cops knowing we've been in here."

Upstairs, in the dark bedroom, Harry stacked clothes in two piles. His father arrived with a pair of heavy garbage bags and dropped them on the floor. Harry noticed that his father had changed clothes and saw a silver gleam sticking from the waistband of his pants. He had seen it before, a stainless steel Colt .380 automatic pistol that his father liked to brandish while he watched television. They must be preparing for a serious trip if he was taking the Colt. His dad picked up his neat piles of clothes and stuffed them into the trash bag. Harry had also pulled from their closet a pair of sleeping bags.

"Good thinking, Harry," his dad whispered. "Bring 'em with you."

He motioned them to get down on the floor. The kids sprawled quickly. Suddenly light beams flashed in through the windows. "It's the cops, again."

"What'll we do if they come in here?" Harry asked.

"They didn't get out of the car, last time did they? They probably won't this time, either."

After a few minutes, the looping lights ended. They heard the

42

cruiser pull away.

Harry's father stood up, his knees cracking. "You each can take some other stuff with you."

"What kind of stuff, dad?"

"You know. Your stuff. Toys, whatnot."

"Where are we going?"

"You don't need to know that. I don't know myself."

TV walked over to the closet and rummaged through piles of Harry's toys. He held up a tee-ball bat, a gift from Harry's grandfather that had remained in his closet for years, unused. TV forbid Harry from playing baseball, saying it was for "pansy queers."

"You like baseball, don't you?" his father asked him. Harry's mouth flew open, but his dad had already headed down the stairs.

Harry took a last look at their room. His family had belonged to few places in their life, and never had much of anything. Small apartments in rundown buildings. Many nights when they had no place to stay but the car they happened to be in. Grandpa Tuck had a huge house with carpet on the floors and furniture so fine that Harry felt uncomfortable on it. Grandpa lived a normal life. So unlike the way they lived. His dad hated Grandpa and never went over there. He truly was not welcome in that house. Grandpa Tuck was a good man and his dad was something else.

Here, in the humble house on Lenore Avenue things had gotten better for his family. Harry had allowed himself to be hopeful in this place. He and Teeny had lived and acted like normal kids. They had their own room and a closet to put their things in. They had new clothes and went to school with other kids. Harry even went home to the same place after school, a house, not a tiny apartment in a slum building, or a van parked under a bridge. He knew his dad was stealing to pay for all the improvements, but his biggest fear was that it would end, which it did when the police came busting into their bedroom last night. Harry wasn't surprised, just disappointed. Now they would live like stray dogs again, with nothing.

He saw his sister rummaging through her toys, creating a new pile on the floor. She was pulling out everything. He walked over to her, grabbed her by the arm and pulled her up. In the dark of the room that they had shared, her enormous blue eyes looked at him with excitement. For Teeny this was a big adventure. The five year difference in their ages made him the adult.

"Take a doll. That's all. We'll be back for the rest later." he said,

43

lying easily, like his dad. He started helping her put all the other stuff back.

A few minutes later, the three of them scrambled out through the basement window and back to the Buick.

Harry looked at his dad bent over the steering wheel column, prying open the metal plate with a screwdriver. He saw his dad twist wires on the ignition. The starter turned and cranked the engine. Harry wondered whose car this was and how they were getting along without it. He thought of the box of toys he had left in his room. Just like me without my stuff, he thought.

His father turned and looked at him, and Harry felt ashamed. Other kid's dads had keys for their cars. He saw anger in his father's eyes. He knew he had made his dad feel uncomfortable just by watching him. His dad did not like being watched and Harry knew why. Why couldn't I just look the other way when he's jacking the car? I'm always catching him in the act, doing something wrong. Harry's cheeks flushed. He braced himself to receive the back of his father's hand. He knew the look and had seen it before. Here it comes, with little provocation. Harry had taken the back of his dad's hand lots of times. Then followed by the familiar words, "That'll teach you something. You know what it's for. Think about it, figure it out." What his dad did not say out loud was, "You shouldn't be staring at me when I am jacking this car that I stole. The next time you'll look somewhere else."

Harry's dad's eyes locked into his, and he knew they shared the same thoughts. His dad hated cowardice worse than anything. Sure, he might get punched for watching him, but if he looked away, his dad would give him a beating. He heard Teeny in the back seat playing with her doll, humming a Sesame Street tune. Harry thought, go ahead. Hit me. I really would like a good reason to hate you. I couldn't feel any worse. Hit me and let me hate you.

They glared at each other across the width of the front seat. The light of the street lamp made them both look ghoulish in the night. Their faces reflected the moonlight, their eyes red and alive. They both shook slightly with the uneven idling of the Buick's engine.

His dad smiled warmly and reached his arm over Harry's head, circling his thin shoulders, pulling him tight in a fatherly hug. "I love you, son. This'll all be okay." Harry's body went limp with relief.

The Swansons headed east and north on route 8, toward Cuyahoga Falls. They turned into the dark empty parking lot of a strip mall and drove around to the back where deliveries were made. Harry's dad parked the Buick and shut off the headlights. They waited in the darkness with the engine snoring like a hibernating bear.

Ten minutes passed in silence before Harry whispered, "Dad? What are we doing here?"

His father stared through the windshield, at a chain-link fence covered with dead vines. The sinews stood out on his wrists where he gripped the steering wheel. By the light of the moon, Harry saw the sinews relax, and he realized that he would get no answer to his question. His father's head leaned back, his body settled against the car seat. Harry heard the rhythmic breathing of a person asleep. Teeny had sprawled out on the back seat. It was way past his own bedtime and he too felt the need to relax and let go of all of his worries. The stuttering rumble of the Buick's engine provided a hypnotic effect. In the past he had to sleep in unusual conditions and the current one was better than some he had experienced. He lowered his head on the seat until it was resting against the softness of his father's hip. Harry drifted off while the stolen car idled on, its tailpipe spewing a powdery gray mist into the darkness.

****

The Buick ran out of gas, jolting them awake. Harry sat upright, making himself dizzy. His father blinked and gasped. From the back seat Teeny said, "What time is it?" in a small and squeaky voice.

Somewhere a dim haze of gray light pushed back the darkness. Harry thought they all looked like ghosts in the pre-dawn gloom. TV stretched his fists and yawned, a move that made Harry duck in the confines of the front seat. He looked at Harry, turned and looked at Teeny. He smiled warmly. Harry had forgotten how warm his father's smile could be.

"What do you say? Let's go over to the Starvin Marvin and get some breakfast."

"Yea!" Teeny piped from the back seat. They climbed out of the car and slammed the doors, destroying the silence of the foggy morning. Cool air blew through Harry's thin tee shirt making him cross his arms against his chest. They walked around the far end of the strip mall into dim sunshine. Across the parking lot, a convenience store's lights beamed. They made straight for it.

When they opened the glass door of the store, the smell of coffee made Harry's mouth water. The clerk scowled at their wrinkled clothes.

"Where'd you folks come from?" The man said. The coffee still dripped into a half filled pot.

"We beat the donut man?" his dad asked.

"Yeah. He don't get here till about 6:30. I got Hostess stuff and yesterday's baked goods."

Teeny slipped her hand into Harry's while they scanned the racks of packaged food.

"You got a can for gas? I ran out a little ways from here," his dad asked.

"You stay in your car 'til now?" the man asked him back.

"What's it to you?"

Harry looked up when he heard the change in tone and saw the convenience store man recoil slightly.

"Nothin'. I didn't hear you come up is all." He went back to fiddling with the stuff behind the counter.

"Do you got a can?"

"Yeah," the man replied over his shoulder. He turned slowly to face his customer. "I got a can I let people use. They either buy the can or leave a deposit. And you got to buy the gas to put in the can," he added.

Harry glanced over at Teeny. She wandered to the other end of the aisle looking at candy.

"How much is the deposit?"

"Fourteen dollars."

"You charge fourteen dollars for a can that costs two bucks, and that's a deposit? How much to buy the can?"

"Fourteen dollars. We're not in the can business." The convenience store man stepped back from the counter and folded his arms. "I've had people leave a ten dollar deposit and take off with the can. Had to raise it to twelve and even that wasn't enough. So it's fourteen. If that ain't enough, it'll be sixteen. Then twenty. And so on. You get the picture, I guess."

Swanson did not reply for several seconds. He exhaled deeply.

"So it's a bargain at fourteen," Harry's dad laid down a twenty. Harry herded his sister toward the check-out, bringing their items. The man tallied on the cash register.

"I took a dollar out for gas. That's about what the can will hold. You can fill it at the pump out there." Swanson took the change and headed out to the pump.

Harry followed his father back to the car. The sun had risen over the tops of distant trees. Swanson walked to the side of the Buick and poured all but a small amount into the tank.

"Go release the hood," he told Harry.

Harry knew how to do that and ran to comply.

TV took the top of the engine's air cleaner off and poured a few spoonfuls of gas into the throat of the carburetor. He closed the hood, threw the empty can into the trunk and climbed into the driver's seat.

"Why did you pour gas in the engine, dad?" Harry asked.

"Because when you run out of gas, sometimes it leaves air in the fuel line. Pouring some gas in the carburetor helps it fire up. Remember that, son. Something that you learned from your old dad."

As if to demonstrate, he played with the ignition wires. The engine turned over, caught, coughed, stopped, coughed again and caught again. Soon the car was rocking with its familiar idle. They drove around the corner of the strip mall to the convenience store.

"Got to give the can back to the man." He recited like a poem. He pulled alongside one of the pumps and filled the car with gas. It was still early. The sun's rays were starting to reach the parking lot. The store was still empty of customers. Through the window, Harry saw the store clerk watching them closely.

TV retrieved the borrowed and now empty gas can and took out the aluminum tee-ball bat. He placed the can on the parking lot's asphalt surface, between the car and the store, and stared at it for a moment.

Harry saw him look up to see if the convenience store man was watching him. Within the darker interior, he could see the curious look on the man's face.

With a move so sudden it was like a strike of a snake, TV slammed the tee-ball bat into the can. The parking lot echoed with the sound of the blow. The can folded in half, and toppled on the asphalt. TV squatted beside it. Another blow folded the can even more. Then again, twice more, four times more. The sound reverberated starkly in the quiet, misty morning, silencing the bird's song and the insect's buzz. From within the car, the two children flinched and watched, without comprehension, their father's senseless beating of the gasoline can. He kept beating the can until he was drenched in sweat and he had flattened the can into metal scrap. He picked it up, hot from the hammering, and stood, breathing hard, staring at the twisted scrap in his hand. Harry's father's eyes slowly followed the path his feet would walk toward the store's door, and up until they linked with the store man's eyes, staring at him through the window glass. His dad's face remained expressionless, vacant. He walked slowly to the store, his steps erratic.

Unable to move the store man backed away as far as he could. TV threw the flattened piece of metal on the counter. It hit with a loud clatter and wobbled unevenly for a second.

"Got your can back, asshole," his voice rasped. "You can keep the deposit."

Chapter 9

The spring of 1980 had seduced Tuck with a familiar hope. Spring had been his late wife Jenny favorite time of year. Spring renewed Tuck's spirits, allowing him to partly mend the wound left by her passing. Having Corky at home gave him hope that he could solve some of her problems. Last night's rescue from the police did little to encourage him, but now she was sleeping it off in the guest bedroom. He thought that if he could keep her husband away, he had a fair chance to pull her through the drug problem. After they retrieved the kids from the county home, they would convert his rarely used office into an additional bedroom. The thought of having his daughter and his grandkids in his house filled him with energy.

But Tuck Wallace had passed an uneasy night, even for him, a chronic insomniac. Lurking fear kept him tossing and pillow pounding all night. But with the dawn sunlight warming his face, the fears of the night now seemed vague.

He stared out the window into the backyard which used to be a showcase of flowers. Tuck had neither the talent nor the patience to keep it anything but functional. If he had planted a few flowers, more like the way her Mom had kept it, it might have had a good effect on Corky.

Corky had been a wonderful energy filled child, whose boisterous nature had turned to rebellion as she lurched toward puberty. Tuck had been a military officer, and she probably resented his authoritarian manner. He hadn't always been home to keep his authority intact. Jenny had tried to maintain a traditional mother-daughter relationship, but raising her had seemed like such a futile exercise. She bit every hand that had tried to feed her. Then Jenny became sick, and Tuck and Corky watched the life slowly leak out of her. Even when she was too weak to get out of bed, Jenny still showered Corky with love and encouragement.

Tuck looked out of the sunny window and talked to Jenny, a habit he had taken up since she died. "I've got a shot at bringing her back, Jen. The bad guy is in the slammer. Corky is home. She's heavy into drugs, but we can get help. She can come back. Ted won't have a hold anymore. The kids will be okay. They're good kids. I need you to get the

Big Guy upstairs to send some of his world famous help this way. I know that you're the sweetest saint in heaven because you were the sweetest woman on earth. Even The Big Guy can't resist those baby blues anymore than I could."

His eyes filled with tears. He could still recall her in his arms. The way she felt when he held her vibrant, living body. Her lips, her eyes, her smile and even her scent were still fresh in his mind.

Sounds from behind made him turn. Corky appeared at the kitchen door, leaning against the door's frame. She was barely awake and had come from the bedroom dressed only in a tee shirt and panties. Recently, her appearance always shocked Tuck and first thing in the morning was no exception. Her body was bloated from all manner of abuse. Too much drinking, eating, taking drugs, no exercise. Her breasts hung like bags of Jell-O. Her stomach was a thick ring of fat. Visible below the tee shirt were tattoos of a lizard on one leg and a coiling snake on the other. Her face was puffy and red. She looked twenty years older than her twenty-seven years.

Tuck had planned to greet her with a cheerful good morning, but his reaction to her appearance caused his authoritarian manner to return. "Corky. Go put on a robe," he said.

"Why?" She squinted against the bright sunlight. Without waiting for a reply, she stumbled back to her room and returned wearing boxer shorts. She squeezed past him in the galley kitchen and slumped down at the kitchen table. Tuck placed a steaming cup of coffee beside her, but she looked at it with no interest.

"When are we going to get TV out?" she said with a raspy voice.

He realized that was why she had gotten out of bed. Her hands shook as she came down from her high. If past episodes were any indication, she would soon begin fidgeting. Restlessness and cramps would follow, then vomiting, and unrestrained groaning. Only now her drug supplier was in jail. Tuck hoped he could get her past the critical stage. Maybe he could get her into a clinic. He made a mental note to look into that later.

"We're going to get the children this morning. I'm waiting for my lawyer to call."

"We got to get TV out of jail."

Tuck looked at his daughter. He might as well have it out with her now. He opened his lecture with his favorite phrase. "Corky. We have only three priorities," he said.

Everything in Tuck's life could be expressed in three priorities. As an officer in the Air Force, his opinion carried the considerable weight, but at home as a father and husband, his authority was challenged by two very independent women. The mention of the "three priorities" caused Corky to roll her red eyes like a teenager.

"Number one. We get the kids. We make sure they're safe. They're probably scared to death right now. I'm waiting for Jim Haney to call. When he does we're driving over there to get them." He took a step closer to his daughter. "You care about them, don't you, Corky?"

She didn't answer him but stared down at the table top.

"Next," Tuck went on. "We settle you in here until this blows over. Your house isn't safe. There were too many bad characters going in and out of that place yesterday."

Corky threw her father a hateful stare. "TV's friends."

Tuck snorted. "With friends like that, you don't need crotch lice. Corky, they were cleaning your place out. Thieves, stealing stuff. Ripping you off. You and the kids aren't safe there. You need to stay with me."

Corky slammed her fist on the table. "Now I know you ain't getting him out. You would never put up with having TV here. I'm not going to live without my husband!"

Tuck shook his head. "The third priority is to get you into drug rehabilitation. You can't live like this."

"I can't live without TV," she repeated.

"He's killing you."

"You're going to let him rot in jail."

"He was rotting before he went to jail."

"You could help him."

"Jesus couldn't help him. Corky, look at how you live. You have crooks at your house every night. You're getting stoned in front of the kids. Ted's a thief and he sells drugs. He's violent and dangerous. Harry and Teeny are going to get hurt. You're going to get hurt, even worse than he's hurt you so far. I know he's hit you and not just once in a while. The kids see it. Is that what you want for your family? Is that how you want to live?"

Tears were running down both their cheeks. Tuck's voice choked with emotion. He fell to his knees and tried to hug her where she sat. The edge of the table got in his way and made it awkward for them both. She smelled like a mushroom factory, a musty smell that even Dial soap and hot water could not eradicate. She did not respond to his embrace.

"You don't need him. You would be so much better off without him," Tuck said, his voice muffled by her tee shirt.

"I'm pregnant," Corky said as if those words would counter all his arguments.

For several minutes he couldn't move except to rock back on his knees. He stood awkwardly, feet and legs tingling. Corky could always find a way to beat him. She had found the awful but unassailable reason for keeping her monster husband around. "Your baby? What have you done to him?"

Corky lowered her head, hiding her face behind stringy hair. "I need him, Daddy." She looked up at her father with unreadable eyes, like a puppy in the animal shelter, scared yet expectant. Tuck felt a heavy, punishing weight fall upon him. He stumbled backwards the length of the kitchen. He walked staggering toward the bathroom, closed the door and turned on the faucet. Splashing cool water on his face did nothing to clear his head. Outside the bathroom, he heard the phone ring. He hurriedly wiped his face.

Tuck came out of the bathroom to see Corky hang up the phone. She turned around when she heard him. Her expression gave him a chill. Her eyes darted away from his, and she inched toward the front door.

"Who was that?" Tuck asked.

"What?"

Tuck glanced at his watch as if time held the answer. It was 10:00 AM. Outside a lawnmower hummed, probably his neighbor across the street, the elderly Mr. Smith, who kept his lawn like a golf course. Somehow the normally reassuring sound of his mower failed to calm Tuck's rising panic. Corky peeled back the heavy drapes on the window. A shaft of yellow light speared the room.

Tuck felt the dread of last night's dream envelope him, rendering him helpless, unable to move or speak. Corky turned at the front door to look at him. Outside, he heard the sound of tires crunching on gravel. Corky quickly opened the door and slipped out. Tuck tried to run after her, but his nightmare seemed all powerful. He forced his leaden feet toward the door.

When he opened the door, he beheld his nightmare revealed.

A gray Buick was parked across his driveway. All the windows were rolled down. Inside the car, his grandchildren were staring at him with wide eyes. Standing by Tuck's mailbox was Theodore Vincent

Swanson, his son-in-law, Ted, who some called TV. Corky stood beside her husband hugging him with drunken enthusiasm. Ted's right arm hung loosely around her. His head cocked to one side, and he grinned like a lunatic. From inside the car, Teeny yelled, "Grandpa!"

Tuck tried to comprehend the impossible scene before him. TV's eyes focused on him alone. His smile disappeared and he gave Tuck an expression that said, "Watch this."

He grabbed Corky's wrist and flung her away from him with a violent twisting motion. She screamed in pain. TV's left hand bunched into a fist and he jabbed his wife in the face. Her head snapped back and she fell to the driveway like a sack thrown from a truck. Ted lunged and kicked her in the ribs. She screamed again. Ted brought his foot back for another kick.

"Stop!" Tuck shouted, rasping, trying to get more air.

"Why, Tuck?" Ted smiled. "Don't want to come between a man and his wife, do you?"

Across the street, Mr. Smith continued to mow his lawn, his white haired head focused on the line of grass. Ted's foot connected hard with Corky's ribcage.

"You'll kill her!" Tuck could barely move his feet.

TV's smile returned and he laughed. "Shit. This is nothing. Tell him Corky. You've had worse. This is a cupcake, right honey?"

"You'll kill the baby," Tuck croaked, struggling with his voice.

With that, TV's expression turned to curiosity. "Baby? What the fuck is that supposed to mean?" He grabbed Corky's hair and jerked her head back. "What'd you tell him? A baby? You mean we're going to have another fuckin' kid?" Corky moaned.

"You are a monster," Tuck said.

"Look here, Tuck." He pulled her hair harder, displaying her head like a visual aid. Purple welts swelled up on both sides of her face. "Tuck, would you fuck this? You got to fuck to make a kid. Hey! You kids listening? This is educational. Yup. You got to fuck to make a kid. I ain't done it. Not since I got stoned and we made Teeny. I can hardly stand to look at her. Tuck, can you stand to look at her? She's ugly and fat. And she smells bad. Even my buddies won't do her. She ain't preggers. That's just some bullshit she dreamed up. Got you pretty good, huh? You think maybe Jesus came and done it? Another Immaculate Conception? Modern Christian miracle?"

Tuck seemed to remember who he was. Cold anger seeped into his brain. His muscles tensed, and he took a short step toward them.

Ted noticed. "Come on Tuck. That's what I want. Come on."

William "Tuck" Wallace charged across the short lawn. Ted straightened up and raised his fists to meet the attack. Tuck stopped short of him and whirled around on his right foot, his left heel rising high, catching Ted full on the face. TV's nose erupted in blood. Tuck's right foot came off the ground, slamming into Ted's chest, knocking him backwards into the Buick's door. Ted made a grin through the blood as if to say, "Good lick, old man."

Tuck had been trained in hand to hand combat while in the Air Force. He became one of their best and frequently sparred with the instructors. They trained him to be careful, to never forget that your opponent could kill you. He needed to get TV down and immobilized. He looked to land the toe of his foot on Ted's kneecap.

Ted reached through the driver's window and whipped out Harry's tee ball bat. Tuck lashed out with his foot. TV swung the bat and caught Tuck on the ankle. The momentum of the blow spun Tuck off balance and he fell, landing on top of Corky. Ted swung again, down at his father-in-law's temple and connected with the end of the bat. Tuck's eyes fell back showing white. Instantly, TV bashed his father-in-law's head again. Tuck lay sprawled on top of Corky, while she tried to crawl out from underneath him.

TV rained two-handed blows down on Tuck with machinelike regularity, grunting like a pig with each swing, staining the driveway with Tuck's blood.

Somewhere faint and far away, Ted Swanson heard a car door slam. He knew that he should try to pay attention to the sound, but there was too much pleasure in the beating he was giving his father-in-law. Suddenly, his arm was halted in mid-swing by something unknown. He turned to look but it was impossible to focus. Slowly, an image came into view. It was Harry hanging on his arm and trying to say something, but his voice was garbled like a bad radio station. Ted wanted to tear into this new victim. Hands flashing, he dropped the bat and grabbed Harry by the throat and squeezed that tender, fleshy cylinder, feeling the little bones, muscles and tendons. TV could feel the tiny, helpless beating of his son's heart. He could hear him gasping and drawing breaths in ragged, wheezing drafts. He could feel his small hands grappling against his own sweaty wrist.

Harry's eyes saved him. TV saw them and read his thoughts. He could not hide from Harry's eyes. It was the same expression he had seen last night. Harry's eyes said, "Go on. Kill me. Give me another reason to hate you."

TV dropped his son and stood up. His lungs were heaving, his arms twitching. Tuck lay on the driveway behind him. Harry sat up rubbing his throat. Corky managed to get to her hands and knees and crawled like a toddler in no particular direction. TV heard the sound of the morning birds and the relentless hum of Mr. Smith's lawnmower across the street.

"Get in the car." He stumbled toward the Buick, and flopped into the driver's seat. Harry helped his mom into the passenger side and climbed in the back next to Teeny.

"Dad, shouldn't we get an ambulance?" he murmured in a low voice.

"Fuck that shit."

TV hit the accelerator. The car screeched forward.

Across the street, Mr. Smith finished cutting the grass. He killed the lawnmower's engine. In the methodical manner of an old man, he removed the bag of clippings and took it around to the back, to the compost heap.

Chapter 10

The Swansons kept to the small rural roads, avoiding both interstates and turnpikes. TV knew the cops would notify every law enforcement organization in the country, but they wouldn't know what kind of car to look for. Certainly, he concluded, Tuck would never rat on him. "That dude was toast!" he blurted against the wind coming in through the Buick's open windows. The rest of the family did not share his enthusiasm. For the last two hours, Harry sat silent in the back seat, not responding to his father's jocularity.

Corky's face displayed a multitude of agonies. Her eyes were stiff with dried tears. Her cheeks, jaw and neck swollen with purple bruises. She chain smoked Pall Malls but could not calm the stronger cramps that knotted her abdomen. Spasms rose and fell, like the waves of an ocean, evoking a low groan every few minutes. She tried to contain the agony, but it grew larger than her fear.

"TV, I need something," she croaked.

TV looked at her, taking his eyes off the speeding highway for only a moment. She wilted from his glance and leaned meekly against the passenger door.

The highway was arrow straight as they headed west through central Ohio. They drove through corn country. Long green lines of ankle high shoots flowed endlessly on both sides of the car. They encountered few cars on the road. Ted Swanson kept his speed moderate to avoid the stray country cop.

Corky whimpered again, trying to stifle all but the most compelling spasms. In the back seat, Teeny started singing "Who are the people in your neighborhood?" from the Mr. Rogers Show, "...in your neighborhood? In your nay - bor - ho – od!"

A cramp doubled Corky over, laying her face against her knees. Swanson hit the brakes hard, swerving the car, leaving S-shaped tire marks on the asphalt. The top of Corky's head slammed against the dashboard with a loud thump. Then he gunned the engine. The sudden acceleration threw her back into the seat. Drool flew from her mouth in a sun streaked strand.

"Ow! That's gotta hurt," TV laughed. "You should wear your seat belt,"

"Dad. I'm hungry," Harry interjected, trying not to look at his mother's twitching body.

"Your Ma here don't need no food, do you Corky? You're getting by on a special scientific diet. Nembutal and cigarettes." He reached in his breast pocket and pulled out a two hundred milligram capsule. He held it up to the sunlight. "One of these is all you need. This and a few other ingredients. You could go for days without eating, couldn't you, Corky?"

Corky looked at the pill. Thinking he might actually give it to her, she reached for it.

Laughing, TV flung it out the car's window. Corky wailed.

Teeny sang without melody, head down, staring at the face of her doll, "Oh, who are the people in your neighborhood? It's the people that you meet when you're walking down the street. It's the people that you see - each - daaaay."

"Dad, there's a McDonalds up the road. I saw a sign." Harry said.

TV replied, "Corky. Do you want to get some food? I'll stop if Mom wants."

"Come on, Mom. Say you want to stop."

"I want some french fries!" Teeny wailed from the back seat.

Corky sobbed. Her face pointed toward the floor with her hair hanging in sweaty strands.

"Well, what's it going to be, Mom? Wanna stop?" TV said.

Corky wept. She jerked with another spasm.

"See. Your mom doesn't want any food. Just because she gets these pharmaceuticals, she thinks the rest of us can get by with nothing. Only look at her. Does it look like she misses any meals?"

In the back seat, the two kids started a pitched begging. Swanson laughed as their cries grew strident. Corky's hands squeezed her skull like a vise. Finally she screamed. "Alright, goddamn it! Stop yelling at me!" The kids' voices ended like a switch had been thrown.

Swanson reached into his pocket and brought out another capsule. He held it in front of Corky's face. She snatched and dry swallowed the pill in a quick motion. She held her hand over her mouth and tilted her head back. Her body jerked three times and stopped. After a few minutes, Corky slid down on the seat and closed her eyes while the warm wind blew through the Buick's open windows.

They drove on for another twenty minutes. They found a busy

McDonalds in Tiffin, Ohio. TV took the kids inside, deciding to leave Corky in the car. She still wore only a tee shirt and boxer shorts and her beat up face would be noticed. "I don't look too good neither," he mumbled at his reflection in the restroom mirror. "Old Tuck punched me pretty hard. Ha! A fat lot of good it did him."

When they returned to the car, Corky was still slumped in the front seat. The kids wolfed their cheeseburgers and fries in the back seat, while TV drove out of the McDonalds. After a few blocks TV hit the brakes. A recent model Buick Le Sabre Estate station wagon, complete with powder blue paint and imitation wood grained sides sat outside a medical office building. He pulled alongside and inspected it. The station wagon gleamed in the afternoon sun. He noticed a child seat in the front. "Good. Momma should be inside with her darling for at least a few more minutes."

His skillful hands quickly unlocked the Buick. He motioned the kids to get into this new car. TV carefully moved the child seat into the Buick Century, as if to say to the unknown owner, "This is yours now." It was easier transferring all their belongings than it was Corky. He wrestled her semi-conscious body into the back seat of the station wagon next to Teeny. That meant that Harry could ride up front.

Jacking the wagon's ignition took less than a minute and they were on the road again. TV gripped the steering wheel, feeling the powerful acceleration of the Le Sabre.

"We got power brakes, power windows, cruise control, sun roof, wide-assed seats and a cargo area. Best of all, there are thousands of these sons a bitches on the highway," he declared. "They won't know who we are. The notorious Swanson family traveling in a station wagon. Them assholes ain't got no clues."

They turned left on Highway 23, heading south, toward Columbus. The station wagon cruised effortlessly. TV stopped at a shopping mall, found a car with Michigan plates and switched them with the Buick's. They took State Route 37 in Marion to avoid Columbus. If the police found the stolen Century in Tiffin, they would never connect it to a Le Sabre wagon in southwestern Ohio, or anywhere else the Swansons decided to go.

Chapter 11

The Tidy Mart in Cedarville, Ohio was a small independent store, located on the north side of Highway 42. Mayor Tydee had recently celebrated the twentieth anniversary of the opening of the Tidy Mart, just one year more than he had been mayor. He owned little besides the store and his modest home on the west side of the town. He was not a gifted storekeeper, but the place was so profitable he could ill afford not to keep it. So he hired local folks to run it for him. Almost every teenager in town had done a stint in the Tidy Mart as a sort of rite of passage. Jim Tydee had no trouble finding someone to work there. Usually it was someone he knew. It was unlikely that a stranger would wander into Cedarville and rarer still, into the employ of the Tidy Mart.

The current store clerk was an exception. He was both a stranger and a foreigner. Mohammed Mohammed Sundarabrani, a native of Pakistan, had been in the United States less than a year. Mohammed Mohammed had come to America with no job and no resources. His uncle, a banker and one of Jim Tydee's business associates, had asked Jim to give his nephew a job. Otherwise, Mohammed Mohammed would never have found his way to Cedarville nor into the job at the Tidy Mart, a job for which he was temperamentally unsuited.

Cedarville, Ohio, was a friendly place, but Mohammed Mohammed, or as everyone in town called him, Moe Two, had managed to alienate everyone within a fifty mile radius. The fact that he was a foreigner did little to offset what everyone perceived as downright rudeness. He treated all customers with suspicion and stalked them as if they had come in to shoplift. He accused them of cheating the store and if they spent more than a few minutes shopping, dispelled them as loiterers. At first the folks in the community tolerated his behavior and tried to teach him the friendly, Southern Ohio way. But Moe Two found their suggestions offensive. Jim Tydee, slow to admit a mistake, probably let things go on a little longer than he should.

Sales dropped dramatically in a few short months, plunging the Tidy

Mart into the red for the first time ever. Jim Tydee tried daily pep talks with Mohammed Mohammed but those sessions left them both tense and sweating. The Tidy Mart had been a cornerstone of the community but now was in shambles, cursed with who everyone in town considered a rude little wretch. The once happy hamlet became a place of bickering and conflict. No one had to look very far for a reason, and everyone expected Jim Tydee to do something about it.

Friday, May 23, 1980, Moe Two had endured another bad evening at the Tidy Mart. Jim Tydee ran the store until five o'clock in the afternoon. Moe Two took over until midnight. He usually arrived anywhere from twenty minutes to an hour late. High school aged boys considered beating him up a community service, so he had to be careful walking to the store.

After he arrived, Jim Tydee's daily lecture always covered punctuality. He also reminded Moe Two to treat the customers with courtesy. He finished up with the need for accuracy on the cash register, all highly familiar topics. Mohammed Mohammed rolled his eyes like a fifth grader in the principal's office. The daily homilies always brought him to the brink of a frenzy.

Jim Tydee had placed the day's receipts into a lockable canvas bag. He had done pretty well. To avoid Moe Two's shift, the town's people preferred shopping earlier in the day. He put about twenty-five hundred dollars in the bag, along with a total sheet for the deposit he would make on the following day. He locked the bag and placed it in the floor safe. The floor safe was his only area of privacy in the entire store. He knew that Moe Two invaded every drawer, box and envelope in his office in spite of the fact that the back room was off limits to him. Jim Tydee was certain that he spent a good deal of his shift back there reading Penthouse and Playboy.

"Moe, could you refill the cold vault? It's getting kinda low." The back of the store contained a cooler large enough for a good sized grocery store. It was usually stacked floor to ceiling with beer and soft drinks. The Tidy Mart boasted "The Coldest Beer in Town." To make good on that claim, he kept his cooler just above freezing. The cold vault was a smaller cooler in the front of the store where his customers selected single drinks. Jim Tydee held scant hope that Moe Two would actually do the task, but he asked anyway.

Moe Two folded his arms across his chest and scowled, waiting for his employer to leave. Jim Tydee obliged him. "I guess I'll drift on out of here. I'll be down at city hall for awhile, then home to have supper with the wife, maybe catch the Reds on the tube. Goodbye, Moe. Have a good night. Don't forget about the drinks."

Mohammed Mohammed went behind the counter and sat down, expecting to spend his shift doing nothing except later he might check out the new Penthouse.

His shift was light as far as customers go. Not many people came in at night. Mohammed Mohammed was rude to them all because it helped pass the time. He was unresponsive, rang them up incorrectly, and gave them the wrong change. When a stranger asked directions, Moe Two indulged in his favorite method of customer torture, bringing out his most unintelligible accent, professing ignorance of any destination whatsoever. On any given night, he rarely had more than a half dozen candidates on which to practice, so he spent his hours in near total frustration. He hated his job, his employer, the town, the state, and America in general.

Around eight, an elderly lady came in bustling all over the store. Mohammed Mohammed rolled his eyes and ground his teeth. She paused by a large stack of charcoal bags and lighting fluid. Jim Tydee brought in a small mountain of the stuff in anticipation of the Memorial Day weekend. She stopped at the candy rack, the potato chips rack, the sundries and the cosmetics. She wandered over to the fountain drinks next to the microwave oven, where customers could heat up a selection of pre-made plastic wrapped sandwiches. At each stop, she seemed about to make a selection. Then she would pause and move on.

The old lady looked up and noticed Mohammed Mohammed staring at her. Unconsciously he stared at all women in America, regardless of their looks or age. He would never get used to the way they dressed. He would never get used to the sight of their faces, their legs, and the contours of their bodies, and it brought to mind a host of sexy thoughts. His customer was a septuagenarian, but it did not matter to him. When she caught him looking at her, she reacted as if she could read his mind. She made a face and quickly left the store, letting the glass door bang with a crash. Moe Two gave her the finger behind her back.

The night wore on Mohammed Mohammed like tight underwear. He checked the clock at least a dozen times an hour, and always it pained him how slowly time progressed.

At last his tedium ended. He looked at the clock. His shift only had another thirty minutes. He was sorely tempted to close early, but recently that had become impossible. Two state highway patrolmen stopped by the store just around midnight. The men were friends of Jim Tydee. If they found the store closed they would, of course, tell Jim. That would make tomorrow's lecture twice as long as today's. Mohammed Mohammed's hands made fists and he growled, "Allah! That man has more friends than a beggar has lice!" It seemed that they were all placed on earth to annoy him.

He counted the night's meager receipts and closed out the cash register. He did not have to anticipate the state highway patrolmen purchasing anything since their coffee and donuts were always free. That was a store policy, a stupid policy, Moe Two thought. Why should those arrogant whores' sons get free food and drink when he had to pay for everything? The fact that he helped himself to whatever he wanted and never paid for anything escaped his consideration for the moment.

He saw the lights of a car pull into the parking lot and line up with one of the gas pumps. Mohammed Mohammed uttered another curse. It was a station wagon, not the police cruiser. He was going to have to deal with another customer. Maybe they would pay with a credit card. If not, he would have to close out the cash register again. Another godless American bastard complicating his life! In three languages he cursed them all.

He saw a man get out of the station wagon and pump gas into his car. As he approached the store, Mohammed Mohammed knew that this man would not use a credit card. He was sloppily dressed in jeans and a tee-shirt, the kind of witless, soulless redneck that always paid with a collection of coins and wadded bills, dug from the depths of their pockets. The man walked into the store like any American, without a dram of humility, like someone who owned the world. The bright fluorescent lights caught his face.

In all of his years in America, Mohammed Mohammed had never seen anyone so ugly. He was tall and lean, although most Americans were ridiculously tall, all towering arrogantly over his own meager height. A bulging forehead hung over deep set eyes. A long pointed nose and a long pointed chin reminded Moe Two of several minor Hindu deities. Hindus! Godless, filthy, ignorant people. Moe Two hated them almost as much as he hated rich, fat Americans.

The customer's expression fell a little when he saw who was behind the counter, a reaction Moe Two had seen many times when a white American realized they would have to deal with a dark-skinned foreigner. The man stared at him long enough to make Moe Two nervous. Where were the state highway patrolmen?

Finally the man spoke. "Say, how can I get to Highway 68 from here?" His voice was typical of the rural local dialects. Moe Two replied with his usual ruse, pretending he could barely speak a word of English.

"Dixit. Prehe-able do por tee doon." Mohammed Mohammed stifled a grin. The man cocked his head to one side, perplexed. "Look. I'm trying to find Highway 68." He spoke very slowly and made waving motions with his hands. Mohammed Mohammed loved it. Everyone had the same reaction. When they could not be understood, all Americans resorted to sign language, as if anyone could interpret their wild gesturing.

"Loo wen der hull diff gel du hide," Moe Two said.

"Do you have a manager? Someone who speaks American?"

"I operspeek definite to for gul hexiden." Mohammed Mohammed smiled.

The man lowered his hands. Moe Two realized the situation was losing its humor. He looked at the clock. Did he hear the state highway patrolmen pulling up? He looked around the man, to peer through the glass window at the front of the store.

"Hey!" The man's voice shouted. "Sand-nigger! I'm going to do you a favor. I'm going to teach you how to speak American in one quick, easy lesson." Mohammed Mohammed's eyes returned to the customer. He saw the muzzle of a gun and the man's sinewy finger around the trigger. The cold look in the man's eyes reminded him of the vicious street dogs in Islamabad, full of hunger and animal fury.

"You have two seconds. How do I get to Highway 68?" He pulled the slide of the gun back with a solid metallic snap. The sound confused Mohammed Mohammed for a precious second. "Hurry, Sand-nigger. Tell me."

Quickly, the words spilled out in a torrent of clarity. "Continue down Highway 42 to Xenia, about 6 miles. There you will encounter Highway 68." His own voice sounded far away, like someone else's. His language skills had indeed improved in the last six months, but nowhere near as fast as in the last five seconds. The man smiled, but there was no humanity in the smile.

"Now. Let's have the cash in that drawer. Just the green bills. You can keep the change." Mohammed Mohammed rushed to comply. He was very familiar with how to open the cash register without tendering a purchase. The drawer flew open striking him in the stomach. He had just counted the bills. The take was pitiful.

The man looked at the amount. "Hmmm. Someone has cleaned out this place already." He stepped around the counter and spied the floor safe. "Open it," he said gesturing with the gun pointed to the floor.

"I cannot. I do not know the combination," Moe Two replied wringing his hands.

The man spied the red plastic name tag pinned to his shirt and read it. "Mohammed Mohammed. Mohammed Mohammed," he repeated, smiling. "May I call you by your first 'Mohammed'?" He gestured at the floor safe. "You say you don't know how to open it?" Moe Two nodded. "Well, kneel down like you do know how to open it. Now!" The last word shot out of the man's mouth. Mohammed Mohammed dropped quickly to his knees, his breath coming in short puffs.

"Now I'll show you the power of the human mind. I'm going to teach you how to open this safe. Look at it."

Mohammed Mohammed stared at the round brass plate sunk into the floor. It had a combination dial on it, but his eyes would not focus. He could barely read the manufacturer's name, engraved in deep letters around the circumference of the safe's frame.

The other man knelt next to him. Anyone who saw them might think they were kneeling together in prayer.

"Open it."

"I do not know how," Moe Two pleaded.

"Yes. You do. Open it."

"No. Truly. I do not..." The barrel of the pistol slammed against the side of his head, making a slapping, clunking sound. The impact knocked him nearly to the floor.

"Look, Mohammed Sand-nigger. Don't give me that shit. Open the damn safe. You lying, stinking, foreign faggot bastard. In three seconds, I'm going to shoot off your nose." Moe Two felt the cold steel circle of the gun barrel against his left nostril. "Then I'll shoot off more parts, like toes and kneecaps, until only your eyes and hands are left. But there will always be enough of you left to hurt. Now, I'm done talking. Put your hand on the dial. One second gone."

Mohammed Mohammed put his shaking hand on the dial. He fondled it with his finger tips like a woman's breast.

"Two seconds gone and you haven't even turned it."

Mohammed Mohammed turned the dial. Each degree of rotation

sent a tiny tremor-like clicking sensations through his fingers. As the tears rolled down his cheeks and his heart pumped out one painful beat after another, Moe Two started feeling a steamy resentment toward his employer for putting him in this situation. He had felt this feeling every night when Jim Tydee had placed the canvas bag in the safe. The safe had a combination, something his boss had tried to keep secret from him. Why should he keep this from him? Didn't he trust Mohammed Mohammed? So, he had discretely watched over Jim Tydee's shoulders until he learned the combination. Many times, when alone, he opened the safe and stared at the bag inside. How many times had he thought to take it and run away? There never seemed to be enough money to last him more than a few weeks. After the money ran out he would be destitute again. And here he was in this country, a foreigner. The police would track him down and throw him into prison. Jim Tydee would visit each week and lecture him for hours on end. That alone made the risk intolerable. Again he felt hatred for his boss. He hated everything in America except the man kneeling beside him holding a gun on his nostril.

"That's good. Turn it, Sand-nigger," the man said, his voice soothing and once again human.

Mohammed Mohammed turned the dial to the right. Then to the left and again to the right. There was a final loud click.

The safe door popped out of its brass frame and swung on an oiled hinge. The large canvas bag lay within the shadows of the floor safe. Moe Two struggled to contain his bladder.

"I'll take that," the man said. Mohammed Mohammed, sobbed out loud. He reached in and pulled out the bag, noticing, for the first time, the small silver lock on the zipper.

"I do not have the key to that. I truly do not," he said apologetically.

"Ha! That's okay, Mohammed Sand-nigger. I'll open that one myself. Now get up and walk to the back." Mohammed did what he was told. The man spied the large door of the cooler and stopped. He opened the door, pulling the horizontal chrome lever. A cool white fog rolled out. Moe Two shivered as he felt the sting of the cooler's air.

"Okay, Sand-nigger. Get in," he said. "Don't shiver now. Wait till you get in there and freeze your ass off." The man laughed.

"It is very cold," Mohammed Mohammed said.

"It's a cooler, goddamnit. It's supposed to be cold." The gun barrel came up until it rested against Mohammed Mohammed's forehead.

"Maybe this'll keep you warm." Mohammed Mohammed dashed into the cooler. The door shut with a high pitched click. The darkness that followed was complete, and the cold immediately penetrated his flesh all the way to his bones.

****

Outside the cooler, Theodore Vincent Swanson turned around and scanned the store. He tucked the pistol in his belt. Although he could loot the store at his leisure, he found, with surprise, that he wanted nothing. But the moment of reverie evaporated. He had to move. Someone was always showing up at these stores, the locals needing milk or bread. If they saw him, they would certainly summon the police. But a voice nagged inside his head, urging him on to do something more. The hands of the clock on the wall pointed to midnight. Midnight was when things always happened. The witching hour. What could he do before someone showed up? He looked around the back room. Swanson saw a messy desk, some stockpiled goods for the store, and an old hot water heater slow-leaking into a rusty coffee can. On his left was a coat rack with a few empty hangers. TV grabbed a couple of them.

He squatted down by the hot water heater. Leaning over until his cheek rested against the dirty floor he spied the gas pilot light. A grin came over his face. Using a length of coat hanger wire, he broke the safety device that shuts off the gas if the pilot light goes out. He blew stiffly. The small blue flame went out. The smell of natural gas wafted out from under the heater. Swanson stood up and turned the heater's control to its highest setting. Escaping gas hissed at his ankles stirring the hairs on his legs. Soon the room filled with the invisible vapor. He took a deep breath of the deadly stuff as if he had immunity.

He quickly went to the front of the store. He saw the stack of barbecue charcoal and the pyramid of lighter fluid next to it. In a minute, he had several cans opened, dripping their contents onto the paper sacks. Several more cans were opened and kicked across the floor, dripping, turning the checkerboard vinyl to a slippery quagmire. Over at the microwave oven, he placed a couple of quarters from his pocket into a box of Ohio Blue Tip kitchen matches. He placed the box into the microwave oven, squirted a generous quantity of lighter fluid inside and closed the door. He cranked the dial up all the way and saw the light come on.

"Time to skedaddle," he said.

Sucking in the cool night air outside made him realize how full his lungs had been with gas. His head was spinning as he staggered across the parking lot to the station wagon. Three pairs of eyes watched him with interest. Harry and Teeny, and remarkably, an alert Corky, all wondering why he had taken so long inside the store.

He walked toward the gasoline pumps, still clutching coat hangers. Moths, attracted by the neon and fluorescent lights, fluttered against the store front window. Inside, the microwave continued to cook.

"I'll need premium for this operation," he muttered. He stuck the nozzle into the top of the metal trash can next to the pumps and started pumping gas into it. The smell of gasolene filled the air. TV took one of the coat hangers and wrapped it tightly around the handle's lever to keep the gas pumping. The gasoline flowed, a vaporous, crystal stream in the night. He quickly went to the other pumping station and repeated the procedure. The numbered cylinders on both pumps spun rapidly. With his hands on his hips, Swanson took a minute to survey his handiwork. All was quiet, except for the sound of the gasoline pumps. "I'm gonna run up a big bill, doin' like this."

He got into the front seat of the station wagon. "You smell like gas." Teeny said from the back seat.

"That's my new cologne. You like it?"

He slowly pulled out of the parking lot, reluctant to get away too quickly. As he reached the stop sign at the end of the block he saw a state highway patrol car pull into the Tidy Mart. The cruiser seemed to pause at the entry for a second as if the policemen, having seen the station wagon, thought for a moment to take a closer look.

Watching in the rearview mirror, TV said, "Go on into the store and get your doughnuts." As if taking his suggestion, the patrol car continued into the Tidy Mart parking lot.

****

Officers Cletus Moody and Tom Wittgenstein were a little late getting to the Tidy Mart that night. They had been chasing a drunk down on highway 35. Although it used to be their favorite stop, neither officer liked going to the Tidy Mart, not since the new clerk had arrived. But they dutifully made the stop, because they promised to look in on things for their friend, Jim Tydee.

67

Every night, they had to make their own coffee. Sometimes they even had to bang on the front door to get Mohammed Mohammed to open up. The little bastard just did not seem to get it. The two men made a lot of jokes about him, agreeing that he was "a piece of work."

It was Officer Wittgenstein who spotted the blue station wagon leaving the parking lot. "1979 Le Sabre Estate wagon. Blue with wood sides. Michigan tag GF-285-L. What's Michigan doing in Greene County, Ohio?"

"How can you even see the damn thing?" Moody responded. "I wonder if the Madman left us any sugar."

"Hold it, Clete. I'm going to call it in. A family car this far south at night? You never know."

Moody nodded, vaguely. Instead of parking up near the store, he stopped the cruiser nearer the street so that his partner could see the retreating station wagon.

"Come on up when you finish your police work," Moody said with a smirk. He opened the driver's side door and walked toward the store. A slight breeze blew from his right, wafting gasoline fumes away from him. Moody saw no one in the store and wondered if Moe Two was in the back room again with the Penthouse Pets.

Inside the cruiser, Tom Wittgenstein listened to the return on the license. The dispatcher told him, "Michigan registry, Joseph Fedderson. '72 Chevrolet Malibu, black. You need the address?"

Wittgenstein sat up. "Say again. 1979 Le Sabre wagon, right?"

The dispatcher seemed impatient. "No. 1972 Chevrolet Malibu. Black. Not reported stolen. No warrants."

Wittgenstein muttered. "Well, the tags are, anyway. Over." He hung up the receiver mike, and rolled down the passenger side window, and yelled at his partner. "Hey, Moody. We got to go after that Buick!" He immediately noticed the overpowering smell of gas fumes. Moody had nearly reached the store's front door when he heard his partner's yell. He turned around. Both men seemed to notice at once that a lake had formed on the surface of the parking lot between them. For several precious seconds, their minds grappled with the puzzle. Finally Wittgenstein slowly got out of the car.

"Go inside and shut off the master switch. Tell that little bastard to call the fire department. We got to go after the station wagon."

Moody nodded and turned toward the store. Through the front window, he saw, rather than heard, the flash of yellow bursting out of the microwave. Within half a second, the entire inside of the store was engulfed in orange flame. In another half second, the wall of glass blew out, shattering into a blizzard of fragments, flying, tearing everything in its path, including Officer Cletus Moody, who fell, his body lacerated beyond hope of living into the spreading lake of gasoline.

The lake came alive, seeming to rise off of the black asphalt like a brilliant yellow dragon, with a crown of black smoke surging into the dark sky. Bellowing, moaning with furious energy, bending, twisting, gorging on everything, living or not.

The concussion flattened Tom Wittgenstein backward into his cruiser. The ball of flame scorched his face and hands, all the exposed parts of his body. For only an instant had he seen his partner, writhing in the flames, before his own sight had been etched out by the wave of heat. The burning liquid, still pumping from the wired nozzles reached his shoe bottoms. It took only one breath, sucked in almost involuntarily, to dispatch Officer Wittgenstein. Pain arched his body. Flames gushed upwards, reaching out for his legs, his arms, his hair and face.

The Swanson family watched from the end of the block. The yellow-orange light reflected off their four faces, the children with open-mouth fascination. TV Swanson started tunelessly humming the Mister Rogers song that remained in his head from earlier in the day.

"Dad, what did you do?" Harry whispered.

His father gave no answer, but took his foot off the brake and started the Buick moving. He watched the glow in his rear view mirror.

The fire grew in strength, fueled by the huge tanks underground. Inside the store, the conflagration centered on the large stack of charcoal. The intense heat caught and passed on its hot life to all merchandise within reach, and soon everything was burning. The goods on the shelves ignited. The Tidy Mart held its last going out of business sale. Everything must go and it did.

For the moment, safe inside the cooler, Mohammed Mohammed felt a curious abatement of the numbing cold. He heard the explosion, dulled by the cooler's thick walls. But soon the compressor stopped. The temperature rose and he began to feel good, even hopeful. The temperature inside the cooler increased to an ideal level, as a short equilibrium was reached with the living hell beyond the cooler's walls. The thawing contents of the cooler began to release their characteristic smells, hot dogs, lunch meats, dairy products. Soon he detected the unmistakable odor of cooking. He heard meats sizzling within their packages. Sweat was streaming off of him now. The heat made him dizzy and he staggered into a hot metal wall. The contact burned him and he screamed. His feet could no longer stand on the floor of the cooler. Every square inch of his exposed skin blistered like a grilled sausage. He toppled over to roll on the super heated floor of the cooler. His flesh stuck to the surface like a badly fried hamburger patty. He didn't last much longer. The screaming stopped, not that anyone could have heard it.

Outside, the fire made a lasting roar, waking the nearby residents of Cedarville. They rose in their pajamas to witness a huge fire lighting up the sky. The fire department quickly responded, but there was little they could do, other than to use their hoses to keep nearby buildings from joining the holocaust. The fire would burn itself out and leave a smoking, smoldering ruin. Nothing of the three victims remained but charred and twisted bones. The police cruiser, blackened and melted like the rest, helped identify the two men in the parking lot. The brutal destruction had also claimed the life of the town's least liked citizen, the nasty little foreigner.

Outside Cedarville, the Buick continued on highway 42 until it reached highway 68. There, the Swansons turned left and kept going south. They crossed the Ohio River at Aberdeen. Once in Kentucky, Ted Swanson discarded the Michigan tags and picked up a new set.

If anyone had asked him where he was going, Ted could not have answered. He pointed the Buick Le Sabre station wagon south, kept to the smaller highways and followed a meandering path.

PART TWO - FRANK'S TALE

Chapter 12

In May of 1980, Theodore Vincent Swanson, alias, TV Swanson, fled the Akron police, and three days later was captured in Juliette, Georgia. At that time, Raymond, a.k.a. "Big Ray" Culp, served as the mayor of Juliette. Big Ray was Remy Robillard's grandfather, Frank Robillard's father-in-law, the father of Lydia Culp Robillard, Frank's widow, and being mayor, he was also Frank's boss.

Since the fateful fishing trip, I had acquired most of all I was ever going to know about TV Swanson's past. I still longed to know how TV's life of crime ended the same day Frank Robillard died. Nothing in the mountain of information on Swanson, the criminal investigation, or the trial in which he was convicted, jumped up to say, "Hey! Brendan, look here." In fact, everything I saw or read tried to convince me that the connection existed only in my imagination. But I wouldn't give up. Not without bothering a lot of folks, making a complete nuisance of myself and driving my boss and coworkers crazy with the single-mindedness of my obsession.

I met Big Ray the following spring. I expected a cigar chomping, good old Southern boy, who was also a crooked politician and shady businessman. Everything was pretty much like I pictured it, except that he wasn't actually very big at all but short like me. In his seventies, Big Ray was a man of considerable accomplishment, rich, renowned and respected.

An ancient and unfriendly African-American butler answered the door and escorted me down a long corridor to Big Ray's office, a library-like, pecan paneled room. There the man sat, as still as a statue, in a leather chair large enough to make him look even smaller. The wall to my left was dominated by a gigantic wooden desk, covered with a respectable stack of ruffled papers. Instead of looking at me, Big Ray stared into space with oblivious serenity, making me feel downright awkward. I waited for someone to speak. The butler broke the silence by announcing my name in a rusty drawl. Big Ray glanced at me briefly. The corners of his mouth raised a fraction and he nodded with the slightest nod as if balancing a wine glass on his head.

The mansion where he lived possessed enough tackiness to remind me that a rich southern gentleman lived here but one for whom good taste did not come naturally. By the time I sat down in his library, I'd had to admire the trappings of his life; the long tree lined driveway, the white pillared porch, marble foyer, curving staircase, and glittering chandelier. His décor spoke of pride and history, the dual markers of Southern culture.

Big Ray kept a long-legged secretary around, and she was easy on the eyes. Ray apparently thought so too. When she entered the room, he kept a careful watch on her ass as if it were about to do something cute. We were not disappointed. Her posterior was amazingly well muscled, and draped in a clinging, revealing fabric. A scoop neckline blouse exposed a generous bosom. It became obvious to me that, at least in Big Ray's house, the usual rules about staring down a woman's blouse were suspended. Under our glaring scrutiny, the woman fetched us iced tea and lemon wedges, placing them on a polished teak table. Then she disappeared through the hallway door without a hint of friendliness or acknowledgment. We both stared after her and shared a mild regret before Ray turned to face me.

The former mayor of Juliette had made most of his money in real estate, but he didn't start from scratch. Many considered his father the meanest man in the state, but he left Ray farms and houses scattered all over five counties. The elder Culp owned several little country banks in the counties north of Macon and had been a hard debt master to the farmers in the area. Most folks breathed a sigh of relief when Ray took over because he treated his clients with some kindness. He turned out to be a shrewd developer, successfully developing many housing projects during the population boom in Georgia. He attracted the attention of the big investors in Atlanta, but he got his nickname "Big Ray" long before that. He pretty much ran Juliette after his daddy died.

Ray's verbal opening was expected, part of a pre-chat protocol we Southerners all must learn. "Pretty hot for March, ain't it?"

"Yup. Had to run the air driving down." I replied.

"We need rain. Hadn't had a drop since two weeks, last Monday. You get any in Atlanta?"

"Some." I nodded my head.

"You with television up there?" He looked directly at me, asking this and then returned his eyes to the empty air between us.

"Yes, Mr. Culp. I'm a reporter for a station in Atlanta."

"Do you cover sports? The Braves?"

"No. No sports."

"What then?"

"Mostly local interest stories. Folklore, legends."

"Folklore?" Ray looked like he did not understand the term.

"Stories about people or things, traditional beliefs, legends, sayings, culture."

"Culture? What culture?" he asked.

"Uh, our culture. What people talk about around here." He was asking all the questions and that made me uneasy.

"What do they talk about?"

"I don't know. I'm trying to find out about Frank Robillard. Used to be your son-in-law."

"Frank? Why do you want to talk about Frank? He's been dead for what? Sixteen years?" He barked a short cough.

"Frank was an interesting guy." I said. "Football player, Vietnam vet. He was..."

"Interesting? You didn't know Frank. If you did, you'd know he wasn't interesting. That boy didn't much give a hoot about anything. Never did. No one asked about him when he died. So why now?" His eyes flicked in my direction. "Frank was just a policeman. I don't know he ever wanted to be anything else. He never tried. Yes, he married my daughter, and because he was my son-in-law... I would have brought him into the business. He was smart enough. He could have done lots for me. But he wasn't interested, never came on board.

"I wish he hadn't married Lydia. I never thought he was after my money or anything. That would have been okay, you know. I could have understood that. That's the kind of husband I wanted for Lydia. Strong willed, focused. Digging, going after things... like the old man's money. But Frank wasn't interested in none of that. Just wanted to be a policeman. I don't recall he ever did anything that mattered his whole life."

We both looked at the glasses of tea on the low table between us. Drops of condensation collecting on the sides. He slowly picked one up and took a swallow. A drop dribbled down his protruding lip.

"Maybe he married your daughter because he loved her. Maybe he was interested in something other than money."

A flick of his half closed eyes answered me. "Yeah? Like what?"

"Juliette was his home town. Maybe he cared for it and the people?"

75

Big Ray shook his head. "I gave him that job. He took it because he didn't have anything else to do."

"A policeman needs courage." I ventured.

Ray snorted. "In Juliette? Locking up drunks. Catching speeders. You think we got a lotta crime in Juliette? Like you folks in Atlanta? You think anyone ever tried to rob a bank in Juliette? We don't have a bank. Nearest one's in Forsyth. They had real police over there, in Forsyth.

"Frank was the best crossing guard we ever had. And we ran a pretty good speed trap over on highway 23-87. I guess he could just about handle that." Ray laughed, although his eyes drifted, seeing things in the dust motes caught in the sunlight beaming through the window.

I smiled as if Ray had said something amusing. He assumed that I knew nothing of his speed trap, but this is where I came into the story sixteen years ago, my brief and only appearance. Ah, my speeding ticket! How clear the incident was in my mind now, resurrected from the grave of long dead memories, thanks to Ray's grandson, Remy.

Chapter 13

FRIDAY, MAY 23, 1980

Officer Frank Robillard sat in a new Ford Crown Victoria Police
Cruiser, trying to enjoy the peace of a quiet morning. He had parked out
on Highway 23-87 behind a large roadside sign to hide his cruiser from
any passing speeders. The Crown Victoria was a gift from the governor
to the mayor of Juliette, Big Ray Culp, his boss and father-in-law. Frank
enjoyed the newness of the car. Running his fingers over the fabric of the
seats gave him an unconscious pleasure. The Crown Vic still had that
new car smell, but he expected it would soon be destroyed by his chain
smoking partner, the other policeman on Juliette's force, Larry Lee.

Frank needed his alone time before the day brought on his usual
worries. Restlessness had chased him from his rented room in the back of
Mrs. Reynolds house while the rest of the town slept. The cot he slept on
was ridiculously tiny for his large body, and the room itself wasn't much
bigger. It was large enough for the pitifully small pile of stuff he owned
after marital separation. Inside the new police car, Frank could stretch
out and watch the sunlight coming through the pines, the mist rising over
the soybean field across the road and listen to the waking songbirds. This
respite renewed him better than sleep on that cramped cot.

He had discovered that if he angled the cruiser in a particular way
and played with the radio buttons, he could receive a faint but clear
signal from the tiny low wattage Atlanta radio station, WRFG. From six
to ten in the morning they played traditional blues, a form of music that
Frank enjoyed. He listened to an old scratchy Robert Johnson recording,
"Hellhound on My Trail." Despite the poor quality of the recordings, he
loved listening to the old blues singers. Lately the songs seemed to
perfectly match his mood.

     "I've got to keep on movin',
     Blues fallin' down like hail,
     An the days keep on worryin' me,
     There's a hell hound on my trail."
Robert Johnson's haunted voice on the old recording kindled fresh

emotions. His days did keep on worrying him. His wife, Lydia, wanted a divorce. She had obtained a court ordered separation, working some slick Atlanta attorney on him like a hickory rod. On top of that, the attorney had the nerve to send him the bill. He already owed his father-in-law thousands of dollars, a debt partly inherited from his father and partly run up on his own. Frank had paid on it for nearly a decade, but the balance had hardly changed.

Lydia wanted to move to Atlanta. After the divorce, there would be little he could do to stop her. She intended to take their son, Little Ray, with her. Frank did not want her to move away, and he could not stand to be away from Little Ray. Frank Robillard shook his head at the notion of her leaving with their son, of how hard he would fight it and of the inevitable, frustrating outcome.

Lydia was the hardest woman in the world to live with, but she had always been Frank's dream. Lydia had been the prettiest girl in town and the daughter of the richest man in town. Since they were kids in grade school Frank had idolized her like a golden work of art. But how she pained him, made him feel small, especially concerning what their life lacked. She hated their rustic existence. He knew his dream was little more than his fantasy, one that no one shared. Frank let out a deep breath, unaware that he had been holding it in his lungs. Like I hold on to everything until it hurts, he thought. And I have no argument against any of it.

Muddy Waters followed Robert Johnson, singing "She's Nineteen Years Old." The song, all about being a slave to lust, made Frank stir. He was a healthy adult man with a healthy drive, something Lydia had matured without. Oh, she was beautiful and men lusted after her, but she seemed to be satisfied with the stirring of that lust and found the act itself distasteful. The marriage was a fountain of frustration, anger, and hurt, but Frank didn't want it to end.

In a span of five minutes, he had gone from tranquility to agitation. Once his worries started, his day would continue along a similar path. In just a few more minutes, he had to attend to the school crossing. Guarding school children on the quiet streets of Juliette's town square was one of Frank's more meaningless duties. The square rarely received more than a few cars before noon, but the mayor and the city manager, Randy Wilbanks, came up with the idea of a crossing guard. Juliette's last pedestrian injury had been inflicted by a horse around the turn of the century. Guarding the kids at the cross-walk ranked right up there with running a speed trap on an empty highway.

Frank raised his hand as if to strike the steering wheel, but the far off whine of an approaching car interrupted him. Instead his hand darted to shut off the radio. He leaned his ear closer to the open window. The sound of a high revving engine tantalized him. Although he was hidden by the road sign, Frank crouched inside the Crown Victoria and stared down the nearly half mile of straight road. Immediately he saw a glint of red paint. A new Mustang flashed by him, and he briefly heard the Allman Brothers through the car's open window.

"One of those new 5.0 Mustangs." Frank checked his radar display. "77.7 miles per hour. That's a violation." The Crown Vic had been idling for a long time. Frank turned on the flashing lights and pulled out from behind the sign. He almost hoped for a chase, that the speeder would continue speeding, letting him open the cruiser up. But the Mustang's brake lights came on as the driver reacted to the flashing lights and siren. The Mustang pulled to the side of the road.

Frank donned a pair of mirrored Ray Bans and grabbed his citation pad. He knew his uniform and sunglasses made him the stereotypical Southern cop, but having fun at the speeder's expense provided a little compensation for the guilt he felt writing them citations.

The walk to the Mustang was only a few yards, but he spotted a dead raccoon on the other side of the road. Road kills were common enough, but had become epidemic since the water started filling Lake Juliette. Driven out of its flooded den, this poor critter wandered to the highway. Frank looked at the brightening sky and saw a dozen vultures circling. They would never descend on the carcass while it was lying on the pavement. They understood the dangers of the highway better than the raccoon. Frank booted the carcass until it was several feet off the pavement. As he turned toward the Mustang, he noticed the driver curiously looking at him in the rear view mirror.

The driver turned out to be a college kid. Probably returning to Atlanta from Macon or Statesboro. His dad sure bought him a nice car, Frank thought. The kid got in the first words.

"Officer, did I miss that light back there?"

Frank did not smile. There was no light for twenty miles. Violators occasionally said something funny, but it was bad form to acknowledge their humor. He might get a chuckle later when he told the guys down at Hector's.

"May I see your driver's license and registration, please."

79

The boy handed them over. Frank appreciated the lack of fumbling. Fumbling reminded him that he did the driver a disservice and that made him nervous as well. "Do you know what the speed limit is on this highway?"

"Uh... fifty?"

"Try forty-five. You were clocked over seventy. Going thirty miles per hour over the speed limit is serious. We can arrest you and tow your car."

"What? For speeding?"

"That's right. I'm doing you a favor writing it for sixty-five." Frank said.

"I never got a ticket before. Can't you give me a warning?"

"You need to be warned about the consequence of speeding?" Frank asked.

"Well... I give you my word that I'll keep my speed down. I..."

"Speeding is part of the American way of life, Mr. uh...Macbean. Is that like 'bean' or pronounced Scottish, like 'Bahan?'"

The college kid blinked behind thick glasses at the question.

"More like 'Bane' but thanks for asking." He added, "My mother was Irish."

"Irish, huh? That must have made for some interesting family situations." Frank handed him the clipboard to sign.

"That's it? I'm ticketed?" the boy said.

"Yup. There is no escape from the law."

Again, the driver gave him a look. "Officer, is there anything I can do to..."

"What do you think?"

"No. I guess not. I'll take my ticket."

"Good. Court date is June seventeenth. Come to the address on the back or pay the fine of sixty-five dollars, cashiers check, no personal checks. And retard that beast to the posted speed limit."

Frank realized that he was now late for the school crossing and hustled back to the cruiser. He pulled out smoothly in the direction of Juliette. Speeding past, he caught a quick look of the college kid's disgruntled expression.

Chapter 14

In full flight, the Crown Victoria zipped past farms and fields, weedy vacant lots and in less than two minutes passed the store fronts of Juliette. He left the cruiser parked in front of Juliette's combination police station, courthouse and city building. As expected, his partner Larry Lee was not outside waiting for him. He charged into the building, past the empty receptionist's desk. Frank stuck his head into Randy Wilbanks's office. Randy was Juliette's city manager. The murmuring of a Christian radio station came from a small radio behind Randy's desk.

Randy looked up from his desk. "Good morning, Frank. Christ be with you. Aren't you supposed to be at the school?"

"Larry's late again."

The front door slammed. "Godamnit, Frank, where the fuckin' hell are you, goddamnit?" Larry Lee burst into Randy's office.

"Randy!" He bellowed, drowning out the gospel radio. "Are you still listening to that goddamn Jesus station? All damn day, every mother fucking day. Don't you ever get sick and tired of saving your goddamn ass? Christ on a fucking crutch! Come on Frank. We gotta get to the mother-fucking school before Randy gets his dick caught in his bible, and he starts preaching us another sermon on the mother-fucking mountain."

"You should be at the school now, Larry. And please, your language." Randy clenched his fists but kept his voice calm.

"Goddamn right, Randy. And we'd be there now if fuck-head here, would get his ass in the fucking police car so we can get both our asses over to help the little bastards get their assess across the street. And, right again, my language is fucking horrible today." Larry lowered the brim of his policeman's hat to his eyebrow and gave Randy a wide smile.

Randy pressed his lips together and took slow deep breaths.

Frank turned and made long strides down the hallway. Larry scooted to catch up. Outside, the bright morning sun slanted into the small city square. Like dance partners, Frank and Larry swung toward the cruiser, trying to match the grace of Starsky and Hutch. Frank slid into the driver's seat..

"Frank, will you stop by Rue's so's I can get me one of them bear claws and some coffee? My stomach is feeling worse than a pig's asshole. Too many shots at Hectors last night." Larry lifted his left leg and ripped a loud, blustering fart. "My ass is shooting flames, too."

Frank stared straight through the windshield, not breathing.

"Larry, we're already two minutes late."

Larry rolled his eyes towards his partner. "Frankie, Frankie, Frankie. I need it. That coffee will wake me up. I need to be alert to guide the little bastards across the fucking street that don't have three cars a day. If I can't get some coffee, I gotta go do a sit-down on the can. We can go to the school after that. Maybe if I take a shit, I won't fart so much."

Frank sighed and accelerated the Crown Victoria half a block to the "Rue's Southern Style Bakery." The gold lettered window announced, "Established 1976."

"Hurry up, Larry."

Larry climbed the brick steps into the bakery. Frank watched him through the glass door. He saw the owner, Rue Harrison, hand Larry the small white paper sack. Frank tapped his fingers on the steering wheel, and was about to get out when he saw Larry coming toward the door.

Larry paused outside the cruiser to raise his leg like a dog and let another fart rip. He climbed in and shut the door, babbling before his butt hit the seat. "Holy fucking baboon dick! That woman looks good today. She's wearing this thin cotton thing. You can see her nipples all puckered up and sticking out. She leans over that pastry counter a long time getting out those bears claws. Oh, them titties are the biggest in town!" Larry made kissing noises. "Then she walks over to the coffee thing and starts pouring, kinda clenching her ass cheeks together. She's got this real sharp wedgie in her crack. Man! I was just about to jump over the counter and have that thing right there!"

Larry placed his coffee on the dash of the Crown Victoria and stared down into the paper sack sitting in his lap. He lowered his mouth almost to the top and muffled his voice in the bag.

"She wants you, Frank." He looked at his partner out of the corner of his eyes.

Frank ignored him.

"'How is Frank today, Larry?' she says. 'Does Frank want a cup of coffee?' she says. She was fingering her crotch, pushing her hips forward-like. She had that look in her eyes, kinda dreamy and hot. You know what I mean?"

"Larry, we're late already. It's going to be your ass and mine if Big Ray comes by and we're not there."

Larry deeply sniffed the contents of the bag and exhaled loudly. "What about Rue? She could close the shop for a little bit. You two could do it now, on the tile behind the counter. Come back, do it again when it gets hot this afternoon. That'd feel pretty good, you know. All that cool green linoleum. Hot pink flesh. Can you do it twice in one day, Frank? You up to that? I know Rue can. There's enough woman for a whole bunch of..."

"I don't care about Rue. I'm not interested. I am a married man." Frank snapped. "And she's..."

"She ain't no man, married or otherwise, buddy boy. Take a look at those titties. Whatta you mean, you married? Lydia? That cold bitch? That ain't married. I'd rather have a hot woman in the bakery than that cold bitch in your big house. Only you ain't in the big house anymore, are you, Frankie? Sorry, I didn't mean to bring that up. That room in the back of Mrs. Reynolds, that bed big enough for you and Rue to do it in?"

"Shut up, Larry. Shut your goddamn mouth. Get your fucking coffee cup off the dash or I'm going to hit the gas and it'll spill on your crotch. Stick that donut in your mouth and shut the hell up."

"Frank. Frank. Your language is terrible today. You're ragging 'cause you're a little tense? Haven't had any lately? That usually makes me cranky. If you're waiting for Lydia's twat to thaw out, you might as well wait for the Braves to win the World Series. There's a hot woman right in there waiting for you. Warm, inviting and already wet. Go for it, man. I'll watch the little weenies cross the fucking street. Just ease on up those steps and have at it."

Frank's eyes betrayed him, darting toward the gold lettered window of Rue's Southern Style Bakery. Sure enough, at that moment, Rue was looking straight at him through the glass. The car's engine was rhythmically throbbing, sending dangerous vibrations through his hands on the steering wheel, warming his body in an uncomfortable way. He tore his eyes away from Rue and stomped on the gas.

When Frank hit the accelerator, the coffee cup flew straight off the Crown Victoria's dash. Larry deftly caught it, but a substantial slug of hot liquid landed in the crotch of his khaki uniform pants. Larry raised the cup to prevent another spill. The distance they had to travel was less than two hundred yards, but the Crown Victoria was already going fifty miles per hour. Frank hit the brakes hard. Another big gulp of coffee sloshed out the front rim of the cup and again landed squarely in Larry's crotch.

Larry Lee spewed cuss words at an astonishing rate, staring at his soaked trousers, holding the bear claw in his right hand and a dripping coffee cup in his left.

A fist fight had broken out in the middle of the street at the precise location of the town's only school crossing. One of the combatants was Frank's own son, Raymond, who he called Little Ray. A crowd of school children and a few adults had gathered to watch. A delivery truck had stopped to avoid running over the crowd. The driver, obviously in no hurry, watched from behind the wheel. Frank reached the sprawling boys, a flurry of tee shirts and denim, grabbed each by the arm and pulled them apart.

"Stop it, now!" They came to sloppy attention at the sound of his voice. "Ray, what's going on here?"

The two dust covered boys glared at each other, but being held apart by a big adult stifled any further aggression. From their expressions Frank knew he would get no information from either, so he stood there not knowing exactly what to do. A second later, Larry Lee climbed out of the cruiser, sticking his baton into his belt. He stood, towering over the kids with an intense scowl on his face. "You two boys are the sorriest pieces of shit I ever saw."

"Larry..." Frank's voice had a warning tone to it but Larry ignored him

"What right do you have to disrupt the peace of this city? You know the law. It's simple. You get your ass out of bed. You eat your goddamn corn flakes, and you walk to school. Which of them things don't you understand?" Larry Lee paced in front of them. "Where does it say that the town needs two boys duking it out in the street and stopping traffic?"

He waved a hand at the delivery truck driver. "You both have violated about seven laws right now. I could haul you down to the jail and leave you there until your parents came home from work. Then when they come to pick you up we wouldn't let you go. No. You'd be in prison for a long time. In the slammer. Hard time. With queers as cell mates ."

"Larry, that's enough."

"Just give me one minute, Officer Robillard. These boys need to learn to respect the law." Larry pointed a finger at Little Ray. "You! Your dad sure told you not to fight in the street on the way to school, didn't he? I know you been raised right. What sorry ass excuse do you have? What the hell do you have to say for yourself?"

A smile crossed little Ray's dirty face.

"Officer Lee. Did you have an accident?" All eyes turned toward Larry Lee's trousers, where the coffee had soaked his pants. "Looks like you shoulda used the restroom." An immediate and loud squeal of laughter erupted from the crowd, made up mostly of school kids. Frank fought off his own smile. Larry's face reddened and he felt a cool breeze between his legs.

Everyone's attention shifted to a gold Cadillac that screeched to a stop in the middle of the road. The car's tinted windows rolled down to reveal Big Ray Culp, the mayor, viewing the scene through squinted eyes. He snorted and slowly climbed out of the car, walking over to where Frank stood. He looked the boys up and down, who looked fearful, now that the real authority in town had arrived. Big Ray frowned when he saw Larry's wet pants. He cocked his head up at Frank, who bent low, moving his ear closer to Ray's lips. Ray spoke in a whisper that only Frank could hear.

"You got about thirty seconds to get this cleared up."

Frank straightened and cleared his throat. His deep voice penetrated the air.

"You kids get on to school. Bell's going to ring any second. Anybody tardy today will stay after school and pick up trash in the park."

Little Ray moved first, sprinting through the crowd, zipping down the sidewalk. Then all the children ran toward the school, their shrill voices piercing the warm morning air.

Frank, Larry and Big Ray remained in the middle of the street. The delivery truck rumbled around them. Larry Lee drew a breath, as if to speak, but was silenced by a look from Big Ray. He spoke, shaking a finger in Larry's face.

"Officer Lee, you command no more respect for the law than some drunk pecker-wood who's pissed himself. You go get changed. Dry those pants. Do something. And don't say nothing. I'm tired of hearing that mouth of yours."

Larry turned and limped toward the courthouse, trying to avoid contact with the wet parts of his clothes. Ray stood for a moment regarding Larry's backside. Then he turned and looked up at his son-in-law. A tight smile crept into the corners of his mouth.

"Who was winning?" Ray asked.

Frank snorted. "Little Ray looked like he was handling the

situation."

The two of them stood in the middle of the street for a few moments. Ray folded his arms across his chest and the slight smile left his lips. Frank looked toward his police cruiser.

"What time do you get off, Frank?" Ray asked.

Frank looked at the shorter man. He reached into his uniform shirt pocket and retrieved his mirrored Ray-bans.

"Shift ends at four. You know that."

"Well, come see me. I'll be in my office." Ray looked down the road. The morning mist had evaporated and the sun heated the asphalt under their feet.

"A little hot for May, ain't it? I need to get my air looked at in the car," Ray said.

Frank wondered, why Ray wanted to see him? His father-in-law barely tolerated him as his daughter's husband. Other than for the city's business, they rarely spoke to each other. The few times that they did speak was when Ray wanted Frank to do something that, more often than not, Frank would not want to do.

"I'll be there."

Ray climbed back into his Cadillac and rolled up the tinted window effectively shutting him off from the sunny street. He made a u-turn in the middle of the intersection and headed toward the city building.

Frank followed the Cadillac in the Crown Victoria, passing Larry Lee inching uncomfortably along the sidewalk, humbled and hunched over. Larry grimaced as the police car roared by.

Chapter 15

Randy Wilbanks, city manager of the town of Juliette, still sat in his office and still had the radio tuned to the gospel radio station. For Frank it was such a commonplace occurrence he hardly noticed. Frank walked into his office with something specific on his mind.

"Jesus loves you, Frank," Randy said. Frank grimaced at his banal voice.

"Jesus loves you too, Randy." Frank leaned over the front of Randy's desk."But if He really loves me, He'd see to it that I get that pay raise this week."

Randy frowned. "Frank. You mustn't use my simple, Christian greeting to blaspheme."

"Asking Jesus to help get me my raise is not blasphemy. Blasphemy means to speak irreverently of sacred things. This subject is most sacred in my system of beliefs, one that I treat with reverence. Ray granted me that pay raise over six weeks ago. Your unprofessionalism and lack of diligence is blasphemous. There's no reason on God's earth why the paperwork couldn't have been completed by now, so I can get my raise."

"These things take time, Frank. Be patient."

"Around here, things take too much time, especially Randy, when you're involved. I'm out of patience. Maybe Ray will have something to say about it when I talk to him later. I guess I could tell Ray about a lot of things." Frank shook his head. "Why would you care? You make three times what I do, and your fat ass never leaves that chair."

Randy recoiled. "Your mouth has become a tool of the devil. It's your association with Larry Lee. You're talking just like him."

Frank took a deep breath. "Randy. You know my situation. I need that raise. I work hard for this city. Long hours every week. I don't get paid overtime. I have to work odd jobs to make ends meet. Your own good Lord knows that I deserve a raise after 5 years on the job without one. You're only here a couple of hours a day. If I didn't do your work, the state and county agencies would shut us down. Is it too much to ask that you fill out the form and let me get my raise? It'll take you all of twenty minutes. If you haven't started it, I'll fill it out myself, without your usual spelling errors, and then all you have to do is sign it. I'll walk it over to the accountant myself. Do you think you can spare some time from your sermon writing to sign the form after I fill it out?"

Randy blushed. At that moment he actually was writing a sermon for Sunday's service. In addition to being city manager, Randy was the pastor of the East Juliette Church of Jesus. East Juliette was an even smaller community on the other side of the Ocmulgee River. Every Monday, he started a new sermon. The rest of the week he refined and practiced it. On Friday, he handed his scratchy, almost unreadable scrawl to Doris, the city's receptionist, for typing. Randy kept all of his sermons in binders, stored on the wooden shelves behind his desk. He often told anyone who would listen that they were really the word of God, and he was just His humble instrument. He preferred writing sermons over city work, and expected the rest of the office to ignore the activity. Frank's remark represented a breach of protocol. "Frank, your obsession with money will only lead you to anger and the occasions of sin."

Frank opened his mouth to respond to that statement, but was interrupted by the phone in the front office. Randy tore his eyes away from Frank's malevolent stare, leaning around him to yell down the hall. "Answer the phone, Doris."

The phone rang again.

"Doris! Get the phone," Randy repeated.

Doris was officially the mayor's secretary, but filled in as Randy's assistant, which meant she typed his sermons after he completed them.

Randy resolutely pushed up from the desk, bustled past Frank and stormed out of the office. The phone rang on.

"Doris! The phone!" Frank followed Randy to the front office.

Doris' desk was empty. From behind the closed door of what she considered her private bathroom, she hummed "The Sound of Music." Her tune ended abruptly. From inside the bathroom they heard Doris' muffled voice. "Randy. I'll get the phone. You leave it be. I'll just be a second."

"We're trying to run a city out here. You can't be leaving your post anytime you want."

With that the bathroom door burst open and Doris came bustling out, twisting her skirt into position.

"Doris. That call might be important," Randy pointed toward the phone on her desk.

Doris halted at the sound of his voice, glaring through teardrop shaped glasses, hands on hips. The phone rang and rang again. Randy raised his fists, his face just three feet from hers.

The front door opened and in walked Larry Lee. He scanned the scene, head moving from left to right.

"Jesus Christ. What the fuck you-all doing, playing charades? I got it! It's the 'Alexander Graham Bell Invents the Telephone' thing. Larry parodied with a deep voice. "Watson! Get your ass in here. I want you." He thrust his hips forward and back rhythmically. Randy turned away, closing his eyes. The phone rang again. Randy reached for the receiver.

Doris growled. "Randy, if you so much as touch that phone, I'll scratch your eyes out." She made claws with her shiny red nails. "It's my job to answer the phone."

"Then answer the goddamned phone!" Randy shrieked.

At the sound of his profanity the room filled with silence. The blood drained out of Randy's face. His mouth hung open. His breath stopped, and for several moments he held himself very still. Then he awkwardly turned toward the door through which Larry had just entered. Larry stood aside to let him pass. Brilliant sunlight filled the room as the door opened and closed softly behind him. The phone rang again. Larry walked over and picked it up.

"Yo!" he said. "Hm... Must have missed the son a bitch. Nobody there." He hung up the phone and walked toward the back office, whistling. Doris returned to her desk and began filing her nails.

Frank returned to Randy's office. On the desk were Randy's sermon-in-progress and notes scribbled untidily on several pieces of wrinkled paper. Nowhere did he see any evidence of the paperwork for his raise. Frank knew the form, a thirteen-oh-one, the same as county employees used. The city of Juliette wasn't important enough to have different paperwork.

He tried the center desk drawer. It was locked, but Frank had a key for every lock in the building. He went through all the drawers and found no thirteen-oh-one. Frank rose and returned to the front office.

"Doris, do you have the paperwork for my raise?"

Doris' first reaction was to give him a glassy stare over the top of her spectacles. She continued the stare while blowing a bubble with her gum. Then, with a display of considerable effort accompanied by a huge sigh, she rose and pulled out a tablet of thirteen-oh-one's from a filing cabinet, which she handed to Frank. Doris picked up a "People" magazine and flopped backed into her chair.

"You mean that Randy hasn't done anything on my raise. In six weeks?"

Doris blew another bubble. "Doesn't look like it, Frank."

Frank went back to Randy's desk and quickly filled in the form, all but the "authorized signature" at the end. Temptation nagged at Frank to raise the amount he had been granted, but Big Ray would spot that in a second. Frank returned to Doris' desk and waited for her to look up from her magazine.

"Yes, Frank. You're back, I see."

"Doris, who can authorize this? Is Randy the only one who can sign it?"

"Randy's supposed to sign for all the city's business." Frank's expression fell. "But Big Ray usually ends up signing everything anyway."

"Why is that, if it's Randy's job?" Frank asked.

Doris smiled, returning to her magazine. "Randy only gets things done when he gets around to it. He ain't had a 'round tuit' for a long time."

Frank returned to Randy's office, and sat in the squeaking, wobbly chair. He pressed his knuckles against his eyes. Big Ray granted Frank the pay raise but had done nothing to push it through, neither forcing Randy to turn in the paperwork nor doing it himself. Why should he? The money came out of his budget, which was nearly the same thing as coming out of Big Ray's own wallet. Frank folded the form and put it in his pocket.

On Randy's desk was the uncompleted sermon. Frank labored through Randy's scrawl. He picked up a pen and scratched a few lines in his own clean handwriting:

"Pride is the fundamental flaw in man that leads to all sins under God's commandments. Pride is the absence of God's grace. Pride compels us to regard to ourselves alone. Pride closes off our love for our fellow man. Pride obscures our sight, hinders our understanding of the plight of others, and our responsibility to them. Pride causes lying. Pride causes fear. Pride is hypocrisy, coveting, jealousy. Pride causes theft, war, idolatry. Pride causes a man to stand before his betters preaching the word of God rather than humbling himself and begging their forgiveness. (Rend garments for effect.)"

Frank handed over the handwritten pages to Doris.

"Go ahead and type this one up." He said. "Randy's just now finished with it."

Doris nodded toward the "IN" basket.

In the back of the city building was another bathroom and a small office which Frank shared with Larry Lee. At his own desk, he typed up the report on this morning's speeding ticket. The sound of Larry's mumbling penetrated the bathroom door. Larry swung the door wide, just as the toilet flushed. He fanned the door back and forth, saturating the room with a wave of warm air, the smell a mix of cigarette smoke and human waste.

"Good Sweet Jesus and MAD RAY DEE HAY-SOOSE! That'n near ripped me a new one. I feel ten pounds lighter. I thought I was going to ask for some help. Ain't had that good a shit in weeks. Fuck me!" He pulled out a cigarette and lit it with his Zippo lighter. Frank winced at the lighter's sharp click and the blast of smoke that rolled across his desk.

"Larry. We have a prisoner downstairs from Recorder's Court. Go take him to Forsyth. Here is the paperwork from Judge Venable." Frank worked the key off the key ring and laid it on top of the papers.

Larry eyed the key and forms.

"Ain't you supposed to go out on patrol this afternoon?"

"I doubt if a major crime wave is about to hit the city. I have paperwork to do. You can take the cruiser."

"Jesus Henry R. Christ! Why do I have to lug that asshole over there? I'll do it tomorrow. Who is it?" Larry said in one breath.

"Martin, David James. You know. Beat up old Clifford." Frank replied. "Judge Venable assigned him to county jail this morning. We've got to get him over there today. You know we can't keep him down in our cell overnight."

"Yeah. Thanks to Big Ray's Daddy, who built that goddamn thing in the basement good enough for Nazi fucking Germany." Larry snorted.

Larry grabbed up the key and the paperwork, stuck his head back into the bathroom, and gave the toilet another flush. He retrieved his black leather gun belt, strapped it on and strode out of the small room toward the basement.

Frank yelled after him, "Bring back the yellow copy. Signed."

Chapter 16

On the afternoon of May 23, 1980, the sun baked the town of
Juliette and added a dose of summer humidity a month earlier than usual.
Because Big Ray refused to air-condition any part of the city building but
his own office, Frank endured kiln like conditions at his own desk while
he tried to whittle away at a pile of paperwork. Every citation,
conviction, sentence, or acquittal generated their own reports and forms.
Doris did little more than basic typing and filing. Larry's meager literacy
kept him off the paperwork detail. Randy knew almost nothing about
municipal documentation. Big Ray mostly ran his own enterprise from
his mayoral office. Big Ray left little doubt that he expected Frank to
attend to the important work. Frank gave no thought about this lopsided
division of labor. He enjoyed making order out of chaos, even if it
saddled him with all the responsibility.

Frank considered Big Ray, Doris, Larry and even Randy like his
family. His mother had died while he was at college, his dad a few years
later while he was in Vietnam. His dad had been an unpleasant man and
a consistent failure, leaving Frank with an inheritance of debt. The house
had been sold to cover some of his dad's obligations, money mostly owed
to Big Ray. Big Ray collected on this debt by deducting payments from
Frank's paycheck.

Frank did not miss his father, but he felt differently about his
mother. From his earliest memories, she provided him more than love.
She introduced him to art and literature and her life's passion, music.
Even while he was still in a crib, she read to him when her husband was
away. Frank's father considered such things just plain foolish and in their
house money was not available for foolishness. But thanks to the library
in Forsyth, they could borrow books and records.

At an early age, Frank learned to read on his own, and his mother let
him go to exotic places he found in books, places she had longed to see.

At age four she took him to the local music teacher, Old Nora
Potvin, a woman who immediately recognized his talent and her own
good fortune. Frank's father allowed the lessons, but demanded Frank
spend equal time playing baseball and football. His mother sold

needlepoint and vegetables from her garden to pay for Frank's violin lessons. While still a boy, Frank gave the town of Juliette something to celebrate. He excelled in the violin, but he also became a baseball star and the captain of the football team.

But sports could never replace Frank's true passion. Nothing pleasured him, excited him like his violin. The Robillards had no money for a decent instrument, but his mother's family owned an heirloom; a treasure, originally purchased by her great grandfather. The nineteenth century Parisian master, Mon. W. Guilliame, had carefully built Frank's violin two hundred years ago, and its quality and tone would have been exceptional in any orchestra. The value of the violin exceeded all the stuff they owned, and Frank treasured it more than any possession.

Frank truly had a gift, and in his hands the violin came alive. His child's fingers found all the right places easily. He seemed to remember every note he either played or heard. He progressed through every piece Miss Nora Potvin placed in front of him.

When Frank was a teenager, the music lessons came to an end. After a recital in Atlanta, his father overheard someone remark about the quality of his violin, something like, "How did that hick kid get such and such a violin?" It started the wheels turning in the mind of the elder Robillard. One day he snuck the violin out of their little house, drove to Atlanta and sold it to a music dealer for about one tenth of what it was worth. The act caused the first and only violent confrontation in the Robillard household.

"Frank, how could you do such a thing?" But old man Robillard offered no explanation.

Younger Frank, who at sixteen was no longer little, confronted his father. "You had no right. That was mine." His teenage voice cracked with anger.

"Nothing in this house is yours," his father replied, but he could not meet his son's eyes.

"You go back and get it. You get in the car and go get it, NOW!"

While sitting at his desk in the stifling office, Frank remembered yelling at his father, recalling that his old man could not look him in the eye, but had no trouble slapping him across his mouth. On a reflex, Frank punched his father in the face, a little harder than he wanted to, snapping his head back with a crack. He landed in a heap in the corner of the kitchen, where he remained for a few seconds. He came up off the floor with murder in his eyes. Frank's mother tried to get between them but he cast her aside with a sweep of his arm. She hit the wall with a loud noise that had stopped them both. Frank remembered her lying there on the floor. It was the first time that he noticed her frail health and what a tiny and frail thing she had become. She hung on to life nearly four years, but her health seeped away past the point where anyone wanted her to live. The violin had been a tangible altar for her desires; her dream that her son would become a great musician, that he could leave the little town in central Georgia and fly to gleaming cities. That she would have played a part in launching him on that journey, had been her dream.

Frank never recovered the violin, and he stopped going to his lessons. Old Nora called several times, and each time he told her he wasn't coming back. She finally quit calling.

Often while alone at his desk, the Bach First Violin Sonata snuck up on his train of thought. Those passionate notes rose in volume until they drowned out all of his memories. The Bach Sonata had been a specialty piece for him. As a boy he mastered the notes until they tumbled effortlessly from his bow. But the piece had mastered him as well. At times he could not shut off the cascading music in his head. It happened to him now while he caught up on his paperwork, in the hot sweaty office, where he worked too hard for nearly nothing.

For the second time in the day, he found himself holding his breath. Eventually his head music faded and transformed into familiar, manageable emotions. The steady clacking of Doris' typewriter came down the hall. She must be typing Randy's sermon, he thought. Her loud "Ha!" confirmed this, as she laughed at Frank's finishing contribution.

Frank heard the opening and slamming of the front door, announcing Larry's return from Forsyth.

"Goddamn, it's hot out there! I thought I was gonna melt like a shit popsicle." Frank visualized Doris refusing to look up, focusing instead on her typing. The wooden chair in front of Doris' desk creaked as Larry eased himself onto it.

"Doris. You busy?" Larry asked.

"Busy as I ever am," she said in a dry, old lady's voice. "Tons of things to do around here."

"Doris. How long you been married?"

After a silence, "Twenty-eight long years."

"Twenty-eight years. I ain't hardly that old. You and Bill still do it?"

The clacking of the keys continued.

"Doris." Larry persisted. Frank imagined her head bent closer to the typewriter, mouth set in a tight line.

"Doris. Do you and Bill still do it?"

"Do what?"

"You know, get it on."

"Larry, that's none of your business." Doris snapped back. "Does your mind ever go anywhere else but the gutter?"

"How many times?" Larry asked.

"What?" Doris said.

"How many times do you do it? You know, like once a year, or something. Hell, I know it's none of my business. But I like to know anyway. I wonder why people get married. My momma wants me to get married. Have kids. Get a house. But it ain't likely. My job is too dangerous." Doris let out a snort at that.

"Well, I like women. All kinds. I get tired of them after a few fucks. They all want too much."

Doris' typewriter clacked for several minutes.

"Doris...?" Larry said.

"What, Larry?"

"How do you and Bill keep it fresh?"

"Who said it was fresh?"

"You mean it ain't?"

"Larry, what do you think? Bill's put on about fifty pounds in those twenty-eight years and he wasn't too slim when I married him. He's got more hair growing out of his ears than the top of his head. His Nauga Hide Lazy-Boy sits about six feet from the television. Next to him is a cooler full of PBR. Does this sound like Paul Newman to you? When he gets home from work he strips down to boxers and a tee shirt and settles into that Lazy-Boy. At seven I bring him a tray full of fried chicken, with a folded napkin. At seven thirty, I take that tray away, napkin still folded. Right after Johnny Carson's monologue, he walks down the hall, does his business in the bathroom and falls into bed with all the grace of a sack of feed. That's how fresh it is."

The typewriter clacked away.

Frank stood and walked down the hall toward their voices. As he reached the front office, the door opened and Randy entered. He closed the door softly behind him and stood there staring at the floor. Randy's eyes rimmed with tears, and his head hung low. He inhaled deeply and raised his head.

"I am glad you are all here," he croaked and cleared his throat. "I have something I need to say. I guess we all get a little tense and angry sometimes, but there was no call for what I said earlier. No call at all. Taking the Lord's Name in vain is a bad sin. From the bottom of my heart, I apologize to Doris for the way I treated her. I am deeply ashamed of how I behaved. I know that I am unworthy of the authority that the city has placed on my shoulders. I don't deserve you-all's respect. But most of all..." here Randy's nearly sobbed and gestured his hand toward Larry still sprawled on the chair beside him.

"Most of all, I am deeply sorry for the poor witness that I have shown Larry."

"Jesus fucking Christ, Randy." Larry drawled slowly. "Nobody around here gives a rat's ass."

Frank suppressed a smile and scooted out the front door.

Chapter 17

Outside in the hot sunshine, Frank looked again at his watch. He had no idea why Big Ray wanted to see him. Big Ray treated him like a good employee, but even after ten years of marriage to his only child, Frank was not family. Ray wanted a good looking, golden haired boy for a son-in-law. One who played golf and brought in a string of business successes. He wanted someone who would join him in his enterprises, someone who also lusted after money and power. Frank had dropped out of college, joined the Marines and served in Vietnam, which Ray considered pretty stupid things to do.

Frank and Lydia's marital problems had done nothing to improve this relationship with Ray. Ray probably was relieved that his daughter had come to her senses. He knew that Frank was responsible for nearly all of the city's work, but because of Frank's lack of ambition, Ray treated him like a servant. Occasionally, Ray gave Frank something else do, usually something unpleasant.

Ray's office was on the second floor, in the back of the city building. He hired carpenters to close the inside entrance, which required visitors to come up a narrow set of stairs on the outside of the building. Frank climbed slowly. Each step sagged with his weight. Big Ray was on the phone when he entered and took no notice of his son-in-law.

Ray's conversation made little sense to Frank so he paid little attention. He stood there, a large presence in the somewhat small room. The office contained many filing cabinets, full of Big Ray's secrets. There was no place to sit down. A hard running air conditioner droned away in the room's only window. The back of the building received the direct afternoon sun. Even with the window unit on full, the heat was winning the battle. Finally, tired of being ignored, Frank moved to stand in front of the air-conditioner. This got Ray's attention. Not only did his bulk cast a shadow across Ray's desk, but Frank's body blocked all the cool air.

"Look, Willy, I got to go. Someone's here to see me."

Ray put down the phone and waved his hand sideways, gesturing Frank to get out of the stream of cool air. Frank stepped aside. Ray mopped his forehead with a wilted handkerchief. He shuffled some papers on his desk, pushed his chair back and turned to look up at Frank. Ray's small round head, only half covered with hair gleamed from the overhead light. He folded his hands over his paunch and squinted up to meet Frank's eyes.

"You still takin' that fishin' trip?" Ray asked. "To Florida?"

Frank eased his weight to the other foot and looked out the window. He knew Ray had little interest in his proposed fishing trip. Frank planned to drive to St. Marks in the Florida panhandle to fish for speckled trout. He'd spend the time reading, lying around, and drinking beer. He usually stayed in a cheap hotel and took his meals at the nearby fish house. After only a few days, worrying about how they were all doing without him he'd return to Juliette. Frank remembered that he had promised to take Little Ray with him one of these days. But school was still in. Duties around Juliette kept piling up and he rarely felt good enough about the state of the city to allow himself to slip away. He thought about Lydia's idea of moving to Atlanta and feared that she might use his absence to do it.

"Well, I don't know."

Big Ray puckered his lips. He stared down, past the tip of his nose. "Well, you should go. We can do without you for a while."

"There's a lot going on." Frank said.

"Nothin' that important. You made your ticket quota last month. Good job. Here, this'll help."

Big Ray reached in his pocket and pulled out a wad of bills. The green of it caught Frank's eyes. Ray pulled off a few twenties.

"There's some extra. You have a good time. Don't drink too much." Big Ray smiled with little warmth.

Frank picked up the bills. "Thanks." He decided to say no more about fishing or going on vacation.

"There's something you need to do before you go," Ray said.

Here it comes, Frank thought. This is the bad part.

"You checked on Old Nora lately?" Ray asked.

Frank let out his breath. Now that the official reason for the visit was exposed, his previous apprehension seemed foolish.

"No. Not lately. Why?"

"She should have been moved out weeks ago. Construction office called again this morning. They have the pump going, bringing water in from the Ocmulgee. The dam's finished. Water going up like an inch a day. Lake'll be full up sometime this month. So we gotta get old Nora outta there."

The building of Lake Juliette ended last month. Plant Scherer, a Georgia Power Company generating plant would begin churning out electricity in August. The engineers impounded Rum Creek, a small tributary of the Ocmulgee River, but the amount of water flowing in that little stream would not fill the lake in a hundred years. The engineers solved that problem by installing a massive pump on the banks of the Ocmulgee River, pumping water into the reservoir. Old Nora was one of few people to be displaced by the lake. The others had been paid off and moved. No one stood in the way of progress, except for old Nora Potvin, and she had refused to move. There would be thirty feet of water over her roof by the end of the summer.

Frank felt the sweat on his neck. Nora had lived in that old shack for fifty years. She buried two husbands in her backyard. The graves were against state and county regulations, but Nora seemed immune to such things. Big Ray let her stay. Everyone in town whispered that she had some power over him. Nora was Frank's old music teacher, and he had been her prized pupil. When he gave up the violin, he had killed her dream, his mother's and his own.

"Frank, we got to move her. The county is getting pressure from the construction guys. If she's still there by Monday, Sheriff Hansley will take her out himself."

"I'll go out and move her tomorrow. And thank you for letting me have that opportunity." Frank said, wondering if Ray would catch the irony.

Ray nodded and pointed his finger up at Frank. "You better get her out of there. They'll do it if you don't, and it won't be nice."

"I'll get her out," Frank started to leave and he remembered the folded up 1301 in his pocket. He had almost decided to put it off to another day when Ray held him up.

"I want to talk to you about another deal." Something in his voice chilled Frank. "It's about Lydia."

Frank's fist clenched around the twenties still in his hand.

"You know Lydia wants a divorce. She wants to move to Atlanta."

Frank shook his head.

"She wants to take Little Ray with her." Ray said.

"No!" Frank leaned over the desk. "She can't take him away from me. He needs me and I need him."

Ray folded his arms. "Look, Frank. I know you love that little boy. But you got to realize a few things. She don't want him growing up a country redneck."

"The country's good enough for you, Ray."

"That don't mean nothing. It doesn't matter what I want. She's not going to leave him here and that's the end of it."

"Well, we'll see about that. We're not divorced. She can't do anything she wants. He's my boy. It's my choice how he's raised, and he isn't moving to Atlanta."

"How you gonna stop her?" Ray pointed a finger. "She's got a lawyer. First she'll get a court order, and then a divorce decree that'll be ninety-nine percent in her favor. And then she'll ask you for the rest."

"I can get a lawyer."

"How you gonna pay for it?"

"How is she?" Frank knew the answer as soon as he asked the question.

Ray let the silence fester for a minute. "Look, Frank. If you love that boy, you'll do what's best for him. What are your plans for his college?"

Frank folded his arms and stared at the papers on Ray's desk.

"How much do you make, Frank?" Ray's voice went cold. He started using his hands and fingers like an abacus. "You make fifteen and a half thousand. After taxes, your take home is about a grand a month. You pay Mrs. Reynolds about $200 for that back room of hers. You ought to be paying her a hundred, but you're a soft-hearted idiot and know she's trying to make ends meet without a husband. You pay four hundred dollars a month on Lydia's house." Ray repeated, "Lydia's house. You're still paying me about one-fifty on your daddy's debt. The court is gonna stick it to you on child support. It's the state law, now. That'll be about six, seven hundred a month." Ray had all his fingers turned up and pinched together. He squinted at them. "In short, you're about five hundred a month short. And that's if you don't eat, don't buy clothes, and don't put gas in that little truck of yours. Nothing left over and a debt that gets bigger every time you take a breath." Ray finished and shrugged.

It stunned Frank to hear his financial position stated out loud like that. He slowly shook his head. "It seems like you all are against me. What did I do?"

Ray snorted. "Ain't nobody against you. You married Lydia, you

100

dumb shit. It wasn't my idea. Now it's time to square things up. She's going to ask for all that and get it."

"Why should she get everything she wants?"

"Because she always does. And because you're the fool who'll go along with it. If she asked you to load the moving van, you'd do it."

A smile drew Ray's lips back. "Let's make this easy. Lydia is going to get the house, but the court is gonna make you pay for it. Let's say I buy the house and give it to her. She don't want it, so she'll probably sell it. Paying child support for eight years is about sixty some thousand dollars, but for a lump sum she'll probably settle for fifty. Then comes college. Every man wants his son to go to college. That will probably cost ten grand a year for, what, four years? Make it five because Little Ray ain't exactly the scholastic type. That'll just about do it for this deal." Ray's smile became genuine.

Frank stared at his father-in-law, not into his eyes but at his bald head. "What do I have to do for all this largess?"

"Huh? Large-ass... what?"

"What do I have to do or agree to for you to do all this?"

"Oh. You don't have to do nothing. You just sign the divorce papers and get your ass out of the way. Let 'em go to Atlanta."

"What kind of visitation rights do I get?"

Ray shifted his eyes out the window. "Well, I don't rightly know, but she is gonna ask for full custody. She's gonna want you, uh, not seeing him much."

"No! A judge won't do that. I'm good for that boy. He needs me."

Ray's voice softened. "You're right again. But being right don't mean jack. Lydia can name a lot of bad influences here in Juliette, things not good for the boy. She can talk about all the fights he gets into, and such. The judge might give you two weeks. Maybe a week at Christmas and during the summer."

"No judge around here will do that," Frank said.

"She won't file around here. She'll do it up in Atlanta. She'll get some Jew lawyer to make Juliette look like a real hick town. That Atlanta judge will think he's doing the kid a favor." Ray held up his hands. "I know you are being hurt in this. You love that boy. But she's going to get her way. You're only going to make it worse if you try to fight it. And you'll run up more debt that you won't ever get out from under. This way your kid gets taken care of. It just makes the most sense. I'm the one who's gotta pay." Big Ray even managed to look a little wounded about it.

The truth hurt Frank more than any bullet he'd taken in Vietnam. If he stood up for his rights, he would get creamed in the courts. If he gave in, all his money problems went away, his father's debt, house payment, and child support. But his boy would be gone. His pretty wife would be gone. The house that currently he did not live in, would be gone. In summary, his life to them meant nothing. He won only if he agreed to this deal and allowed the Culp's to take away his pride, his manhood and his fatherhood.

"Who's going to look after the boy to see that he's taught the proper values?" Frank's voice cracked. "Who's going to teach him the things a boy needs to know? How to throw a ball? How to tackle? Who Ted Williams, Mickey Mantle is? Who's going to show him the woods at dawn? Do you think Lydia will do any of that?"

Ray shook his head.

"Do you see Lydia bringing up Little Ray and have him turn out right?"

Big Ray snorted. "Hell no. She'll have that boy prancing around like a Claxton fruitcake. I'm just being honest. Little Ray has no say. You have no say. That's what you are giving up."

"You want me to give up the only thing that matters in my life. My boy. My pride in seeing him grow up. Just so he can go to college."

Ray's face turned stern, and he leaned forward in his chair. "So he don't grow up ashamed of his old man for having nothing. For doing nothing."

Frank's eyes widened as if Ray had just punched him. Ray's statement drained his last shred of hope. The idea that eventually he could save his marriage seemed idiotic to him now. Lydia was in the driver's seat. Ray put most of this deal together. Lydia told her daddy what she wanted, and he gave it to her. Frank looked into father-in-law's eyes and saw Ray's face melt into a smile, a salesman's smile.

Frank wanted to say something, but no thoughts or words came into his head to save him. His hand moved to cover his heart, and he felt its heavy pounding. His fingers probed the pocket of his shirt, and he pulled out the folded thirteen-oh-one, the form for his long overdue raise. Hands shaking, he laid it on the desk in front of Ray.

"I was supposed to get this six weeks ago. Randy's done nothing. Will you sign it?"

Ray looked at the form and then up at the bigger man. His eyes narrowed.

"You don't ask for much outta life, do you Frank?" He took his pen and scribbled on the form.

Frank squeezed through Ray's office door and somehow avoided slamming it.

Ray shouted after him. "We're gonna do everything for that boy! You don't have to worry! He'll get everything he needs."

Chapter 18

Little Ray expected his dad to pick him up at six o'clock to take him to the baseball field. He darted around his room grabbing socks, shirt, pants and cup. Tonight their opponents were the Cardinals. So far this year the Indians had won every game. It was because Little Ray's team had the best coach in the world, his dad, who knew how to run a team of ten year old boys. He knew how to let the guys have fun. All the kids loved his dad and wanted to be on his team, but only Little Ray had the privilege of being on Frank Robillard's team every summer.

Little Ray enjoyed putting on his baseball stuff. He even liked wearing the cup to protect what the guys called, "the family jewels." Only a couple of years ago, the state baseball association made a rule requiring this protection for all players. The new rule was greeted by a considerable amount of comment from both the adults and the kids. Of course, the kids teased each other without mercy, describing what the cup was protecting, its vulnerability, utility, and of course size.

The Juliette league baseball games involved the whole town. Nearly everyone who wasn't working would be sprawled on the hills surrounding the baseball park. With little else happening around Juliette, parents and non parents joined in prepping the field, running concessions and other fund raising activities to provide equipment and uniforms. All of Juliette loved the baseball games. Not Lydia, of course.

Little Ray's mother lacked appreciation for the game or Little Ray's enthusiasm for it. She even sniffed at his uniform. "What's so great about it?" she said. "The pants don't flatter you. The shirt's too big and so is the hat. Besides you get those horrible stains all over." Little Ray felt exactly the opposite. The Indians had the coolest jerseys and caps with the red and black "Indians" emblem stitched across the front. He had number seven, a lucky number. The black baseball cap had the Cleveland Indians Wahoo character on the front. The caps were adult sized, so kids adjusted the plastic strap to fit their smaller heads, making the caps seem billowed at the top. All the boys had creased the brim to an inverted "V" shape. The pants were supposed to be white, but the red Georgia clay had soaked into the cloth past the point where laundry could rescue them.

Not that his Mom even tried to get the stains out. She paid someone else to do the wash.

Ray stomped out of his room deliberately causing his cleats to make the loudest possible sound on the hardwood floors in the hallway. Flecks of red clay fell off the dirty black leather. Usually his mother yelled at him to quit making so much noise and to stop grinding dirt into her Oriental rugs, but today, she was completely absorbed in entertaining her guest.

Lydia and her guest sat out on a small screened porch she called the verandah. Little Ray avoided the verandah because his mom had decorated it in pure white wicker furniture and overstuffed pillows covered in a flowery pastel print. Any hint of dirt on the verandah would send her into a frenzy.

Her guest ran a store in Macon that sold decorative home objects. Ray referred to him as "Decorator Boy." They were having what his dad called a "tea party" and they had been at it all afternoon, talking, laughing and talking some more. Decorator Boy's plump posterior would be wedged into the white wicker chair until well past dark. Tomorrow there would be another guest and another tea party.

Little Ray glanced out the window, but saw no truck coming down the road. He glanced at the clock and smacked his fist into his glove. His dad was never late for a game.

But many minutes later, there still was no truck. In the hallway he pretended to scoop up a hot grounder and pretended to fire a sizzling throw toward first. He pantomimed various baseball moves until he heard the unmistakable coughing and wheezing of his dad's little Datsun pickup truck. He looked out the front window again and saw the truck bouncing down the road, groaning to a stop at the end of the driveway.

His dad did not live there anymore, and he could no longer enter without permission. Little Ray hardly thought anymore about how his mom had driven his dad out of the house. His dad didn't live here anymore and had to drive across town to pick him up.

Little Ray grabbed his bat and headed for the front door. As he passed the verandah he yelled at his mother. "Hey! Mom. Dad's here. I'm going to my game. "

"Bon Jour, Remy," came her dark, contralto voice.

Little Ray muttered an obscenity under his breath. Only his mom called him that. Unless you counted any kid at school who wanted to fight.

"Oh! But it's 'Beau Soir.' late enough for 'Soir' my dear," came the higher voice of Decorator Boy. His mother's guest poked his broad and pasty white face out of the verandah. "Bye. Bye. Remy, uh. Little Ray. Who are you playing tonight?"

Ray stopped with his hand on the doorknob of the front door. "The Cardinals," he said patiently.

"Oooohh! They... are... tough." Decorator Boy said, separating the words.

"We already beat 'em twice," replied Little Ray. He turned the doorknob.

"Oooooh! You guys are really good." His mother's guest eyed little Ray's uniform.

"Uh. Thanks." Ray bolted out the door.

His dad's enthusiasm for baseball games usually exceeded even his own. They both thrived on the competition, but the look on his dad's face told him that something was wrong. As he approached the truck, his dad stared past Ray toward the house. Ray turned around and saw his mother's tea party guest sticking just his head out the front door, smiling at him.

"Who the hell is that?" his father asked.

"That's mom's friend."

"How long has he been here?"

"He was here when I got home from school."

For a minute he thought his dad was going to get out of the truck and go up to the house. He gripped the steering wheel, as if trying to pull it off, working his jaw back and forth. Ray climbed into the passenger's side, and pulled the door shut. The door creaked and groaned. His father still stared through the bug soiled windshield.

After several long seconds, Frank put the truck in reverse and backed out of the driveway.

"How you doing, dad?"

"Fine."

"You okay?"

"Yeah, just great."

Little Ray feared to say more. His mom had told him they were moving to Atlanta, which to him was a disaster. First his father moved out of the house, and now his mom wanted to move him away from everything he knew. At the moment Little Ray did not know what his dad was angry about, but their current situation sure seemed to fit his

106

mood. Ray wanted the old days back. They all had been happy once. He remembered his dad and mom laughing together. Why couldn't it be like that again?

He rode the hard seat of the old truck and watched the pines whistling by through the windshield. His aluminum bat bounced between his knees with every lurch of the truck. He glanced at his father driving down the road, large hands strangling the thin steering wheel. This wasn't going to be fun. Not tonight. Usually they discussed baseball strategy, lineups, how to pitch to certain batters, but tonight they traveled to the ballpark in silence. Little Ray thought, baseball should be the priority, not divorce, not moving to Atlanta.

Tonight, his dad had neglected to make out a lineup. He just sat silently in the dugout, oblivious to the game. Little Ray made out the lineup, asked for his approval, and not getting it, submitted it to "Blue", Mr. Feherty, the crazy old coot that officiated all their games.

Little Ray pitched and held the Cardinals scoreless for the first two innings. The Indians however scored in the first and two more runs in the second. In the third, Ray walked the leadoff batter, who stole second. The next batter hit a hot grounder past the second baseman, allowing the runner to score. Little Ray thought, that ought to get to him, walking the leadoff batter. But his dad sat on the bench, thinking his own thoughts.

Little Ray mumbled to himself. "Okay, Ray. You got no outs and a man on second. He glanced over to the third baseman who secretly gave him the finger, shielded by his fielder's mitt, their signal that the runner on second held a big lead and that their second baseman was sneaking in to cover. Just as the Cardinals coach yelled at his runner, Ray whirled and threw. The ball arched gracefully into the second sacker's mitt and he tagged the runner.

"You're out!" Blue's ragged voice sang.

Ray looked over at his dad, proud of himself, waiting for the inevitable smile of approval. His father's face still held the angry expression.

The next kid up was the Cardinals youngest player. Ray took advantage of him by throwing a fastball in near the kid's chin. The batter hit the dirt. After that the batter stayed well off the plate, and Ray easily struck him out. Again, no reaction from his father.

The game crept along, and the Indians played with no coaching from their coach. When Ray tried to talk to him in the dugout, his dad only returned grunts. The Cardinals tied and still Ray's father took no action. Soon the Indians played with the same indifference as their coach. The Cardinals took the lead just before the game ended. The players crossed the field in parallel lines, shaking hands, muttering hushed comments. Nobody suggested that they go to the ice cream parlor.

His dad kept his thoughts to himself while driving Little Ray home. The headlights of the truck lit up thousands of mayflies, a blizzard of lacey wings.

In the driveway of his house, Little Ray hopped out of the truck.

"Thanks dad, for the..," Ray began. He could not finish the sentence. Thanks for what? For the fun time? For the crap he would have to take in school Monday? For not patching up his marriage with mom? A strange feeling grew inside of him. There seemed to be simply nothing for him to say at all. He shrugged and turned toward the house.

"Ray," his father said. Ray turned around. His father climbed out of the truck and walked a few steps toward him. He noticed for the first time how funny his dad looked in his Indians shirt, baseball cap and blue jeans. The shirt was too small for him. The heat of the night and the dust of the game had covered them both with patches of red clay. The swirl of mayflies in the lights of the truck made his father look like he was walking through wisps of smoke. His dad stood looking at the house, which was all dark except for the well lit verandah. Voices of Lydia and her guest could be heard along with the clink of glasses. Ray's mother's laugher skipped like music across the lawn.

Suddenly his dad sank to his knees and hugged his son crushing the breath out of him.

"I'm sorry, Ray," he said in a whisper.

Little Ray patted him on his back. "It's okay, dad. It's only a game. You always tell me that. So we lost."

"No, son. I lost..." His father's voice dropped to a whisper until the chattering of the night crickets smothered it.

He pulled his head away and even in the shadows cast by the harsh headlights, Ray could see tears in his dad's eyes. He felt his arms tighten around him again. Their baseball cap brims collided, knocking the hats off both their heads. Frank turned away from Ray, picked his cap up and walked back to the truck holding it in his hand. The truck sagged on its shocks as he squeezed himself inside. The door banged shut with a squeal of hinges. The truck backed out, rattling and clunking as the wheels went over the curb at the end of the driveway. Little Ray watched the red tail lights until the truck vanished into the dark swirl of mayflies.

Chapter 19

Just outside Juliette, Hector's Grill and Bar crouched beside Highway 23/87. Three decades ago, the old concrete block building had been built for storing cotton bales. Since then it has housed many types of businesses. Hector wandered into town a few years ago, established a store, thereby saving the building from demolition. The place badly needed paint. The door frame was low, so that most visitors ducked when entering. A single small window, covered with brown and yellow soot, offered only dim views from either direction. Hector had painted the crooked, unlit sign above the roof, long before he had much command of English, thus the "Grill" came before "Bar," and no one had bothered to correct it.

The locals found it hard to define what Hector sold, as it differed from one day to the next. He had bread, milk, soft drinks and other stuff that he obtained at the Piggly-Wiggly in Forsyth. He sold beer, wine and whisky by the drink but had no license for that trade. Hector carried bait and tackle for fisherman who wandered by, but anglers were rare on the Ocmulgee River and no one considered half-filled Lake Juliette very promising.

Most afternoons Hector donned a dingy apron and cooked up barbeque, slabs of ribs, a whole, half or quarter chicken, sides of white bread, and Hector's own concoction of baked beans. For this, he began with institutional sized cans of Van Camps which he poured into a cast iron cauldron and added whole bottles of molasses and Tabasco sauce, chopped onions and an undetermined amount of black pepper. The state health inspector had never seen Hector's kitchen, otherwise he would have been fined, jailed and deported to the unknown country of his origin.

On weekdays, locals crowded in front of Hector's tiny counter, where tantalizing smells turned them into a jostling mob. Most of Hector's barbeque was sold in an hour.

Around 9 PM, Frank and his friends drifted in to sit on boxes, snack on the leftovers and sip a few beers.

The night of Friday, May 23, 1980, Frank came late, pulling his clanking Datsun truck into the dark parking lot of Hector's Grill and Bar. Earlier Larry Lee had arrived in the Crown Victoria and parked between Clyde Hembree's new pickup and Eddie "Blue" Feherty's fire truck.

A cloud of smoke, glowing yellow from an interior light, seeped through the open door of Hector's Grill and Bar. Frank's friends looked up when he entered. "Who won?" somebody asked him. His eyes adjusted to the smoke and dim light. Larry and Eddie "Blue" Feherty had cigarettes going. The yellow light came from a bare 60 watt bulb suspended from a cord, over the counter.

"They did," Frank replied.

"What's the score?" asked Hector. Hector's son was on the team, but Hector rarely came to the games.

"Nine to six."

Eddie "Blue" Feherty sat backwards on a folding chair, with a beer in his hand. The "Blue" moniker came from the fact that Eddie earned pocket money as the little league baseball umpire. To fill in his vast amount of spare time, Eddie ran the Juliette Volunteer Fire Department of which he was the only volunteer. Eddie could have answered Hector's question a while ago, but Hector hadn't asked him and Eddie, who off the baseball field rarely said a word, hadn't volunteered the information.

Clyde Hembree sat on a rickety cardboard box, holding two fruit jars. The one in his right hand contained a few ounces of bourbon, the other held spit from a ball of snuff he held between his lower lip and teeth. In the dim light, the two liquids looked nearly identical. After a few minutes he would expectorate into one jar and then take a sip from the other. Frank often wondered if he ever got them mixed up. Clyde earned his living plowing other people's fields with his big John Deere tractor. He also harrowed, seeded, tilled and harvested. Clyde moonlighted as a guide to hunters and fishermen from Atlanta.

"Hey, Frank!" Larry's loud voice cut through the smoke. "We're bullshittin'."

Hector pulled a beer from the ice filled barrel and handed it to him.

"Really? What about?"

"Well..." Clyde offered. "Sometimes what your folks have told you ain't always the truth. Like my daddy used to say, 'No one ever got anywhere except from hard work.' And my Granny would say, 'Never sow under a full moon.' But none of them ever worked at night, no how. And my daddy, he didn't work hardly at all."

"Hah!" Larry laughed. "You're just like your daddy, Clyde. You don't do much besides building tree stands. My crop is wild oats. I plant 'em under a full moon, or a new moon, or any moon for that matter. I pull her legs wide apart and plow my..."

"Stop your bad mouth! You talk filthy in my store and drive away customers!" Hector's anger sounded genuine, but as usual, Larry ignored it.

"Ain't nobody leaving." Larry said. "My daddy told me, 'Say it straight and loud. So they can hear you."

"You knew your daddy?" Clyde asked.

Frank observed that arriving late had caused him to miss the inebriation train. "That's the theme for tonight?"

"Well, Frankie, we were getting serious there. We're telling a bunch of lies because we're too drunk to remember the truth. Nobody ever always tells the truth. So how can you tell when somebody is telling the truth? You can't. 'Cause they most never are." He took a long pull on his beer. "Except when they're sober."

"Sometimes I tell the truth," Clyde said.

"Not often, you don't," Larry replied. "How many goddamn twelve point deer stories have we heard from your lying lips? Jesus! There ain't that many deer in the goddamn, mother-fucking woods."

"What about you? To hear you tell it, you've screwed every woman from here to Brunswick. And the truth of it is that you probably ain't had it in a year or two." They all laughed except for Larry.

"That ain't true. I've had it plenty. Women line up to get a look at my pretty dick. You guys don't know shit. You'all a bunch of fartheads, and you can't trust a fart or a farthead."

Clyde gave him a look. "What the hell's that supposed to mean? How would you trust a fart?"

"Well, just think about it. A fart is God's way of making you do something stupid. But you got to be careful with them things. There are umpteen million ways to have a fart go wrong. Maybe you got a special delivery building in your pants, blowing your ass up like a balloon. It's always the worst time, like you got to be around civilized people. Maybe even some gorgeous city woman. You try to act with a little dee-core-rum, but the damn thing slips out anyway. It ain't gonna do you no good putting the moves on her, cause she's a thinkin' that you smell like a goat's asshole. You can never trust a fart."

Something in Larry's statement inspired Clyde. "Right! And how many times you think that it was just a fart and it turned out to be something else? Then you go through the whole day with strewn Jockeys."

"Stop!" screamed Hector. "All that vulgar talk will drive away my customers!"

"What customers?" Larry and Clyde said together.

Clyde asked. "Frank. What causes farts? Momma used to call them, 'breaking wind.' Why do people call farts breaking wind? How can you 'break' wind?"

"That's easy," Larry took a deep pull on his beer. "Eatin' causes 'em. You eat. You shit. The more you eat, the more you shit. Farts smell like shit. They come out your ass. They're shit gas." Larry squared his shoulders.

"That right, Frank?" Eddie asked. They all looked at him. Eddie rarely spoke except at the ballpark.

Frank had not had enough beer to take this conversation seriously, but they were all eyeing him expectantly."Larry's correct. Farts are gas. The gas builds up in your intestines, actually your rectum where you store solid waste until... well, until you do a number..."

"Until you take a shit. Goddamn it, Frank. Quit pussy footin' around. Just say it, for Christ's sake."

"Right," Frank said. "Human waste contains hydrogen sulfide and methane. Hydrogen sulfide smells like rotten eggs, while methane has no smell at all."

"Then that ain't what's in yours, Larry. Yours smell like a month old cat box." Clyde observed.

Frank continued. "Both gasses are produced by the decomposition of food. Vegetables are made up of carbohydrates, like starch and cellulose. Starch is a carbohydrate. Cellulose, is a polysaccharide. Your stomach has hydrochloric acid, which breaks down the food. Other enzymes in your intestines add elements to the starches to make sugars, mostly glucose, which can be assimilated by the body..."

"Finally we're getting down to the ass," Larry said. "Goddamn it, Frank. We don't need no chemistry class. Tell us about the farts."

"Shut up, Larry," Hector said.

"Methane and hydrogen sulfide are produced by decomposing organic matter. That's why dead animals bloat. That's why it stinks in the swamp. That's what makes swamp gas or foxfire.

"I seen my cousin light his farts," Clyde said. "With a Zippo. Set his pants on fire."

Having heard it before, nobody laughed.

"That's the methane and the hydrogen sulfide. And hydrogen. It all burns pretty good."

Lecturing his friends on flatulence turned out to be thirsty work. Frank had drained his beer and half consumed the second. But apparently the silly-talk stage of the conversation was winding down. For the moment, they all fell silent.

Frank felt Larry watching him in the dim light. Larry lit another cigarette. Frank's eyes drifted toward the ancient white porcelain cooler, the top of which served as a counter for Hector. Frank had never identified the dust covered items inside, visible through the dingy window in the front of the cooler. He suddenly regretted coming here to be with his friends when he had so many things on his mind. But he had nowhere else to go but here or the tiny room at Mrs. Reynolds house.

They were his guys, and he knew them better than himself. He knew the split second when Larry would open his mouth, almost what he would say to get Frank going on the next topic, something other than a dissertation on flatulence. No one wanted the evening to end. No one really wanted to go home, either to their wives or their empty, rented rooms. He heard Larry inhale and knew what was coming.

"Hey, Frank. Tell us about Benny."

Frank did not look up. "I don't want to talk about Benny."

The others stirred. Frank felt the energy in the room rise.

Clyde offered, "Yeh, Frank. Tell us about Benny. He won a medal, right?"

"I don't want to talk about Benny,"

"I did not know him. They say he was our town's biggest hero," said Hector.

"He made the national news." Larry said. "He was in the Atlanta papers."

"He saved all the guys in his squad. Won a medal for bravery. I never thought he'd had it in him." Clyde spit into his spit jar and took a swig from the other one.

"He was lazy," said Larry, looking at Clyde. "He got fired from every job he had. He just about told every lie there was. That boy never owned up to anything in his life. They said he stole that guy's ridin' mower. Harriman's mower. What did he need a ridin' mower for? He wasn't gonna cut no grass."

Frank got up and crushed his can in his fist, tossed it in the trash and reached into the icy barrel to fetch another. He returned to his seat and sat down heavily. His eyes glanced again at the defunct cooler with its collection of dusty artifacts.

"He was likeable, but about as worthless as a stray dog," Frank said.

"That right, Frank?" Larry asked. "He was still in high school when you went to 'Nam."

"Benny," Frank said. The name hung in the thick air. Larry exhaled a cloud of smoke. Eddie lit another cigarette from the butt of his current one.

Frank needed to talk of something besides the complete catastrophe of his life.

"He was good enough for the Army, although how he ever got accepted, I'll never know. Or how he got through basic training. But there he was in 'Nam. I saw him, good old Benny, from Juliette, Georgia. His hair was buzzed off just like the rest of us. I found him in the hospital at Binh Dinh. He wasn't there because he was hurt. Jungle fighting scared him so he used every excuse to get out of going on patrol. Benny and I spent an hour catching up on what was happening back in Juliette. I was amazed when he told me about getting married! But, you know, same old Benny.

"What a screw up! The Army is always giving you jobs to do, but Benny went after the safe, easy jobs. And he'd screw them up and have to go back to being a jungle grunt. His unit and mine trucked out in the same convoy, going toward Dak Pek, near the Laos, Cambodian border.

"It was my last few months. I was on what they called a 'short stick'. We just sat there on the Cambodian border with no orders, doing nothing.

"One day, I found Benny hiding behind the mess tent trying to wolf down a cake of soap. That's right. He was eating the damn stuff. 'Benny, I know the chow's shit around here...' He looked up and smiled like a little kid. 'Hey Frank.' He spit out the soap and shook my hand. 'Naw. I ain't that hungry. They want me to go out on patrol. This'll make me puke in the Med tent.'

"'Benny,' I said to him. 'Patrol around here is cream puff. Charley's across the line." I pointed north.

"They want me to go into Cambodia on a special mission." Benny said looking scared enough to shit in his pants.

"That scared the crap out of me so I made it a point to find his sergeant, and almost got in a fight with him. Turned out that he knew all about what a first class fuck-up Benny was. He said, 'We got two boys going home end of the week. Good boys. Faced Charlie a hundred times while your homeboy was lounging around the hospital. Those guys deserve to go home. He don't. I hope he gets his ass shot off.'

"So Benny went on that patrol and I heard the rest of the story from the few that made it back.

"They were supposed to blow up a supply dump, but right after they planted all the charges, they were attacked in force by the Viet Cong. As usual Benny hid somewhere out of the firing.

"The patrol was outnumbered and totally pinned down. One by one our guys took bullets. It was only a matter of time before they all got it. Then suddenly, there was Benny walking toward the Viet Cong! They stopped firing, probably out of surprise. Benny was mumbling some nonsense, like 'How's your mom and them.' The Cong shot him. Benny fell down on one of the planted charges, held a grenade next to it. Set it off. The rest of them went off and blew away most of the Viet Cong. What was left of Benny's patrol made it back, and they gave him the Silver Star. Posthumously."

Frank finished with a moody silence. The other men in the room stared at the floor. Outside, crickets sang.

Clyde stretched and yawned. "Well, Benny was a screw up. But that was a brave thing he did."

They all nodded and grunted.

"I got to get up in the morning," said Larry.

They tossed their beer cans in the trash and slowly filed out the door, leaving Frank sitting on the crate and Hector standing behind the counter, looking like a cigar store Indian. Larry, Clyde and Eddie stopped when they heard Frank whisper. "The jungle sounded just like this, like a hot night in Georgia. I remember being there, lying on my cot, listening to the insects and the water dripping off the leaves. Tree frogs. Critters and such."

He followed the rest out into the humid night.

****

Around two in the morning, Frank Robillard lay on an old mattress in the rented back room of Mrs. Reynolds's house. The room had lost little of the day's heat so he lay in his underwear with a fan blowing on

116

him. A bright, near full moon shone through the open window. He watched the shadows on the ceiling, noticed the intricate cracks in the plaster that wandered across its span.

May 23, 1980, had certainly not been one of his better days. In a few hours, Saturday's sun would rise. Certainly, he thought, tomorrow's got to be a better day.

PART THREE - JULIETTE'S TALE

Chapter 20

More than the first interview with TV Swanson, I dreaded interviewing Lydia, but I had to talk to her to see what she knew about the death of her husband. On her fell the role of villainess. She did our hero wrong, and ruined her own son, Remy's life. I allowed myself plenty of negative attitude about Lydia, and as a reporter, I anticipated hammering her.

What did I know about Lydia? She was a year younger than Frank Robillard. That placed her in the bullseye of middle age, the forties, a tough time for a former beauty queen. When she was sweet sixteen, she won the title of "Miss Silver Queen" at the Monroe County Autumn Festival.

Lydia, an only child, received lots of attention all of her life. Big Ray ran the town, and his golden haired little girl strode every pedestal he could put her on. Her friends elected her high school Homecoming Queen a couple years in a row, as well as head cheerleader, and so on. She must have grown very comfy having everything her way.

She married Frank after his return from Vietnam and gave birth to Remy in the early 70's. According to Big Ray and Remy, the big city lights beckoned, and she abandoned the town of her birth and the love of her high school sweetheart. Let's be fair; why should she stay in a hick town, married to a hick, who wanted to raise his boy to be just like himself? It was a classic conflict, one that troubles many a marriage. Lots of women in that situation skedaddle. Remember the song, "You picked a fine time to leave me, Lucille"?

Getting the interview turned out to be unexpectedly easy. I looked her up in the Atlanta phone book and then called. She suggested that I come over, and she didn't want to wait. She could clear her calendar for a real television reporter.

But on that phone call, the sound of her voice affected me in a strange way. When she hung up, I just sat there saying to myself, "Huh?" Her voice, low pitched with sultry Southern sophistication, gave me a heavy dose of goose bumps. I had been prepared to hate her, but my hostility evaporated. Anyone with a voice like that... how bad could she be?

After Frank's death, after leaving Juliette, she settled in Morningside, a really cool Atlanta neighborhood filled with old, architecturally splendid homes. Bright flowers and a sunny day bedazzled her stunning house, situated on a quiet foliage-lined street. The dogwoods and azaleas were running full tilt. I parked my Toyota in front. As I got out of the car my feet tingled like they were asleep and my heart pounded with excitement. I smelled honeysuckle and carnations and thought, what am I so excited about? Then before I knew what was happening, Lydia appeared right in front of me. I immediately judged her to be an extraordinary beauty. The mid afternoon sun set her hair ablaze with a burst of yellow. Her pale blue eyes beamed up at me with friendliness and grace. I fell head first into her trap. Her well proportioned little woman's body made me an Olympian by comparison. I actually towered over her. A great ego burst, that. Frank Robillard must have felt like Mount Rushmore.

I don't remember coming to my senses much in the next few hours. She had me completely dazzled. She took my arm, led me into a parlor and had tea poured quicker than a spider rolls up a fly. She seemed to take for granted the effect her first impression had on people, particularly men. She treated me like her dearest friend, like a genuinely lovely, charming person instead of the villainess I expected.

We chatted for a good thirty minutes about utter nonsense, which, if I recall any of it, included Atlanta politics, the Braves, how hot the summer was going to be, but wasn't it lovely weather now, and so on. I enjoyed that time with Lydia. I felt witty and handsome for a change. The episode was so pleasant and fulfilling that I couldn't imagine spending my time doing anything else. But pangs of guilt spoiled what could have been a perfect afternoon. I finally remembered that I was a television reporter who normally conducted tough interviews on wary subjects. I controlled nothing here. This was all Lydia's scene. What had happened to my goal of hammering this charming woman? Her life appeared to be nothing other than sitting, sipping tea with a friend. But I had to turn this off, fun as it was and get down to business.

With absolutely no grace at all I started in on the subject of Frank. Our pleasant afternoon went south in a heartbeat.

"You left Juliette around 1980, didn't you?" I said. Her sparkling blue eyes turned frosty and dark, like a rain shower approaching.

"Juliette? You mean the town?" Her chin drew back, exposing a loop of wrinkled skin under it I had not noticed before.

"Yes. The town."

"I lived there when I was growing up. I don't remember when I moved up here."

"You were married to Frank Robillard?"

Her hand flew to her forehead like a headache impended. "Yes. I was married, a long time ago."

"How long were you married to Frank?" I asked.

"Ten years or so."

"You had a son?"

"Yes. Still have. He lives here in Atlanta."

"How did your marriage to Frank end?"

Lydia's eyes drifted up, over the top of my head and she stared at the wall behind me for a long time. I could not remember what was on that wall, and turned to look. It was a large, gold framed photo of the Eiffel Tower. I remembered her father, Big Ray commenting on her obsession with French culture and noted that the place was well decorated with Impressionist art hanging on the walls, flowers in vases on pedestals and furniture, in a French style, draped with the appropriate lace.

"He died in an accident."

"How was your marriage with Frank?" I rolled on, like the storm trooper reporter I was.

Lydia ran the tip of her tongue across her upper front teeth. Her lips twisted, as if the last sip of tea had gone bad. Then her eyes locked onto mine and I shrank from her frosty disdain.

"Why do you want to bring that up? He's been dead, what? Sixteen years, now? Seventeen. The marriage wasn't all that great. Who cares? Neither of us was famous." She shrugged her tiny shoulders.

That was a good point, but I was on the attack and could not back off. "Well, Frank was a hero," I said. She responded with a merry smile.

"No! A hero for what?" She tossed her head back. Her laughter pealed like elfin bells.

"He was a war hero. Vietnam. He won decorations, medals."

She waved that off with a physical gesture. "Oh, the war. It's over too, you know. Who's famous from that war?"

"Didn't he capture a dangerous criminal? When he was a

policeman?" I asked.

She did a double take. "I don't know anything about that."

"Wasn't he smart, almost brilliant?"

She raised her eyebrows. "Sure. He was very intelligent. But lazy. He never used his head at all, either before or after being in the army."

"Marines." I corrected.

"Whatever. He hung out in that little town with his buddies and didn't do a darn thing. I urged him to do more, but he wouldn't. He could have gone back to college and been an architect or an engineer, a doctor. But he didn't. He was happy with his simple, little life. We didn't have a thing, not even money to buy clothes for myself or my child."

I looked around the room. "You seem to be doing all right."

Lydia arched her eyebrows again and sighed. "Mr. Macbean, it has been a long time since then. We're all doing better. Doing better wasn't in Frank's language. He thought we should all be happy living a simple life."

"But that was not for you. You wanted to live in Atlanta."

"I like Atlanta. I like New York. I like lots of places. Chicago, London, Paris." She raised her face with a tight smile, waiting for my next challenge.

"Were you planning to move up here before he died?"

"What difference does that make?"

"Well, it's one thing to be a widow. It's something else to be a divorcee."

"What are you getting at? I got nothing from Frank's death. We had nothing. I told you that. I didn't like living there. I didn't like our position. I don't want to say anything bad about Frank. He was a good man, in his way. We wanted different things, that's all." She folded her arms.

"You didn't know about him capturing a dangerous criminal?"

Lydia shook her head. "I don't remember a thing."

"You never heard of TV Swanson?"

"No sir. What'd he do?"

"Killed a bunch of people. He was caught in Juliette just before Frank died. Frank had a hand in capturing him... maybe."

"He took his job very seriously," she replied. "He took everything seriously. I wanted out. I wanted out of Juliette. I wanted out of the marriage. I wanted my son to grow up away from that small town."

"Away from Frank?" I asked.

122

Lydia looked out the window. There was no sadness in her eyes. No tears. "Yes. Away from Frank."

"Wasn't he a good father?"

"Depends what you mean." Lydia said, turning her frosty blue eyes on me. "He taught him how to play ball, about fishing and all that."

"Making him into a good little redneck," I offered.

"Exactly. I do loathe those good old boys, sitting around the cracker barrel, drinking beer, dipping snuff. It's the ugliest picture I can think of. I didn't want my son growing up being like that. I didn't want him being like Frank. You didn't know him. I knew him for more than twenty years. He was quite a smart little fellow once. When we were in school as kids, he won all the awards. He was way out in front of the rest of us. In grades. In lots of things."

"Music?" I offered.

She frowned. "Oh. Yes. I had forgotten. His violin. He played when he was a child. His parents took him to Atlanta all the time for concerts. My parents wouldn't take me, even though I begged them to. My daddy only took me when I needed specially fitted shoes. I loved the city. I loved the buildings, but I had to stay in Juliette. The only contact I had to the big, outside world was through the Atlanta papers."

"So Frank got to go all the time. And you didn't?" I asked.

"All the children loved Frank. All our friends. When we were kids he always led our play activities and games. But he was running off with the boys most of the time. You couldn't pin him down. Everyone made a fuss over Frank. I hated him sometimes, for all the attention paid him. When we got older, Frank was in sports. I went into cheerleading and found ways a girl could be a celebrity too. My daddy let me enter a few beauty contests. Then in high school, Frank and I were kind of thrown together. He was the captain of the football team. I was the head cheerleader. Yes. High school was fun. He was a pretty good athlete. And I was the most sought after girl in school.

"After high school, he went off to college. My father wanted to send me to Forsyth College, that little hick school just down the road. I refused. I wanted to go to Agnes Scott, Emory or someplace in Atlanta. So I was left to rot at home. I tried other beauty contests like the Miss Georgia Pageants. Ha! That wasn't going to work for me. I'm too short. They all like the real tall girls. I didn't have a chance.

"After high school, we dated for a while. He got hurt playing football. Then off he went to Vietnam. He was home only for a short time.

"We got married. Seemed like the whole town wanted us to. I went along. Everyone in Juliette remembered his big days, when he was giving all those concerts and later, when he was a football star. Our son Remy came along. Frank gave up everything and doted on that boy. He just wound himself down into one big disappointment."

Her eyes drifted off again. Her voice dropped to nearly a whisper. "Frank never went back to college. He took a job as a policeman. Like Juliette needed a policeman! Juliette didn't have a police force until my daddy made one. Juliette didn't have a fire department until my daddy made that too. Juliette wasn't even a town until my daddy made it one. All those people owed everything to my daddy. Even Frank. Especially Frank."

Chapter 21

Like every other day, Eddie "Blue" Feherty rose early on Saturday. At the first glimmer of light, he rolled out of the cot in the loft above the old wooden building that served as the fire station. His family had been farmers for generations. Early rising was in his blood. Although he had lived on his father's farm from childhood to middle age, Eddie "Blue" Feherty was not a farmer. His father died and left the farm to him. Eddie had not wanted the heavily mortgaged, hard to run place and had let it fall to its creditors.

Blue cleared a little money from the foreclosure. He had nowhere to stay and few possessions, but managed to buy a rundown old pickup truck. It was dented on all sides and the driver's window wouldn't roll up. He cleaned it up as best he could and with a few dozen cans of spray paint, carefully painted it red. On both doors, he hand lettered the words, "Juliette Fire Department." After the citizens of Juliette overcame their astonishment that Blue could write, no one had much praise for the results. He drove the truck around town, waving, head and elbow out of the driver's window. Every now and then a fire did pop up in an abandoned house or field. Blue showed up in his red truck and usually had it put out before the arrival of the real firemen from Forsyth.

Blue's only source of income was the meager wage he earned as the Little League baseball umpire. On summer evenings, he would race the truck to the baseball field, blasting the horn and flashing the headlights. Everyone would know that Eddie "Blue" Feherty was coming. After the games, Blue would drive to a vacant lot out on Juliette Road, open a can of pork and beans, smoke dozens of cigarettes and sleep under the truck or under the stars if the weather allowed. Blue tried to keep things simple. He never considered whether he was happy or not. He had reduced his life to the level of a stray dog, and it was okay with him.

Such situations never last.

Big Ray was developing a trailer park a few miles out of town. For months he had studied the state regulations specifying what size lots to build, how much water, electrical power and sewerage were needed. It took him a total of three months to build the Vanair Trailer Park, which was later renamed the Vanair Mobile Home Park, when that became the preferred term.

The Vanair was an instant success. Within a week, Big Ray had dozens of leases signed. The prospects of a good hookup made the Vanair in such demand that it soon built a waiting list. Ray's lots could be rented for six months or a full year. You could move your trailer in yourself or Big Ray could get Clyde Hembree to do the hauling. If you were a good citizen and paid your rent, you were left in peace. Big Ray's rates were the best within the five counties, even if his amenities were a little sparse. If you failed to pay on time, you were given a terse warning, then a quick eviction.

The advent of the Vanair and a random, seemingly unconnected event changed Eddie "Blue" Feherty's life forever.

One of the Vanair's tenants, Collie Burdell, habitually paid his rent late, a distasteful shortcoming in Big Ray's doctrine. After several months, exhibiting what he considered extraordinary forbearance, Ray called on Collie's trailer to collect and/or evict. Collie begged and pleaded to be spared, forgiven and extended. Ray took in the five kids and a pregnant wife who all lived in the thirty foot trailer and took pity.

"Collie, I'll give you till Friday. If you don't have the rent then, I'm evicting you. That's it. You got that, boy?"

Collie nodded his head. "Thank you Mister Ray. You can count on it. Friday it is, no problem."

Friday came and nearly went. Late in the day Big Ray drove out to the Vanair. He was about to knock on the trailer door when Collie snaked out through the bathroom window. Collie hit the ground and high-tailed it. Ray ran to his car, but the man on foot was fleet and nimbly disappeared into the forest behind the trailer park. Big Ray gave up and drove back to town.

He summoned Frank.

"Frank, old Collie has given me the slip, but he'll turn up sometime. Go pin him down and call me. We're going to have a 'Come to Jesus' meeting."

Big Ray's phone rang an hour later. Frank had Collie holed up at the Amoco station on the Macon Road. Ray drove out there to confront his renter. Collie's eyes rolled back and forth looking for escape, but Frank blocked the door with his arms folded. Big Ray strolled in, maybe not exactly savoring the moment, but knowing that he had Collie treed, and all the elements were favoring victory.

"Collie, it's Friday. Where's my money?"

Collie smiled, trying to make the best of a bad situation. "Are you sure, Mr. Ray?" he ventured.

"Sure, I'm sure. Dig deep and hand it over." Ray held out his pudgy hand.

Collie squirmed in his seat. "Well, I thought you'd give me till the end of the day."

Big Ray snorted. "This is the end of the day. Your day ended when you sneaked out that window. You're out of the Vanair. You been nothing but trouble since you moved in. You're late with the rent. Not just once but all the time. I'm coming back tomorrow. You either hand me the money or I'm hauling your trailer out to the highway."

Collie blinked. He looked to Frank, covering the door. Frank stared at the girlie calendar on the gas station's wall.

"What do you mean by that Mr. Ray?"

Ray bent over and put his face close to Collie's. "Haul your trailer out to the highway. I'll ask Clyde Hembree to bring up his tractor. He'll hook it up and pull it up to the highway. Off'n my property. If it goes in the ditch, so be it. Then I'll call the State Highway Patrol. Tell 'em that it's out there on the road, blocking traffic. They'll come and put it in the impound lot in Macon. You won't have nothing left inside but scrap."

Collie sat there and considered the consequences. "But what of my family? My kids?"

"I ain't gonna hurt your kids. I'll make sure they're out of the trailer, that they're somewhere's else. But you!" Ray pointed to Collie with a fat little finger. "Better get out of the way. You ever seen Frank here evict someone? He played football for Georgia. He's a strong man." With that Ray turned and left the Amoco station.

Collie shouted after him. "It ain't fair. I'm good for it. Just give me a few more days"

Ray turned when he reached his Cadillac. "My money or the highway. It's up to you."

Collie worked on his trailer all that night. When Ray arrived the next morning, along with Clyde Hembree driving the John Deere, he saw several of the Vanair's citizens standing with Collie, viewing the damage to Collie's trailer.

"I don't understand it Mr. Ray. Someone upped and stole my hitch last night," Collie said pointing to the scarred front end of his trailer.

The evidence was plain. The V-shaped steel beams that formed the front of the trailer had been cut through with a welding torch. The hitch was gone, although Ray suspected that he could find it in the woods nearby. There was no way Clyde could haul the trailer to the highway.

"I heard them welders cuttin' all night. Almost called the police." Someone said in a sleepy voice.

"Who would do such a thing, Mister Ray?" Collie kept a straight face, but triumph was plain in his eyes. No hitch. No hauling out to the highway.

Ray stared at the hitch for a full minute. Then he looked at Collie with a smile that chilled the little man's guts.

"That's okay. I got something, don't need no hitch," Big Ray said.

He turned and spoke a few words to Clyde Hembree, who stood there hanging on to the straps of his overalls. Clyde wrinkled his forehead, and Big Ray had to repeat his instructions. Finally Clyde shrugged, climbed onto the tractor and drove off.

Big Ray leaned against the front fender of his Cadillac and lit a cigar. Collie's neighbors inched away. No one offered him any support. By the time Big Ray's cigar was about half gone, they all heard the grinding of a very large truck entering the Vanair Trailer Park. Clyde had returned with a huge flatbed trailer carrying a front loading Caterpillar, commonly known as a bull-dozer.

Clyde took the chains off the Cat, and lowered the thick steel ramp in the back of the flatbed. Slowly he climbed on top of the big yellow Cat. The morning birds sang a few last notes before the whirring of the starter motor began. The Cat's engine exploded to life followed by blasts of sooty exhaust from the powerful diesel. The ground shook from vibration.

Collie's mouth moved but no one heard him. Big Ray tapped his cigar, and threw a cold look at Collie. Ray then nodded at Clyde, high atop the yellow Cat. On that signal, Clyde gunned the Cat's engine. The sound became a war of noise that made everyone back up. The power of the big Cat shook the leaves on the trees around them, the ground under their feet and made the air so charged they all struggled to draw breath. Big Ray, unaffected, blew a few smoke rings.

Collie stood there, his feet glued to the red clay, his shoulders slumped. He finally turned and went into his trailer. Moments later he emerged carrying a tiny bundle in his hand. He walked over to Big Ray and handed him his money. Big Ray counted the money slowly while Clyde continued to destroy the world with the Caterpillar's noise. Finally Ray folded the money, put it into his pocket and nodded again to Clyde.

Everyone was relieved when Clyde killed the engine. The sound under the trees became quiet again, although no one expected to hear the birds singing for a couple of days.

Collie was defeated, and Big Ray had his trailer repaired and eventually evicted him. Collie devoted himself to vengeance and called a relative in Atlanta, who knew of someone who worked on a state regulatory board. Within weeks, Big Ray was visited by state inspectors and his Vanair Park was put under continuous scrutiny. Big Ray weathered most of it. He had done his homework. The Vanair Trailer Park met all the minimums required by the state.

Except one. There was a state rating system that evaluated developments according to their distance from a fire station. Without a fire station nearby, insurance companies could raise the rates for his tenants. At the time Ray built the Vanair, there had been such a fire station within the required distance in Forsyth, but that city had moved the facility to the west side of town which put the Vanair in a less favorable category. Ray called the State Insurance Commissioner, who just happened to be a friend of his.

"Bill, the rates are going so high that my tenants can't afford to live in the Vanair."

Bill was sympathetic. "Ray. I'm sorry. I can't do anything about it. Regulations are regulations."

The situation plunged Big Ray Culp into a mood. He drove his Caddy around Juliette not stopping or speaking to anyone. The Vanair was a big money maker. He hated to give it up. He sat at the ballpark one warm evening, letting the car's air-conditioning cool his balding forehead when Eddie Blue Feherty came thundering down the hill, blowing horns and flashing lights, in his ridiculous red pickup. The lights came on at the ballpark about the same time they came on in Big Ray's head.

Ray called the commissioner, again. "Bill, can you give me a few months before my rating gets downgraded?"

"Heck no. That fire station closed four months ago. The ratings'll change immediately. It's the decision of the insurance companies, and they usually raise the rates when they get wind of it."

So Ray had no time. He went to see Blue the next day and found him sitting in the shade of an oak near the edge his favorite vacant lot.

"Blue, Juliette needs a fire department. A real fire department."

Blue made no effort to respond. He lit a cigarette with the butt of his previous one. It was impossible to tell what thoughts cycled through his head, if any. He squinted back at Ray with a watery red eye.

"Blue, I want you to run it. I'll get you some equipment. I'll get a building. Blue, are you hearing me?"

Blue looked away. He had the same expression on his face as when kids' parents argued with him at the baseball field over some call they didn't like.

"Blue. You get to run it. The Juliette Fire Department!" No response came from Eddie "Blue" Feherty.

"I'll pay you," Ray said. Not even a flicker. Blue refused to meet his eyes. "Blue. Don't you want a fire department? Something better than...." He might as well have been talking to a squirrel in a tree. Ray turned away, hands stuffed in his back pockets. His whole life depended on making others do what he wanted. What could he do with Blue, who at the moment seemed content with his job as the village idiot?

"Blue. I'll get you a new truck. You want a new truck?" Blue scanned the sky, the road, his fingernails, which were caked with a darkness that defied identification.

"With a siren, Blue. The new truck will have a siren." For a moment, Ray entertained the idea of making a sound like a fire siren, but he saw he now had Blue's attention.

"Play Ball," Blue said with a slight smile.

Big Ray was a man of his word, but he limited his largess to the least amount of money he could get away with. He bought a small fire truck from the Forest Service in North Georgia. The truck was larger than Eddie's old pickup and in fair condition. It had flashing red lights, assorted fire-fighting equipment such as ladders, axes, boots and helmets, 200 feet of three inch hose, a 500 gallon tank, a water pump, and most gloriously, chrome sirens mounted on each of the dented front fenders. The sirens put out a terrible wailing that brought a smile to Blue's leathery face.

Ray chose one of his many properties to be the site of the new Juliette Fire Department. The weeds had all but taken the place over, but Ray got Clyde to cut them. The simple frame building, built of rough sawn timbers, barely held the truck. A loft over the garage became Blue's sleeping quarters. The distance from floor to peak of this "room"

130

was only a few feet, so Blue had to crawl when he was in it. He cut a large hole in the floor of the loft near the back and although he couldn't find a brass pole, he installed a twenty foot length of galvanized steel pipe. Blue only used the pole a couple of times. He found that his knees painfully gave way when he landed, and that the surface of the pipe cut his hands. He fashioned a ladder out of 2 x 4's, and used it to climb up. Big Ray provided him some paint, which he used to spruce up the building's outsides. In a couple of weeks, the place didn't look too bad.

"There's no way in hell I'm gonna certify this outfit as a fire department," said the state inspector. "Has that man ever had any training?" he said, pointing to Blue.

"That man is a respected member of the community, and he has saved lots of lives puttin' out fires."

The state inspector looked skeptical. "Look, Mayor, you can't receive certification this way. You have to have trained firemen, equipment, facilities. I don't see none of that."

Big Ray had been studying the regulations. "What about a volunteer fire department? We don't have the budget to fund a regular fire department anyway."

"Volunteer fire departments are not certified by the state. We don't care what you do, really. There are few regulations that govern their operations, you know, to keep us from getting sued. But it's the insurance companies you need to worry about."

Big Ray smiled. "I know. They test you and if you pass, you can get a better rating. And the insurance rates will go down."

"They could," the state inspector nodded, eyeing the nearly bald tires on the old fire truck.

Big Ray got Frank to take the written test and received the highest score ever recorded for the "National Firefighters Association's Standard Fire Prevention and Safety Readiness Examination." It was a remarkable achievement. Big Ray started receiving job offers from fire departments all over the country. Even the most experienced firefighters were happy to merely pass the SFP&SRE. In spite of having not earned it, Blue proudly hung the certificate on the wall of the fire station. Big Ray received the ratings he needed for the Vanair Trailer Park and things should have pretty well gotten back to normal in Juliette.

Except that Blue's simple life had by then all but vanished. He became another victim of government bureaucracy. Big Ray installed a phone in the fire station. It had neither rotary dial nor push buttons, so

Blue could not use it to dial out. But people could dial in and dial in they did. They rang Eddie "Blue" Feherty up with merciless frequency. The phone, mounted on the wall of the garage, always seemed to ring when he was either up in the loft or out in the yard. It took him a while to climb down the 2 x 4 ladder. Each strident peal raised his blood pressure several points. Big Ray required him to answer every call. It just might be a fire.

Blue answered all the calls with a poor attitude and a loud, "Fire station!" Then he'd fall silent. It didn't matter if the caller asked Blue a question or made a statement. Blue would respond with heavy breathing until the caller hung up. And of real emergencies there were few.

The firefighters from the nearby town of Forsyth arrived once a month to check the charges on his fire extinguishers and attend to other state regulations. Blue found the inspections nerve wracking and intrusive. Sometimes such visits left Blue with work to do. If he failed to do any of it, Big Ray, fearful of losing the insurance rate equilibrium he had so carefully established, would be down there in a flash scolding him like a naughty child.

Since he paid Blue twenty dollars a week, plus room, plus board, plus transportation (the fire truck) and utilities, such as phone and water, (there was no heat), Ray felt entitled to have Blue run errands for him, which Blue did without comment or enthusiasm. Blue accepted this shift of his life into high gear with obvious petulance but yearned for the old days of sleeping under the truck.

On days when Big Ray didn't show up with a list of errands or the Forsyth Fire Department didn't come to check the fire extinguishers and the phone didn't ring, Blue puttered around the fire station or drove the roads of Monroe County in the fire truck with no discernable destination.

Saturday, May 24, 1980, turned out to be one of those days. Blue set out early to avoid what little attention people paid him. Juliette was a community of early risers, but few noticed Blue in his red truck.

At the turn of the century, Juliette had been famous for being the home of the world's largest water powered grist mill. The Ocmulgee River had powered a mill at that location for over a century. From a small wood and stone building, the mill had grown until it was a four story, steel and concrete building with complex gears and pulleys turning nearly fifty large stones. Alas, someone built a larger one in Europe. The town lost its pizzazz, and the mill shut down in 1957. The building still stood across the river from the town, dark and abandoned. The mill had employed nearly a hundred people, and many small frame houses were built to house these workers.

The forest swallowed most of the mill houses in the twenty-three years since the mill closed. Trees now grew in places where people would never plant them, and weeds grew everywhere else. Their once white paint had faded to the deathlike gray of abandonment. Once or twice a year, one of these houses would go up in flames, and it never occurred to anyone in Juliette that it was a natural occurrence.

Blue had brought an old tire with him. Inside the tire, taped to the inner ply, was a device of Blue's own design. It consisted of a small medicine bottle attached to an emergency road flare. Inside the bottle was a mixture of potassium permanganate, powdered sugar and magnesium. Also inside the bottle was a small latex bladder with a teaspoon or so of plain water. The latex bladder was cut from the tip of a balloon and secured with a wire tie. Electrician's tape held the whole contraption together. According to Blue's tests, it took the water about 15 to 20 hours to leak through the walls of the latex bladder, and when it came into contact with the potassium permanganate/sugar/magnesium mixture, a reaction took place that produced a flame and a lot of heat, which usually ignited the road flare. The road flare would burn for about thirty minutes, more than enough to ignite the old tire. The tire would burn for hours, setting fire to and keeping the dry-rotted timbers of the house alight.

On that Saturday morning, Blue drove to a particular house that he had had his eye on for some time. This house was situated away from the occupied homes in Juliette, but close enough that a fire would catch someone's attention. The flames would create a beacon of yellow and orange light. Blue's friends and neighbors, dressed in their pajamas and bathrobes, would gather just beyond the heat and smoke, to watch the monster fire and the lone man courageously battling the flames. Blue stirred in the seat of the truck just thinking of what was coming.

Sometimes though, his device didn't work. The timing wasn't exact, and he would wait with increasing anxiety. If the call did not come, he would have to retrieve the contraption, find the flaw and make another. He'd wait a few weeks and try again. Some nights when darkness silenced even the crickets and tree frogs, images of fire crept into his thoughts. Blue would light another cigarette, squinting against the smoke that clung to his cheeks, watching the glow in the darkness of his sleeping loft.

The house he had chosen stood back from the road, obscured by small saplings and brush. Few would have bothered to look at the mildewed spotted walls, the fallen in roof, and shattered panes of glass. The front door hung off its hinges. Blue carefully made his way inside. He placed the tire behind a peeled and cracked wall in the center of the house. He stood there and stared at the tire leaning up against the wall. It looked out of place, but it was highly unlikely that anyone was going to come in here and see it.

Eddie "Blue"Feherty skipped across the loose boards of the porch beating a hasty retreat back to the truck. He furtively looked from right to left. He saw no one. The trees, leaves and vines surrounded him. The slanting rays of the morning sun heated the dew into wisps of fog. The noise of Blue slamming the truck's door shocked the stillness. Blue took a last look at the dilapidated old house. He imagined how it soon would shine with its own light. He had Saturday morning baseball games to umpire but afterward he planned to get plenty of rest. He would need it.

Chapter 22

TV Swanson drove the Buick station wagon through the night. By dawn the morning, Saturday, May 24, 1980, the Swanson family had left Ohio, crossed Kentucky and Tennessee. The kids slept bundled in their sleeping bags, Harry in the front seat, Teeny in the back next to her unconscious mother. Having tired of her complaints, TV had given Corky enough pills to make her bonkers, hoping she'd stay in her own world.

Ted loathed the weaker part of his character, the part that gave him doubts and fear. The black night seemed to naturally churn out negative scenarios; of him getting caught and punished. He had crossed state lines, but that would not hinder the police. They would alert other law enforcement agencies to be on the lookout for him.

If those idiots figured out who did the gas station...., he thought. How would they know? The explosion and fire probably left nobody alive. Those troopers might have seen the car, but I can get a new car... and new plates.

TV thought: Low Profile Ted. That's my name.... only I might need a new name. I'll get the kids new names, too. That won't be easy, but they'll do what I want, what I tell them. What else? I need somebody to help me who ain't in trouble. I need new stuff and a hideout. Nobody's gonna do that, you ugly son of a bitch. You scare the living shit out of everybody. Who's gonna take you in?

The enveloping darkness and swirling bugs massed in the Buick's headlights, but the insects splattering his windshield offered no clues. To drive and keep on driving seemed to be the only answer.

****

The beautiful red clouded sunrise saw the Swansons heading into Georgia. Harry and Teeny murmured with waking sounds. The glittering lights of an all night gas station drew their attention. After filling up, they drove across an empty highway to a McDonalds and bought breakfast, parking in the back so TV could transfer the license plates from a stranger's car.

Harry munched on an Egg McMuffin and looked up at his father. Fatigue and stress etched his face. He wondered how much longer his father would drive and what would happen when he reached his limit. He knew nothing about what they were doing. They were on the road, an existence more familiar to him than any house he had lived in. His dad had said that they were going on vacation, but Harry expected little entertainment on this trip. So he rode shotgun in the front seat of someone else's big blue Buick station wagon, and they continued down the highway, driving into the red sunrise. Teeny danced her doll against her mother's unmoving backside while the station wagon skirted Atlanta and continued south.

Harry watched the painted lines on the highway without thinking. He noticed the car drifting left over the center of the highway. His dad often drove recklessly but Harry felt that this time, he might be losing control. His father's chin slowly inched down, and his eyelids drooped. Then his head jerked upright, eyes wide for a second. Once recovered, he drove with renewed focus.

Harry had only a vague idea of their location. He knew that they had driven around Atlanta and its suburbs a while back. He could see thick pine forest whizzing by on either side of the highway. Occasionally the pines were interrupted by a billboard, advertising "Paw Paw's Country Bar-B-Q" or "Dewey's Auto Fix-it." Beyond that, he saw little evidence of city life. They were out in the sticks of Georgia. He felt the Buick's speed come down a little.

Harry's dad slammed on the brakes, spinning the station wagon nearly around, leaving black streaks on the empty two-lane asphalt. The Swansons bounced around inside the car like a tipped basket of fruit. TV shoved the Buick into reverse and hit the accelerator, leaving more tire streaks on the road. They careened backward nearly a quarter mile until he made another abrupt halt in front of a small billboard. The station wagon rocked for a second. The rear bumper of the Buick stuck into the weeds on the highway's shoulder and the front of the car rested at an odd angle over the pavement, but there was no traffic on the highway. Harry and his father stared at the roadside sign through a bug-streaked windshield.

The sign seemed crude, even to Harry. A photographic image of a grinning preacher, dressed in a Sunday-best suit, white shirt and black string tie, holding a book with the word "BIBLE" in gold letters. The

136

caption had been lettered in a movie-poster font; its message blared out, "Your sins can be forgiven! Nothing is beyond the Power of the Lord! Salvation is near! Come and hear the Word of our Lord Jesus Christ! Randy Wilbanks, Pastor, East Juliette Church of Jesus."

"Where the fuck is the East Juliette Church of Jesus?" TV asked, leaning on the steering wheel.

"In East Juliette, Dad," Harry said. His father slowly turned to look at him. Harry noticed the deep red of his eyes, but the eyes themselves glowed bright with moisture. Harry tensed for either a punch or a hug. But his dad's eyes softened, and a smile crept into the corner of his thin mouth.

"Ha!" TV looked back at the sign. Nothing but a solid wall of trees lined both sides of the road in front and behind. "Where's the fucking East Juliette?"

Harry smiled back at him. "That would be east of Juliette, Dad."

"No shit, Sherlock." He turned and grabbed his son's head and they rolled and tickled each other on the front seat of the car.

Chapter 23

The speed trap had always been his favorite place to think, but contrasting yesterday's simple doubts, on this Saturday morning Frank Robillard had come there to worry. The deal with Big Ray was done. Frank would give up Little Ray. Lydia would move them both to Atlanta and allow him little contact. Nothing justified the punishment of losing his son. Or his wife. In Atlanta, Lydia would blossom like a flower left too long without water. She'd be happy there and of course, she was miserable here in Juliette. Big Ray would pay for Little Ray's education. But Frank wanted them to be happy here in Juliette. Was that too much to ask? But only a fool would ask it, he thought. They'd both be better off with this arrangement.

A hay wagon lumbered by at such a slow speed, it seemed to Frank he had first heard the tractor's hammering engine an hour ago. That would pretty much kill any chance of getting a speeder, he thought.

Lydia wanted him to have no influence in Little Ray's life. She would make visiting Little Ray increasingly more difficult. Whatever Lydia wanted, Big Ray had the power and money to see it through. If Frank didn't go along, he'd get hammered by her father.

Was it so hard to figure out, really? Frank wondered. She wants more than to leave Juliette. It's me she really wants to get away from. And she wants the big city. Atlanta had society. Atlanta had arts and culture. Atlanta had restaurants, professional sports, nightclubs, country clubs, and glittering parties. Little of that interested Frank. He might have enjoyed concerts, libraries and museums, but he could give it up for.... for what? If you lived in Juliette, you had to live under Big Ray who eventually got around to controlling everyone. And Frank was one of his lifelong projects. He remembered the ill fated results the last time Big Ray had offered him a deal.

After his college football injury, Frank had spent the summer rehabilitating, spending long hours thinking about his future. He stumped around the town, at first on crutches and eventually a cane. Everyone in town greeted him with enthusiasm and advice about what he should do.

As the summer wore on, his knee healed, but not his irresolution. On a hot July day, Big Ray approached him

"How's the knee?" he had asked.

"Coming along," replied Frank. Frank could walk without the cane, but he still sported it because he thought it would stop folks from asking about his knee. Apparently not.

"What are you doing this fall?" Frank had grown to be a big man. Big Ray had to look up at him.

Frank had little use for fathers, even Lydia's. He knew Big Ray to be a master manipulator, and that he probably had some plan for him.

"Why?"

"Are you going back to the University?"

"I'm not playing any more football, if that's what you mean." Frank said.

"You're not?"

"No." Frank braced himself for Big Ray's blast of disappointment. His mind filled with retorts, mostly sarcastic.

Big Ray took a deep breath and looked around the town. The streets, hot with Georgia sunshine, were empty.

"Well. That's good." Ray said.

"You don't care if I quit football?"

"No. You'd be stupid to go back, and you ain't stupid."

"Everyone wants me to play. There'll be big disappointment around here if I don't hunker down this fall."

"Let 'em be disappointed. You don't owe them that. You ain't no football player, anyhow. I don't care how good you are. Why get yourself hurt again? Your assets are in your brain." Big Ray touched his own head.

Frank looked away and shrugged. "I'm glad you approve."

Ray made his move. "You could be pretty big. You got good grades, don't you?"

"I have a four-oh." Frank replied, with little pride in his voice.

"So you could get something besides a football scholarship?"

"Academic? I'd have to apply for it, but yeah, I could get a full boat. Why are you concerned, might I ask?"

Big Ray looked mildly hurt. "Why, I like you, boy. You're the brightest kid to ever come out of this town. We look up to you." Big Ray waved toward the town's center and kept his arm rotating until he had turned a full circle. "These people love you like their own son. What you

139

do is important to them. It's important to all of us."

Frank wondered if that included Lydia, his daughter. Frank wanted her like every boy in the county wanted her. She was the most beautiful girl within a hundred miles, the daughter of the richest man in Monroe County. But Frank wanted more than her beauty. He wanted to see her sweat with a passion that matched his own. But he had never seen even a hint of it. She was like a porcelain statue on a parlor table, that never moved or changed, that everyone saw and wanted to touch, far too exotic to possess. She hadn't quite rejected him, but she hadn't welcomed him either.

"Well, I know the folks around here want to see me succeed. I always thought that it meant football."

Ray shook his head. "It doesn't have to be football and if I were you, it wouldn't be football. You're too smart for that. You got a brain. I'd like to see you do something big after you graduate. Make this town proud."

"Like what?"

Ray squinted from the sun moving behind Frank's head. "Well, what do you want to do?"

The question made Frank uneasy. "Be a doctor, I guess." Frank offered.

Ray snorted. "Hah! I guess you could do it, too. Being a doctor takes a lot of work. You put in some long hours and start small."

Frank said, "You wouldn't go that way?"

"No sir." Ray shook his head. "They make a ton of money. You could be a doctor, but that ain't what I see in you. What I see for you is the practice of law, at least at first."

"Law," Frank said. "Why law?"

"Because with law, you can go anywhere, do anything. The law is the power in America."

"But don't you have to become a lawyer?"

Ray was tuned into his sales pitch, not sarcasm. "Sure you do. You could finish up a pre-law degree at Georgia in about two, three semesters. There ain't nothing to that. Then you go to law school. UGA's got a good one. Or you could go to Emory or even Vanderbilt. Then you pass the bar. No problem for you. You could probably pass it now, but you need the degree. You could hang your shingle in Macon, "Frank Robillard, Attorney at Law.""

"Then what?"

Ray looked inward, visualizing his plan. "I give you a few cases to start you off. Some that will do me good to win, you know. Oh, and you'll win them. I know you will. You build a reputation as a good lawyer. But being a lawyer is not the end of it."

"It's not?" Frank grimaced. His leg was healed, but something was causing it to twinge.

"No. Then you run for the state legislature. We can get you into the house in about ten, twelve years. By then everyone thinks of you as an up-and-comer. You do that for a while... you can help me a lot in the state house too. Then we'll see what we can do about, maybe something bigger. Something national." Ray pumped his hands in the air. "Washington! We get the governor to help us. Frank, what do you think?"

Frank stared at him for a full minute. Had he really heard Ray suggest that he become his lackey? He would face a lifetime of serving the man's schemes. Ray had just offered Frank a huge opportunity, but the cost was his freedom.

"Look, Mr. Culp. Law school scholarships are different from regular curriculums... difficult to get. I could apply for law school, but I haven't campaigned for it. Anyway, I don't have the money. It might take me a year or more to get caught up to that track."

Ray waved him off. "Don't worry about paying. You just been awarded a scholarship. Uh... the Raymond Culp Memorial Scholarship for bright young boys who live in Juliette." Heh, heh. Ray sniggered. "Boy, your school's paid for from now on. But that's not all. I'll get you a car and an apartment in Athens. I know that you'll catch up the book stuff in no time. You're smarter than all the rest of them. You can do it. What do ya say, Frank?"

Frank's head swirled with endless tableaus: late meetings with Big Ray, money-making schemes, power moves against people that were in the way and writing foreclosure letters to folks who fell behind in their payments. Frank's life would be one of conflict and confrontation. But for him to not take Ray's offer was also a problem. No one in this town stood against Big Ray. If he turned him down, he would become Ray's enemy. Ray always won.

An empty melancholy settled over him. Big Ray, at least has plans, Frank thought. He may be greedy and avaricious. He may be missing a little generosity and compassion for his fellow man, but he has purpose. He gets up in the morning with something to do. He goes after what he wants and nobody turns him aside or puts him off his goal. He doesn't sit and wait for what he wants. He doesn't hope. Big Ray doesn't need hope.

Frank could see no way to decline the offer. Ray would take his life from him and use it to his purposes because there was nothing inside of Frank that could stop him. He had no real direction, no ambition large enough to absorb the enormous gifts with which he had been born. Ray was willing to provide the will, the direction and the money.

Frank stared at the bright blue sky. He looked down at the man who wanted to be his benefactor, his boss and eventually, his father-in-law.

Frank's long deliberation strained Ray's amiability. Frank could almost hear the thoughts going through his bald head. "What's the problem? Ain't I offering this big cracker a lifetime meal ticket? He came from trash. His pappy was a poor fool. His mom, rest her soul, was a nice enough girl. Did he want to be poor all his life? I don't have to do this. This ought to be an easy decision."

"Ah. Look. Mr. Culp. I need some time to think this over. Can I let you know tomorrow?"

Big Ray smiled. "Sure, boy. Tomorrow then, we'll talk." He nodded and walked toward city hall.

After his mother died, Frank and his father didn't speak very much, so it was no surprise he didn't discuss this with him. Frank spent a sleepless night and left the house at dawn. Three hours later, he found the Marine Corps recruiting office in Atlanta. He signed his name with a shaky hand. By the time the semester started at the University of Georgia, Frank was slogging through the mud at Parris Island.

It seemed to Frank as he sat at the wheel of the Crown Victoria police cruiser on Saturday morning, May 24, 1980, that Big Ray had gotten what he wanted after all. Frank had become Big Ray's lackey anyway, only now he was going nowhere and had nothing. Everything that he valued seemed to slip from his grasp, and there was very little left.

The hay wagon labored past him, the sound of its engine too loud for the quiet mist rising over the soybean field. It was time to leave the shade of the billboard and get to the office. He pulled the Crown Victoria out on the road behind the tractor. The farmer crept along at barely a slow walk. Frank pushed hard on the accelerator, shifting lanes to pass, into a cloud of dust raised by the hay wagon's wheels.

Out of the dust loomed an oncoming car. He saw the grill, headlights, windshield coming at him. Frank hit the brakes with all his weight. He swerved back behind the hay wagon, the front wheels locking, the tires screeching in agony. The rear end of the Crown Victoria swung completely around, until it pointed cross ways on the road. The big car lurched to a stop and laterally rocked on its axles.

To Frank's right the tractor and hay wagon kept on its lumbering course. A Buick station wagon, powder blue with wood grained sides, flashed by in front of him. The driver turned and stared at Frank. Thin lips stretched into a spectral smile. A hand came off the steering wheel in a jaunty wave. Frank's mind saw a skeleton dressed as the Grim Reaper, its bony arm waving an invitation to the grave, its teeth rattling in a bare jawbone, grinning at him, telling him that his time had come. Oh, maybe not at this moment but soon. Very soon. Frank shook his head to clear the terrible vision. The station wagon flew by in an instant leaving a cloud of red-brown dust.

Frank gunned the Crown Victoria's engine. The rear tires bit into the soft shoulder sending gravel, dirt and weeds flying. He felt the rear end waggle, unable to get any traction. The wheels churned with a devil-raising racket, but the car shuddered, not moving. Cursing, Frank put the Crown Vic into reverse and gave the accelerator a slight nudge. Then forward again, he felt the tires gain some purchase. He rocked the car back and again forward. Slowly the police cruiser came free from the road's soft shoulder and headed in pursuit of the station wagon.

The Crown Victoria sped away from the town of Juliette at reckless speed. With an animal fear gripping him, Frank chased the Buick and the scary looking driver without knowing why. His heart pounded in a way he had not felt since Vietnam. After a mile or so Frank came up behind the pickup truck of Evan Waters, a retired local plodding along just a little faster than the hay wagon. Frank pulled alongside and rolled down the passenger window.

"Evan. Did you see a Buick station wagon go by here?"

"Hey Frank. You pulling me over? I ain't speeding. Can't get this old truck over fifty. Just won't go that fast. Huh?"

"Buick station wagon." Frank repeated. "Did you see one go by the last few minutes."

"Buick? No. Ain't nobody on the road this morning. Glad I'm not speeding, though."

Frank debated for a second. Evan might have missed the Buick. Or its driver might have pulled off on any of a number of dirt roads. Why would the guy pull off the road? Is he expecting pursuit?

Frank left old Evan Waters and sped up the road. He tried to recall what he had seen. He remembered seeing a powder blue station wagon with wood grained sides. Such a car was common enough. He thought he had seen other shapes inside the station wagon, which meant other occupants. But after another ten minutes, Frank knew that he lost the Buick. He turned the Crown Victoria Cruiser around and headed back to town. Along the way, he looked for tire marks where the station wagon might have pulled off on a side road between here and Juliette. He saw no such marks, but by the time he got into town, he was certain that the station wagon and its occupants had escaped somewhere in the woods outside of Juliette. Frank also knew that the forests around Juliette now concealed a very bad man.

Chapter 24

Randy Wilbanks rarely came in to the office on the weekend, but he came in that Saturday. Doris always had the weekends off. Larry Lee was not scheduled to go on duty until after lunchtime, but Randy could hardly care less about when Larry worked. He sat at his empty desk with nothing before him but his elbows and the neatly typed sermon Doris had placed there yesterday.

The tiny red light flashed on the answering machine, indicating it held messages, but Randy never listened to them. Frank would check them when he came in, and then Frank would take care of any problems. Randy had no time for messages. He needed to contemplate the remorse that clutched at his heart.

Randy lived his life by the Lord's rules. It was not a happy life but Jesus had called him to the ministry, and that was not an easy path. The Lord had seen fit to burden him with some pretty bad defects of character. For him the lure of sin was strong, and on occasion, he gave into it. When Randy lost control, he sinned quickly, uncontrollably.

Yet God had called him to stand before his flock and preach of the rewards of virtue and punishment for sin. Randy alone knew a sinner dwelt deep in his heart, unfit to preach to the simple folks of Juliette. He had sinned the bad, go-to-hell kind of sins, but as a minister of God, he had sought to redeem his soul.

Punishment follows sin, just like a hangover will follow a bout of drinking. In that moment of anger, yesterday's profanity had slipped out, and Randy needed to know why. He had taken the Lord's name in vain and abused his authority as God's teacher. He had shown Larry Lee, the community's most public of sinners, a poor example. It would take weeks of spiritual agony to undo what he had done, but not until then could he feel like he deserved the warmth of God's love.

No one in Juliette knew about the sins of his past, but there were others in the world who knew. God knew, of course, but God forgives. Men have long memories and do not forgive. What if his parishioners found out? Fear clutched at him like a physical force, hammering his heart. That's good, he thought. Pain is punishment and punishment

145

cleanses the soul.

Randy heard the front office door slam. Upset at the intrusion, he almost got up to close his door, but it was too late. Frank had charged down the hall, into his office.

"Frank, I'm busy in here." Randy said.

"Randy. I didn't know you were here."

"Well, I am here, and I need my office."

"Randy, the red light is blinking. We have messages. I have to get them."

Frank reached past Randy and hit the button on the machine. Randy leaned out of his way, pushed back his chair and folded his arms. The answering machine's small speaker emitted high pitched blips as the tape rewound. Most of the messages were not too important. One message came from the Monroe County prosecutor's office directed toward Randy Wilbanks, City Manager, that the arrest reports were due, overdue in fact.

"Frank, when are you going to get those to me?" Randy asked, over the sound of the next message.

Frank shrugged. "A week ago, last Friday. They're in your 'In' basket."

There was a message from a farmer who lived nearby, about somebody playing their radio too loud and waking him up at night.

Then the machine spoke in a voice that they both knew, and it immediately got their attention.

The tape hissed, "Frank. This is Lydia. I need to talk to you. It's important. Can you come by tomorrow afternoon?"

It was the last message on the tape. The machine went silent and then clicked as it rewound. Both men held their breath and watched the turning wheels of the recorder.

"What are you going to do?" Randy said.

Frank turned toward the door.

"Frank," Randy said. "A man promises to love and cherish his wife, but a woman needs to love, honor and obey. You must make her obey you. Only then will you find the Lord's blessing on your marriage."

"Shut up, Randy. Shut your goddamn mouth."

"Taking the Lord's name in vain. You'll never get to His kingdom that way."

Frank pointed at him. "You seem to know something about taking the Lord's name in vain, Randy."

Randy blushed, opened his mouth to respond, but Frank had already left.

****

Frank walked back to his own desk. Behind the teletype a length of yellow paper had piled up. Whenever police units in other parts of the country wanted to communicate with a large number of law enforcement agencies, they were usually sent by teletype. Frank read through the first of several dispatches, all dealing with the same crime. "Oh, my God," he said.

The dispatches described the deaths of two police officers and a huge fire in Cedarville, Ohio. An entire city block of a small town had been destroyed. The police had little to go on, besides a license plate called in by one of the slain officers. It was concluded that the car or plates were stolen. There was a list of contacts, among them, a detective Kevin Neri, with a 216 area code. Frank pondered. "216" was northeast Ohio. The crime took place in central Ohio, west of Columbus. Why were Cleveland police involved? On a hunch Frank called Neri's number. It turned out Neri was a member of the Akron Police, a city in the same area code as Cleveland.

"Why are you calling me?" Neri asked.

"I read about the fire in Cedarville. You were listed as a contact, but according to the map, the fire was over a hundred miles away, wasn't it?"

Frank heard a blowing sound through the phone. "What's it to you? I'm kind of busy here."

Frank held back an equally impolite reply. "The fire was in Cedarville. You're Akron police. What's the connection? Why are you listed as a contact? That's all I want to know."

"What was your name again?" Neri asked.

"Frank Robillard, of the Juliette Police. Juliette, Georgia."

"Do you know how many calls I got on that damn fire?"

"No. How many?"

"I really don't know. Maybe somebody did something right. When I heard about the fire, I called in and talked to a State Patrolman in Cedarville. They probably put my name on the contact list because of that."

"Why did you call them?"

147

He heard another blowing sound, but this time it sounded more like a heavy sigh.

"I'm after a guy. Robbery and drugs. Maybe nothing to do with the fire, but I had a hunch. I arrested him Thursday."

"What is it about that fire that made you call down to Cedarville?"

"We arrested my suspect Thursday night. Somehow he got out. Then lots of bad things happened. My guy beats people to death, and he doesn't seem to care about it. Before we arrested him, I didn't know he was like that. He got out. I don't know how. We had him. Now we don't. Then this fire seemed like someone pretty angry. He's got wheels. The slain officers in Cedarville were caught in an explosion. Before he died one of the cops said something about a station wagon."

Frank jolted. The image came clearly to his mind: a Buick station wagon blasting out of a cloud of dust heading straight for him.

"A powder blue Buick LeSabre wagon with simulated wood grain sides. He's got Georgia plates now."

"The cop in Cedarville mentioned a Buick."

"Your guy knows how to switch plates."

"Where did you say you are?"

"I'm in Juliette, Georgia. That's an hour south of Atlanta. Tell me about your guy."

"Theodore Vincent Swanson. Alias TV Dinners. Lots of priors. Two stints in Ohio State and Lima. Lima's for the looney crooks. We had him for possession of stolen property, over a hundred thousand dollars worth. We had him for drugs. Grand theft auto. I could go on. We've been working on this case over a year. We finally got him off the street, and someone turned him loose."

Frank stared at the page of notes he had taken. The last thing Neri said to him was a warning. "I know that you're probably a good cop and all, but don't mess with this guy. He's a killer and he doesn't play by any rules."

Frank thanked him and hung the phone up. He heard Randy slam the front door. The daily calendar on his desk told him it was Saturday, May 24, 1980. "Nora" was written on the left side of the calendar.

"Damn!" he said, bolting for the front door, in Randy's wake.

148

Chapter 25

The Buick station wagon zoomed through the rust colored cloud of dust, thrown up by the tractor and hay wagon. "Dad! Look out!" Harry screamed. Without thinking, he had pointed toward the oncoming car, and his finger collided with the windshield. Harry couldn't tear his eyes away.

"Kill us all, you goddamned son of a bitch! Kill us all!" his dad screamed, bracing his arms against the steering wheel, legs straight, pressing hard on the accelerator. Shafts of sunlight speared through the dust cloud, making the vision seem unreal and dreamlike. Harry took his last breath and held it.

With tires moaning and smoking, the car ahead of them slid out of their way. They sailed past the stricken car. Harry saw that it was a police cruiser. His dad waved jauntily at the astonished policeman, then kept his eyes on the rear view mirror.

"Oh yeah, he'll come after us. Did you see that look in his eyes?"

Harry turned around and saw the police cruiser's rear tires spewing gravel.

"Got his tires stuck in the mud or something," his dad muttered.

Heart hammering, Harry looked down at his legs, still there, still alive and attached to his body, his hands and arms, twitching, but still living. He heard Teeny sing-songing in the back seat. They flew down the highway, between hedges of forest on both sides. Harry looked at his dad. "Dad...?"

His father turned to look at him with vibrant eyes, full of a strange light. "Man! That scattered my shit, back there. Did that scatter your shit?" He bellowed over the sound of the engine. He turned back to the road. The station wagon slowed to a fast walk. They turned off onto a weedy, dirt road, lurching and rocking on the uneven surface. TV held his chin only inches above the steering wheel. Tree limbs reached out for the Buick as they passed, slapping against the windshield. Shafts of sunlight pierced the foliage, marking their passage with strobe-like green and yellow flashes. Harry looked into the back seat. His mother and Teeny bounced around. Teeny smiled at him and hung on like they were

149

on a kid's ride at Cedar Point.

The road narrowed and ended abruptly in a small clearing. Before his dad could stop the car, the nose of the Buick plunged several feet into a thicket. Harry's head snapped back against the seat. Brushy leaves and twigs layered over the windshield. To his right lay the clearing, a tiny sunlit theater surrounded by deep forest. An old campfire lay in the center, cold, black and already under siege by weeds. TV let the engine run for a few seconds, then reached under the steering column and jerked out the wires. The Buick shuddered to a halt. After several moments of silence, they heard the sound of wind blowing in the trees.

The place was as isolated as any place could be. Harry got out of the car, wanting to stretch some life back into his legs. He turned to look back at his father, still sitting in the driver's seat, staring straight ahead into the thicket that pressed against the car's windshield. His father's head turned slowly until he looked at Harry with unfocused eyes, his expression like a wretched, cornered animal. The look frightened Harry. His father seemed like an animal on the verge of a fit. He had seen this look before. It usually preceded one of his dad's rages. Only minutes ago he had driven the car straight toward an apparent head-on collision, and just now he had jerked the life out of the Buick. Who or what would he destroy next?

Chapter 26

Nora Potvin sat in a rocking chair on the porch in the front of her tiny house. Her house was a shack, just boards over a bare frame. The paint had faded, peeled and been eaten by mildew. The house only had two windows, on the side and in the back. They were festooned with curtains, made and hung long ago, now faded and settled with dust and spiders. The rug in the front room had lost its original color, as had the wallpaper, the pictures hung on those walls and the slipcovers covering her few pieces of furniture. Like Nora, the house had seen better times, and they had both paid their dues.

Her rocker lacked a few canes in the back and the seat, and it no longer even rocked. One of her nephews had fastened some boards to the runners to make it stationary. Her feet hurt all the time now, and her feebleness prevented her from pushing against the worn planks of the porch.

Had Nora's sight been better she would have seen the devastation around her. Until recently she had been surrounded by hardwood forest and bright meadows. The engineer's chain-saws and earth-movers had cleared the land for the building of the reservoir to be named Lake Juliette. All the trees had been chopped down with the exception of a thirty yard swath of forest they left standing along the bottom of Rum Creek, which passed by only a stone's throw from her porch. Well, about seventy years ago at least, she could have thrown a stone that far.

The engineers had told her that they left the swath of trees to provide fish habitat. Fish like to hide in shady areas. How she had laughed when she heard that. Fish don't live in trees she had said. The engineers thought that was funny, and they had all laughed together. No, they explained, it was for when the lake filled up and the water flowed over the trees. They would stock some fish in the lake and the fish would flock to the cover those trees provided. When the fish caught on and multiplied, they would attract sportsman to catch them.

The new dam and Lake Juliette was just the latest attempt to grab her land. Ten years ago, the state had needed some to make a wildlife management area. Who's going to manage it, she had asked? Why, the

State Game and Fish Department, they replied. It made no sense to her, but that didn't matter. Telling her she couldn't stand in the way of progress, they still paid her a lot of money for her land. They also told her she would never have to worry about some big land developer trying to grab it. She would always be surrounded by state managed forest and state managed wildlife habitat.

That promise was soon revoked. She had no worry about land developers. The biggest one around was Big Ray, and she had him under her thumb. But Georgia Power moved in. The state reneged on their promise and again forced her to give up this tiny plot of land, on which her tiny shack stood, next to the grave of her last husband. Her last husband had died here, and would remain even if she couldn't. The engineers couldn't move his grave if they couldn't find it. Big Ray interceded on her behalf, letting her stay until the end. But the end was near. She knew it. She had known it for a long time.

Nora made a sign in the air with her left hand. It hurt to raise her arm, but she had to, to put the hex on the construction engineers. This hex was for allergies to get in their nostrils and clog them up, make it hard for them to draw breath. They would tire quickly, and their bosses would have trouble meeting schedules. There won't be enough pseudoephedrine in all of Monroe County to clear up their lungs and noses. Oh, Nora knew about medicines. She had her kind and the drug companies had theirs. Drugs wouldn't clear up this problem. Maybe they'll choke and give up.

She winced at the pain shooting up her shoulder as she made another sign. This would make the crews unlucky. They would dig into an endless number of yellow jacket nests. Angry insects would be swarming over them, stinging, getting in their food. And mosquitoes and noseums. But in spite of her incantations, Nora knew that the end was coming. She only hoped to delay them long enough for her to die before they moved her out.

All her life Nora used the gifts of the spirits, wisdom, sight, the ability to change herself and to make spells and hexes. When Nora was a young girl, an aunt noticed her talent and guided her into learning the craft. She pledged to use the gifts and powers only for good purposes, but vengeance was a strong temptation. The poor construction workers and those foolish engineers were innocent. She had sown and now she must reap. Payback was a bitch. Payback was pain and feeblemindedness, and living just long enough to lose your home after

152

fighting so hard to keep it. Payback was a stint in hell after she died.

They were coming today to move her out. She had read the signs. Somebody she knew was about to betray her. Somebody she loved. Big Ray didn't have the nerve to come out there and move her. She had the goods on him, and although he had starch, he did not have that kind of starch. Ray wouldn't even let them send in the Monroe County sheriff. The signs told her that it would be somebody she loved. Who remained on this earth that she loved?

Her life had given her many lovers. When she was younger, she attracted lots of men. Nora Potvin had received an unusual amount of education for a woman of her day because she possessed the gift for music. She had played in all the parlors of Charleston and Savannah, entertaining the rich and famous. Nora had traveled to London and Paris and performed for royalty. She loved her music more than the wealthy and famous men who courted her. So much that her father worried about her becoming an old maid. When she was in her twenties, he married her off to a well-to-do cotton farmer. At her new home there was little to do but cook and clean the house. She rode the horse coach and later the bus to Macon, where she found students willing to learn the mysteries of the violin.

Lovers she had. Her first husband succeeded raising cotton but not at keeping her at home. She found interesting times with more exciting men in Macon and Atlanta. Decorum of the times required her to use discretion. Her husband never knew. The man died in a fire when their farm house burned to the ground. Nora moved into the shack, a former slave cabin they had used to house the occasional itinerant laborer. The farm never raised cotton again after her husband's death. The fields returned to hardwood and pine forest.

After a brief mourning, she took up with a man nearer her own style. He was a traveling man, a salesman, what folks called a drummer. She suspected that he had a few girls in the towns where he drove his Chevy, but that didn't bother Nora. She still had her jaunts to Macon. Her second husband didn't seem to care about her activities either. When he was home, they had a good time. When he was on the road, Nora did pretty much as she wanted.

You can't live the life without paying the price. It was Big Ray's daddy that caught her coming out of a hotel in Macon. He threatened to expose her to the community if she didn't do what he wanted. What was that, she had asked? He had replied, same as those men in Macon. She hated the elder Ray Culp. It wasn't so much what her husband would do if he found out, it was her reputation. She loved teaching music. Big Ray, the elder, could put an end to it all.

About that time, her salesman got shipped off to war and like lots of other husbands, came home in a box. Little Ray, soon to be called Big Ray, drove the casket in his pickup from the train station and helped her dig the grave.

By that time Daddy Culp was an old man and she middle aged, but she was young and fresh to him. Love and compassion did not enter into his crusty old heart. He still held her in control with his blackmail tactics. Nora soon reached her limit and began to plot the old goat's death.

She knew how to do it. Her aunt showed her how, but warned her that there was a huge price to pay for exercising such power. Using the herbs and incantations, Nora began the decline of Daddy Culp's health. Just as she started to slowly poison him, Ray, the son had burst into their room and filled his eyes with the sight of them in bed. Daddy Culp laughed at him and said something about him being a "Momma's Boy."

Nora went to the younger Ray the next day. She came right to the point. "We've been together for a while. I guess you should know." She told him.

"I don't need to know nothing about it. What he does is his business." Ray replied.

"You don't mean that, Ray. It's your business too."

"You aren't the first. He's had women for years. He likes taking advantage of them. Nora, you're not young," he said without malice. Still, the remark made Nora wince.

"He could get a younger one, but he's after your property. He'll get it in the end and have his fun in the meantime. He's done it before. He's made my mother suffer for it. You might as well know that he's got a court order on your land. The State will condemn the property and build a landfill in about two months."

It shocked her to learn that even as she poisoned him, he plotted to get her land.

"Ray. You know how to stop this, don't you?"

Ray looked at her. He was fresh home from the war. Although he was no longer in uniform, he still had the GI haircut. Ray had his daddy's strength, but lacked his mean spirit.

"I guess I do, but why would I do that?"

"I'll give it to you if you let me live there. All you got to do is stop the seizure."

Ray looked at Nora. "Miss Nora, you sure you want to do that?"

"Ray. I need your help. I don't want to lose my place."

"Why should I help you? You and my Daddy are messing with Momma's memory."

"You don't like him any more than me," she said.

"Maybe I don't, but I've been living with it a long time. He's gonna leave everything to me anyway. There's nobody else he'd leave it to. I just have to bide my time."

"Ray. Draw up the contract. I'll give you the land right now. You keep it from your pappy and let me live there as long as I want. Put that in the contract. Promise that you'll never come after it while I'm alive. Help me beat your Daddy in this. It's all a victory for you."

"What use's the land to me if you're still on it? I can't make no money on land you occupy." he asked.

"You can use the land. Just let me live there and don't build a landfill."

"You get to remain there as long as you want?"

She nodded.

"I get the money if we sell some off and have control over the rest?"

Nora nodded.

Ray looked thoughtful. "Come back at five. I'll have something for you to sign."

Nora did so. She and Ray had a contract. The old man croaked a few months later. Nora had her vengeance watching him suffer. At the funeral, Ray couldn't look her in the eyes. Everyone knew her reputation, and he had to wonder if he had unknowingly bargained for his daddy's death.

He inherited his father's businesses. Now he was Big Ray. His reign began.

Decades had passed since Daddy Culp's death. Ray's fear for Nora had not declined. He sold off her land and left her with just one tiny plot, a small shack now surrounded by a red dust bowl and rising water.

Quite unexpectedly, her greatest happiness and her greatest pain came just a few years after Daddy Culp's death. The tarot cards had given her a vision. She was about to encounter a prodigy. The spirits were going to give her a gift beyond anything she could have hoped for. She was to be the tutor of a mage, in the words of the tarot, a person with such gifts as to transcend all others. He would be hers to raise, to

155

educate, to bring to full strength.

Nora saw him on the street in Juliette walking with his mother, a little more than a toddler then. Frank Robillard, a golden child had looked up at her with big solemn eyes. Nora fell in love with him at that first sight. Nora persuaded his mother to begin his music lessons immediately.

Frank became everything that the tarot predicted and more. He took to the violin like a dolphin takes to swimming. He flew through everything she put before him. Nora knew how to teach. Nora had received her music training from men who had learned from the romantic masters of the nineteenth century. Little Frank soaked it all up. His capacity was astounding. Nora dropped her visits to Macon. She dropped all her other students. She set her goal on getting Frank into Juilliard.

Her obstacle was Frank's father, a suspicious dullard with no ear for music. The elder Robillard opposed Frank's development. She went around him at every chance, enlisting the boy's meek mother as an ally. Nora succeeded in getting Frank recitals in Macon and Atlanta. His reputation grew.

By the time he was in his teens, Frank had transformed into a huge talent, more than she had ever hoped. Nora held no illusion about her abilities. He had progressed well beyond what she could teach him. She continued his lessons, but now they were more like recitals. How she loved to hear him play! The next step was Juilliard. She sent off letters and résumé's. She received curt replies saying thanks but no thanks. Nora would not give up. She sent out more letters, begging for a tryout. Juilliard began to relent. She located contests and signed Frank up for them. Then what had become the foundation of her world, crumbled.

One day he stopped coming. She was offered no explanation, but Nora knew what had happened. She knew the villain was the boy's father, and would have sent a demon to rip out his cold heart, but the spirits refused. Frank's absence pained her in the extreme. She had lost the child she never birthed, losing a relationship more fundamental than that between a mother and son. Nothing she did, none of her powers helped her get him back.

Nora let the years go on, trying to avoid memories of Frank. She knew the town gossiped about her. It was rumored that she had secrets that would curl your toes. Young boys would sneak up on her house at Halloween and throw eggs or try to soap her windows. She saw them coming and hexed them with massive doses of pimples or arranged for their mothers to catch them masturbating.

That Saturday in May, 1980, as she sat on her porch, she thought of her violin. It sat on the shelf in her front room. Her fingers were so stiff and painful that she could only play the simpler pieces. Losing Frank had taken away her joy of music. She hadn't seen him in years, and hadn't been to town in a long while. Big Ray sent a boy out with groceries every now and then. Life after Frank quit coming was merely an earthly hell. Something kept her from dying and going to the spiritual punishment that she knew awaited her She was a powerless old woman who could only sit here and let it happen.

She heard the car coming long before it appeared at the cleared edge of the forest. Already the water had risen and now threatened the small road that led from her house to the highway. The engineers told her that fifty feet of water would cover the spot where her house stood. Good, she had thought. I'll stay here and it can cover up me and my memories. But they weren't going to let her do that. Drowning an old lady would definitely give Georgia Power an image problem.

She looked toward the sound of the car, but her eyes saw just a white blur. Her nerves jangled; the time had come. She gripped the armrests of her chair, feeling like she should fight for her life. She smiled in spite of the fear that gripped her. Who had the nerve to come out here and do this?

She saw a man get out of the car, just a blur of motion, but she could fill in the details, obviously a policeman. The man awkwardly clambered down the slippery dirt and mud slope, waded the shallow water that covered a section of the tiny roadbed and approached the shack. As he approached, she realized who it was, and her heart thudded like a drum on Judgment Day. She hadn't seen him in over a dozen years. She had only heard of him in short, non-complimentary comments from Big Ray when he came out to check on her. All the love and warmth that she'd ever felt for that boy bloomed again, giving her strong, rapturous emotions. Why did Ray send Frank? Why this cruelty, after his years of kindness?

She saw Frank pause in front of the shack. For them it had always been a place for making music. He obviously saw it as it was, rundown, almost abandoned except for her sitting there. Did he feel the same devastation she felt; the calamity in her heart, the loss of their dream? So many wonderful and good feelings had been born in the little house in the woods. Did he see her, as she was now, still and tiny on the little

157

porch, staring with nearly blind eyes? For years, she had successfully blocked the dreams and memories of their bond. Now the dreams and memories were released to torture them again.

He stood there in front of the porch, not speaking although she sensed in him several attempts to say something, as if there were words appropriate for this reunion.

"Nora...." he ventured, and again, "Nora." He had remembered to call her Nora, like before. To everyone else she was "Miss Nora."

"That you, Frank?" Her voice gurgled like leaking air.

"Yes Ma'am."

For years Nora had longed for Frank to come back and when he didn't, she had cursed him for destroying their dream and rendering both their lives a failure. Frank had turned his back on his potential. He had done it for what? To appease a man whom he hated. He had pissed away a gift so large, so valuable, that its absence depleted him. The enormity of that act stood between them now and rendered them both mute.

Nora took pity on him, but it was beyond her to forgive him. The boy had always lacked spunk. Now he was frozen in his tracks trying to find the right words, those impossible words that could have healed them both. But Frank had come there to conduct his father-in-law's business. Let them get on with it.

"Frank. Let it go. Forget it." Her voice was barely strong enough to break the stillness. The hot spring breeze blew, bringing the smell of newly sawn oak and pine.

Frank looked at the ground. "The water's rising. It's time to go."

She had practiced a long time what she was going to say.

"Go away. You're wasting your time."

"Nora. I can't do that. You know I can't."

"Yes you can. You can leave me and let the water come up. I'll stay here, where I belong."

"I can't do that. They won't let it happen," Frank said. "If not me, then they'll send someone else. You want someone else, Nora?"

"I don't give a damn." The word tasted bitter.

Frank pushed his policeman's cap back on his sweating forehead. "Well, I can't leave it to someone else. I'll have to be the one to move you. I won't avoid my duty."

She tried to look into his eyes. She had been looking at a point far away, but the steady gaze of her stare stopped him. Then she uttered the last words that anyone would ever hear her say.

"It doesn't matter who does it; the act is cursed. No one should be forced to die away from their home. No one should be forced to leave their place of peace. Whoever does this will be damned to a violent fate and their scion damned likewise."

She turned her eyes again to a point far away, but her inner vision saw the effect her words had on him. She saw his expression evolve from hurt to anger. He stepped up to the porch.

"Nora, there's no call to be saying that."

Chapter 27

Big Ray had prepared a very comfortable place for Miss Nora at the Vanair Trailer Park. After carrying her to the police cruiser, they had driven in silence to the Vanair. She stumbled into the trailer without word or gesture, looked around briefly and sat down in a chair. Frank awkwardly backed out of the trailer mumbling to call if she needed anything.

He rushed to the back room of Mrs. Reynolds house, the place where he lived. There he showered, shaved and put on his best parade uniform, with creased pants, shirt, shiny black belt and shoes. Finally, he splashed on some cologne.

He drove to the Police Office to turn in the Crown Vic so that Larry Lee could go out on patrol. Little police work would get done this afternoon, but Frank was obligated to turn the cruiser over to him anyway. He expected Larry to spend the afternoon reading comic books, harassing citizens or cruising up and down the country roads.

When Frank arrived at the office, he discovered to his horror Larry Lee sitting at Randy's desk listening to the messages on the answering machine. Lydia's sultry voice oozed from the tape. "Frank. This is Lydia. I need to talk to you. It's important. Can you come by this afternoon?" Frank stood there in his parade uniform, closed his eyes and sighed heavily.

"Frank. This is Lydia. I need to talk to you. It's important. Can you come by this afternoon?"

Larry rewound the tape again and pressed the button. "Frank. This is Lydia. I need to talk to you. It's important. Can you come by this afternoon?"

Larry looked up at Frank and smiled.

"What kinda fucking bullshit is that?"

"That's none of your business." Frank dropped the Crown Vic's keys on the desk. "If you know what's good for you, you'll keep your mouth shut."

Larry stuck out his lower lip. "Why Frank, I wouldn't say shit if it wasn't for your own good. Why else would I stick my dick into your

160

affairs? But you ain't having no fucking affairs, are you, Frank?" He took a deep sniff. "And do I detect the great smell of Brut? What in fucking hell are you thinking?" Larry parodied her voice, "'Frank. This is Lydia.' Who the fuck else in this town talks like that? Voice like all hell. 'I need to talk to you.' What the fuck she's got to say? Huh? 'Come over to my house.' Why the hell doesn't she come down here like everybody else?"

"Larry, I'm warning you." Frank said. "You'd better not..."

"Bullshit!" Larry slapped his palm against the desk. "Bullshit. Bullshit. Christ Almighty, mother fucking bullshit. You get a phone call from the frozen bitch of the West and it puts you into a fucking tailspin."

"What are you talking about?"

Larry shook his head. "You fucking kill me, Frank. Look at you. You're all showered and face shaved smooth like a baby's ass. You come here in your pressed khakis and you got enough aftershave on to turn a bucket of a cow's shit fragrant. Do you think you're going over there and straighten her out? Ain't nothing going to make that frigid piece of ass do anything nice. You're just cruisin' for a bruisin'. Ain't you been humiliated enough? Huh? Ain't you given up enough of your shit? She ain't gonna give any of it back. She's gonna ask for more. You wait and see. Old Larry may have a huge dick and no brain, but I'm smarter than you when it comes to women." He folded his arms.

Those same exact thoughts had been nagging Frank ever since he heard the message this morning. "Maybe she's not going to ask for more."

Larry made a raspberry sound with his mouth. "Like fucking hell, she won't. What could she possibly want, Frank? The phone number to the tooth fairy? The good goddamn fuckin' Lord don't know what she wants. But she's going to think up something that she don't have, and that's what she's gonna want. Just ask yourself what. Don't go out there until you have at least answered that." Larry pointed the fingers of both hands at Frank, alternating them like pompom guns. "You don't owe her nothing. Not money, not respect, not friendship. Not your dirty, shit-streaked underwear. She's done everything for her goddamn self and not a fucking thing for you. You've been fucked once, twice, and you're gonna get fucked some more."

"She's Little Ray's mother... I..."

"Uh-huh, I'll bet that's the last time you had it, too, when the two of you made Little Ray. She's gonna ruin that boy. You'd be better off stealing him away and going over to Alabama. That's what you should do, Frank. Raise him yourself."

"A boy needs both parents." Frank felt stupid for saying it.

"A boy needs his dad. You're his fucking dad. A boy needs his dad to teach him things. Not his mom. His dad. Who's gonna teach him to spit like a man. Cuss. Belch. Fart. Piss standing up and shake it before he zips up. Who's gonna do that?"

Frank shook his head. "We'll work it out about Little Ray."

"It's already worked out, ain't it, Frank? Ain't it a goddamn done fucking deal? Frank, take your boy. Get over the state line. Her daddy won't reach you there. Those lawyers won't do nothing about it if you were in fucking Alabama."

"I can't go there. This town needs me."

Larry stared at him with bloodshot eyes. "We don't need you, Frank. This town... It's the truth. We love you but we don't need your sorry fucking ass."

Frank stood there long enough to take five slow breaths. He owed none of this dialogue to Larry, and his reservoir of patience neared the bottom. Larry had hit on exactly what Frank wondered himself. He made many sacrifices for the town, for his marriage, for his son. But they all could get along without him.

He turned and headed for the front door, with Larry's voice pursuing him.

"Don't go, Frank. There's nothing but more shit waiting for you at that house."

Frank slammed the door hard enough to rattle the glass.

Outside, his little red pickup flirted with failure. The battery gave out nearly its last watt trying to turn the engine over. Finally it caught and rumbled like an old man just out of bed.

As soon as he turned in the direction of Lydia's house, he saw Clyde heading in the opposite direction. Frank held out his left hand, flagging him to stop. They both lowered their windows and spoke to each other with their trucks blocking the main road of the town.

"What's up, Frank?" Clyde asked.

"You been out to Miss Nora's?"

"Nope. I know I'm supposed to get her stuff, but I ain't had the time, and her being still there and all."

"I moved her out just now. You need to go get her stuff. The water's nearly up to the floor."

Clyde whistled. "Already? It wasn't hardly any water last week."

"They're pumping it in from the Ocmulgee. It's supposed to be full by Wednesday." Frank said. "It can't wait until tomorrow."

Clyde made a face, like he had something else he wanted to do. Frank changed the subject. "Looks like you got a full load already," he said pointing to the back of the truck. The bed of the pickup held a full load. A common sight in Juliette was Clyde's truck piled high with junk.

Clyde nodded. "Ran through them empty houses on my way back from plowing. Found a bunch of stuff people left behind. Old jars, tires, you know."

"Well, you better go unload it and get on out to Miss Nora's. She's in that trailer that Ray set up."

"I'll go get her stuff but I ain't gonna bother her tonight. I'll bring it to her tomorrow. I guess she's none too pleased about movin' anyway."

"No. She wasn't too happy about it, but she didn't put up too much of a fuss. Anyway, I got to go."

Frank put the Datsun in gear and Clyde did the same with his truck.

****

Clyde drove out to his trailer in the Vanair Trailer Park. He unloaded his truck, putting most of the stuff under his trailer.

He spied the trailer next to his where Miss Nora now lived. Curtains over the windows hid the interior. The only sign of life was the whirring air-conditioner.

On his way out of the Vanair, Clyde put on his turn signal to head over to Miss Nora's house, out near the future Lake Juliette. He sat there for a long time, a debate raging in his head. He desperately wanted to go into the woods and look for deer sign. Miss Nora's house was five miles in the opposite direction. He only had a couple of hours of daylight left, not enough time to do both. Maybe he could get her stuff in the morning. He turned right and headed for the forest.

****

Three miles away, on the other side of Juliette, Frank drove toward his former house, toward Lydia's. He parked his truck in the street because the reverse gear was unreliable. He loathed the idea of standing at the front door, waiting to be invited in, but her message had sounded calm, even hopeful. Everything had been already stripped from him. What could she possibly ask him for now?

By the time he had pulled up to her house, he had half convinced himself that she no longer wanted anything from him. She might even be trying to extend an olive branch of some kind. He rang the doorbell and waited. After a suitable period of time, he rang again. Finally he heard footsteps coming down the hall. Little Ray opened the door. He looked surprised to see his dad.

"What are you doing here, dad?"

"Hi, Ray. Your mom asked me to come by."

Little Ray nodded. Frank stepped into the foyer of what used to be his house, one for which he still made payments. Being inside gave him no comfort, and he and Little Ray stood shifting from foot to foot, staring at walls and ceiling.

"Could you go tell her I'm here?" Frank suggested.

"Yeah, I guess," Little Ray hustled off.

Frank had several minutes to study the house. What he saw brought memories, both good and bad. There were a sizeable number of additions; pictures of Paris, photographs of Provence, Impressionistic prints. Peering into the living room, he could see much of the extravagant Louis XVI furniture that Lydia had insisted upon last year, for which he still made payments.

After several minutes, he heard someone coming from another part of the house. Lydia rounded the corner and when he saw her, his heart began pounding. She approached him and held out her hand, smiling as if she were the governor's wife.

"Frank. Thank you so much for coming by." Her voice flowed like warm honey, causing an uncomfortable vibration inside of him. Why couldn't he just hate her? It would feel so much more right than what he was feeling. What was he feeling?

"Frank, thank you for taking Little Ray to his game last night. I was tied up with so many things I couldn't go."

Her statement brought him back to reality.

"Would you like to come to the porch and have some tea?" she asked.

He felt a sudden stiffness in his neck. He straightened up and folded his arms.

"No, thank you. I have to get back."

She nodded. Her face turned serious. "Frank, you know all this furniture will have to go on the truck, next week..."

"What? What truck?"

"Why the moving truck, of course. The moving truck will be here Monday and..."

"You're moving now? I thought that was a month or so off. Little Ray is still in school." Frank's cheeks reddened.

"Well. Now Frank, don't get mad. You knew we were moving. It's just a little sooner than expected."

"You can't take Ray out of school. He's going to have testing in a couple of weeks."

"Remy's school is not an issue. Besides, he's going to stay with Daddy for the time being."

"So why is the truck coming Monday?"

"Daddy's found me the most delightful house in Morningside. That's north, in Atlanta..."

"I know where it is. What do you mean that Ray's school is not an issue?"

Lydia sighed and put the back of her wrist to her forehead. "We closed on the house last week. I have to get it ready."

"Ready for what?"

Their divorce had not yet been filed, but Frank had already agreed to everything. There was no purpose for her staying in Juliette. Lydia stared at him. "Clyde is bringing the moving truck here on Monday. You know we paid a lot of money for this furniture. I thought that you would want to help load it so it doesn't get scratched up, that's all."

Frank felt sweat beading inside his clothes. His hands dropped to his side, made fists, and he clamped his jaws together. Frank could hardly move his mouth. "You want me to help you move?"

"Well, I wouldn't put it that way. You made such a big deal over the cost of that furniture, I thought you'd want to make sure the movers didn't damage it."

"Even though you get the furniture..." Frank smiled, shaking his head. "...you thought I'd want to help you move it. That's what was so important?"

Lydia pursed her pretty lips. "Well, I can see that you are taking this entirely the wrong way. I told Daddy that you might have a bad attitude. He said he had a talk with you and that you were okay."

"Did he tell you what we talked about?"

She looked down at the floor. "Well, I guess he talked to you about

165

the way things were going to be."

"He told me. Why couldn't you do that?"

"Frank. We argue too much." She tossed her head, a flying wave of blonde. "I thought he'd have better luck talking to you."

"You couldn't ask me to give up my kid, but you could ask me to help you move. Is that right?"

"I don't know what you're talking about. I thought you'd be concerned about the furniture. That's all."

Frank took deep breaths through his nostrils.

"Well, I'm not going to do it."

"You're not going to do what?" Lydia frowned. From the expression on her face she looked worried, as if he were going to renege on Big Ray's deal.

"If you think that I'm going to help you move, you're completely loony." Frank folded his arms again. He towered over her by nearly a foot, but he tensed as if she would strike.

Lydia stamped her foot against the polished hardwood floor.

"It's just like you to skip out on your responsibilities. Just when I need your help, you refuse over some petty disagreement. You're angry, and this is your way of trying to get back at me."

Frank opened his mouth and closed it. He shook his head. "Lydia. Look, this may come as a surprise to you. But I don't want you to move. I don't agree that you should move. I don't want you to take Little Ray out of Juliette where I can't see him. I goddamn well am not going to help you move. Is that too hard to understand?"

"You don't have to yell, and you don't have to use that kind of language."

"I am not yelling. When I yell, IT'S! LIKE! THIS!" He emptied his lungs, just inches from her face. The chimes in the grandfather clock rang with his voice. Lydia winced and turned her head, as if he had slapped her. She held that pose for a second, then faced him.

"You'd make Daddy pay to move your furniture."

"Your furniture, you mean. You'd think that between the two of you, you could come up with twenty bucks and hire a couple of blacks to move your stuff. Why you'd think that I'd care about that goddamn furniture is completely beyond me. You must be mentally ill." Frank backed up a step, because he knew that he just played one of his few trump cards. All her life Lydia had feared losing her mind.

She pointed a finger at him. "You're one sorry son of a bitch. Daddy was right about you all along. You'd never amount to a thing. You never did a thing that somebody didn't force you to do. Just like the rest of your family. Okay, buddy. If that's the way you want it, then that's the way it's going to be. I'll go in there and call Daddy. He'll make you do it. If I ask him he'll make you and the whole town will see it."

Frank allowed himself a tiny smile. "Go ahead. Call him. He already told me I could have the week off to go to Florida. I'm leaving tomorrow." He backed up another step and made contact with the front door.

The veins bulged on Lydia's forehead and made her look like an angry child. Frank could not resist making it worse. "Nothing is more satisfying than seeing a spoiled brat, not getting her way for once."

Frank left, slamming the front door hard enough to knock some of the photo's of Provence off the wall. As he reached his truck, he heard the door open behind him. He expected to see Lydia coming after him with a fireplace poker. But instead of Lydia, he saw Little Ray running after him.

"Dad! Wait." Frank's hands still shook. As much as he loved his son, next to Lydia he was the last person he wanted to see.

Ray looked up at him, his face also red. What had he heard? "Dad, take me with you."

Frank's head burned. Of course, the answer was simple. Take him, like Larry Lee suggested. Larry and Little Ray were not geniuses, but neither Larry nor Ray considered the consequences. Big Ray would certainly come after him. No matter where he went, Big Ray could hire lawyers. He could hire private detectives to come and grab Little Ray when Frank wasn't looking and drag him back to Lydia. The hunt for them would never end and they would have to wander forever, like fugitives. Frank could not subject him to that. The current problem was only temporary anyway. In a few years, Little Ray could himself declare where he would rather live, and then they might get back together. Maybe. If his mother hasn't poisoned his mind about him. If he took Little Ray, it would queer the deal with Big Ray, the one that paid for everything, including his son's welfare and his debt. But none of that meant anything to Little Ray.

"Take me with you to Florida," Little Ray said. "You said you would."

Oh, thought Frank. To Florida. Not for the rest of your life. Not that taking him to Florida would change anything. It would still queer Big

Ray's deal. He would have to come back to Juliette sometime. Other than the sixty dollars that Big Ray had given him yesterday, he had less than a hundred dollars to his name. He could not take Little Ray to Florida, or anywhere else and expect to avoid the long arm of the Culp's vengeance.

"Ray, I can't." His eyes focused on the shiny shoes of his best parade uniform.

"Mom's making me move to Atlanta. I don't want to go. You have to help me."

"Ray, I can't," Frank whispered.

"Why, Dad?"

The early evening light merged their shadows on the freshly cut lawn. Little Ray must have noticed the tears in his father's eyes. Tears welled up in Little Ray's eyes too and leaked down his cheeks. He turned his head to one side and wiped them on his tee shirt.

"Okay Dad. It's okay." Little Ray's voice was hoarse. "I'll... I'll see you around sometime, okay?" He sprinted around the house to the backyard, leaving his father standing there fighting an urge to run after him. Frank felt clammy sweat soaking his undershirt. He turned and walked to the truck. He turned the key in the ignition, but the engine would not turn over. He spent several minutes cursing and beating the steering wheel while his own tears flowed down his cheeks. The horror of having to go back to the house to ask to use the phone haunted him like a demon from hell, laughing, making the ridiculous suggestion over and over again in his mind. Finally, the engine caught and he carefully eased it into first. He drove the truck toward the setting sun with the clutch slipping and the gears grinding.

Chapter 28

Clyde drove his truck cautiously down the twisted, potholed woods road. Few people used this road, which was fine with Clyde. He didn't care to run into folks while scouting for deer, but with some disappointment, he noted fresh tire tracks in the roadbed. The weeds in the center track had recently been bent and broken by a vehicle's passing. Lots of people coming into the forest might spook that big buck. Sometimes he ran into teenagers drinking and sometimes just their piles of cans. Sometimes poachers. Whoever had made these tracks had driven in too deep to be teen drinkers. They only had to pull off the main road a short way. Whoever drove their car way back here had a strong need to hide.

Clyde toyed with the idea of turning around and coming back another day. Maybe he could still get over and pack up Miss Nora's things. But he kept driving, mostly hoping that the maker of the tracks had already left. The road did not really go anywhere. It ended after a couple of miles in a small clearing. If anyone was at the end of the road he'd make the best of the situation.

He pulled his truck around the last bend and looked into the clearing. He spied the Buick station wagon before he saw any people. It looked odd that the front end of the Buick stuck into the brush, like the driver had misjudged the distance and couldn't stop in time.

He pulled his truck behind the station wagon and turned off the motor. He looked around but did not spot anyone. The interior of the Buick was covered with the mess of traveling people, but nothing moved inside. A pair of children appeared and cautiously walked around the front of the station wagon.

Clyde approached them. The boy looked to be about ten and the girl half that. They faced him with solemn eyes.

"Hey, kids. Your momma or daddy around?" he asked. The kids did not answer. He tried again.

"Is your momma or daddy here?" He asked.

The children stood at the front of the car and continued to stare at him without speaking. He saw the little girl look past him, over his shoulder. Something moved behind him. He turned around and got the scare of his life. A man stood several feet away, the ugliest, scariest looking guy Clyde had ever seen. His hair matted down on one side, like he had slept on it. Clyde kept telling himself to calm down, that there was nothing wrong. It was only an ugly looking man. He had kids with him. How bad could it be? Besides, the man smiled at him.

"Howdy. My name is Ted. Sure glad you happened along, just now." He stuck out his hand.

"You are?" Clyde replied. "I mean, where you folks from?"

"Up north. We drove back here to camp a little. I know we's trespassing or something."

The man's voice sounded Yankee. The Buick's plates were from Cobb County, but Clyde began to think that nothing about this setup was right. "You-all are a little off the road, ain't you?"

The man called 'Ted' kept smiling. "Yeah. I guess we are. By the way, do you know where the, uh, East Juliette Church of Jesus is?"

"Yup. It's in East Juliette." Clyde couldn't resist the local joke.

"Is it far?"

"No sir. You go back to the highway and turn left. Go about three, four miles. You come to the bridge across the Ocmulgee. Don't go across the bridge, but take the left road just before the bridge. That's J. H. Aldridge Drive. That road winds a bit, but the church is on that road. You know the pastor?"

"I think I do. Told me to look him up if I ever get down this way."

"Uh-huh," Clyde mumbled. He felt it was time to ease on out of here and maybe go get Frank. The man came a little closer and stood beside his truck.

"You broke down or something?" Clyde asked.

"Huh?" the man replied.

"Said you was glad I happened along just now."

Ted looked puzzled for a second. "Oh. Yeah. My car's broke down. She won't go. My missus has taken sick. I need to get her to a doctor. Can you take us?"

Clyde turned around to look at the station wagon. The kids remained where he had first seen them. He tried to peer in to see the 'Missus' but saw nothing, just a dark form in the front seat.

"I can't carry you all in my truck. How's about I go get you some help and fetch 'em back here? It'd only take me thirty minutes. I'll bring

170

the doc and somebody to get your car going."

Ted's smile broadened. "No need to do all that. The kids can ride up front with you. Me and the missus can ride in the back."

The man looked in the truck bed, where Clyde stored his tool box, a spade and a pair of post-hole diggers. The man called Ted started to lift the spade out of the truck bed. "Just need to make some room back here."

"Hold on there, buddy. Don't go unloading my truck. I said I'd bring someone back. No, just put that shovel back." Clyde took a step toward Ted.

Clyde saw the spade swing at him. The flat of the blade caught him on the side of the head, making a clank sound. He staggered and his vision of Ted multiplied many times. He missed seeing the next blow of the shovel, but felt the impact. He toppled and rolled clumsily on his back and lay there unable to move. He did hear his truck start and heard the sound of tires churning the dirt road. He felt his breath leak through dusty lips, and then he felt no more.

Chapter 29

The Reverend Randy Wilbanks sat in the tiny sacristy of the East Juliette Church of Jesus. The room held his minister's robes and a single wooden chair. The sun beat all day on the outside walls of the room, making it like an oven, but for him it was as good a place to hide as any.

Earlier, Randy had taken a couple of hits from his whiskey bottle he had hidden behind the paneling. Now he struggled against the temptation to take more. The whiskey had added not only to his list of sins, but to his misery as well. His head throbbed from the alcohol. In a few minutes his parishioners would arrive for Saturday's six o'clock prayer meeting. Yet he sat there half drunk, unprepared, and sweaty.

God must be angry, not only for his slip of the tongue yesterday, but for all of his past weaknesses as well. Only the Almighty knew why those memories surfaced now. He seemed doomed to commit the same sins over and over again. Randy was good about atoning and seeking forgiveness, but could not seem to stay on the path of righteousness. His anxiety of the last 24 hours had driven him to seek the pint of Old Overholt.

In the past, during bouts of uncertainty, Randy consulted the bible. Although he often quoted chapter and verse, his references often lacked exactitude and authenticity. He still revered the Word of God and believed the bible was that Word. When he found himself completely at odds with a situation or needed a question answered, he used the bible like an Ouija board, where he'd ask a question and then open the book at random, hoping somehow divine guidance would direct him toward a blessed answer.

Without thinking, Randy took another hit off the bottle. Then he picked up the bible and casually opened it. With his eyes closed, he ran his finger down the paper until he felt a spiritual nudge. He opened his eyes and read 2 Corinthians, chapter 12, verse 7: "To keep me from becoming conceited because of these surpassingly great revelations, there was given to me a thorn in my flesh, a messenger of Satan, to torment me." The words turned his bowels to ice.

"A messenger of Satan?" Randy mumbled. Coming to torment him? That could mean lots of things, but none of them good.

He heard the sounds of people arriving for the prayer meeting. Randy's sweat-soaked shirt clung to his flesh like translucent flypaper. At that moment he felt the least qualified person in the community to be the pastor of a church. He pulled his sermon from his pocket. The whiskey bottle went to his lips almost of its own accord and he drained it. He swirled the liquid like mouthwash and forced it down his throat. He staggered through the small door into the main room of the church, where his friends and neighbors gathered, remembering at the last second to set the empty bottle down before he entered the sanctuary.

Randy's knees shook as he walked the few steps to the altar. He grasped the lectern tightly and stared at the sermon's pages. The words lay on the paper like strangers, offering no familiarity or comfort. He managed to raise his eyes to the assembly only through a strong effort of will. His friends and neighbors waited with passive goodwill for the service to start.

He searched his brain for the right opening. He had intended to say something like, "Brothers and Sisters..." but at the last second substituted the word, "Brethren..." since it sounded more biblical. He paused, trying to finish the sentence, since there didn't seem to be a feminine version of that word.

"...and cisterns..." A noisy belch erupted from his throat, echoing in the room like a gunshot. The noise got their attention. The congregation stared back at him. His hair stuck up in random wet spikes, and his eyes had turned red and watery. He drew in a deep breath. It felt so good he drew in another which resulted in a wave of dizziness.

"Let us begin, by praying the way Jesus taught us to pray. 'Our Father, who art...uh..,'" Dumbfounded, he could not remember the rest of it. However, his congregation did and they droned on through the Lord's Prayer as if on autopilot.

"...for thine is the Kingdom, and the Power, and the Glory forever. Amen." Their voices ground to a halt. The prayer had been a poor start. He knew his listless voice lacked conviction. He sensed a growing restlessness of his flock. They shifted in their pews. The word "flock" flew through his brain. His mind filled with off-color jokes about farm boys and sheep, and he shook his head to clear those sacrilegious thoughts. His parishioners stared at him now, knowing something was different. He decided to plunge into the sermon and take their minds off of his suspected but now visible shortcomings.

Doris' typed pages lay before him on the lectern. "Lust," he began reading, "is the basic sin of all mankind." He looked up. He had their interest now. Lust was always a good topic for getting attention. He took a deep breath and spoke the word again, forcefully, "Lust!" The crowd winced as if they could smell his hot breath.

"We all lust after many things. And it controls our lives if we let it. Lust for each other. Lust after women. Lust after men. Lust for things we want." He pronounced the words with emphasis, 'whee-mon,' 'mee-ann,' and 'thangs.'

"We all want those things. We feel we gotta have 'em. Sometimes our lust shuts us out from the people we love. Our family. Our friends. Our neighbors. Our children. Our lusts become more important than all of them." His arm swept through the air. His parishioners' faces followed the movement of his hand, but he could not be certain that he really had their attention. They wanted him to get to the good part, the flesh, sex and adultery. He wouldn't disappoint them.

"Sex. Adultery. Sins of the flesh. That's what we want." His voice rose. "We know we shouldn't have 'em, but we want 'em. The FLESH!" he screamed out, but the effort made him dizzy. His hand went to his head. The parishioners drew back from his words as if from a fire. Randy felt hot blood rush to his genitals. He suddenly found himself swelling down there. It made him blush.

"The flesh will destroy you." Randy lowered his voice. The parishioners leaned forward to listen. "It will destroy us all. Does that make lust bad? No! No! Not bad. Good, not bad." His unwanted erection grew with exquisite lethargy. Rocking his hips forward, he pressed it into the wood of the lectern.

"God created all things, therefore He created lust. It is those feelings that, in the proper circumstances provides for the multiplication of the species. The proper circumstances. That means, a man. That means a woman. That means a Christian marriage. That means their desire for children. A family. In the proper circumstances, it is right for them to procreate. God's plan calls for men and women to do this in the sanctity of marriage. But not for others to use lust to their sinful purposes. To enjoy the pleasures of the flesh. To enjoy the pleasures of the flesh over and over and over again." Randy hands gripped the top of the lectern, pulling it toward him. He drew in a deep breath, pressing himself against the wood. Waves of sexual tumult lanced through his body. His voice crooned now, like a lover's whisper.

"Outside of marriage. Outside of their... OWN. HOLY.

MARRIAGE!" Randy roared at them, shaking them awake. "This does not please God. It makes him angry that we would use our bodies in such a disgraceful way." He pressed his stiffened shaft harder, entering a dangerous zone, his eyes closing halfway. He felt that he could explode with just a few more thrusts. He must cool off. He took two deep breaths, letting them out slowly, inflating his cheeks. The words of the sermon came from his guts now. The parishioners' eyes fixed on him.

"It hurts others and brings them pain. Husbands cheating on their wives. Wives cheating on their husbands. Single people fornicating in front of a laughing Satan. Ahhhah."

The name reminded him of the verse from the bible. The warm feelings of pleasure building in his groin suddenly retreated. The bible verse foretold that soon, he was to receive the thorn, a messenger of Satan sent to torment him. Clammy sweat seeped from his brow, and his stomach gave a lurch. He studied the words in front of him and tried to focus on the sermon. He knew that it lacked spiritual insight. He knew that his sermon was poorly constructed and had no literary merit, not even good enough for the humble folks who came to his lowly little prayer meeting.

He heard the door in the rear of the church open and he looked up.

Randy's faith was not good. His belief in God was only marginal. He suffered profound doubts about his calling. But at that moment his faith in a higher power was stunningly fulfilled, for he beheld the messenger of Satan, standing at the rear of the little church. The congregation seemed not to notice, but Randy saw him and almost believed that he alone could see the awful figure.

The messenger appeared in the form of a man dressed in dirty, wrinkled clothes. His hair flew in all directions. His forehead was broad like the devil's. His chin pointed forward like a goat's. Randy knew him and remembered. He remembered those days, many years in the past, when he had gone about the country doing missionary work. He remembered, too, visiting the prison and indulging in all those hideous acts. He had been tempted, not so much by lust alone, but more by the profound lure of wrongdoing. It was Satan's messenger then, and now he stood before him. Randy's worst nightmare revealed itself, a complicated scenario, containing both his doubts about God, and the return of this messenger to proclaim to his community that he was a fraud, that he was not a holy man. That he didn't even believe in God, but held instead a firm faith in the devil. The messenger stood in the back, smiling at him with recognition.

Randy glanced at the sermon. The paper had soaked up the sweat from his hands. A sea of faces swam before him, his flock of sheep with a wolf behind them. He held the last page, and felt he must finish the sermon. The messenger now awaited the final words before he pounced and dragged Randy to hell.

"...the image of Satan..." Randy repeated the phrase, his throat choking. The messenger's face brightened.

"Is it lust that God loathes the most in all of the sins of mankind? No. No. My fellow sinners it is not." He panted like an exhausted dog. Not recalling what he thought worse than lust, Randy glanced down to the pages to see what he had written. The word was, "Pride..."

"Pride," he said, "...is the fundamental flaw in man that leads to all sins under God's commandments." He did not remember finishing the sermon, let alone what he had written. "Pride is the absence of God's grace. Pride compels us to regard ourselves alone. Pride closes off our love for our fellow man." Randy's mind rang with the righteousness of the words. Wasn't he proud, after all? Hadn't pride brought him to this downfall?

"Pride obscures our sight, hinders our understanding of the plight of others, and our responsibility to them." Damn. This was good stuff! But he had to stop that kind of thinking. His own pride was making him think that he wrote these words, when it had been the Holy Spirit who had guided his pen.

"Pride causes lying. Pride causes fear. Pride is hypocrisy, coveting, jealousy." Randy fell into the rhythm of the words. His voice rose. "Pride causes theft, war, idolatry." He raised his right hand to the ceiling and glanced at the last words on the page.

"Pride causes a man to stand before his betters preaching the word of God rather than humbling himself before them and begging their forgiveness...

"Rend garments for effect!" he cried out and before he realized what he was doing actually moved his right hand over to tug on the pocket of his shirt. His parishioners sat frozen in their pews.

Several moments passed. The silence blended in perfect harmony with the church's stifling hot air. Randy swallowed several times and looked around. The man who was the messenger of Satan had not moved. The others in the church grew restless with the inactivity.

"Well, is this prayer meeting over or what?"

The messenger's voice rang out like the clang of an iron pipe. Several parishioners turned around to look at him. They turned back to the front, to Randy. Randy did not know what to do. He knew that the messenger of Satan had come to torment him and the others were not to be involved. His heart grew cold. It was time to dismiss them and get on with it.

"Friends and neighbors. Go with God's blessing," he said. The congregation stirred. Where were the familiar parts of the service, the church announcements, the final prayer? With mumbles and with a few quizzical glances back at their pastor, the small group of people stood up in their pews and filed out of the tiny church.

In only a few tortured minutes, Randy was alone with the man, whom he remembered from so long ago, whom he now believed to be a messenger of Satan, as the bible had predicted. Why else would he have had so many failings recently? God allowed him to be weak, succumbing to drink at the moment of his greatest peril. No, Randy reminded himself. God had nothing to do with him hoisting the drink. He had been responsible for his own undoing. And not just the drink. In the last thirty minutes, Randy had managed to commit nearly all of the seven deadly sins in an accursed torrent of transgression, even while conducting a prayer meeting in a church. Surely God would punish him for that!

The stranger leaned against the back of a pew, arms folded, staring like a cat focusing on its prey. Randy held onto the lectern, shielding himself.

"Do you remember me, Reverend?" The man asked.

Randy not only remembered him but his mind filled with images of the sins he committed with him. He recoiled from the memory of those acts, feeling his heart clamoring. He had allowed himself to believe that those days had ended, that the degradation too, had ended, forgotten with the passage of time. He had finally come to rest with the magnitude of those sins and felt that God had passed on punishing him for them. He now realized how foolish that had been. For most of his life he had yielded to every major temptation that had come his way. He paraded himself around town as a righteous person, giving witness and counsel to his neighbors, acting as a minister of Christ. But all this time he had been living the life of Satan's fool. The worst place in Hell was reserved for the likes of him, and here was Satan's messenger, come to bring him home.

"Reverend?" the man persisted.

Randy swallowed again. "I... Uh. I seem to remember."

"Reverend, it was back at Lima. Long time ago. The Lima State Hospital for the Criminally Insane. Back there in Ohio. You was there with a bunch of ministers. Priests and such. You came to save us sinners in prison. We was the crazy ones. You remember?"

"Uh. Yes. I remember. It was missionary work." Randy's voice cracked.

"Missionary work, was it? Ha! You'd pray over us. For a week or so. Hold prayer meetings. Read the bible. Talk about Jesus and saints."

"We...We...We... were trying to bring the word of God to those... wr..wre..wretched... Uh. Trying to help you find the light of God...."

The man took a step forward. "Save that for those dumb asses you preach to. I ain't buying that crock. Do you know what things were like at Lima, Reverend?"

Randy shook his head. His jowls flapped with the motion.

"Do you know how we were treated?"

The man took another step. Randy's knees trembled.

"ANSWER ME, PREACHER!"

Randy recoiled from his voice. He tried to conjure a picture of the prison.

"It...it seemed clean."

"Shit! Clean? You saw what they wanted you to see. That place was a filth pit for fifty-one weeks a year. Only when they had visitors coming did they clean it up. Made us clean it up. Work us like dogs to clean it up. And they'd clean us up too. So's they could provide some 'wretches' for you to pray over. They'd never bring out the really bad ones. Some of them dudes in there would cut your heart out. There were some real mean dogs in that place. They gave you guys like me to pray with. Why me?"

Randy's mouth moved but no sound came out.

"Why me, Preacher?" the man's voice roared. He took a step closer.

"Because... Because, they thought you could be saved. That you'd listen to the..."

"Goddamn Bullshit! They put me in there because I wouldn't cut your heart out. Why me, Preacher? Because I would do anything to get out of where they had me, that's why. Where did they have me, Preacher?"

"I don't know," Randy's arms hung limp.

"They had me in the little houses, that's where. The little houses

178

inside the wall. They had about a dozen of them little houses. They were about this high." He held up his hand a little shorter than his own height. "They were about this wide." He held his hands a little narrower than his own width. "That's right. No way near big enough for an outhouse. The little house was just big enough to stuff a single prisoner, but not big enough to sit down in. There wasn't no place to sit down. There wasn't no floor in it. Just some wire screen on the bottom, so your shit and piss fall out the bottom. So's they don't have to clean 'em. The shit just fell out and the piss. There was a pile of shit and piss underneath. In warm weather, there'd be flies and a pile of frozen shit in the winter. Does that sound good? You think you'd like that?

"There'd be a door in the front. They'd only open it to drag my ass out once a week and beat the livin' shit out me with broom handles. Then they'd throw me in again. I'd stand in there, couldn't sit, you know, 'till they'd drag me out again. They'd throw a few clumps of food in every once and a while, and I had to catch it before it fell, 'cause it didn't have a floor, and if the food didn't fall out like the shit, I couldn't reach it anyway cause I couldn't bend over. Place wasn't big enough for me to bend over.

"No heat or air-conditioning. You could freeze to death, and a couple of guys did every winter. It's Ohio, you know. But the worst of it was how your body hurt from not being able to move. You'd scream for them to kill you. When they dragged me out for a work over, I begged them to kill me, so's I didn't have to go back in there. They'd laugh and beat more shit out of me, and throw me back in the little house." The man took another step, now just a few feet away from Randy's lectern. Randy felt the heat from his breath.

"Then the prison bosses offer me a chance. All I had to do was agree to meet with some ministers. Preachers, come to pray over us. All we had to do was agree to meet with some missionaries, like we were niggers in Africa. It sounded pretty goddamn good to me. They took me out and didn't beat the shit out of me. They put me in a hospital. I got to eat some food and get over havin' the runs. They cleaned my ass up and gave me some clothes. I got a shave and a haircut. I started feeling human again. What a deal! All I had to do was listen to some preachers praying over me. A good fucking deal!"

The man's eyes stared at memories of a different time. Suddenly his focus came back. "Only it wasn't just praying over us, was it, Reverend?"

At that moment, Randy could no more utter a word than he could

179

grow wings and fly through the roof.

"We'd agree to the whole thing, just to get all those favors," the man said. "We also had to let you religious guys do your thing. You know what thing I'm talking about. I never understood why you had to do it, with them being bad sins and all. We went along. It was easier to put up with a dose of butt-fuckin' than to go back to the little houses. It's common enough in prison anyway. But, tell me preacher," the man smiled. "Why would a man of God come to prison to preach the bible and want to do it to the inmates? How come you're not above that kind of stuff?"

Randy took the question seriously, one which he had often asked himself. His voice felt as dry as his mouth. "We were there to save your souls for... Uh, Jesus. We tried to show you the light and the way out of darkness. We..,"

He chuckled. "Well, your words have led this sinner out of the darkness. I am here to receive your divine blessing and to take the Lord as my personal savior. What do I got to do to get saved?"

Randy felt like rubbing his ears to clear them. "You're here to be saved?"

"Well, sort of. You said to look you up when I got out. I'm just getting around to looking you up. See, reverend. I'm in a little jam. I need your help."

Contrary feelings of relief and suspicion buffeted Randy's thinking. Maybe this was just a man after all. He wasn't here to claim him for Satan, but was just grubbing for a handout.

"What kind of help?"

"I'm in a little trouble. I need to hide some."

"What kind of trouble? Hide from whom?"

"Felonies. Murder. Flight to avoid prosecution. That's all."

Randy took a step back. "That's impossible. I'm the city manager around here. You must surrender immediately. I'll see you get a fair trial."

The man's hand struck like a snake, gripping Randy's throat, knocking his head back and forcing him to his knees.

"I'll see to it that you don't get a fair trial. You with the police? Maybe you can get me new ID. You can get me money and new wheels. Preacher, you can help me a lot. And you are going to do it because, you see, I don't care much for rules or laws. I'm not afraid to squeeze..," he closed off Randy's windpipe. "...'til I get what I need. I don't care who gets hurt. You got a wife or family. You want to see 'em hurt really bad? I can do that. I..."

The sound of a car outside the church stopped him, although he held onto Randy's throat for a few seconds. The man's head turned to listen. He released his grip, and Randy fell to the floor, dragging painful breaths.

"Preacher. It looks like I have to go, but you don't forget me. I'll be back to get what I want."

The man headed toward the back of the church and slid through the door of the vestry.

Frank Robillard came in through the front door. Randy rubbed his throat. Frank knelt beside him for a moment and then headed for the back door of the church. He came back in a few seconds.

"Whoever that was jammed the door."

Outside they heard the sounds of a truck starting. Frank bolted for the door.

Randy screamed in a shrill voice, "The man's a murderer!"

Chapter 30

Seeing Clyde's truck parked outside the East Juliette Church of Jesus, had triggered alarms in Frank's head. Clyde should have been over getting Miss Nora's belongings, but the last place Frank expected to find him was at church. Frank jumped into his Datsun, fearing the old truck would choose this emergency to display its worst behavior. To his surprise, the engine turned over and caught. He waited an impatient few seconds letting the engine settle in and headed in pursuit of whoever was driving Clyde's truck.

Spring twilight filled the sky with red and gray streaks. When he reached the highway, he spotted his quarry driving rapidly across the bridge over the Ocmulgee River. Clyde's truck headed in the direction of Lake Juliette. Frank reasoned that he probably stole the truck from Clyde, who had the bad luck to run into this stranger. TV Swanson. That was the name the Akron detective had given him. Had he hurt Clyde to get his truck?

Frank wished he had a radio in his pickup. He knew that Larry was lazing around the station, bored, probably reading magazines, and would have loved to get involved in a car chase, but Frank could not afford the time to stop and get him. Clyde's new truck had a powerful engine. If the man chose, he could easily out-distance his little Datsun pickup. The two trucks headed west on Juliette Road, just a few miles from the intersection of highway 23-87. If he turned left, TV Swanson would be heading toward Macon, about thirty miles to the south. If he kept straight, he would be heading toward Forsyth, Interstate 75, and possibly into the arms of the State Highway Patrol. Frank hoped that, in his ignorance, Swanson would head toward the Interstate. If he turned toward Macon, he would also be driving past Lake Juliette. Macon was a long way and the big truck could disappear in the gathering night along highway 23-87. Frank followed at a distance and kept his lights off hoping that the man in the lead would not spot him.

Clyde's truck arrived at the intersection as the light turned green and smoothly turned left toward Macon. Several seconds later, the little Datsun's tires squealed as Frank made the turn at the same intersection.

The bigger truck accelerated ahead of him. He floored the Datsun's gas pedal. The engine missed on several cylinders trying to produce a grudging acceleration. In the dark, Clyde's truck became a dark rectangle framed in red tail lights. The rectangle faded into the gloom and after a minute, Frank concluded he had lost his prey.

Then a miracle occurred. He saw the bright red of the truck's brake lights come on. The truck turned right and disappeared onto one of the many side roads that lead off the highway. Frank let his truck decelerate. When he reached the dirt road, he down shifted into third and also turned right. This road ended at the impoundment of Lake Juliette. Did TV Swanson know that? Frank had to be prepared for the possibility that the man might lay an ambush. He drove the Datsun slowly, looking for signs of the truck. The rough road was less than a mile long, but at low speeds it took precious minutes to negotiate. The trees spread their limbs over the road, blocking the faded sunset colors in the western sky.

Soon, he saw a lighter darkness ahead; the cleared area of the lake. Frank parked the little Datsun truck and looked out upon Lake Juliette. There, a hundred or so yards away, near the edge of rising water was Clyde's truck. The driver's door was open, the interior light on. Frank couldn't see anyone either inside or outside the truck. His quarry could be lying down on the seat, waiting for him.

Frank opened the Datsun's squeaky door with infinite care. He crouched down and duck-walked to the truck hoping to remain unseen. When he arrived, he quickly made sure that there was no one inside. He stood up and risked using his flashlight for a brief second. The brief light showed Frank a few tracks in the dirt leading in a westerly direction, away from the water and toward the woods. Frank crouched and followed the tracks as well as he could in the dark. He avoided dark shapes, such as clumps of debris, piles of brush, and tree trunks, left behind by the engineers. Each dark shape could have been TV Swanson, hiding and waiting. He moved slowly, ears straining for any sound in the night. Frank reached the trees at the edge of the lake about the time when his knees were close to giving out from the squatting. Swanson could not have traveled far into the trees. He didn't know what kind of experience the fugitive had. The smell of the forest and the humid, warm night brought memories of Vietnam. Ahead, Frank's ears picked up casual thrashing sounds, like someone stumbling through the brush in the darkness. He inched toward the sounds on his hands and knees taking care to make no noise.

Frank's eyes adjusted to the deep gloom. Swanson's thrashing decreased, and the sounds coming from his direction became more orderly. He certainly knew now that he was being followed. The area was unknown to him. He would find a place to ambush his pursuer. Frank moved a few more silent steps. The night was still and quiet. Frank inched closer and could make out the soft sounds of the other's breathing. He squinted in the darkness. After several seconds, he made out the gray shape of a man crouched against the trunk of a big tree. Frank could see no weapon, but he must assume that there was a gun or at least a knife. Moving by single steps, he crept closer. TV Swanson shifted in his crouch, making a small cracking sound that froze them both.

Frank's legs cramped. Mosquitoes and other insects attacked the exposed parts of his body. Leafy twigs tickled his face, but Frank knew that the other suffered just as much. He paused and waited for Swanson to relax a little. Minutes passed. Frank saw the man's head nod and shift a little. Slowly the shoulders slumped and the head dropped a little more. Frank continued to wait. Brush screened part of the figure of TV Swanson, and Frank judged that he could get no closer. He dug his fingers into the noiseless leaf mulch.

Frank sprung, arms out forward, fingers spread to grab. TV Swanson tried to stand and face him. Frank's arms went around his ribs, and his shoulder pounded him against the trunk of the tree. Swanson's breath came out in a hard, whooshing sound. His head slapped against the trunk of the tree. Frank wrestled him sideways to the ground.

Swanson bucked like an alligator against the larger man. He dug his nails into Frank's neck and raked, pulling the skin away. Frank butted his head forward and found Swanson's nose. Black drops of blood flew. Frank swung his fist heavily into TV's throat and battered his forehead again into the man's face. TV scrambled, kicked, rolled and gouged wildly. Frank fought to keep his arms pinned. He brought the elbow of his freed arm sharply down on TV's breastbone.

Frank rolled off his opponent and they both raced to their feet. Frank kicked hard at the other's kneecap. He kicked again, his steel toed policeman's shoe landing into the other's body with a meaty thunk. TV slumped to the ground, blood marking his face like a minstrel's makeup. Frank fell on him, pinned his wrists behind him and clicked on handcuffs. Frank stood and swung another kick into Swanson. He lay still with his face in the dirt.

"Where is he, asshole?" Frank growled. There was no answer.

Swanson rolled over and struggled to get to his knees. Frank swung his foot again, knocking the man down.

"What did you do with him?" Frank asked again.

"Goddamn it, you motherfucker. Who the hell..."

Frank rolled him over.

"The guy you got the truck from, asshole."

TV spit out a mouthful of dirt and blood. "That boy's done joined the angels, you motherfucker. Rats are gnawing at his balls right now."

"Where is he?"

"He's in the woods out there. Go find him, shitface."

Frank stood up, his chest heaving. He took deep draughts of air, and struggled to make his mind work. Swanson tried to sit up. Frank kicked him again, and dropped his knees across TV's chest. His hands found his victim's throat and he squeezed. TV's breath grew ragged.

"You gonna kill me, fuckin cop?" he hissed.

"That's right. You're going to die. It won't take long,"

"Go ahead. Do it. You'd not be the first..." Swanson tried to draw a breath. "...that tried. It won't bring your buddy back. I don't give a raw fuck."

Swanson's face was a mess of blood and grime. Franks big hands tightened on the man's throat, but he knew it wasn't in him to kill Swanson this way. His hands relaxed.

He jerked his prisoner to his feet and pushed him in the direction of the trucks.

When they reached the clearing of the lake, Frank looked to his right and saw, not far away, the dark outline of Miss Nora's shack. There was no light on inside the empty house. In the darkness it looked like something discarded, just the shape of the shack and nothing but the bare dirt of the lake bottom around it.

Chapter 31

In the darkened attic of the Juliette's makeshift fire station, Eddie "Blue" Feherty lay atop his bunk. An old AM radio murmured the broadcast of the Braves game, and he smoked his eighth cigarette since the opening pitch. Charlie Liebrandt was on the mound for the Reds. His favorite Brave, Dale Murphy, was coming to bat. Earlier Eddie had cursed Bobby Cox for putting Jerry Royster in at short-stop, but Luis Gomez had sprained his thumb and now sat on the bench, not even available as a pinch-hitter. Royster had already turned a couple of crisp double plays, but he was a zero at the plate. Murphy launched a deep fly ball toward right center, but it was caught by the Red's Randy Foster.

The phone call would come, and he waited for it. It was not an exact thing, but it would happen. Even now the water seeped through the latex bladder, dripping onto the potassium permanganate. The mixture would smolder for a second and then ignite. The phosphorus material from the road flares would burst into flame setting the tire and eventually the dry wood of the abandoned house on fire. Somebody would see the glow of the flames. The call would come.

Blue had spent the afternoon readying things. The truck was gassed up. The hoses were neatly coiled. The brass had been polished to a blinding shine. The pump checked out and the water tank filled. He knew the fastest route to the house where he had planted his fire bomb. He could be there in five minutes.

The inning ended. The Braves managed to give up a couple of runs in the sixth. Johnny Bench came to the plate with runners in scoring position and he hit a line drive over Glenn Hubbard's outstretched glove. Eddie "Blue" Feherty never liked Glenn Hubbard, who he thought was too short to play second base. Blue wished Ted Turner would fire Bobby Cox and get a good manager. His cigarette oscillated on his lips as he mumbled a curse and rolled over.

The phone rang, and it startled Eddie enough that he fell off the cot. He crawled to the ladder on all fours to avoid bumping his head on the roof rafters. He was out of breath by the time he managed to climb down and answer the wall phone. He thought briefly about his fallen cigarette glowing on the wooden floor of the loft above, but he grabbed the phone and yelled, "Fire station!" The caller's urgent words were gibberish to him.

"On my way!" he yelled and slammed the phone down. He crawled back up the ladder, and reached for his dropped cigarette. He picked it up and took a deep drag.

Eddie clambered down again and swung open the doors of the fire station. The truck started with a flick of the ignition. His heart pounding he fought the gearshift into first, let out the clutch, and got under way.

****

Officer Larry Lee spent the evening of Saturday, May 24, 1980 in the city of Juliette police station reading magazines. He listened to Skip Carey calling the Braves game on Frank's beat up AM radio.

"Ken Griffey steps in, stands deep in the batter's box. Larry McWilliams delivers. Fast ball over the inside of the plate. Umpire calls a strike. I don't think Ken was ready because he gave umpire Harry Wendelstedt a look. But anybody named Harry, can't be all bad, right Dad? Griffey steps out, checks the sign. Now he's ready to go. The count is one and one. McWilliams winds. Line drive down to third base! Horner snags it, throws to Chambliss and the inning is over. So Bench is stranded at second after driving in a run. It's the middle of the sixth inning, the score Reds 4, Braves zip."

Larry Lee ignored the game, looking instead at a copy of "Easy Rider" Magazine. His shift lasted until one AM, during which the city expected nothing much of him except to answer any emergencies that came in. Even most of those, Larry ignored. The phone had already rung several times and gone unanswered. The recordings left on the answering machine indicated that none of them sounded too urgent. Larry listened to the messages a couple of times and went back to his magazine.

He had just settled into his chair again when the front door opened. Larry groaned with annoyance. Only Frank, Doris, Randy and Big Ray had keys, and he welcomed none of them. Larry got up to see which one it was.

He saw Frank standing there, dirt and debris soiling his uniform and his face covered in blood.

"What the fuck you doing here?" Larry asked. "How'd you get so

187

fucked up?"

Under the streaks of grime he saw the expression on Frank's face.

Frank took a deep breath to calm his nerves. "Larry. I got us a bad one out there. Go get your shotgun."

"A bad what the fuck?" Larry said. "Who is it?"

"We got a guy who is wanted by the police all over the country. I think he's done something with Clyde. I chased him to the lake and caught him in the woods out there."

Larry opened and shut his mouth a couple of times. "That'd be why you're covered in shit."

Frank nodded. "He was driving Clyde's truck."

He tried to look around Frank, out the front door. "Where the fuck is he?"

He followed Frank out the front door. Larry could see an unmoving human form in the back of Clyde's pickup. "Is he dead?"

"Not dead but he's sure shut up on me."

"Ain't you afraid he'll get away."

Frank shook his head. "This son of a bitch is not going anywhere but into the cell downstairs. Go get your shotgun and put some number nine in it." Larry charged back inside and returned with the Remington pump shotgun, shoving shells into it.

"What'd he do with Clyde?"

"I don't know and I don't know where Clyde is. He said that he killed him."

"Killed him! Killed Clyde?" Larry's face contorted.

"Larry. I don't know that. He said it, okay? But he was just talking tough. He doesn't know who Clyde is. Maybe he didn't even see Clyde, just stole his truck. We got to get him into the cell downstairs and then call Clyde's house. Don't worry about Clyde just yet. Let's get this son of a bitch secure and then call some people. Okay, Larry?"

Larry looked at the form in the back of Clyde's truck. "Yeah. Let's put him up." He jacked a shell into the shotgun's chamber.

TV Swanson lay on his side, eyes open but not moving. He looked like a mad dog, but he did not make eye contact with the two policemen who stood on either side of the truck's bed.

"Frank, you got him tied up like a chicken."

Frank had looped bailing wire around his ankles, and had wired his feet to the rear gate of the truck. Larry placed the cold muzzle of the shotgun against the guy's cheek.

"Did you read the cocksucker his rights?" Larry asked.

"I just did, and you heard me, right Larry?"

"Sure did. Nice of him not to need an attorney. You feel that gun, asshole?"

Frank lowered his mouth near to the prisoner's ears. "Officer Lee has a shotgun pointed at your cheek. In the past he has had the pleasure of killing several men who tried to escape. If you make any attempts to move, Officer Lee will shoot you. There may be an inquest but don't worry. We won't get into any trouble over it. You'd be less trouble to us dead. Do you understand me?"

Like a stunned animal, TV moved neither his eyes nor head.

"I'll take that as a 'yes.'" Frank said. "Larry, wait here. If he moves, shoot him."

"You got it, chief." Frank ran into the building.

"Hey cocksucker. Where did you get the truck?" There was no reaction from the prisoner. "Clyde don't let anyone use his truck. You steal it? You a dirty thief?" Larry moved the barrel of the shotgun over the top line of his body, from his cheek to his groin. He shoved the muzzle deep between his legs.

"Maybe this'll get you talking, fuckhead. Now where is Clyde."

There was no answer. Larry shoved the shotgun in deeper.

"Come on, shit eatin' cocksucker. You want me to blow it off? Might wake a few people up, but I don't mind that. It's just you and me, here in the night. Tell me where my buddy is."

His voice rattled like gravel, deep in a well. It snapped Larry into a realm of cold fear. He had not seen the man's mouth or lips move.

"Your buddy's in hell waiting for you. You be there soon," then nothing but the silence of the crickets chirping and the moths battering against the streetlight.

Larry backed away a step.

Frank came out of the police station with a red hand truck. He glanced at Larry's white face.

"He say anything, Larry?"

"He said he killed Clyde. That guy's all fucked up."

"Larry," Frank said forcefully. "Larry! Get your mind back on the job. We have to move him. Got to put him in the cell."

Larry Lee shook his head. "All right. Let's get the asshole loaded."

Frank grabbed Swanson by the ankles, and roughly pulled him until he fell out of the pickup. Larry covered him with the shotgun while

189

Frank loaded him onto the hand truck like a large sack of spuds. He taped the prisoner to the dolly with a length of duct tape.

There were four steps going up to the city building and fourteen steps going down to the basement, where their single holding cell was located. Both Frank and Larry were sweating by the time they reached the bottom.

The door to the cell stood open. They wheeled TV Swanson into the steel cage that stood in the center of the basement room, surrounded by gloomy dust covered stacks. "I'd leave him on the hand truck, but if I don't cut him loose, he's going to lose his hands and feet. I guess the cell will have to do until we get somebody to come and get him.

Larry stared at the prisoner, his face blank. "Let the fucker's hands rot off." He spat out the words.

Frank shook his head. "Well, we can't do that. We have to do everything by the book from now on, Larry."

So while Larry held the shotgun on the prisoner, Frank pulled off the tape. He secured the prisoner with floor-mounted steel chains and removed the cuffs. TV Swanson lay inert.

Frank backed out and slammed the door. He handed the keys to Larry.

Frank went straight upstairs to the office. From the quantity of numbers he dialed, Larry knew Frank called a long distance number. It was past eleven on Saturday night, but someone answered.

"Detective Neri. This is officer Robillard down in Juliette, Georgia. I spoke to you this morning."

Frank waited a few seconds before continuing. "I have your man, Swanson. Caught him in a stolen truck."

Larry heard a vocal buzzing from the phone.

"I caught the man you wanted, uh... Swanson. Captured him. Put him in a jail cell. He's here."

Frank's voice cracked. "Detective Neri. This may be the most amazing coincidence in the history of police work. It was your guy I spotted this morning. I saw him again tonight in a stolen truck. I went after him and caught him."

More buzzing on the line, this time a long string of questions or statements, during which Frank nodded his head, glanced up at Larry and attempted to speak. Finally he said, "Yup. He's not going anywhere."

Larry heard what he guessed was that other detective's astonished response.

"Frank. Call me Frank." Frank said. "He had nothing on him. He fits your description. I have a lot of things to run down and I'll get a report off to the Feds in Atlanta. I'll fax you a Polaroid in thirty minutes or so."

More buzzing on the line.

"I have to attend to some things around here first. It will be about a half hour or so," Frank said. "Right. Right. I'll call you back." Frank hung up the phone.

"I'm gonna kill that son of a motherfucker if he did anything to Clyde." Larry said.

Frank did not respond. He picked up the phone and dialed Clyde's number. There was no answer.

"No answer at Clyde's," he said.

"That cocksucker's done something to him. Took his truck. Clyde'd never let him do that."

Frank was about to speak when the phone rang. Larry picked it up before Frank could grab it. It was Big Ray.

"Goddamn, Larry. Is Frank there? I been looking for him everywhere."

Larry handed the phone to Frank.

"A fire? Did you call Blue?" Frank listened for a few seconds. Finally he hung up and looked at Larry. "There's a fire at Big Ray's trailer park. I got to get down there."

"A fire. Who's trailer?" Larry asked.

Frank shook his head. He reached into his bottom drawer and pulled out a box of film for the Polaroid camera.

"Larry. Listen up. Go take five or six good photo's of our guy downstairs. Make copies of them on the copier and fax them to this number." He scribbled on a piece of paper. "This police officer in Akron, Ohio, is looking for him. He wants to identify him."

Larry had done it a few times before. He was happy to have something else to do than to go fight fires in the trailer park.

"We doing work for them Yankee cops?" he asked.

Frank was already headed out the door. He turned and yelled back at Larry, "Call the Forsyth Fire Department. This one sounds too big for Blue."

And then he was gone.

Chapter 32

Eddie "Blue" Feherty pushed the truck as hard as it would go with sirens splitting the darkness. The truck's colored lights splashed against trees and houses with flashes of red and blue. Long before he neared the abandoned house, Eddie knew something was wrong. There was no glow in the night sky, underneath which should have been the blazing house. The occasional car he encountered sped in the opposite direction. He even passed Clyde's truck, also opposing his progress and to his surprise, did not yield to the emergency lights and siren. Both vehicles swerved violently to avoid a head-on collision.

Eddie soon concluded that all that traffic was headed to a fire and he wasn't. He pulled the fire truck into a dark and unused driveway and slammed into reverse. He gunned the accelerator. The truck lurched back and stopped so abruptly that his face was thrown into the steering wheel. He felt the truck tilt as its rear wheel backed into a hole. The wheels spun, kicking up dirt and weeds but the truck wouldn't move.

****

Driving Clyde's pickup as hard as it would go, Frank nearly crashed into Blue's fire truck headed the wrong way. The night sky in the direction of the Vanair glowed orange and yellow, with clouds of angry smoke surging upward, blotting the stars. Frank turned into the entrance of the trailer park and had to steer around a scattering of cars and trucks whose owners had haphazardly parked there. Apparently the fire had attracted nearly the whole town, with more still coming in. Frank leaned out of the open window to yell at the pedestrians cluttering the Vanair's drive.

"You have to move your cars. Pass the word along. Eddie's coming with the fire truck. Tell everybody. Get back here and move your cars. If Eddie can't get back in here, the whole place will go up. Go! Pass the word!"

His throat ached with the effort of yelling the words. His friends and neighbors nodded stupidly and plodded toward their cars. Frank drove a little farther and saw the blaze. Clyde's trailer burned like a volcano, every foot of it squirted flames. Frank noted how close the adjacent trailers were.

A few of Clyde's neighbors had gotten out their garden hoses and were impotently spraying the fire with puny streams of water. Frank approached the nearest one.

"Don't spray Clyde's house. Spray the one next to it!" His voice roared in the man's ear, but the fire smothered his words.

"Huh? Hey Frank's here!" the man yelled. Frank repeated himself, and the man nodded.

Frank looked around for Clyde's wife. He finally spotted her. She stood there next to a man who had his arms around her shoulders. Frank realized with a start that it was Clyde. One side of Clyde's head was bathed in blood. A flap of his skin hung across his scalp. His face twisted with pain, but Clyde's eyes were clear. Frank shouted at Clyde's wife. "Get a neighbor to take you and Clyde to the hospital in Forsyth. We'll take care of your house."

She looked at him without comprehension. He had to say it again. She nodded and the two lumbered off, arms around each other.

Frank spotted Big Ray and ran over to him.

"Ray! Get these people moving on saving these other houses. They got to get out their water hoses and wet down the trailers. Where is Blue?"

"Hell if I know. I called him half hour ago!" Ray shouted back.

At that moment, they both heard and saw the fire truck inching its way down the obstacle filled driveway. In a couple of minutes, Blue had parked the truck near the burning trailer and started uncoiling the hose. Frank motioned vigorously at a couple of men standing nearby with their hands in their pockets.

"Come with me!" He shouted and ran toward the truck.

Frank took the men to the back of the fire truck. He pointed to a few shovels and stacked bags of chemicals stored in the back of the truck. The bags were the size of cement bags and contained a dry flame retarding compound.

"Take these to the fire and shovel them onto the flames. Here, I'll show you." He ran up to the burning trailer carrying a shovel and a bag of the chemicals. The intense heat seared the skin of his face. Breathing was nearly impossible. He threw the bag on the ground and opened it with the blade of the shovel. A spade full of crystals thrown onto the fire

193

started a painful hissing where it landed among the yellow coals. The heat turned the chemicals into another kind of smoke but seemed to have little effect. Following Frank's lead, the other men began throwing shovelfuls of chemicals. To Frank's left, a powerful stream of water poured in from Blue's fire hose.

The scene came straight from a nightmare. They worked the hose and the chemicals long after their muscles cried for a stop. The flames grew larger and hotter. Others ran to their homes and brought back their own shovels. They hammered at the fringes of the fire as if they could beat it to death, but the fire continued to burn no matter how much water they poured onto it.

A new sound split the air. Flashing red and white lights caught everyone's attention as the Forsyth Fire Department arrived with a massive tank truck. The men of that fire department deployed thick hoses alive with more surging water. The cold streams slammed into the yellow flames, producing huge columns of smoke and steam. Gradually the fire cooled and subsided. When the water tank on the truck of the Forsyth Fire Department was nearly exhausted, the final flames died. Clyde's trailer was a smoking pile of rubble. As the last flame went out, the trailer park went dark, lit only by the white beams of the Forsyth Fire Department's fire truck and the weaker beams of Eddie's.

Frank's muscles twitched with exhaustion. Clyde's home was completely destroyed, but he had seen them both, so there was no point looking through the rubble for bodies.

With a start he looked up at the adjacent trailer where only this afternoon he had placed Miss Nora. Her trailer stood a few yards away from Clyde's. He had completely forgotten about her. Her trailer was blackened from the heat and he realized with a sickening feeling that she was probably still inside. Frank slogged through the mud and ashes that covered the ground. He reached for the knob on the front door, and it burned his hand. Holding the doorknob in his shirttail he managed to open the door and stick his head inside. The hot air of the trailer blasted through the open door. Nothing could have survived the heat. He took a deep breath, covered his face with his arm, and plunged into the trailer feeling his feet sticking to he floor where the soles of his shoes melted. He quickly looked in every room, and finally burst out the front door gasping for air. The outside air was cool and delicious. Frank breathed deep.

Blue coiled his hose near the fire truck. The attraction of the fire gone, the crowd drifted away. Only a handful remained, staring at the columns of white smoke rising out of the wreckage.

"Have you seen Miss Nora?" he asked the nearest one.

"Who?"

"Miss Nora. She was in that trailer."

They all shook their heads and turned away toward their own homes.

Hunched over like a thief, Collie Burdell, also tried to sneak away.

Frank yelled at him. Collie stopped, turned and smiled. Above him a full moon broke out behind the clouds.

"Collie. Did you see Miss Nora. She was in that trailer." He pointed at the heat darkened wreck behind the blackened hole that had been Clyde's.

Collie looked up at the trees overhead, dark against the white smoke and moonlight.

"That old lady?" he asked.

"Collie. I don't have time to shoot the breeze with you. You know who she is. Did you see her?" Frank said.

"Uh. Well. She was walking around earlier."

"Earlier? When?"

"About supper time."

"Where'd she go?" Frank asked.

"She walked up to the road." Collie pointed to the long driveway of the Vanair Trailer Park.

"She wasn't movin' very fast. Don't think she could get far."

Cursing, Frank ran to Clyde's truck, ran by Eddie, who stood watching the efficiency of the Forsyth Fire Department packing up their equipment. Frank yelled at him as he ran by.

"How come you were late?"

Blue looked up and shrugged. Collie ambled over and stood next to Blue. They both watched Frank heading toward the highway. They saw the truck's brake lights and the left turn signal come on. The truck did not stop, but made the turn and disappeared into the darkness. The sound of the truck's engine quickly faded.

PART FOUR - THE LOST CHAPTERS

Chapter 33

From Brendan Macbean's journal:

Frank's story lacked a proper resolution. Frank Robillard drove out of the Vanair Trailer park, turning left on Juliette Road, looking for Nora and was never seen again. I'd obsessed over this story since that fishing trip three years ago. Still I found no hint of what happened to him after the fire. The mystery continued to keep me awake at night. The time had come to let go of it. After all, weren't mysteries more mysterious if left unexplained? Maybe to some, but all of the unanswered questions kept me mentally paralyzed, unable to work on much else.

Big Ray told me about the fire at the Vanair and about Collie, Eddie "Blue" Feherty, Clyde and a few others. They all had their own pieces of the puzzle, but no one could tie the whole thing together. It was very frustrating. Larry Lee told me about Frank bringing in Swanson on his last night alive.

What had happened to Corky? She disappeared during the Swanson's flight and nobody saw her again either. The State Patrol found Harry and Teeny wandering near the road the next day, but no one in Juliette knew who they were. No one asked TV about them or asked them about him. After what must have been a frustrating interrogation, they were "reunited with relatives in Ohio" as the police report said, but according to Bill Wallace, they had no idea of the whereabouts of their mother.

William "Tuck" Wallace, had barely survived his beating at the hands of our villain. Tuck took the kids in and reared them. He told me that Harry never said a word about his mother. Neither did Athena, a.k.a. Teeny. Tuck suspected that TV knew more than he was saying, but even Tuck Wallace couldn't keep the authorities on the trail. Police did some searching, but found nothing. So, Corky was a loose end.

The story left too many unanswered questions.

What had happened to Frank? According to Collie, he had gone after Miss Nora. Had she returned to her shack in the rising lake? Did they tangle and both drown? That's what the folklore says, that he found her at the shack and she banged him in the head with a frying pan. No one ever recovered their bodies. They did find some pieces of Frank's uniform in the water, which contained bloodstains. Back in 1980, there was nothing like the technology we have today for analyzing such things. But what would that have told us? Three thousand acres of lake is a lot to search, but they find bodies all the time in Lake Lanier, another Georgia lake that's a hundred times bigger and deeper. It must have seemed easy to conclude that he was in the lake. After searching, they concluded they'd never find his body. They did find his old pickup truck, sunk and crumpled, down near the bottom of the dam. The place where Nora's house had stood was completely bare and beneath 60 feet of water. The officials told me that there were acres of deep silt on the bottom of Lake Juliette, where houses, trucks and bodies could remain hidden forever. The official report says "death from drowning."

I searched exhaustively, but never found any death certificate on Nora Potvin. No investigation was ever conducted. No one mounted a search for her, not even Big Ray. When she disappeared, he probably breathed a sigh of relief, and hoped that she never turned up again. As Remy said, not hide nor hair, nor a set of dentures.

After three years of continuous research, I had talked to just about everyone who might know anything. There seemed to be nothing left to discover. I initially intended to put the story on television. A viewer who knew something might come forward with more information about Frank.

Of course my producer, Bud, turned it down. He not only rejected the piece, he admonished me for spending so much time on it.

"Bren, you're losing it. Go back to kittens and babies." He thought my work was fluff, and of course, some of it was. But I made my career trying to seek out quaint and interesting stories about people like ourselves. It was my job to show the world that there could be more to television news than the Atlanta Knife and Gun Club, the Global War Society, or the Stock Market.

His rejection made me more determined to prove him wrong. Bud is a dullard, who spends his time looking at ratings. The Atlanta Gun and Knife club may disgust us but gets good ratings. Bud doesn't care if he likes a piece, he'll put it on if it can drag in customers. Anyway, I was hooked on Frank's story and determined to answer all of the questions, and in answering them, I'd have a story so compelling not even Bud could say no. For three years, I rationalized my motives with words like this, unaware that I was in the grip of a full scale obsession. I never got close to putting the story on television. I drove a lot of people crazy with phone calls, and allowed my other work to deteriorate while chasing the Frank story.

A big shakeup occurred when the CBS and FOX networks switched their locally affiliated stations. A bunch of people were laid off. I found my name on a pink slip. Bud didn't apologize, but I felt that he was truly sorry to see me go. Who would argue with him now?

So the end of the year saw me out of work. Being a low maintenance kind of guy, I didn't suffer financial hardship. My friends call me cheap, and I invest a little. The market was booming, so I managed to get by. But the loss of my job saddened me. It took away my prestige, my pride of working in television, where such jobs are rare and hard to get. I lost daily contact with my coworkers, which I have to admit, I greatly loved. I still did some occasional work, writing for the Atlanta paper or prepping someone else's scripts. But the professional isolation took a big adjustment on my part.

Obsession is a form of delusion. The delusion was that somebody cared about Frank Robillard's story besides Remy and myself. But delusion is unhealthy. I continued to believe in the real world. I had to go to the grocery store and dry cleaners. My car ran low on gas and I had to refill it. If I hit my thumb with a hammer, it hurt, all those comforting imperfections of normal life. While working on the Frank story, I had something to do. I went to the library, made phone calls, asked questions. But each day revealed a little more that I had become a strange little man, weird, and maybe trying too hard to be liked.

Around Thanksgiving, I received a certified letter from a law firm. An attorney informed me that Raymond C. Culp had passed on and bequeathed me nothing but the contents of the enclosed letter, addressed in his own hand. Big Ray dead? How did that escape my scrutiny? I tore open the letter and read Ray's last words on the subject:

> October 25
> Dear Mr. Macbean,
> I know that you have been searching for information on Frank Robillard for quite a while now. You have been asking around, more than just with me too, upsetting folks who would rather let the dead stay where they are. I'm asking you to honor

a dying man a final wish and leave it be. Frank is dead and gone, and that is what he would have wanted. You will do nobody any good, the least of which his family, who wish his memory to remain as it is without you telling a bunch of lies about him and stirring up old wounds.

The times you and I talked, you seemed like a reasonable man. I appeal to you to find something else to do with your time. The doctors say I'll only have a few more weeks. Who knows? I will rest better if I knew you would give it up.

Sincerely,

Ray Culp

Where does he get off calling me a "reasonable man?" Receiving this letter was like a bomb going off in my head. I asked myself, why did he write it? Was he really trying to comfort Frank's family? Or did Big Ray have something else buried beneath Juliette?

So I obsessed with this for a few weeks until another event took my mind off of Frank.

My mother passed away in her sleep a few days before Christmas. She had been in a nursing home for a decade and for years had not been able to recognize her only child. Was her death a mercy to me or to her? Thus I joined that other group of orphans, Harry, Teeny, Remy and Frank himself.

On New Year's Eve, I went to bed early after staring at but not really watching a football game. I couldn't bear the Times Square thing with Dick Clark. Too many cheerful people. Too much celebration. I was the one who needed cheering up.

So on New Year's Day, I called Larry Lee. Larry, Frank's old friend and coworker, had long ago been forced out of a job when Juliette ceased to be a city. After Frank's death, and with the declining health of Big Ray, there seemed to be no one interested in keeping the town alive. And it surprised us all that along with Juliette's demise came the demise of East Juliette. Larry had moved to Atlanta. He now worked as a security guard at the Gold Club, a high class strip-joint in Buckhead. Over the last three years, I had pestered him about Frank so much that we became friends. I called him frequently, but always at the wrong time. That New Year's day, he answered the phone as if just waking up.

"Puff! Puff! Ah, fuck. What the fuck?" he gasped. Larry remained the most profoundly foul mouthed person I have ever known. His profanity knew no censorship, passing fluently from his brain to his mouth, swifter than normal speech for the rest of us. He is the Picasso of the cuss word, the Louie Armstrong of smut, the Baryshnikov of filth. I liked him because there is never a thought in his head that you don't hear about immediately.

"Larry, it's me, Brendan." I waited for the stream of villainous words to end.

"Why'd you call me so early?"

I glanced at the television screen. Glorious New Year's parades were on every channel. I guess it was a little early. The Gold Club must have had a historic party last night. His eyes must be falling out their sockets and his head splitting.

"Sorry. Look Larry. Why don't you come over and watch football? The beer is cold. We'll bet on the games."

Larry had no wife or girlfriend. He lived alone. I only visited his apartment once. I'll never go there again. Roaches and flies found it unsavory. Monkeys and wild dogs might have kept it cleaner.

There was a pause. I could still hear him breathing, regularly, like he had gone back to sleep.

"Larry....?"

"Oh, fuck. Shit. Damn. Okay." He hung up.

When Larry arrived, the New Year's Day glut of college football was in full swing. When he did not slouch, Larry towered over me. His face, although aged in a mid-forties way, was still cheery and youthful. His blonde hair receded up the slope of his forehead. He had gulped too many beers, too many bar meals, and his body had labored through too few workouts. His eyes were outrageously red from last night. Although his job requires him to intimidate the strip bar patrons, usually his face had a sloppy grin on it.

"Goddamn, Bren. Don't you get your mail?" As a familiar visitor, Larry had let himself in. He handed me a thick wad of stuff from my mailbox which I had probably not emptied since Christmas. I quickly scanned it. Hiding in the stack of junk mail was a menacing sight: two envelopes exhibiting the bleak stationery of the Ohio State Department of Corrections. One letter had been addressed on a printer, the other, handwritten in a tiny, backward slanting scrawl. A chill passed through me.

201

For a moment I forgot Larry Lee was in the room. I tore open the handwritten envelope. The single page letter held only a few lines, also written in that skewed script.

Dear Mr. Macbean,

It has been a while since the last time we talked. I used to look forward to your visits since we do not have much else to do around here. Now because my time is short, I wish to ask you a great favor. Could you please come here again? There is something of VITAL IMPORT that needs to be discussed.

The LORD has restored my soul and instructed me to talk to you. You are the only one who can save me.

Please look into your heart for this. I need for you to come here. I do not have many more days.

Very Truly Yours,

Ted Swanson,
Inmate # A175467
Southern Ohio Correction Facility

I sat there holding the letter as if it was a dead snake, expecting it to smell rotten. I had tried so hard to get over the tale that nobody cared about. But it seemed the story itself was unwilling to let things rest. Through TV Swanson, it was saying, "Not so fast, buster. We're not done with you yet."

What could he mean his days were short, a reference to him being a condemned murderer? Ohio had not executed anyone since 1963. The life expectancy of death-row inmates in Ohio was longer than for the rest of us. But, I recalled, a few months ago, TV Swanson had "volunteered" to go to his execution. In declaring that he was willing to face his punishment, he gave up further legal reviews and appeals. The state sets a date, and when it comes, he will be snuffed. Last year, there were more than a dozen "voluntary" executions in our country. Ohio was about to have its first execution of any kind in over thirty years.

Normally, the public is outraged when the state prepares for an execution; even more so when the guy asks for it. The prisoner must be crazy to ask for death, and the state will not willingly execute a crazy person. But from time to time, a voluntary execution does happen, accompanied by the usual public outcry, protests with guitar wielding folk singers and candlelight vigils.

His letter said that he wanted to talk to me and that I could save him. What did that mean? Years ago, I made several trips to interview TV Swanson. Every time, the man just plain scared the hell out of me. He enjoyed it, took pride in scaring me. After the third interview, he relaxed a little and after that he had become much easier to talk to. But I never relaxed. You couldn't be sure what his mood would be from moment to moment. Those prison visits with him rank among the all-time most frightening experiences of my life. To my vast relief the day came when I no longer had to visit him. Now, I'd rather face a pack of rabid dogs. He volunteers for the execution that he so richly deserves but says that I can "save" him. That quote about the Lord restoring his soul made my head spin. What's all that about?

The second envelope, answered none of these questions. The letter came from the Ohio State Director of Corrections, inviting me to be a witness to the execution of Theodore Vincent Swanson, to be carried out at the time of 1:00 AM EST, on the date of February 18. My hands shook as I read the invitation for a second time.

"You wearin' sweat pants, again?" Larry Lee's blaring voice cut through my morbid fixation. He returned from the fridge with a couple of beers. Although it was barely past midday, I accepted the bottle and forced my face into what I hoped was a cheerful expression.

"You need to get out more, Bren. Sweat pants just says your fucking Levi's are too tight." He flopped down on my couch. "The only goddamn exercise I'm gonna get today is smoking out on your patio, shivering my ass off."

I tried to be a fun guy watching football with a buddy, but fever brewed in the back of my mind. I faced sleepless nights and a weekend of turmoil until I could make some calls on Monday.

So I had to suck it up and at least try to have fun with Larry. We watched the New Year's Day football games like a pair of regular guys. We bet on plays, on scores, on calls made by the officials. We cursed and drank beer. We belched and passed gas without inhibition, consuming handfuls of potato chips, pretzels, and peanuts along with cocktail weenies stuck with a toothpick and dipped into barbecue sauce. We slapped the surface of the couch with the flat of our hands and emptied our lungs at the outcome of plays. I had a great time, the letters from Ohio forgotten for a while, except for a dull heat I felt in my cheekbones. After this, I had something I had to do and I itched to get at it.

During half-time, my mind wandered off football and having fun. Now released, my old obsession grew in strength. I felt like an epileptic knowing a seizure was coming on. I stared at Larry, while he made lewd remarks about the college cheerleaders.

It occurred to me then, that he alone saw Frank and TV together that night in 1980. I kept thinking that he had to know more than he told me. He saw me facing him out of the corner of his eye. He turned and said, "What the fuck you looking at? You turnin' queer or something?"

I "owned" the television remote control until the end of halftime. I shook my head and hit the mute button. I knew what I was about to ask him would do neither of us any good, would in fact hurt us and stay with us like food poisoning, but I could no more hold my tongue than I could stop the coming of the night.

"Larry, you remember when Frank brought TV Swanson in?" I asked in the new clean silence. In my peripheral vision the quiet television gyrated with colorful motion.

Larry rolled his eyes. The expression on his face said, "Not this again."

"What's that shit? You still on that? Give it the fuck up, Bren. Your skin'll clear up." He turned back to the cheerleaders.

"You and Frank took him down into the basement cell. You kept him handcuffed and locked up, right?"

"Yeah. He was chained, not handcuffed. And you know that I let him escape. Goddamn it. I haven't talked to anyone about it. Just you. None of that got out. It was so long ago. It don't matter to anyone anymore... but you."

"You went down there to take his picture, like Frank asked."

"Shit yeah, after I called the goddamn Forsyth Fire Department. I took the Polaroid down there to get his picture. When I got there, he was all wrapped up in his chains. Had 'em around his neck. His face turned blue. He looked dead, not that I gave a fuck about that. He was so dark that I thought the picture would turn out bad. Frank'd get mad at me if he was dead. I went in to unwrap the chains and he struck like a fuckin' snake. He had me down and the chains wrapped around my neck and now I was going to die. I was never so fuckin' scared in my whole goddamn life. The chains diggin' into my neck now and... and I gave it up."

The afternoon of fun had evaporated. Larry's head hung low over his spread knees, as he recalled this event. He looked up at me, as if to apologize for letting TV get away, his expression sorry and distant.

"I came to, I don't know, hours later. It was dark, and I woke up scared. I was alone. I don't remember much about getting out of that basement, just that I had to find Frank, or Big Ray. I called the State Police and the Monroe County Police. I was willing to take my medicine, you know, for letting him go, but we had to get that motherfucker back in jail.

"Looked all over, but I couldn't find nobody. The sun was coming up. I drove the Crown Vic to Frank's, where he was staying. He wasn't there. I drove out to the trailer park. Nobody. I drove to Big Ray's house. He wasn't home."

"You went to get Randy Wilbanks, the city manager," I said. I remembered my interview with Randy, years ago. What an asshole! He tried to take credit for capturing Swanson. The last time I saw Randy was at his run-down house in Juliette, dressed in a dirty tee shirt, unshaven, smelling of booze, apparently a victim of self-afflicted dissolution.

Larry shook his head. "Yeah. I went to get that sorry son of a bitch. I knew that he'd be home, getting ready for Sunday service. Fat lot of good I expected of him. He never did nothin'."

"He was at home and had just got up, like I said. When I told him what had happened, the chicken-livered asshole wouldn't even go with me. Told me to find Frank. That it was Frank's job. I physically had to drag his ass back to the police station.

"And, son of a fucking bitch, like a wet dream, the State Patrol was waiting for us outside city hall with that mother fucker sittin' in the back seat of their cruiser, cuffed and subdued. They'd found him up on the highway. Can we watch more football, now?"

I had experienced this reaction before. Where I could have talked about this all day, Larry couldn't. Nobody could. Recalling the bad memories hurt him. Why couldn't I let it go? Big Ray was right. This hurt people and stirred things up.

Halftime ended and he grabbed the remote. Football sounds again filled the room. We both turned to face the television, but our former enthusiasm became a distant, impossible dream.

I studied Larry's profile and saw his mind working on something. To my surprise, he powered off the set and turned on the couch to confront me.

"Why the fuck you still on this Frank story? Didn't your ass get fired?"

I shrugged. "I didn't get fired for that." I replied. "More like not doing anything else."

Larry shook his head. "You need to get off it, Bren. It's killing you. He's gone. You're still here. You still got a life to lead."

"You call this a life?" I quipped.

"It could be. You know I loved that man. If anybody ever said that I loved a man, I'd kill him, but I don't mind saying that I loved Frank. Frank was good as gold. He put up with my shit, like I was good too. But he didn't become the superstar he shoulda been. And then he got killed, in spite of all his smarts. It was a fucking waste is what it was. He wasted his life on nothin'. And now he's got you sucked into it. It killed me when he died, but I'm over it. It's killing you now, and you didn't even know the son of a bitch. And you keep sucking me back into it. All that ever came to Frank Robillard was sorrow. He was the saddest man I ever knew and he made those who loved him sad. Get over it, Bren. You never knew him. It's not your story anymore. Go get yourself a woman. Screw your brains out, missionary style, doggy style, monkey style... whatever that is, and get over it."

"Not sure it'd help. Anyway, no chicks on my radar screen, Larry."

He snorted and gave me a look.

"I could fix you up with Gwen. You know, over at the Club."

Gwen was an exceptionally gorgeous young woman who nightly made hundreds of dollars flaunting her body in front of men who checked their brains at the door and had an endless supply of cash and drool. Larry took me occasionally to the Gold Club, reputed to be the best of its type. The Gold Club had a sumptuous interior, treated customers like Persian Princes, offered women that were visual works of art, miracles of biology and surgery. Because Larry was an insider, all the girls made a patent fuss over me. Gwen showed special attention. I guess she took pity on me and didn't have a millionaire on a string at the moment. But the thought of spending an hour alone with Gwen scared the living crap out of me.

Larry saw something in my eyes and chose, mercifully, to let it go. We faced the television and went back to the mind-numbing football. The rest of the afternoon and early evening, we stared at the television without thinking about football, lost to our own private anguish, knocking back beers to numb our minds against the brutal memories that lay within.

Monday could not come fast enough. I called my agent and told her about the execution. She said she would see what she could do, her dry way of saying that I might get an article or two. Witnessing an execution was indeed a rare ticket. Ohio planned to execute the first inmate in thirty-six years. It would turn into a national event and create a frenzy for the press. Reporters of all stripes would be clamoring for elite positions. Summoned as it was by the officials, I had a leg up. I knew I could get an article for Time or Newsweek. Maybe a book. Out of thousands of reporters, the condemned himself asked to see me.

So a week later, I found myself going to Ohio again. It was the dead of winter and cold as hell. I landed in Columbus, and drove out of the city in a rented car.

Things were a little different this time. The Ohio Department of Corrections kept their death-row prisoners at the Mansfield Correctional Institution, in Mansfield, Ohio. Executions were carried out at the Southern Ohio Correctional Facility in Lucasville, Ohio. Nearing his execution, TV Swanson had been carted down to the SOCF. So instead of heading north on Interstate 71, out of Columbus, I headed south, through Waverly, Ohio, and then on to Lucasville. Momentarily, I thought about taking a side trip west to Cedarville to see if they had rebuilt the Tydee Mart.

I arrived at the penitentiary with a sickening wave of déjà-vu. The SOCF was a different prison but invoked nearly the same feelings. Execution death-row was completely different than waiting-to-die death-row. The prison officials had also undergone attitude adjustment because my new guide, a Mr. Rhodes, had been taught some manners. I capriciously asked him if he knew Bedoe, the guy from my previous visits to death-row at the Mansfield Correctional institution, and received from him a curious stare. I didn't pursue it.

Again we went down elevators and halls through locked doors and sliding steel gates. Everything smelled better now for some reason. Maybe the prisons were using a new disinfectant. Maybe I was just less frightened this time. When we arrived at a place they called the death house, the same feelings of foreboding and fear swept over me, but the place had an atmosphere of competence, newness and anticipation. There were only eight cells, all but one empty. TV's would be the first execution for everyone involved. Considering the light of publicity that would shine on this one, the prison crew wanted no mistakes, nothing left to chance.

When the Supreme Court reinstated the death penalty in 1976, every state had to rewrite their capital punishment statutes. Ohio had a rough time with this, because the US Supreme Court had not approved Ohio's law until October 1981. TV's trial was still going on then, and he wasn't convicted until Christmas Eve, 1981. His sentencing took place in April of 1982; otherwise he would have received a life sentence. Talk about bad timing!

Mr. Rhodes took me to the interview room where we waited. This was a very nice room with carpet, taupe painted walls and decent furniture. Again, a massive, stoic guard sat at a wooden desk reading the newspaper. Mr. Rhodes waited for Swanson to arrive rather than abandoning me like Mr. Bedoe had done three years ago.

The door opened before I had a chance to work myself into an emotional wreck. In walked Theodore Vincent Swanson, as casual and at ease as anyone. He looked well groomed, and although in prison whites, seemed to be in pretty good shape. When he saw me, he actually smiled in a warm and friendly way and stuck out his hand. I would have rather placed my hand into a shark's mouth, but I shook it anyway. His shake was dry, and strong.

"Thanks for coming Brendan." I again noted his West Virginia accent.

I nodded and gulped for a word. "Uh, you're welcome."

I had no idea what had prompted TV to send for me. He said in his letter that I was the only one who could save him. I concluded that TV had asked for voluntary execution as the only way to extend his life, crazy as that may sound. All his appeals had been exhausted. The Ohio Attorney General set his date. Thanks to the A.C.L.U. and some other organizations who protested capital punishment, he had an army of lawyers working nonstop to save him, including a pack of psychiatrists shrinking his head. Nothing worked. His scheme had failed. His date was firm, and the high paid talent working their asses off for him would not prevail. He was going to the gurney.

Years ago, Ohio had allowed lethal injection as a method of execution, as an option to the electric chair. With lethal injection, the condemned lies on a gurney and receives a poison shot rather than electrocution. The condemned man makes the choice. You'd have to be truly crazy to select the chair. It is painful, it burns, breaks bones and makes your body look like you were dragged through a forest fire. With lethal injection, you just go to sleep and never wake up. But, "getting the gurney" lacks the same romance as "getting the chair."

I had a suspicion that Swanson would try a con on me again. I was TV's last hope. Somehow he hoped to manipulate me into publicizing his plight and getting him that stay of execution. Years ago when we met he fed me a bucket of bull, complete with conspiracy theory that led to false conviction. What crock would he feed me this time?

We sat in comfortable chairs, not bolted to the floor as they were at the other place. He smiled at me for nearly a minute before turning toward Mr. Rhodes. "Garret, can you give us a few minutes?" he said in the most civilized tone possible under the circumstances.

To my surprise, Rhodes nodded and waved to the guard. They both slipped out. The door closed softly behind them. I was alone with TV Swanson, vicious killer. Sweat broke out on my forehead.

The killer turned to face me. He looked up at the ceiling and when I followed his gaze, saw video cameras mounted there. He wanted to reassure me that I wasn't truly alone with him, that somebody was watching. How considerate of him!

Somehow I had difficulty matching up the man before me with the one I had interviewed three years ago. Then it hit me. I knew what was different. The man three years ago was a mass of fear and self-loathing. He viewed everyone as a potential attacker, a threat or a mark. I saw none of that now. Incredibly TV Swanson had become a nice guy and could be reasoned with. Unbelievable. He spoke first.

"Brendan, you look different now." He seemed genuinely concerned. It made me nervous, that he could have been so discerning, that he saw something in me, maybe my unhappiness and dissatisfaction. How could he do that? He should be screaming inside with tension and fear. I remembered that on our first meeting, he had disarmed me with his observations. I struggled to control myself, to show no reaction to his words.

"You know that they're going through with the... ah, do the deed, in a month," he said, trying to state the fact without being affected. But it had caught him in mid-sentence. He looked at the floor for a moment before turning to face me again, with the look of a man under considerable control.

I too, did not know how to react to what he faced. I thought that I wanted this man dead. I wanted the benefits to society his death would bring. And others like him. But staring into his face, I could neither bring myself to want his death, nor comprehend my sudden feelings for him.

"It's okay. Look, Mr. Macbean, Brendan. I have acknowledged my sins. I have confessed to the authorities and admitted my crimes. That's right. I am ready to face the Big Eye in the Sky."

I almost believed his calm and serene voice. I found myself cynically thinking, Okay. What's the deal? Did he have one last heist before he blew life?

"About a year ago, I sat in my cell thinking. Gosh..." TV smiled again, an expression that weirdly contorted his ugly face. "I've told this story so many times! The lawyers had just visited me. We were talking about another appeal. I just felt weary of it all. I thought of doing myself in, you know, ways I might snuff myself. I wanted to go. Nearly seventeen years on death row. I didn't want to go through all that court stuff again. And it came to me. Not so much like a voice, but a thought in my head." He tapped a finger against his temple. "I had a choice. I could look forward to more pain on earth or I could get my just desserts in the hereafter. God promises to forgive all our sins..." he added, "I thought about it for many days. In the end it was an easy choice.

"And after making the decision, God started sending me more information. Like the computers we have in the library, a stream of data. It was all truth. I didn't have to figure what was right or wrong. It was all God's truth.

"He, God, said that I would have to confess. Stop trying to pretend I was framed. I wasn't innocent. Tell them I did it. Let 'em take me to the chair. Only now you can get a shot instead. You go out easy, like sleeping, which is a lot better than the people I killed got. I am ready to pay for what I done. Do you understand, Brendan?"

I was too shocked to speak. I nodded my head like a dumbass.

"God told me that I had to confess it all. Those people at the convenience store, two cops and the sand nigger in the cooler. I did them. They died because they were there, and I was pissed at the world. I told the state DA and his crew about it and they all took notes and questioned me for days. Suddenly they believed all the stuff that they had used against me in the trial. I wanted to make a clean breast of it and go to my execution. No more delays. No stays. Tell the governor he can go to bed early. No need making the last minute phone call to save my sorry ass.

"Then I learned a lesson. I tried to tell them about the guy that they sent to kill me in the Akron City jail. Nobody seemed to know about him. When they looked into it, it caused a lot of trouble. You see, that guy didn't exist. They told me that it didn't happen. You got to have a corpus delicti. No body. No crime. It caused too much trouble. Then God said it did not matter if they believed me. You see, The-Big-Eye-in-the-Sky doesn't tell you the easy way. He just tells what you need to do. He don't give a rat's ass if it's hard on you. I had to clam up about the other ones. I tell about them, they'll open up an investigation, more lawyers and trial. More shit hits the fan. It will be another 10 years before I get to go. So I don't say nothing about the rest of it.

"But God says to me, 'Not so fast, Ted. You gotta tell it all.' But I can't tell them, you see? I have a problem."

The last pieces of the puzzle began moving, turning. Yeah. He's got a problem… with me as the answer. That's why he wanted me. It was the opportunity of a lifetime! Literally. This is what reporters live for. The big scoop. To be on hand for a story that has everything. Ohio's first execution in 36 years. Notorious criminal gets religion at the last minute. Death penalty protesters outside the prison wall. Used-up reporter gets a chance to redeem himself. TV had more to confess, but he couldn't tell the authorities because it would delay things. He's tired and wants to die. He wants to confess to me. Pathos, baby! This would be big. I felt that familiar sensation, like when Remy offered me the story of his father three years ago, only I knew immediately that this one would cause no problems with Bud. He'll be on his knees begging me! But what would be the price? What changes would this one put me through?

"TV ..." I started. He held up a hand.

"Please, Call me Ted. I never liked that name."

"Okay. Ted. You said that I could save you. What did you mean?"

Ted looked at me with his permanently veined eyes. I could see his struggle to express something complex and mystifying.

"God has put the thoughts in my head. Those thoughts are the truth. I have to pay for the bad things that I did and confession is part of that.

"There's more," he whispered, looking around at the door. "I got more to tell and I need to go. Been in this life too long. I don't want to wait any longer. You don't know what it's like living like this."

We both looked around the white room. I saw how clean and well lit they had made it. Death Row looked pretty cushy.

"Come on," he said. "I'll show you something. Come on, it's okay."

With that he grabbed my hand and led me to the door. I followed like a lamb going to slaughter.

Rhodes and the guard were waiting outside the interview room, leaning against the walls of the corridor. They both straightened up when we came out.

"Garret, I'm going to show Mr. Macbean my cell."

"Sure, Ted." Rhodes nodded.

We walked past several steel doors, rooms for other condemned prisoners, to his cell, which was only about twenty paces away. His door was open. It was solid steel, with a letter sized window near the top. A cot lay in the corner of the cell next to a wash basin and a toilet. These appointments made the room seem cramped. Above us was a flush, steel meshed covered light set into a drab ceiling. The room's walls were smoothed concrete painted in a color that I cannot remember.

Ted invited me to sit on the cot. I did. He backed out of the cell and closed the door. Immediately I went into a sweating panic. Was this a joke? My body wanted to claw at the door, but I sat and waited, growing angrier by the second. The air grew so heavy my lungs could not draw it in. Tears welled up in my eyes, and only through the most extreme self control I kept from wailing and screaming and pounding the walls with my fists.

Ted opened the door. My forearms ached when I let go of the cot. I rushed out into the corridor, brushing the condemned man aside. Outside, I saw Rhodes and the guard standing up the hall. While I heaved to catch my breath, they smiled at me, as if they had just witnessed a common hazing ritual, perpetrated on rookie reporters and outsiders. To them it was no big deal and only mildly entertaining.

I looked back at Ted. He too smiled and that really pissed me off.

"Is it funny?"

"No. Not at all, but imagine twenty years of it. Hours and days in that cell, except for a few moments, like now. I only get to go outside about five times a month."

"You're not supposed to like it here."

"No, I guess not. Well I don't, but that's beside my point. I want out of it. I don't want to be set free, except in a spiritual manner. I want to pay for my crimes. God's truth says I gotta tell it all and that's why I asked you here. Then I can go. I'm ready after that."

He looked up the corridor at Rhodes and the guard. They paid us no attention. By the time we returned to the visitor's lounge, the panic of a few minutes ago had left me.

"Brendan, you must promise that you'll tell no one until after the... Uh, the eighteenth of February."

I stared at him. I knew that technically I could get into trouble, but I doubted that anyone would prosecute me for withholding evidence or whatever. I was being handed a golden story.

"Ted. You're going to make me a millionaire," I said.

He stared at me for a few seconds.

"Good. Not that I give a shit about that. Do good works with it, is the thought God's putting in my head right now. You ready?"

I nodded. The prison officials had allowed me to keep my notebook. Everything else, including my belt, wallet, watch, and college ring were resting in a locker, in a room, where I had been searched before coming down here.

Ted told me about a guy he encountered that Saturday in May, 1980, in the woods. He beat the man to death with a shovel and then took off in his truck.

"Wait a minute," I said, excited. "The guy's name is Clyde Hembree. Ted, Clyde's not dead."

Ted blinked at me. "Not dead, you say?"

"No. He recovered. He's got a big scar, but he's doing fine. He knew you stole his truck, but he's okay."

Ted took a deep breath and smiled, like a man discovering that the massive debt he owed was slightly decreased.

"Well damn. I am mighty happy to hear that. What was the name of that town?"

"Juliette."

"I got more to tell you."

My head spun. Was I going to get all the answers? Would it be what I needed?

I spent the rest of the day with the condemned man, getting what he had, writing small, so that I didn't fill up my notebook with the awful details of his story.

The next day, I flew back to Georgia. I had a few weeks before my return to Ohio for the execution. I needed to close some loops before then. I sat down and sent Tuck Wallace a long e-mail, feeling he needed some release too.

A week later, someone knocked on my door. I opened it to see an ancient white-haired man, leaning on a cane and a younger man standing beside him. Tuck's blue eyes sparkled at me and I immediately knew him.

"Mr. MacBean, I'm Tuck Wallace and this is my grandson, Harry."

Our conversations were short, almost as if the mission that lay before us was too important for words. In an hour, the three of us headed

213

out of Atlanta in their rented Jeep, me driving, Tuck to my right, and Harry chain smoking in the back seat.

We spent the mild winter day driving around Juliette. Although it meant nothing to Tuck and Harry, we visited Frank's grave, which the town's folks had placed in a tiny graveyard on a hilltop near the East Juliette Church of Jesus. Off in the distance, a mile or two away from that hill you could see through the hazy white sky, the towers of Plant Sheerer, which had been generating electricity since just after that fateful time. Frank's marker was non-elegant, just his name and his dates incised into a plain granite slab.

We searched every dirt road we could find. Long ago, I had asked Clyde Hembree the location in the woods where he had been attacked, but he had quit going in the woods, and he would not remember.

We turned down a little road that the forest had almost reclaimed. Like the other roads, it turned and twisted to match the contours of the terrain. The woods claimed more of the trail as we progressed, until I forcefully drove the Jeep through a gauntlet of protesting saplings. At the end, the forest opened up into a small clearing, dominated by a large overgrown thicket. I turned around to look at Harry's face. His eyes quivered, as he scanned the place through the car's window. I nearly turned the Jeep around to go back to town, but Harry's eye caught on something, and he held up his hand. I got out and approached the thicket, while the other two stood by the Jeep.

With shaking knees, I waded into the brush. My heart pounded as I pulled back a branch and saw the powder blue paint, nearly covered with twenty years of accumulated sap. I saw the simulated wood grained sides of the Buick. I wondered if anyone else had seen this car since May of 1980. I came closer until I could peer into the old vehicle. I pulled away the limbs and twigs and opened the car door.

Nothing but the musty smell of a space long kept from the air. Twenty years of mold covered the inside of the car. My heart nearly hammered out of control as I backed out of the thicket.

A light rain began to fall, spattering, the sound of tiny drummers beating on a thousand leaves. I turned and faced my new friends, Tuck and Harry. Harry scowled, his face frozen with horrible memories. He collapsed to his knees, bent over and landed on his hands in the leaves and dirt. His sobs came from a reservoir that seemed to have no bottom. Tuck knelt next to him, his arm around Harry's heaving back, knowing that no comfort existed adequate to what that boy endured.

Much later, back at my condo I heard Harry's story, and the three of us cried together. They stayed the night before catching a plane back to Ohio.

****

My agent received a steady stream of good offers. She advised me to wait a couple of weeks to see what additional temptations would come in, and then she'd close the deal with the highest bidder. So far, Newsweek looked better than the rest. Book offers from big house publishers, all promising hefty advances came pouring in. Things were looking good. Maybe this was going to work itself out. Working on the article and a book provided a channel for my energy and might just be what the doctor ordered, a prescription for my gloomy obsession. My days of idleness had ended. I had writing to do. My next event would be the witnessing Ted's execution.

****

February 17 arrived, an early spring-like day, amazing for Ohio. My plane landed in Columbus, in brilliant sunshine, exactly twelve hours prior to Theodore Vincent Swanson's finale. I tried to have a nice lunch in a decent restaurant. Everything was fine until the food came. I thought about Ted eating his last meal. Besides the benefit of eating it, what good would that food do? There was not enough time for him to digest it. The governor had refused to stay his execution. The local papers carried articles, mostly lamenting the immorality of capital punishment. When I arrived at the Southern Ohio Correction Facility, quite a crowd had assembled around the place, hoisting signs. People with guitars sang in the sunshine. Oh great, I thought... Woodstock. They apparently assumed that I was an official arriving for the execution and booed me as I drove past them.

Arriving slightly late annoyed the prison officials which they made little effort to conceal. The State burdened each witness with a huge amount of official business to go through before the execution. I had briefings, where the actual process was told to me several times in excruciating detail. I signed papers releasing the Department of Corrections and the State of Ohio from any liabilities if I were to be grossed out by anything. I signed off on dozens of disclosure and non disclosure agreements without reading them.

The Department of Corrections had prepared a waiting room for the witnesses, a nice and comfortable place, very much like an airport hospitality room. I hung out there with the other witnesses, while the clock wound on toward midnight. Our group contained members of the press, state and federal officials, members of the legal profession, the police, the A.C.L.U., and a single family representative, who turned out to be a second cousin of Ted's. In all, about two dozen people were going to witness Ted's execution.

The room held several televisions, tuned to CNN and FOX. One camera gave us a view of the actual death room, but we saw no activity. The image showed an empty gurney, draped in brilliant white sheets. Occasionally, a uniformed orderly would bustle through the camera's field. The brief activity caught everyone's attention.

It alarmed me that the clock on the wall seemed to be flying ahead with supernatural speed. Every time I looked up, another half hour had passed. It also surprised me that in some way I dreaded the upcoming event. The hours must be flying by for Ted as well, only for him, they were actually his last.

A loudspeaker in the ceiling blared out, startling me with a huge noise.

"Mr. Brandon Macbean. Will you please come to the information desk, immediately." and then the noise repeated.

My name is Brendan, I thought to myself. Almost everyone gets it wrong. As I left the room, a man came up to me, a tall, swarthy skinned man with a rat-like face. He put his hand out, not to shake mine, but to halt my progress.

"Macbean. Are you Macbean?" he asked with what I considered typical Yankee rudeness.

I looked at my name tag to see if I had pinned it on upside down. "It's really me. Who are you?"

He smiled, almost imperceptibly. "I'm Kevin Neri, Detective, Akron Police." Now he did put out his hand to shake. "We talked on the phone a few times."

"Detective Neri. Glad to finally meet you. How did you manage to get tickets?"

His blank stare evolved slowly to a look of mild annoyance, and he gave me another perfunctory smile.

"I had to lobby hard to get this appointment. The tree huggers outside almost trashed my car when I came in. I guess they're mad at me for arresting the guy. Did you hear the basis of his latest appeal?"

I shook my head.

"They say he's retarded. We should not execute the retarded, they say. What are we, Nazis?"

"Ted's not retarded," I replied.

"Hell, I know that. He's smart and plenty dangerous. We'll all be better off when he's dead, don't you think?"

At that moment, my feelings on the subject were too complex, and my summons had said to "report immediately." "It's hard, though. I don't think I could do it."

Neri looked like he also had plenty to say on the subject, but he clamped his mouth shut. He nodded and politely let me go. I hustled out.

Garret Rhodes stood in front of the information desk when I arrived. "Mr. Macbean. Come with me. Ted wants to see you."

I followed him, stunned. The possibility that I would have to see Ted face to face just minutes before he would be killed had somehow completely escaped my preparations for this event.

Ted paced in a room much like the witnesses' room, except it was mostly bare of furniture. The prison officials had given him a standard hospital gown with short sleeves. The insides of his elbows were painted with Betadine. I couldn't take my eyes off of those red-brown stains, where they would stick him with IV's in less than an hour.

He saw what I was looking at and remarked, "Don't want me to get an infection, do they?"

I was unable to smile at his joke, unable to say anything. I'm sure that my face looked ghastly.

"Look. Brendan. I ain't got much time." His hands and arms made small, jerky motions that had nothing to do with communication. "I ain't got no family left that I care about. That guy out there, my cousin. Hardly know him. Nobody wanted Harry or Teeny to come to this." He waved his arm at the room we were standing in.

"But they wouldn't come visit me. I tried to get them to come, to tell them I'm sorry and all that. They wouldn't come. You gotta help me."

His pupils were large and darkly vacant as if he had just taken eye drops to dilate them. We both instinctively looked at the clock on the wall. Ted had about 50 minutes left. My heart started pounding in sync with the second hand, heavy like a kettle drum. He tried to comfort me.

"Brendan. It's okay. Come on now, I need you."

"What..." My voice sounded dry and unused. Ted handed me a tissue. I used it to clean out my soaking eyes. I was the wreck. Where did he find the courage?

"I want you to tell them for me. I'm sorry… for all of it. You can put any words around it you want. Promise me you'll do it." His eyes blazed with the perfect logic of the damned. His hand gripped my shoulder, painfully hard. I felt more sadness at that moment than I felt I could bear. I had to live in this world after he left it. I had to help him clean up another mess, his mess. Anger filled me. I thought, why me? Why did he choose me? Then I realized that he hadn't chosen me. I had chosen him.

"Yes, Ted. I'll do it. I'll go see them. I'll tell them."

He lowered his hand. Tears were running out of his eyes in a stream that made his cheeks shine.

"You're what they call a friend, Brendan. I know I ain't no friend of yours, but you are a friend of mine. Maybe the only one I've ever had. Thank you. Thank you. Thank you."

Ted and I stood there for an awkward moment where, if we were friends we would have hugged each other, but my foolish uncontrollable mind laughed sadistically, "Sure, like he's going on a cruise or something." I saw a longing in his eyes, an emotion dredged up from some part of him deep inside, the human part longing for the touch of another, a reassuring touch, telling him something, anything. I backed away a step. And then another. I could not breathe as I left him. He watched me go, his head hung, looking at me like a child who had gotten into trouble and now had to be punished. After I left the room I turned to the wall of the empty corridor, covering my face with my forearm, hot tears filling my eyes, spilling over. It took an eternity before I felt I could walk again or even think about facing the other witnesses. Through this curtain of sorrow, my conscience nagged me for many things I should have done or said, but now I had to hurry. Hurry, there weren't too many minutes left.

I stumbled back to the waiting room and arrived just as they were herding the witnesses into the execution theater. This room could hold several dozen people, seating them comfortably in cushioned chairs. We saw a wide glass window that took up most of one wall. I sat in the front row, a place of honor. Curtains obscured the window on the far side of the glass.

We were hosted by no less than the Ohio Director of Corrections, himself. He explained the procedure to us, although we had been more than thoroughly briefed earlier.

"The condemned is strapped to a gurney, much like a normal hospital gurney. He will be restrained by the head, chest, ankles and wrists. The attending physician will start two saline IV's, directly into veins in both arms. On the other side of the curtain," He pointed to the glass. "...the condemned is now on the gurney and the IV's are being inserted. The condemned's vital signs are measured by a cardiac monitor and a stethoscope. He pointed to a display showing a spiked line marking Ted's heartbeat. A quiet beep accompanied each spike

"At this time, the chaplain is with the inmate. The warden will come into the room to read the sentence and record the final statements of the condemned, if any. At that time the curtain will be opened for us to watch the proceedings."

He nodded to the telephone on the wall. "This phone is a direct line to the governor's office and residence in Columbus. If the governor issues a stay of execution, the condemned will be returned to his cell and a date for a case review will be established."

It occurred to me that the director had polished his delivery pretty well for this to be the state's first execution since 1963.

"At exactly one minute after one AM, The warden will come out to this room and announce that the execution is about to begin. He will then return to the death chamber with the condemned. At that time, a quantity of sodium thiopental will be injected into the condemned through the IV's. This puts the condemned into a deep sleep. After that, pancuronium bromide is injected into the condemned. This drug is a strong muscle relaxer, which will cause the condemned to stop breathing. Finally the third drug, potassium chloride, is injected to cause the heart to stop. When the heart stops, he will be examined so that the state may be certain that the execution has been successfully completed."

On cue, the warden entered the room. We all jerked our heads to look once more at the clock on the wall. When I returned my gaze to the window, I saw that the curtain had opened, and there lay Ted, being fussed over by a couple of white coated attendants. He appeared to be calm. He stared up at the ceiling, awaiting his death.

"The execution of Theodore Vincent Swanson, convicted by a jury of his peers for the malicious murders of police officers, Cletus Moody, Thomas Wittgenstein and a citizen, Mohammed Mohammed Sundarabrani." The warden read off a list of appeals and hearings, all of which had upheld the verdict and sentencing.

"Said condemned prisoner has voluntarily accepted his sentence and given up all further appeals. The governor of the state of Ohio has ordered that the execution be carried out on this date at this time."

The Warden retreated back to the death room, appearing in the window. Noticing the warden's return, Ted raised his head, but only an inch because of the straps,. We heard the warden's voice through a speaker. He repeated the same short announcement to the condemned man. He added one question, "Theodore Vincent Swanson, do you have a statement, or anything you would like to say, before sentencing is carried out?"

Ted kept his head raised, and he cast his eyes about as he sought to fill his last moments with visions of this world, as sterile and bizarre as what he was seeing must have been, the lights, the room, the window full of onlookers come to watch his execution. His eyes locked onto mine. I do not know if the window was transparent on his side. There seemed little point in allowing a condemned man to stare at his witnesses. Nonetheless, his eyes bored into me as he spoke his last words.

"God has forgiven all my sins. Can you, when you remember me?" Everyone in the room heard his voice, but he spoke only to me.

He lowered his head, but kept his eyes open. The warden nodded to the two attendants. My eyes darted between Ted's face and the bumpy line making sharp peaks on the heart monitor.

Some movements are never seen. Whatever happened to start the injection of the chemicals that would kill Ted went unnoticed. We all sat there, expecting something to happen, but Ted's death approached us slowly, creeping and uneventful.

Perceptible changes started to occur in him. His eyelids grew heavy and a slight smile spread across his lips. His hands relaxed, the fingers curled. I could not see if his eyes closed all the way, but the peaks on the line of the heart monitor grew further apart, and its beeps less frequent. The second injection, again unnoticed, caused barely perceptible results. The tempo of the monitor slowed to a languid gait. For many long, thick minutes, his heart continued to beat, like the organ of a reptile will continue, even after it is removed from its body. It tortured me to hear the monitor's beep, again and then again, each one weaker than its predecessor and apparently not the final beat. It seemed impossible that Ted's heart could produce still one more spasm, that his body would even try to cling to his miserable and defeated existence. At last, when we all held our breath, the monitor's line went flat. The two doctors allowed this to continue for an eternity before they went to the body, which was no longer condemned, and announced Theodore Vincent Swanson dead at 1:14 AM.

What were we supposed to do now? We sat there as if we were restrained. No graceful closing ceremonies had been prepared. I wanted none. I just wanted to get out, but my reporter's duties kept me there, observing. The prison officials saved us by piling on more paperwork.

Hours later, I returned to my hotel room, finished the Newsweek article, and uploaded it to my editor. Ted Swanson's hideous face would haunt the newsstands of the world a week from Monday, and that issue would, in my humble opinion, cause a sensation. Offers on the soon to be finished book were getting out of hand. Apparently, the public lusted after stuff about condemned criminals, which contrasted my growing weariness with the topic.

I didn't think I could sleep after that, but I was wrong. Fate spared me the dreams I should have had, and I awoke after several coma-like hours feeling nearly as dead as Ted himself.

Could this story get any sadder?

Chapter 34

[TV Swanson, wife Corky and children, Harry and Teeny, while driving through rural Georgia encounter Frank Robillard, in his police cruiser on a highway outside of Juliette. TV eluded him by pulling off on a little used woods road. He drove down this to a remote clearing in the forest. There he disabled the station wagon.]

Corky Swanson swam in a black fluid, where there was no light, no sound, no feelings, no thoughts, gripped by a sense of peace that eluded her when she was conscious. She knew changes were coming, the effect of the drugs ending, and when the trip ended, the pain would return. Pain pursued her always, from one drug trip to the next. Drugs allowed her to swap painful life for insensate life. At the end of the trip, pain returned and her thoughts fell from the lofty and fantastic to the horrible, the guilt ridden and self defeating.

She felt herself coming back into her body. Her lungs needed air, but ached with the effort, her head pounded. Her body felt stiff from laying for hours without moving.

Waking up and not knowing her whereabouts was commonplace for her. Cracking open an eyelid she caught a confusing picture of her surroundings. It looked like a car, but she didn't know which car or when she had gotten into a car, or even where the car was. She could feel the sun beating in through the windows. She drew in another thick breath, and her head exploded with several violent sneezes. She rolled off the back seat onto the floor. She blinked tears away and caught another glimpse. Trees, sunlight, whatever. Her bladder screamed for attention.

Waving her arms like a cripple, Corky brought herself to a sitting position. Her head whirled like a carnival carrousel. Without looking, she reached for the door handle and pulled it. The door of the Buick swung open, and she crawled out head first like a tired old dog. She found herself outside the car, on all fours, her hands clutched at clumps of dirt and leaves. Slowly she went to her knees and then stood on shaky legs.

The hangover blinded Corky to the beauty of the clearing. The forest surrounded her, the warm, humid air caressed her body, offered her a dank, natural smell. The sun came through the canopy of trees from overhead. She heard sounds of birds and insects. Mosquitoes discovered her arm and circled for a landing.

She felt alone. Had TV left her here out in the middle of nowhere? If that were the case, she would die. She had no illusions about her ability to survive by herself. *That dirty SOB left me to die in these goddamn woods where no one will find me.* Her next thought, did he leave any stuff in the car?

Her nature call came first. She walked a few feet toward the center of the clearing, squatted and let her water flow. The act seemed to take hours and burned her painfully. Her stomach jerked and kicked, but she ignored it. She finished, rose pulling her underwear over shaking knees and waddled back to the car. She stood with one hand on the fender and looked around again. Maybe they had gone for a walk and would be back soon. She had the car to herself and it made her think a devious thought. Corky knew that TV had a stash of drugs. He had teased her with it yesterday... or last week, she did not know. He probably left it in the car. She looked around the clearing and saw no witnesses to what she was about to do.

Corky searched the car. Her head spun, but she managed to go through the glove compartment, feel under the seats, and the cargo area behind the rear seats. She found sleeping bags, some clothes thrown into plastic bags and a few of the kids toys, but no drugs. She looked through everything again and found nothing. Panic filled her head. *The dirty son of a bitch left me here and took everything with him,* she thought.

She fought the urge to cry. Corky needed her husband. He treated her worse than a dog, but it was part of the package. Nobody's perfect, and she needed what he could give her. From the beginning, her parents had hated him, but that just made her love him more. Corky had had lots of would-be boyfriends in high school, but she rejected all those preppy, pimply boys who her father liked and befriended, guys her mom might have made cookies for. Disgusting straight laced, tight assed, kiss my father's ass kind of guys, who wore hair cream, kept their mustaches trimmed, dressed nice, shined their shoes. Her dad would have loved for her to bring home one of them. He would have taken him into the family business, whatever the hell that was. Old dad would have sprung for a nice wedding and a new Chevy to drive around in, sent their kids to school, where they would get good grades and "student of the week" awards. TV and his friends always had a big laugh over that picture when they sat around and ridiculed her old man, while smoking weed and knocking back tequila straight from the bottle. The guy she went after wouldn't kiss her father's ass all the time. She needed a guy who would kick her father's ass....

Corky looked up at the sun. A songbird somewhere nearby sung a sweet little tune and repeated it over and over. The tiny green leaves twisted on their stems, fluttering in wind rustled shadows. The sun shone warmly on her face. It felt good. The warmth quieted her stomach, and her hands shook in rhythm with the wind. She bit her lip till it hurt.

Kicked her father's ass. That's what he had done.

Kicked his ass and beat him into a gore splattered mess until he resembled an animal road killed and then traffic battered until you could no longer tell what kind of animal it was. Corky pulled her head out of the shaft of sunlight that warmed it, and lowered herself into the shade behind the Buick, falling forward until her knees sunk into the leaves beside the wheel. Her hands brushed the leaves and she hung her head until her unkempt hair draped against the earth.

Beat him. Killed him.

While she watched. And did nothing. And later blotted out the memory with a drug high.

Corky thought she hated her father and now discovered another kind of feeling. She hadn't wanted him to die. She only wanted him to feel what she had felt. That he had made her feel when he went away. Other girls had their fathers at home every night. Whenever she needed her father, he'd be away. Now he had gone away for the last time.

And she felt fear for herself: her husband was a murderer. He killed before her eyes, and the family was on the run. Corky had no idea if they were a half mile away from the murder or a thousand miles away. She knew that her husband would save himself and leave her to die if it came to that. TV might kill her if he thought it would improve his situation. And how could it not? She had big, special, expensive needs. He did not need to kill her. He could just leave her to die on her own. If he left her without drugs, her addiction would kill her or she might become so tortured that she would kill herself.

Corky struggled to a standing position. The movement made her dizzy and after it passed, she made another frantic search for drugs. In the luggage area near the rear of the car, she found a compartment she hadn't looked in before. Raising the carpet covered door, she discovered all kinds of stuff.

There were no drugs, just tools and a nest of unidentifiable paraphernalia. A shiny pistol rested alone in the center. Corky picked it up. On its side she read the letters, "Colt .380 auto," engraved like someone's proud initials. She held it in her hand and stared at its silvery surface; stainless steel, with a black checkered handle. The gun felt alive to her like a tiny but powerful pet, seeming to shiver and tremble in her grasp. The gun had substantial weight, which unbalanced her, pulled her forward. She stepped to follow its lead as if it were a divining rod pulling her toward a discovery. She stepped again, away from the car, into the forest clearing.

The possibilities spun in Corky's head. She had problems. The gun gave her answers. She turned it so that she could look down into the muzzle's dark circle, feeling the terrible danger. She took another step, a headache forming behind her eyes. Have to get away from the car. The car is big. They'll find... I don't want to be found.

She looked around the quiet clearing in the woods. Nature, at least looks happy. I am the only thing in the world not happy, not meant to be. She turned the Colt another few degrees. She could see down the barrel and where it led. There was light at the beginning of the tunnel, a shining ring of the sun's brightness at the barrel's end. Spiral groves wound counterclockwise into the interior. She could fall into it and keep turning, spiraling until all the pain went away.

Corky took another step, not watching where she put her feet and stumbled over the uneven surface of the clearing. There were obstacles like sticks and brush that grabbed at her ankles. But she took halting step after step, continuing to stare into the barrel of the Colt. Her feet collided with something soft and alive. She stopped and looked at the ground. There, on a hastily strewn sleeping bag slept Theodore Vincent Swanson, alias TV Dinners, her husband and the murderer of her father.

Corky looked around, suddenly suspicious that someone could see them. She saw nothing but the forest and just TV asleep at her feet. She could see his chest rise and fall with an even rhythm. He lay flat on his back, sunk into the loft of the sleeping bag. He looked as if he hadn't moved for hours. She saw him in a pose that she had seen many times before in their bed. His mouth was open and his head tilted back. His arms were at his sides, legs slightly apart as if he had been laid out on the cooling board. Many times, in her dreams, she had been summoned to the morgue to identify him and he had been lying in this exact pose.

Corky's gun arm dropped to her side. Mosquitoes parked on his face and filled with his blood. His open mouth had attracted a fly. Her husband lay peacefully, completely unaware that she stood at his feet with a gun.

With a gun... Corky's thoughts ran toward the incredible. Her despair of a moment ago had departed, but not the fear. Her brain kept flashing the thought, to turn the gun on him. Turn the gun on him. Turn the gun on him. It would be so easy.... he's just laying there. He doesn't know that I'm standing here with a gun. He can't hurt me if he's dead. He can't hurt anyone again. If he's dead.

Her arm raised the Colt by inches. She lined it up with his body, looking straight down the short barrel, focusing on his vital parts; his genitals, his stomach, his heart, neck and finally his broad forehead. Corky knew nothing about guns. You pointed and pulled the trigger, but missing would be a disaster. She moved closer. Another step, she leaned over, slowly until her hands were only a foot from his nose.

Her mind ran through all of the last ten years. This was her husband. She had arrived at the end of her life, too. End it. End it. Do him and then do yourself. She looked for the last time at his resting face. Slowly her finger tightened.

TV's eyes opened like a flashbulb, two blazing points of light, freezing her, flushing her face with an unnatural heat. All of the power and energy inside of him came through his eyes like a laser, burning her where she stood, filling her with fear. He was very much awake, and she knew he knew what was happening. His features relaxed slightly although his eyes lost none of their intensity. His thin lips curved with a smile.

"Corky. Corky." His voice sounded low and soothing. Corky's hands started to shake. The barrel of the gun danced before his face. "I see you found the gun but not the drugs. I know why you're doing this. I know what it is." His voice vibrated like a cat's purr.

"You do?" she said, her words hissing out in a phlegm filled stream of air.

"Sure. I'm the problem. Get rid of me and it all goes away."

She said nothing in reply to this. The muzzle of the Colt waggled in small circles. Her arms ached with the weight of it.

"It's true. I'm the one. Without me you got no worries. Think of your life without me, Corky. Think of waking up every day and I'm not here. Going to bed every night and I'm not there."

Tears welled up in her eyes and she blinked to clear them. The drops circled around her cheeks. Her mouth wrinkled.

"Corky. Corky listen to me. Do the world a favor. I've caused you more pain than a woman should bear. If I live another day, it's gonna get worse. Just squeeze that trigger and do me in. That bullet'll take a big bite outta my face. I'll be in the promised land. The only promise that life keeps. You live like hell. You die like hell. You go to hell. Put me in hell, Corky. I've had my run."

More tears ran down her cheeks. She worked to make a word, several tries before she could say it.

"No."

TV smiled a little more. "Yes." He left his mouth open a little when he said it, like a baby wanting to suckle.

"No... Oh," Corky said.

"Yes. Yes, you ugly bitch." His voice still crooned, but now with icy bitterness. "You're a pus wound that fucks up everything. You ain't worth shit. You never been worth shit. Your dad wasn't worth shit and he was so much better than you. You ain't fit to hold that weapon. It's a fine gun and you're nothing more than a fat, ugly piece of shit.

"You want the drugs? They're in the spare tire. Ain't no air in the spare, just has the drugs in it. There's heroin, speed, mescaline, some good Colombian buds. Enough to last you the rest of your life, so much that you'll probably kill yourself. There, I've told you. Now you got no reason for me to live. Pull the goddamn trigger, you disgusting, dried up old whore."

Corky's tears stopped. His words had no effect. She had heard it all before. But she needed the drugs. Somewhere within her some anger sprouted. She had been holding her breath. Yes, she had anger. She had had it for a long time. The gun came up and pointed at TV's nose. Her finger tightened on the trigger.

"Pull it, Corky." TV said. "Pull it. Pull it. Pull it." TV repeated, chanting the words. It had a hypnotic effect on her and soon she could not stop her finger from tightening... tightening.

She pulled. She pulled hard. She pulled with all her strength, until the metal of the trigger bit into her finger. But the trigger didn't budge. So fast, it seemed that it had not really moved, but impossibly his hand smacked the gun from her hand, sending it flying through the air to her right to land in the leaves. In a second he jumped to his feet, towering

227

over her. Corky wailed a cry of pure terror and tried to back away. Her feet stuck to the ground. His eyes blazed into her, turning her brain into a lake of fire and fear.

"You know you got to cock them things," he said casually.

"Oh God. Oh God. Oh God oh god oh god oh god. God God God," she cried.

"YEAH!" TV declared, raising his arms like a victorious prize fighter. His face reflected the sun, his skin glowed gold. He reached his arms out for her and took her shoulders in his hands. He squeezed her flesh sending spasms more of terror than pain shooting through her body.

"Corky," he said. "Do you know what's gonna happen now?" Her mouth froze open, lips stretched against her dull teeth. She remembered the baseball bat raining blows down on an already dead body. She saw him do that, but knew he could do worse. She felt her heart slugging inside her chest and she closed her eyes squeezing out the tears.

"Corky!" He shook her, jerked her hard, like he was punishing a small child. "Say it. Say what's gonna happen to you now."

Corky looked into his eyes, like telescopes trained on the sun, looking into the eyes of a roasting, swirling chaos. Her mouth moved, but no sound came out, like in a nightmare, unable to move or scream, her voice mute and impotent.

"Say what's gonna happen now, you worthless sack a shit, sleaze cunt...." TV's nose zoomed toward her face. Her cheeks roasted from the heat coming off of him.

She tried to back away, but his fingers bit into her shoulders and he drew her closer.

Suddenly, TV pulled her to him, gently. Her swollen breasts felt his hard chest, his arms pressing her into an inescapable embrace, encircling her body. His hands caressed her back, his fingers manipulating the folds of fat. He held her for a full minute before he whispered into her ear with the voice of a lover. "Corky. It doesn't have to be like this. I know it's been bad. But we can make it better." He continued to caress her flesh and murmur into her ear. She had not heard those words ever from his mouth in all of their life together. Like whispers from her dream while swimming in the black fluid, "Not to die. After all, not to die." Her brain registered nothing else. A heavy sense of relief seized her, and she sobbed into his shoulder, her tears wetting his shirt.

They stood there while the sunny breeze wove the strands of their hair. Gradually her body's tenseness released. She hugged him back and they gently rocked and swayed. She felt his hands slowly run up her back, along her spine. The feelings sent goose bumps and chills tingling throughout her body, to the tips of her toes and fingers. He took her head in his hands and gently pulled her head back to look at her tear ravaged face. She parted her lips for a lover's kiss.

"TV, I love yo....."

Corky's words ended with a loud crack as he twisted her head forcefully to the left. He twisted it the other way and again her neck made a sound like the breaking of a tree limb. TV centered her head so that he could look into her face. Her eyes still stared into his, her mouth frozen on the word that she had been about to speak. Her breath leaked out from her lungs in a long sibilant "Ahhh... Ahhha."

TV quickly put an arm under Corky. He carried her back to the car, awkwardly in a bear hug, opened the front passenger door and heavily dropped her onto the seat. He laid her limp skull against the head rest. He lifted her legs one at a time into the car and closed the door.

TV froze when he heard a loud metallic click coming from behind him. He turned around to see his son Harry holding the Colt. Harry had pulled the slide back, just like he had seen on television. TV could clearly see the automatic's hammer lying horizontal like the ear of an angry cat.

"Where's your sister?" TV asked calmly.

"What's wrong with mom? I saw you carrying her."

TV shrugged. "She's high. She needs to sleep it off." He pointed to the automatic. "What are you going to do with that, little dog?"

Harry did not answer.

"You're not dumb like your mom. You know what to do, and that little thing looks like it's all ready to shoot. You goin' shoot me, Harry?"

Harry kept the gun pointed at his dad, his eyes locked into his father's stare.

"You goin' shoot me, Harry?" TV asked again. "You could save the world a lot of trouble, by shooting me. A whole lotta grief for yourself too. Shoot me and then take your sister back to that town. You'll be okay. You'd be a hero. Shoot me, Harry. It would be easy, son. There's eight shots in that gun. Two or three shots would do it. One might if you was lucky. The best way is to make your first shot here in the stomach." TV pointed to his abdomen. "That'll put me down. Then come up and put one in my head." He pointed at his skull. "Right here. Then empty the gun in my head. You got nothin' more to worry about."

TV could see the horror racing through his son. Then he saw the angry expression return to Harry's face. Harry's judgment. He was doing it to him again, judging him, watching him when he was doing something bad. The look on Harry's face said, "That's great, Dad. Make me like you, a murderer. Give me no other choice. Make me shoot you, my own dad, and then I have to live with it."

"Don't be weak, Harry. I didn't raise you to be no weakling. You're smart. You know what to do. Be a man and do it. You got to do it. Sometime. You. Might. Never. Get another. Chance." Space grew between his words as if his batteries were depleting. TV's eyes drifted off of his son and across the clearing. Something had distracted him, and he stared off into the woods. He started walking, almost stumbling in that direction. When he reached the edge of the trees, he stopped for a second and looked again at his Harry. The sound of a vehicle coming down the road distracted them both.

TV stepped behind a tree and disappeared from view.

Chapter 35

[After the fire in the Vanair Trailer Park, Frank Robillard discovered Nora Potvin missing and left in Clyde Hembree's truck to look for her.]

Smoke from the fire still swirled in the cab of Clyde's truck. Frank rolled down the window as he left the Vanair Trailer Park, relishing the much cooler night air flowing around him. His mind feverishly calculated where Miss Nora might have gone. Of course, she wanted to go back to her home, the shanty out in the bare lake bed. She wanted to die there rather than in a strange place. Did she have enough strength to walk the six miles? The rising lake water now lapped at the foundation of the little house. If Collie had seen her at suppertime, nearly five hours ago, she might have gone quite a distance, even in her condition.

He turned toward the lake, and drove slowly so that he could look for either a white shrouded woman stumbling along or a limp body lying on the side of the road. She might have collapsed in the tall weeds somewhere between the Vanair and the lake.

But he didn't spot her along the highway. He eventually came to the long narrow road that led to the lake. Only hours ago, he had been on this same road pursuing TV Swanson. The dark forest immediately swallowed the truck as he drove down the woods road. The unimproved road bounced him around pretty good, but unlike his own truck, the springs on Clyde's reduced the jostling.

He arrived at the edge of the forest. Before him in the moonlight lay the half filled Lake Juliette. The band of sloped earth between the edge of the forest and the rising water had narrowed considerably. In the bright moonlight, Frank could see the shack in the distance, a football field's length away. The water had risen past the foundation now making it look like a semi-sunken houseboat.

Frank drove around the edge of the lake toward the shack and left the truck parked in an area above the waterline. He walked toward the shack, wetting his legs to the knees. The coolness soaking into his shoes made his toes curl. He climbed the steps to the porch, made slippery by the muddy water. He pushed through the front door and sloshed into the small room.

Over fifteen years had passed since he had last seen the inside of Miss Nora's shack. The moonlight coming in through the window gave everything a gray cast. Frank sensed immediately that she was not here. His memory told him that not much had changed over the span of years, those days when they were both in this room making music. The foot of water covering the floor made the only difference.

Frank recalled the happiness that he had felt here, happiness that seemed to have ended when he stopped coming. Ignoring the urgency of his current mission, he took a moment to look around the room and felt sadness for a promise that had never been kept.

She lived a sparse life. The only furniture was a straight backed chair, a cast iron wood stove older even than Nora, and a small table where she took her meals. A door in the back led to her tiny bedroom.

Still high above the water, a shelf held Miss Nora's violin case. Frank stared at it, dark against the whitewashed wall. His fingers curled at his side.

Fifteen years passed him by since those miraculous days of music, an age of exile and denial. Her violin was a fine Italian made piece and could produce a loud, exceptionally bright tone. Nora's playing the violin could be an irresistible spectacle: the motion of her thin fingers flying over the black ebony fingerboard, or the way she would toss her head to get more force out of the bow. In her hands the violin had shaped so many sensations. Nora had shown him how the violin could both weep and thunder. She had shown him how to summon the emotions of love or happiness or sorrow. She showed him how to cast a spell over his listeners, or if there were no listeners, to cast the spell over himself. He had known that she was a witch woman as no one else had known her, and he had learned even better than her, the ecstasy of casting that spell, the love, the strength, the happiness that it could bring.

The water touched a sensitive spot on the back of his knees.

Frank waded over to the shelf and holding it high above the rising water, opened the violin case. The violin lay in a bed of dark green velvet that looked nearly black by the milky light of the moon coming through the window. He picked it up and marveled at the lightness of it. His hands were larger than Miss Nora's, but as a child, he had been able to learn her fingering technique. As he grew, Nora showed him how to use the size of hands to stretch to the farthest reaches of the fingerboard, to play note combinations others could not play.

He plucked each string, and found them only slightly out of tune. The naked notes sounded shrill in the darkness, and raised the hair on the back of his neck. Frank turned the tuning keys. His ear shrugged off a decade and a half of disuse and guided him to the right timbres. He picked up the bow and placed the lower bout under his chin. The violin felt warm and alive against the stubble of his beard. The first scraping of the bow across the strings brought forth a fountain of sentiment, hidden away inside him all these years. In his mind he saw the face of his mother, weak and shrinking, sitting in her chair, nodding and smiling to his music. He scraped the bow on another note and then held the next note long and warm, adding vibrato and glissando, climbing an octave. Then he played the C major scale followed by the G, and so forth through the cycle of fifths.

Frank Robillard, violinist, stood there wet nearly to his thighs, breath barely entering his lungs. He could still play. He could still play, and the joy of that revelation clutched at his groin like a lover trying to seduce him. He welcomed the feelings, the sensations, the warmth. He took a deep breath, and his lungs shuddered even before they were full. And they shuddered again, but he filled them and held the air.

He played the first movement of the Bach Sonata for Violin in G minor. The opening double notes he held long and mournfully, as had been his signature in those days when he played. The opening movement was a long and sorrowful song, full of double stops and tricky intervals. It seemed that no time had passed since he had last played the piece, so fluid were his fingers, but it had. Time had passed, a great deal of it, and with few moments of pleasure for Frank. But his body remembered this, the playing of the violin, pure pleasure and joy. He knew then he had been placed in the earth for no other reason.

For three minutes and forty seconds, the world waited for him. If there had been anyone within earshot of the little hovel, now awash in Lake Juliette, they too would have stopped and listened to the haunting melody coming out of the cabin in the lake. The moon seemed frozen in the sky, casting its blue white light down on the scene through the window; the light uninterrupted by cloud or breeze. At the end, painful tears filled his eyes and flowed down his cheeks, leapt off of his jaw and nose, and dropped to join the water lapping at his waist.

Frank lowered the violin and bow and let his head drop.

"That was fucking beautiful."

233

The voice seem to come from the other room. Frank looked up to see TV Swanson charging, swinging something at him. Instinctively, Frank raised his arms to ward off the blow. A steel poker from Miss Nora's wood stove, crashed through the violin, creating a shower of splinters. The first strike landed weakly. Frank saw the second coming as Swanson backhanded the poker, a swish of air, a crunching of hair and skull, an explosion of pain.

Frank dropped to the flooded floor. Darkness reached out for him. He felt his body floating in the cold water. He grasped for something to steady himself, gulping water that immediately went down his throat. He coughed and tried to get up, tried to take a breath. He saw his assailant raise the poker again, but he held his arm in mid strike.

TV Swanson stood over him in the rising water. He dropped the steel poker, and it sunk swiftly to the floor. Frank felt him rifling through his holsters and pouches, finally finding the handcuffs. Powerless, Frank felt one of the loops clasped around his ankle. He heard a water-muffled click as Swanson had fastened the other handcuff loop through one of the filigreed holes in the foot of the cast iron stove. Frank's arms reached out impotently to stop him, but he rolled on his back and struggled to get air.

His assailant stood over him for only a second. "That'll give me a little time. Give you a little time too, I guess. Then you're gonna be fish food. No hard feelings, asshole, but you're now fucked, and I'm still king of the world."

Frank heard him wading through the water and then heard nothing else but the unmusical ringing in his ears. He could feel throbbing darkness coming over him. He floated only a few feet below the cracked ceiling of the little room, but he gradually lost focus of it.

Hours could have passed, or minutes, he could not be sure. He bobbed at an odd angle. The heavy cast iron stove below him anchored his foot to the floor. The back of his skull bumped against the ceiling. He noted that all pain had left him. No air space above him meant he had nothing to breathe. He had no use for breath anyway. His lungs had long ago filled with water. It surprised him to discover that he had been wrong about something else. Miss Nora was there in the house with him. Although he could not turn his head to see her, he saw or felt the glow of her light as she moved about the room, making her home in the water. Nora, not chained to anything at all had indeed returned to where she belonged. Frank remembered her words and again feared their reunion. But for now she paid him no more attention than if he had been a piece

234

of her furniture.

Chapter 36

Harry's mother had not revived. In fact, her only movement had been an inert settling where her body slumped shapelessly against the car door. Harry and Teeny had bedded down in the back of the station wagon. Harry had lain awake most of the night, but Teeny dropped into a deep sleep after an afternoon and evening of hunger for them both. They had looked but found little to eat but a half pack of vanilla-filled cookies and a few cold french fries.

Harry spread the sleeping bags in the back of the car amid the clutter. They turned in early with night dropping through the trees. Sleep came immediately for Teeny, but not Harry. He worried that they slept with a dead woman. It had taken him a while to realize that he had witnessed his dad kill his mother. The lumpy form in the front seat had not moved, and he had been too afraid to try to shake her awake. In the darkness and quiet of the night, he isolated the sounds of his own and his sister's breathing, but he heard nothing from his mother.

His mother's dying presented another problem. Having seen enough road killed skunks and 'possums, Harry realized he had to bury his mother. He spent last night's sleepless hours recalling what he knew of the process. You dug a hole in the ground. It had to be deep enough to keep the animals from digging her up. A grave was supposed to be six feet deep, an apparent traditional depth, but deep enough for him to get trapped in the hole.

He could not move her very far. She weighed more than twice as much as he did. Even getting her into the hole would be hard. At funerals, several men carried the box that held the body. They lowered the box into the hole slowly to maintain dignity. Harry did not have the resources for a funeral.

The dawn found him groggy from lack of sleep. The smell in the car drove him out early and he wondered how Teeny endured it. He spied the shovel his dad had used to overcome the man who had come into the

236

clearing yesterday. Harry had thought that his dad had killed that man too, but he had lain there for a couple of hours, eventually stirred, rolled over and got up. Harry and Teeny watched him from behind the thicket. The man had looked around dazedly, head wound still seeping blood. He turned toward the road and slowly walked off. The shovel lay on the ground with blood still staining the blade.

Harry picked up the spade and went to a spot in the middle of the clearing. He tried the spade in the earth. The blade caught on rocks and roots that the forest had already buried there. Long grueling hours of work lay ahead of him, but he knew he had to stay at it until he finished.

Teeny came out of the car to stand beside by the growing hole. "What are you doing, Harry?"

Harry thought of all the answers he could give, but only one made any sense.

"I'm burying Mom." He threw another shovelful of red dirt on the mound beside the hole.

"What's 'burying?'"

This question also challenged him. Any answer would beget another question and each question would make him think about what he was doing. He would rather have avoided the truth, but Teeny was all the family he had at the moment. From now on, it had to be the truth. He had to bear up to it. Like yesterday's notion of killing his father, this was too much responsibility for a ten year old kid.

"Mom's dead. I'm digging this hole. We have to put Mom in the hole and fill it up with dirt. Cover her body up with dirt," he corrected. He wrestled another spade full up out of the hole. His hands were getting raw from the rough wood of the handle.

Teeny stood there silent long enough for him to remove several more shovels full.

"I don't want Mom to be in the ground," Teeny said.

Harry stopped for a moment. He didn't want his mother in the ground either. He hadn't wanted her to be a drug addict. He hadn't wanted his father to be a thieving murderer. He hadn't wanted his whole family to be such a disgrace. He wanted to be like his friends who lived in clean, sparkling, loving, church-going homes where everyone grew up wholesome, laughing at good things, not painful things. His family lived in cheap, dirty rentals, sat on stolen furniture, wore mismatched clothes. Harry hadn't wanted any of this. He wanted his mother to be alive and striving to overcome her problems. He wanted his dad to be law abiding and have a good job, respectable, but barring that... to be gone from their lives.

"I don't want Mom in the ground either, but I have to. She's dead."

"Dead," Teeny said.

"Dead. He struggled with a root that burrowed straight across the bottom of the hole. "Like the 'possums on the side of the road."

Teeny turned to look at the lump in the front seat of the station wagon. Her mother's face pressed against the window glass. Steam had collected inside the car, like a hot shower fogs a bathroom. While she stared, Teeny started to cry, a thin cry, toneless and high pitched. Harry looked up and felt a heartbreaking sympathy for her. Her thoughts had arrived where his had been for some time, just realizing how things were and how they would be from now on. He longed to step out of the hole and hug her, but the Swansons were not a hugging family and Harry had never gotten the hang of it. Teeny faced him with tear stained cheeks. She turned to look again at her mother and slowly descended into a sitting position, sitting at the edge of the hole, lowering her head so that her tears fell into the dirt.

The hole grew slowly, and Harry became lost in his misery. His hands were bleeding when hours later he deemed the grave big enough. He climbed out and lay on the ground exhausted, muscles twitching, mind dizzy. The overhead sun made the clearing hot. His sweat mixed with the dirt and he knew that he looked like a total mud-stained mess. But he was a grave digger. Weren't grave diggers supposed to be dirty?

It took several minutes before he could stand up. He retrieved one of the sleeping bags from the rear of the car and dragged it over to the passenger door of the station wagon, where he spread it on the ground. Teeny came over to stand next to him. He slowly opened the door. The heavy weight of his mother's body pushed the door open faster than Harry wanted. The dead Corky seemed to lunge at them. They both jumped back.

His mother's body dumped itself halfway onto the spread sleeping bag. Her legs hung on the bottom frame of the door. Harry tried to pull more of her onto the bag, but she barely moved. His mother's flesh felt like nothing he had ever touched, and an icy chill drove from him the heat and exhaustion he had felt moments just before. After an intense struggle, he managed to get her on the bag. Harry gathered up the corners of the sleeping bag and connected the halves of zipper. He fought with the zipper until the bag was nearly closed around her body. Her face was the last part of his mother to disappear inside the darkness of the sleeping bag. They both stared at her for a minute. He had seen the expression on her face many times before, tranquil, lost to the world. Her lips were closed and straight. Her face had turned light gray in death, erasing the wrinkles from her forehead making it look smooth, ghostlike. Even the darkened circles under her eyes had faded.

"She is so beautiful," Teeny said.

An emotional storm burst in Harry's chest and he felt his composure violently slipping. He looked at his sister, angry that she could summon such a deep emotion from him when he had nearly exhausted all his strength to contain it. His mother wasn't beautiful. She was ugly, even dead. But Teeny's eyes held their mother's face in an enchanted stare, and Harry suddenly saw his sister in a new perspective. His sister was the truly beautiful one, the only one in their whole family. Her skin was perfect, creamy. Her eyes were lined with dark brunette lashes that could barely conceal her eye's brilliant blue. Her solemn expression showed her ignorance of the complexities of their situation and a simple faith in him. At that moment, he felt such an intense love for his sister, he thought it might kill him.

He pulled the zipper the last few inches, closing the bag, but stranding a lock of his mother's mousy gray streaked hair. Teeny looked up at him, so he opened the zipper again and gently tucked the lock inside. Pulling the heavy bag over to the hole proved difficult to do, but he finally got it done. With his heart beating like a freight train, he pushed the load into the pit he had so laboriously carved in the rocky, root infested ground.

It surprised Harry to find that his hole barely had enough capacity to hold the body of his mother. Some of her actually stuck out above the top of the hole, but gravity slowly pulled her body down. Harry shoveled dirt, filling the hole quickly. He piled the excess dirt on top as he had seen them do in Western movies. When he finished, there was quite a mound over the grave. Harry scattered leaves and sticks over it to look as natural as possible.

Harry stepped back a few feet and collapsed to his knees. Again, dizziness overcame him and he heard a roaring that had nothing to do with any wind. Teeny came over and put her arms around his neck. The warm touch of her flesh electrified his body, bringing back distant memories of his mother's touch that must have come from when he had been a baby. Or maybe it had been his grandmother who touched him.

He didn't remember who had done it, but he remembered that he had once been loved like a normal child. Maybe he hadn't been raised in a house where there was hugging, but he could learn. Teeny knew how to do it.

Harry nuzzled his cheek against his sister's chest. The gesture felt right, given the time and place. Hot tears came out of his eyes and soaked into her tee-shirt. He felt nausea in his abdomen accompanying the whirling in his head, but his sister's arms were warm and he felt her lightly padded breastbone and the cool cascade of her brunette hair, which fell, mixed with his sweat and flood of tears. In a moment Harry would have to be her big brother again, but for now, for all too few innocent seconds, he could allow himself the memory of his mother's arms.

EPILOGUE

From Brendan Macbean's journal:

Spring is the best time of year in Atlanta. Every neighborhood sparkles with blooming color and every surface gets covered with yellow pollen dust. Although I worked feverishly on the book, my mood when not writing kept the winter alive and well, thank you. My agent reveled over every chapter. We both admired the contract she negotiated, and although I shared her enthusiasm, I couldn't shake my funk. I still grieved over a man I didn't know who died nineteen years ago and another whom I would rather not have known, who died while I watched. I felt extreme sorrow for Corky, who died after a short and unhappy life, but who had such a noble burial during those sad events. Her father had chosen to relocate her remains to the family plot, so there was another funeral coming up. I grieved over two boys and a girl, kids who grew up without their fathers and two fathers who had lost their daughters.

And speaking of kids, what of Remy? Did I answer his questions about his dad? I don't know. I haven't seen or talked to him since that dim-witted fishing trip three years ago. I don't even know where he is or if he still works for the television station. It seemed unusual that he never asked about our project. What faith he must have had to have left me unsupervised on this most important thing in his life. During the last three years, I never realized that while I obsessed over the Frank Robillard story, I ignored the reason I started it in the first place.

In April I attended one of Lydia Robillard's splendid parties. Much of Atlanta's glitterati attended that fine spring night. By now I totally loved this middle-aged little princess. She lit up the room in her shiny cocktail dress, stood as tall as she could in four inch heels and her hair, in the words of Warren Zevon, "was perfect." I always received a lavish greeting from her upon my arrivals, like I was a Russian Prince, recovering from a grave illness. Dostoyevsky anyone?

"Brendan! How wonderful to see you. Are you okay? Your color looks a little pale. You need to get more sunlight. Tell me about your work." I knew she would only listen to me for about thirty seconds before flying off to another local star with a brighter corona. I intended to hang about her party, knowing no one, feeling more depressed by the minute, and looking for a way to slip out, go home and feel even worse.

Later that evening, just as I inched toward the exit, Lydia surprised me by again gracing my presence. She gave me a concerned look, but she couldn't know or care about the real reason for my condition.

243

"Brendan. What is it? I've been looking at you all night. You look terrible. Did your dog die or something?"

"Don't have a dog." I mumbled.

She pursed her pretty lips and cocked her perfect head. "Come on. Tell Lydia. What is it?"

What could I say? I felt the urgent need to tell somebody, but it seemed all so stupid. No way could I tell her, Hey Lydia, I'm gloomy because of a story about a man I didn't know. He's been dead and gone nearly twenty years, and oh, it was your ex. At that moment, the whole thing seemed ludicrous. Except for Frank Robillard's remarkable gifts, I had not found him the least bit likeable. His life had inundated me with its gloomy, incredibly sad and tragic details. I felt cut off from Lydia's shiny world, especially since she had fought so hard to escape Juliette and Frank. How could I explain to her in the next twenty seconds, which would be just about all the time I had left?

"I... I...Uh, well...."

She held up her tiny hand flashing with jewels and cut off my prattle.

"Bren, you need to get out more. You brood too much, like one of those poets or something. You need a vacation. I like to go to London or Paris when I'm feeling blue and buy a bunch of stuff." She looked pensive for a second.

Lydia grabbed my elbow and led me to the parlor where we had had our first chat. She sat me down at the Louis XIV chair in front of the gild-framed picture of the Eiffel Tower. She held one tiny finger to my face, but her eyes rose to stare behind me at the picture. As I watched her face, her expression transformed from probing to breakthrough.

"Wait!" Like a flash she left and returned with a piece of paper.

"Here, this is a friend of mine, Bettye Le Boutilliere. She lives in Paris. She teaches English in the schools over there. Get a plane ticket and a hotel room. That's all you'll need. She'll take you everywhere. You'll forget everything in a week."

Apparently Lydia must have called her friend, because in a few days I started receiving phone calls from Bettye. She called me almost daily, sometimes leaving messages on my answering machine. She knew the hotels where I should stay, what we would do. On every call, she would ask, when could I come? She spoke terrific English, which was a relief, since I had no French beyond, "Bone-jur, mon-ser."

To my surprise, our overseas conversations became pretty darn entertaining. She delighted in my being a man of letters, as she called it. For her English students, she collected examples of American colloquial speech, which I had in abundance. Before I knew what happened, I sat in a jet, flying to Paris one evening in May, for a week of vacation with the energetic and assertive Bettye Le Boutilliere as my guide.

I had a few preconceptions about Bettye, but found myself delighted with her as soon as I walked off the plane. In order, I noticed Bettye was shorter than me, a great dresser, and an attractive woman. She greeted me with hugs and kisses as if we were old friends. I noticed that she carried a French copy of Newsweek with Theodore Vincent Swanson's ugly mug on the front. She held the magazine out to me with a pen.

"Monsieur, would you sign it please?"

It was my first autograph. I can't tell you how happy it made me feel, jet lag and all.

She gave me until that evening to get my internal clock set to rights. I napped in my hotel room until about 7 PM. I met Bettye in the lobby, dressed in my most expensive suit. Bettye made a face and immediately bought me another necktie in my hotel gift shop.

"Hey, my mother gave me that tie!" I protested while she stuffed my mother's gift in an ornate trash can. Out of the corner of my eye, I saw the gift shop clerk nodding approval. Bettye gave me one of her twinkling-eye smiles.

"You should always respect your mother. She is not in Paris, no?"

"Not the last time I looked." I said and managed a feigned pout.

"The last time you looked?" A confused expression preceded her whipping out a notebook to write something in it, a pattern she would often repeat and I would relish in the days to come. Anytime I said something cute, upon receiving my explanation, she'd write it down, presumably to share with her English students. I endured this, because it let me stare into her lovely gray eyes without making her too uncomfortable.

"It's sort of a joke. We both know that my mother isn't in France, right? I just say, 'Not the last time I looked' as if she might have snuck up on me or something." Bettye thought about it for a half second and then laughed, a sound like tiny bells tumbling down a waterfall. She shook her head and took my arm to escort me to the cab.

"Put on your new tie, Brendan." The way she said it, like 'Brel'n-dahn.' Her pronunciation of my name required nose and throat maneuvers I could never hope to master, but it tingled my spine every

245

time. I felt like a million bucks. Make that a million bucks with a new French tie.

We ate at a place called, L'Espadon in the Ritz Hotel, where I enjoyed the most fabulous meal of my life in one of the most beautiful rooms I have ever graced, spending more than my monthly grocery budget. The cook, a guy named Guy Legay, noted Parisian chef, came to the table and asked for my autograph. Bettye explained that it was a huge honor, since he was such an _artiste_. The Newsweek article had made a tiny sensation in France. The French both admired and were appalled by everything American. There is no capital punishment in France, so the voluntary nature of Ted's execution created a national, morbid fascination. I deserved this brief renown as official chronicler. I loved this place.

The next four days went by in an uplifting daze. A tonic for my deflated condition, Bettye's cheerful attitude expanded my soul, like the wonderful cuisine filled out my waistline. After that first night in a fancy restaurant, we continued to eat marvelous food in less pretentious cafes at a fraction of the cost. Bettye did all the paying and tipping in addition to gently guiding my humble behavior, since a lifetime is required to understand the strange rituals and laws governing Parisian dining.

We furiously attempted to see everything in Paris. In quick succession, we visited the Pompidou Centre, the Arc de Triomphe, the Eiffel Tower, the Cimetiere du Montparnasse, the Mussee Picasso, d'Orsay, de Cluny, du Louvre, the Dome Church, Le Sacre-Coeur and Notre Dame. This routine finally bent me over nearly as much as Quasimodo. By Saturday, I begged for a quiet night at a bar with a few beers.

"Oh, Yes, Brendan." she said giving me a squeeze. We were huggin' buddies by now. "But tonight it is Opera National de Paris at the Opera de Paris Bastille."

"The opera who de what?"

"The Opera National De Paris, the finest in the world, of course!" she replied.

"Maybe after the Atlanta Opera, it is."

She gave me that look, making me feel like the redneck I was from that hick town in Georgia. It seems that if you compare anything, even a French toilet seat, to something in America, you are offering the gravest insult to a Frenchman. Anyway, I knew nothing about opera. Atlanta had one, but it probably couldn't rank anywhere near what Paris had to offer.

I wasn't giving up easily.

"You French people got it pretty good. But you ain't got nothing like Lenox Mall!"

Alas, there was not much in Atlanta French visitors wanted to see, but they never missed Lenox when they came to town, American culture being what it is. Anyway, an opera sounded pretty peaceful, like I could catch a good nap, while Brunhilda with the Viking helmet tried to hit a high C.

I could not do justice to the history Bettye gave me on the Opera Bastille. Apparently, the building opened about ten years ago, and the French hailed it as an example of world class architecture. I recalled the movie, "The Phantom of the Opera," took place inside the Paris Opera. That's got to be an older building, doesn't it? Bettye set me straight.

"That is the old Opera. It is still there in the Opera district."

"But we're going to the new opera house," I quipped, "and it is not in the Opera District?"

"Oui, monsieur." That phrase, spoken in a husky female voice with a French accent, is deeply lodged in every man's fantasy. I went along meekly with her plans.

The Opera Bastille is located on Rue de Lyon, but when we got into the cab, Bettye told the driver something like, "Plastic lobo steel." I found out that meant, Place la Bastille, which is a large square, absolutely choked with pedestrians and traffic. Several big streets in Paris intersected there, and French law required every driver to honk the horn when he drove through, several times for good measure, making it, the noisiest place in the city. Unusual, I thought, to build an opera house here.

The Opera Bastille was an impressive building covered with brilliant mirrored glass, but five days in Paris had blunted my appreciation for French architecture. Our seats were in the balcony, close to the front rail and not too far from the stage.

Bettye read her program. "This is for the tourists." she lamented. "But it was the only opera they had scheduled during your visit." She rolled her eyes toward the ornate ceiling. The program was in French, of course, but at least I could read the title. Puccini's "La Boheme." I was not an opera lover, but at least I had heard of it.

"What's wrong with that?"

She shrugged. "Oh, I have seen 'La Boheme' many times. It is beautiful, but there are so many others that might be more interesting.

The composer was not even French."

Again I was tempted to say, "What's wrong with that?" but I resisted. The lights dimmed and people rushed to their seats for the opening.

La Boheme completely blew apart my expectations. Not that I could have made any sense out of the plot synopsis in the program. They sang in Italian, a major concession for the Parisians. Above the stage, the producers flashed super-titles in French, which didn't help me much. I could only watch the actions and listen to the music. La Boheme has no Viking women in brass bras. No horned helmets or spears, just a bunch of guys running around a dingy apartment, trying to duck the landlord, just like back home. Women came in and the guys tried to put the make on them. Finally after a bunch of nice songs, the curtain came down and the music ended.

I turned to Bettye and said, "That was very pretty. Where are we going to eat tonight?"

She gave me that look again and smiled. It took her a moment to judge my statement was not a joke, but that of a total fool.

"No. No, my Brendan, La Boheme has four acts. Is it not beautiful?"

I nodded as I scrunched down in my seat, embarrassed. Looked liked no one else in the theater made the same error. I thought it seemed a little short for an opera. The curtain came back up in a hurry and we saw a pretty bistro street scene.

The lively music framed the Latin Quarter, in nineteenth century Paris, urchins, and keystone cops running around, Molly Malone selling cockles or whatever. I know I misinterpreted the whole thing. The guys from the apartment were cutting up, having fun. More women show up and they sing. What else? Since I knew that two more acts are coming, I didn't get restless when the curtain came down. But Bettye stands up to leave and that really confused me.

"Come on, Brendan. It is intermission."

We walked to the sumptuous lobby where French custom required everyone to have several Gitanes burning. Bettye handed me a flute of champagne, and we sipped while standing around looking stylish.

And we talked. Actually Bettye did, on the subject of French poetry, particularly Henri Murger, whoever that was. I hardly caught any of it so mainly I looked into her eyes, and noted the features of her face, the subtle curves of her fine skin stretched over delicate cheek bones. I felt a strong inclination to drop my eyes and take measure of deep crevice between her breasts. While resisting with all my willpower, I noticed a change come over Bettye. I heard her voice, like a kind of fine music barely registering in the background and wham! It hit me. Bettye was showing interest in me. Yes, in <u>that</u> sort of way. Her eyes bored into mine, only now they did not turn away. It seemed in the past week, she had gone out of her way to avoid giving me the wrong signals. Women! They change the rules anytime they want. But things had turned around, and suddenly I concluded that maybe, just maybe, she more than liked me.

She chatted on with no attempt to be clever, her mouth on autopilot, but her eyes sending out the unmistakable semaphore of invitation. My heart fluttered and my face blushed. She noticed and smiled slightly, knowing that her signal had been received. Sudden fire surged through my red-blooded American veins, but my brain prodded me with an endless supply of stupid things to say that would surely ruin both the mood and my chances. I am poorly trained here. You see, women do not offer me much encouragement, and it rattles me when they do. I have many women friends, who only wish to be friends. I'm not shy, but I know what I look like. My parents passed me the short, cute geek genes. The thick glasses and goofy grin I came up with on my own. I'll never be the tall, good looking stranger, who women fantasize about. I don't stand out in a crowd. In fact, in a crowd, most people trip over me if I don't keep moving. Reporter rejection is not the same as personal rejection; it hurts when a woman I am interested in says, "No thanks," but thinks, "You're short and not very attractive." So I just don't play. No point in confusing anyone.

But Bettye gave me those signals and in my head, confusion reigned. She put a velvet gloved trio of fingertips against my lips to stifle the verbal blunders that strove for release.

"Brendan, we must return to our seats, now."

No confusion at all in the way she took my arm and pressed her body against mine as we walked back to our seats. Back in Atlanta, somebody might holler, "Get a room!"

Once in our seats, my arm somehow found her delicate shoulder, and her head came to rest on mine. Her perfume spun my head like a top.

Again the curtain jerked up and the music jolted me back to the opera. I didn't know how I could sit through another two acts of light hearted, rollicking fun, with the prospects of making it with Bettye looming. I wanted badly to be in the back of a darkened cab, tasting her lipstick, heading for my hotel room. This time, I'll throw away the tie.

The opera lay unavoidably before us, but its mood swung completely south. The music became somber and questioning, the scene on stage turned gloomy. Dark gray winter, snow falling. A walled city, with a guarded gate. Sad soaring music and then back to the apartment for a death scene. The opera ends and the crowd's sudden applause drew me back to the present.

I don't think I have ever seen anything like it. I clapped like crazy until I happen to see something near the stage that makes my hands stop, frozen in mid air, inches apart.

At first I thought I didn't really see it. I wiped my eyes on a tissue that Bettye had turned soggy.

In the orchestra pit, in the last row of violins, a gray haired man pulled sheets of music off of the stand. On the stage above him, the cast members bowed while ovations and bravos surged down from the audience. The conductor also bowed and turned to ask the orchestra to rise for their tribute. He stood taller than the other musicians and suddenly the most hideous, appalling, and wonderful thought went through my head. I looked to my right and noticed that the stranger next to me had a pair of small binoculars hanging around his neck by a velvet strap. I did not know how to ask, so in my haste at pantomiming the request, I probably jerked them off of him somewhat abruptly.

The binoculars didn't help much. What I saw was too tantalizing, too impossible. I turned to Bettye. She looked at me with alarm, possibly forming an apology to the man with the opera glasses.

"Bettye. I've got to get to the stage. I have got to get down there."

She looked at me with a strange expression. She could tell this was no joke. I probably gripped her hands with painful strength.

"No. No. It is not possible. No one can go there." She shook her head.

"Bettye. Please. We must try. If you interpret, I'll make the request."

"It cannot be done. It is not done. No. Why do you need this, Brendan?" Her look was full of concern.

"I can't tell you. I just have to get back there. I've got to see if its real."

"What is real?" She asked.

We tried. Bettye was right. Stupid but efficient security men guarded the backstage door. No amount of entreaty or bribery prevailed, but they could not realize how foolishly persistent Americans can be.

"Bettye. The orchestra must come out somewhere. Let's go and wait for them."

She shrugged. We tried several places, running like alley rats door to door around the huge Opera Bastille. Bettye, in heels slowed me down and I almost let go of her hand. We finally spotted some folks walking away from the building carrying instrument cases. Breathless, Bettye asked them questions in French. They pointed to a door, through which a steady stream of musicians exited. A light misty rain started to fall, and I could feel Betty's mild panic since we had neither overcoats nor umbrellas.

At last I saw him, recognized him, although it was night and the light dim. I knew he would be tall, but he looked little like his pictures. How could I not know him?

He must have known that this day would come, but how strange it must have been exiting his place of work, as he had done hundreds of nights to be confronted on this night in May by two people standing in the rain staring at him. For nearly twenty years, nobody noticed him at all. He stopped a few feet away while the other musicians swirled around him. He stared at me, his dark eyes calculating, questioning everything, his mind working to come up with an answer. I saw his expression change from mild curiosity to understanding, as if he magically figured this all out, this impossible thing that had just happened to him, to me, knowing it would happen, and even knowing that somehow I would be the one who found him. He found the first words.

"Macbean. Isn't it? Did you ever pay that fine?"

His voice came to me as if out of a dream, hardly a trace remaining of his southern accent. A musician's ear would adapt to the speech of the locale. My mouth struggled to say something, working without sound, until I took a few great breaths.

"The speeding ticket? Well, yes. I did. At least I think I did."

I wished that I could have come up with a quotation that would have rung out in our lexicon like Stanley's "Dr. Livingston, I presume." But in this drama nothing he or I said would live in anyone's memory.

Frank signaled us to follow him and we did, meekly like well behaved children. He hustled us two blocks to a warm and inviting cafe. We all felt dry and cozy inside. I introduced him to Bettye, and felt strange in doing so, because there was little familiarity between us and I hadn't even introduced myself. He barely knew me and had spent the last twenty years hiding from anyone who knew him. We seated ourselves at a table.

"Why were you looking for me? And how did you find me?" Frank Robillard asked.

"I wasn't. I mean, I was. But not anymore. I sort of stumbled on you."

"You're the author of the Newsweek article about Theodore Swanson." He smiled, the first time I saw his smile. All of the pictures I had of Frank showed him frowning. His had been a life where you could count the smiles.

"Last month, the article came out. I certainly remembered TV Swanson, and then you; the speeding ticket back in Juliette. Red Mustang. That was a terrific article. Even when translated into French."

We both turned to Bettye to see her pretty lips turn down. Frank guessed that she knew English. He said something to her in French and she smiled again.

"How did you come to be here, in Paris?" I asked.

Frank shook his head. "Long story."

"You went back to playing the violin."

"Yep."

"Just a few months ago, Ted told me he left you handcuffed to a cast iron stove in Miss Nora's house. How'd you get out of that?" I asked.

Frank Robillard smiled painfully, a smile that did not count towards his life's allotment.

"He pretty much left me there for dead. The water had filled that place. I must have been unconscious. Suddenly everything started moving. My first thought, was it was an effect of dying, like a total relocation. But then I realized the dam had broken, and the water was flooding downstream. But everything moved in a circle. The old shack came apart, boards flying everywhere. Suddenly my head broke the surface and I took a deep breath and then got dragged under again. Eventually I hit something pretty hard and blacked out. When I came around, I was floating face up in the shallows. It was still dark. The lake was calm."

"The whirlpool." I said.

"Something like that. Before they built the dam, I tried to tell the engineers about a big underground fissure. I suggested that they drill some holes and plant some charges, blow it up. They ignored my advice.

The water must have flowed into that fissure. Anyway, when I woke up, I still had the handcuffs on, but the cast iron stove was gone. Probably smashed against a rock."

"No one saw you again. They thought you were dead."

Frank nodded. "I walked to town. It was still dark. I did some soul searching along the way and decided that the town and everyone in it could get along without me. And I could do without all of them. I concluded that we could all be better off."

"Your son..."

He held up his hand, as if to stop the pain. He looked at a spot beyond where I sat. "How is he, Little Ray?"

"Rem... Uh. Ray is fine. The last I saw of him, he worked at a TV station in Atlanta."

We talked for over an hour, until Bettye's head fell on my shoulder. I learned from him how after hiding out for a few months, he sought violin training at a music school in New York City, not Juilliard, but the Brooklyn Academy of Music. He worked on his chops and moved to Europe. He traveled from orchestra to orchestra, and had been with the Opera Bastille about six years. After so long a layoff he had been unable to elevate his playing enough to sit with first violins, but sat instead in the back row. He found contentment in what he did and knowing that Little Ray had been well-taken care of and eventually buried the pain of their separation.

I told him the story of the fishing trip and how I had been hooked into learning about him by Little Ray. And now his son wanted to know about his father, the one he had missed knowing for 19 years. Frank stopped me.

"Don't tell him. It won't do either of us any good. I just want to know that he is happy."

"He won't be happy unless he finds out about you. For him, you'll always be lost, and he'll keep trying to figure out who you were... are. I wasn't happy until I found you and I'm not even your kin." I said.

Frank considered that. "From what you said, he has a life. I've one as well. I made my choice back in '80. I don't go fishing anymore or watch baseball. What good would it do us to resurrect me or anything else?"

What Frank said made no sense to me. Why wouldn't he want to see his son? I answered my own question.

"Because you left him when he was ten years old... to a conniving mother and a controlling grandpa. That boy went through hell. He loved you. You were his hero," I said softly, cruelly. "Is it pain or guilt, Mr. Robillard?"

Robillard took the rebuke with a grimace, nodding slowly.

"Both. But I was very much a different person back then. As Little Ray grew older, he wouldn't have thought me such a hero. I was a failure. And as long as I stayed in Juliette, I would have remained that way. If I had gone to Atlanta... followed after Lydia and Little Ray, with the meager choices I had, it would have ended up the same. I don't know how much you know, but if you knew Lydia and her father, you know the situation."

I nodded, like I knew everything, but I had not planned for this meeting. It had never been an option: what if I met the man I pursued for the last three years, who was supposed to be dead? What do you say to him, to explain... anything you've done or thought? Did you expect him to have any answers?

Frank finally terminated the interview. He stood and held out his hand, which I noticed was only a little bigger than mine, contrasting the rest of his size. Do you need smaller hands to play the violin?

"Mr. Macbean. You have obviously invested a lot of time in chasing the story of Ted Swanson. I'm certain that there is a book coming, right? Make it about him, not about me. Nobody wants to know about me. I died and want to stay dead. Beausoir, monsieur."

At his spoken French, Bettye's head came up, although her gray eyes remained a little unfocused. When I turned to look at Frank, all that I saw was his back. He walked out of the cafe into the rainy Paris night and I never saw him again.

Nearly a week later, back in my condo in Atlanta, I shamelessly napped in broad daylight to get over the awful flight home. I had decided to spend an extra few days in Paris. You know... Bettye. Frank Robillard had ruined my life for the last three years. I wasn't about to let him ruin my love life. Bettye and I were wonderful together. We parted more than just friends, we promised to celebrate Bastille Day in Atlanta.

But now I had more reasons than Bettye to be jubilant. Tons of anxiety had been lifted off of my back. I could finally look forward to ending this Frank business. Maybe now I could get a decent night's sleep.

But it wasn't over. Long after my jet lag departed, I still lay awake at night. I couldn't get the inequity of the whole deal out of my head.

Remy had started all this out of a longing for his dad who he thought dead. He got me involved with the fishing trip exposing me to the whirlpool and the ghost of old Miss Nora. This obsession had pulled me in every direction but up. And in spite of losing my job, I came out all right.

But not Remy. Even though he hadn't been pestering me for the last three years, he had a right to know about his dad. And what about Frank? To survive he made decisions and abandoned his child to the awful influences of Lydia and Big Ray. His terrible choice came with a high price. He may have found peace and some fulfillment but not happiness. What right did I presume to mess with the balance of things? Every right, I concluded. I had more than paid my dues for being an unwilling interloper in this whirlpool of strangers.

I thought about it for a week and, on an impulse, tried to call Remy. His phone had been disconnected. I tried directory assistance. Nothing. I asked contacts at my old television station. No one knew where he had gone. I did an internet search and found an article in the Macon paper dated June 18, last year. How could I have missed it?

"Police Conduct Search for Missing Boater."

The article said in part:

"Monroe County Sheriff deputy, Paul Waddell, said that his department had called off the search for the owner of a boat found drifting on Lake Juliette. The boat was registered to a Raymond Robillard of Atlanta. Mr. Robillard could not be contacted. The sheriff's department conducted a brief search but found no evidence of accident or foul play. His relatives were notified, but they had not been in recent contact with the boat's owner."

"We got no reason to believe anything bad has happened to him. He might have just tied the boat up and gone off somewhere. And it just drifted out to the middle of the lake." Waddell said.

My chest turned to cold stone. Images of the ghostly Miss Nora swimming in the dark waters of Lake Juliette came to my mind. Old Nora had gotten her revenge at last, snatching Remy out of the boat, pulling him under, and now she waited for his father to return.

That would have been a great ending, but it turned out not to be true. I found Remy a couple of days later. He had moved to Alabama and worked at a music recording studio in the town of Muscle Shoals. Things aren't so mysterious after all.

But I didn't call him. After all, he hadn't pestered me for the last three years about his father. Why had I been so obsessed if he wasn't interested? What if he really didn't want to know about his dad? That would make all my obsession and depression seem pretty stupid. And how could I face him now? In spite of all my effort, I hadn't proved that Frank was a hero or even very likable. But it pissed me off that now that I had the complete wrap-up, Remy wasn't beating down my door to get it.

So I sent him a letter. It was really more of a package, containing a copy of the Newsweek article and a draft of the book. I wanted Remy to come to his own conclusions and decide for himself who his father really was.

But the article and the book were written before my startling discovery in Paris. I revealed this to no one, not even in the book. The world still thought Frank was dead. So in the package I included a round trip plane ticket to Paris, the refundable type that he could use anytime, and Bettye's phone number, in case he needed help when he got there. It was the only way of leaving him the choice of getting into it or not. I knew Remy might find this package confusing. He might wonder, who's Bettye and why should I go to France?

So I added something that I found folded up in the coat pocket of my suit when I took it to the cleaners. It was the program from the Opera National de Paris, for the night of May 15. Along with the cast, the names of the musicians were listed. Under the heading *Seconds Violons*, I had circled the name: Francois Robillard.

Author's Note: The real-life community of Juliette lies just north of Macon, Georgia. Juliette is a delightful place and actually shares a few characteristics with the fictional Juliette depicted in this story. However, much of the fictional Juliette has been borrowed from nearby villages and placed there for convenience. Alas, Lake Juliette has no whirlpool but otherwise is a charming body of water where the fishing is usually pretty good.

Author John Wilsterman was born in Ohio and migrated to the South after college. Always an avid reader and storyteller, he took to novel writing after finishing a long career with IBM. Beneath Juliette, his debut novel is a culmination of stories, locations and characters he has encountered in his wonderful, magical and often peculiar adopted homeland.

Mr. Wilsterman lives in Townsend, Georgia, and is currently working on a new novel, *Next to Life Itself.*

Excerpt from John Wilsterman's new novel, Next to Life Itself, available soon:

Chapter 1

Podunk isn't really in Iowa.

It's located in cow and grass country where roads run straight west, east, north and south. There are no railroads or interstates, just a two lane ribbon of asphalt in and out, a blinking light stop sign surrounded by a few buildings, a bank, grocery, hardware-feed store and pharmacy. A lonely bus station and a good auto mechanic guarantee no one really gets stuck there. If you need anything else you went elsewhere. Nobody went to Podunk except to get lost.

"Podunk" means small, remote and unimportant. The name itself might have attracted attention so the town wasn't really called that, which made it ideal for WITSEC, the Federal Witness Protection Program.

WITSEC knew how to hide people, but they outdid themselves concealing the first great villain of the twenty-first century, the architect of the biggest corporate swindle of the new millennium, the brains behind the so-called, "Hole In The Wall Street Gang," a man once known as Wylie Schram, disgraced CFO of the doomed oil conglomerate InCorps, now buried in profound obscurity under his new name of Daniel Conklin.

WITSEC had faked everything about Daniel Conklin. They gave him fake credentials to go with his fake story. They altered his face so he looked like a bad police sketch from an unreliable witness. They plunked him in a community where he was a stranger to work a profession for which he was not qualified. They tied his federal leash so short he could hardly flush a toilet without incrementing a bureaucrat's computer in Washington.

Four years ago Wylie Schram died in a horrible traffic accident. News coverage showed enough close-ups of the twisted wreck to convince the most die-hard conspiracy theorists. The media would have outdone themselves staging a lynch-mob at Wylie Schram's trial, but his closed casket slid quietly into the ground and in a few weeks America stopped talking about him.

Even more quietly, the feds launched the newly minted Daniel Conklin in the small town that wasn't in Iowa. And although it wasn't called "Podunk" either, the place qualified for its namesake. The town's street names ended with Second Avenue and B Street at a point where the landscape resumed its monotonous farms, pastures and prairies. Daniel Conklin's house stood on across the road from a cow pen holding a few head of sullen Black Angus. The feds bought the house cheap, not that they cared about saving taxpayers' money but more to fit into the town's concept of normal.

WITSEC had made him a pharmacist's assistant, a pill counter who could fill bottles with drugs only under the supervision of a licensed pharmacist. The town's real pharmacist owned the drug store. Federal agents pretending to be rehabilitation therapists had persuaded him to take Dan Conklin on as a project as a man recovering from a severe accident, who needed a low-stress job in a quiet place. The town, the pharmacy and the job fit WITSEC's criteria, and no one there knew the Justice Department was involved.

Dan Conklin played the part to perfection. The Feds gave him an app for his smart-phone enabling him to serve as a short-study pill counter. The drug store thus became the number one employer in the small town.

He had been warned by his WITSEC handlers not to get close to anyone. Friends could be nosey and they talked. Information could get back to someone looking for him. In that little town he was known by the clichés, "He likes to keep to himself," "He's the quiet type," and "To each his own."

Having exchanged hard time in a penitentiary for prison of a different sort, Daniel Conklin settled into a tolerable existence, bearing his burden with quiet stoicism. But he lived with the possibility that one day the people looking for him would step around the corner and put a bullet in his head. Or worse.

Uneventful days turned into months and then years. If he had expected a quarterly WITSEC newsletter or monthly statement from the feds, he didn't get them. His disappearance seemed complete. Even phone solicitors couldn't find him.

The newness of his new life dissipated and he settled into an existence where little changed. Every day he shaved and showered and ate a bowl of oatmeal from the microwave. He would walk to work because the half mile up the slight hill was all the exercise he'd get.

Because it was his nature, Daniel Conklin devoted his days at the pharmacy making subtle improvements to the business. He easily mastered the cash register and the store's computer. He'd surveyed the pharmacy software, and installed much needed upgrades. He connected the store's data to the state medical record system. And without anyone taking much notice, he revolutionized the drug store into the town's first twenty-first century's business. In fact the pharmacist had noted the improvements and tried to thank the rehab therapists who had recommend this exceptional employee, but he couldn't find them. Conklin's recommenders had been federal agents, now reassigned.

Daniel Conklin would stroll home after work, enduring the baleful gaze of the cows at the end of Second Avenue. He'd pop something into the microwave, open the first of three or four beers, turn on the TV and wait until his eyelids drooped.

The memory of being one of the most powerful financiers in the world had receded, as did the memory of barking orders at his staff, pulling all-nighters studying financial data, filling notebooks with strategies, and monitoring worldwide markets, shifting millions of dollars around the globe. Gone were the meetings, the negotiations, the handshakes and deals. Gone was Wylie Schram's unique talent of generating huge piles of money to feed a cash-hungry enterprise.

Instead, thoughts of Denise beat through his head like the unrelenting tick of a clock. Tautological threads of conscience twined through the lattice of lies and logic that had lead him to his current circumstance and deprived him of her.

He had loved Denise deeply. He had devastated her with his crimes, the disgrace the world heaped upon him, and his ultimate betrayal, the lie about his death.

An innocent woman, this woman he loved. And she had returned that love with passion and loyalty, even after his arrest. She probably still loved him, or at least the memory of him. Denise had known the real Wylie Schram. She knew him intimately… or thought she did.

Thoughts of Denise sent pangs of guilt through his chest that even piles of empty beer cans could not dull. Denise had given herself to him and he had deceived her. He hadn't trusted her with the secrets of his crimes. He had allowed her to believe he died in that car crash. To save his own worthless neck, he had to keep the truth from her that he still lived.

On the nights when his dream came, it was always the same: Denise loving him, forgiving him, wanting to know why he waited so long. And he recalled how warm and vulnerable she felt, how she smelled and tasted, the way her body energized his, making the thought of another woman seem like sacrilege. His dream woke him at the cruelest hours of the morning, heart pounding, sweat soaking his sheets and tears his pillow.

In the sobering light of another day he knew he lacked the courage to tell her he still lived, or show for what he had traded a life with her.

Each day a single temptation tormented him. Wasn't it possible for her to steal away and join him, here in the little town that wasn't in Iowa? Had WITSEC had boxed him in so tight and was the danger that great?

Four years after he arrived in the little town, his loneliness reached a sort of critical mass. Conklin spent another painful night struggling with a desire to reach out to Denise. The difference between this night and all the nights preceding it was it ended with a plan.

He visited the local public library and used his computer savvy to hack into the library's computer. He looked through their catalog for likely titles and found two that suited his purpose, "Love Lives On" by Louis Legrand and "Looking for a Godly Man" by Keith Mitchell.

He created an entry in the library's database showing that Denise had borrowed these books which were now past due. The library's computer sent a request to their processing service in a city hundreds of miles away, a place with railroads and freeways.

Denise was mailed an overdue library notice concerning books she never borrowed, from a library in a town she didn't know existed.

A day later, Conklin snuck back into the library and erased all evidence of his intrusion. If the Justice Department ever discovered what he had done, they would have grabbed him up and relocated him under a new identity. But days passed and then a week and then two with no response. Either she hadn't received the overdue library note or she hadn't deciphered its message.

Or so he thought.

One day after two weeks, Daniel Conklin made an ordinary trip to his mailbox, and there was the letter he had longed for and dreaded. Out of habit he looked up the street and down to see if anyone was watching. Then shrugging off his paranoia, he took the letter inside to read it at his kitchen table.

A minute later he knew he had to call Bentley.

Bentley oversaw many duties for the Justice Department, which included the federal witness protection program. Because Wylie Schram was such a high profile criminal, Bentley had handled his disappearance personally. He alone knew who Wylie Schram really was and where he was.

Conklin's call was answered immediately.

"Leave a message," and then a sharp tone. Conklin spoke his message.

The following morning his cell phone showed a voice message waited for him. It said, "Go to work as usual. We will contact you with specific instructions."

He didn't know it then, but it would be his last day in the little town that wasn't in Iowa and his last day in WITSEC.